JULIAN MACLAREN-ROSS
SELECTED STORIES

JULIAN MACLAREN-ROSS
SELECTED STORIES

selected and introduced by
Paul Willetts

dewi lewis publishing

First published in the UK in 2004 by
Dewi Lewis Publishing, 8 Broomfield Road
Heaton Moor, Stockport SK4 4ND
+44 (0)161 442 9450

www.dewilewispublishing.com

ISBN: 1-904587-17-8

Design & artwork production by Dewi Lewis Publishing

Printed and bound in Great Britain by
Biddles Ltd, King's Lynn

10   9   8   7   6   5   4   3   2   1

First Edition

Cover drawing:
Sketchbook drawing of a Soho pub-scene
by Ruth Willetts, c.1952 © Paul Willetts

Contents

Introduction

Julian Maclaren-Ross was the quintessential Soho bohemian. Flamboyantly dressed, feckless, egotistical, pill-popping, alcoholic, and more often than not hard-up, he possessed an intriguing combination of saturnine good looks and unflappable movie star panache. During the 1940s and 1950s, which coincided with the heyday of Soho as London's equivalent to Greenwich Village or the Left Bank, he was one of that area's most celebrated personalities. Since his premature death in 1964, aged only fifty-two, he has been portrayed in memoirs, novels, and histories of the period as a stereotypical doomed artist, squandering his time and talent. However alluring this image of him may be, it's far from accurate. Worse still, it distracts from his achievements as a writer. True, his life *was* tinged with tragedy, and he *did* fritter away inordinate amounts of time and money in Soho's array of pubs and basement drinking-clubs. Even so, he fulfilled much of his abundant literary promise. For most of his adult life, he was a productive professional writer, his diverse output attracting many illustrious admirers, among them Evelyn Waugh who hailed the 'rare accomplishment' of his work. Although self indulgence and free-wheeling excess were the hallmarks of his life, he remained capable of writing with paradoxical restraint and poise.

In the wake of the posthumous publication of his classic *Memoirs of the Forties*, Maclaren-Ross became best-known as a chronicler of the bohemian scene which he'd observed with such acuity through his ubiquitous aviator-style sunglasses. But it was as a short story writer that he rose to prominence a quarter of a century earlier. At their best his stories, thanks to their rare verve and vivacity, retain the freshness that made them so conspicuous when they first appeared.

Like all the most talented writers, he habitually portrayed a distinctive world with which he is now synonymous. He also possessed an equally distinctive literary voice. The world of Maclaren-Ross's writing tends to be the dingy, down-at-heel world of smoke-veiled bars, rented lodgings, blacked-out streets, and wartime army garrisons, first-hand experience lending his work a frisson of authenticity. Of course his preferred settings overlap with those of near-contemporaries such as Patrick Hamilton and Gerald Kersh, but his treatment of them could scarcely be more different. Varied though the stories I've chosen for this volume may appear, they share the same wry tone, the same attitude to life. Whether they're narrated in the breathless, slangy voice of an uneducated soldier, or the clipped cadences of a colonial expat', whether they're set on the French Riviera or wartime England, they're imprinted with Maclaren-Ross's unmistakable literary logo. The prevailing tone is casual, matter-of-fact and laconic, characteristically mordant, humorous asides failing to conceal the melancholy that seeps through their hardboiled surfaces.

Ever since he was a carefree teenager, Maclaren-Ross had nurtured artistic ambitions, yet it wasn't until the latter half of the 1930s that he began to veer away from painting towards writing. His resolve was tested by several years of frustration and penury before his eventual breakthrough. This came with the publication of one of his short stories in the June 1940 issue of *Horizon*, Cyril Connolly's seminal magazine. But Connolly, fearing libel action and charges of obscenity, had first insisted on censoring the story which opened with the line, 'Absolute fact, I knew fuck all about it...' Entitled *A Bit of a Smash in Madras*, the story was written in a snappy, ventriloquistic style that vividly evokes both its exotic backdrop and the personality of Adams, its gruff narrator whose surname may well represent an allusion to Nick Adams, the youthful protagonist of Ernest Hemingway's early stories. So convincing is everything about the piece, you'd be forgiven for assuming that Maclaren-Ross had lived in India. He had, instead, based the whole thing on conversations with a former expat', newly returned, like Adams, from the subcontinent.

A Bit of a Smash in Madras prompted immediate interest from publishers who earmarked its author as a rising star. Despite betraying the influence of Dashiell Hammett's staccato rhythms, James M. Cain's demotic brio, and Hemingway's terseness, his writing was startlingly original. Here, at last, was a genuine English counterpart to the vernacular American style. Over the next few years Maclaren-Ross continued to mine this vein in many of the stories he penned about army life, their realistic barrack-room language provoking further censorship wrangles. His army stories, inhabited by a familiar cast of characters, became a popular ingredient of most of the leading literary magazines and miscellanies which were, courtesy of wartime conditions, enjoying huge sales and comparable prestige.

By the time Maclaren-Ross was discharged from the military in August 1943, following his desertion and subsequent imprisonment, he was already regarded as one of Britain's most promising young writers. He went on to consolidate his growing reputation with *The Stuff To Give The Troops*, a collection of his army stories. I've selected eight of these, including *This Mortal Coil* which Cyril Connolly rated among the finest pieces to feature in *Horizon*. The stories in question extend from lightly sketched, anecdotal tales—typically composed in a single session—to longer, more self-consciously literary ones. They were all culled from Maclaren-Ross's army experiences, yet their narrators aren't always straightforward authorial surrogates. In both *The Tape*—his earliest fiction about service life—and *They Can Have It*, he demonstrates his flexibility as a literary stylist by convincingly mimicking the voices of the working-class soldiers with whom he found himself.

Taken as a whole, his army stories present an unrivalled and apparently accurate impression of what it was like to be on the lowest rung of the military hierarchy. His jaundiced accounts of malingering, incompetence, and nightmarish bureaucracy are a far cry from the propagandistic depictions of wartime heroism and Home Front fortitude seen in countless movies. If anything, his dark, subversive view of the army has more in common with the Vietnam-era cynicism of the Robert Altman movie, *M*A*S*H*.

Less than a year after the release of *The Stuff To Give The Troops*, Maclaren-Ross's second collection was published. Adept at devising catchy, idiosyncratic titles, he called it *Better Than A Kick In The Pants*. It brought together some of his early work, along with more recent examples, set in the hurly-burly of Soho. Of the ten stories that I've plucked from this collection, eight of them draw on wide-ranging aspects of his civilian existence. The other two consist of *A Bit of A Smash In Madras* and its companion piece, *The Hell of a Time*. As if to signpost the absence of the usual autobiographical component, he placed them in a section entitled 'The "I" in These Stories is Not Me.'

The theme of the former expat' who finds himself transplanted from Madras to England recurs in his dazzling 1947 novel, *Of Love and Hunger*, which fictionalises his pre-war stint as a door-to-door vacuum-cleaner salesman. *I'm Not Asking You To Buy*—among his more bleakly amusing stories—appears to have been part of an early version of the novel, though that doesn't prevent it from being satisfyingly self-contained. Two of my other inclusions, namely *Nichevo*, and *Happy As The Day Is Long*, also focus on the cash-strapped inter-war years. Their crisp, sometimes witty dialogue, sparse descriptions, and downbeat endings ensure that they're still resonant and evocative. All the remaining stories lifted from *Better Than A Kick In The Pants* take place in the South of France, where Maclaren-Ross spent the tail-end of his childhood. Their levity, charm, and breezy acceptance of the less pleasant aspects of pre-adolescent life anticipate his treatment of similar subject-matter in *The Weeping and the Laughter*, his luminous childhood memoir.

In 1946, by which stage the once flourishing British market for short fiction was in steep decline, his publisher released *The Nine Men of Soho*. From this volume, destined to be his final collection before he shifted his attention to other genres, I've picked *The Far West*, another delightful story about his childhood. In addition I've selected two Soho tales, an old army story called *Lulu*, and *The Swag, The Spy and the Soldier*, dramatising the unlikely sequence of events precipitated by his friendship with a fairground roustabout.

My favourite story from *The Nine Men of Soho* must be the poignant *Welsh Rabbit of Soap*, the first writing by Maclaren-Ross that I came across. I remember being captivated by the casual intimacy of the opening sentence, by the sadness visible behind the façade of jaunty forbearance. Unusually for him, that sadness shades into self-pity towards the end of the story. In an epic, sinuous sentence that accrues emotional substance through the type of fast cinematic montage which he often deploys, the narrator concludes that his former girlfriend was 'just another neurotic' and that 'neurosis, not happiness, lay in wait round the corner'. It proved an all too accurate prediction for Maclaren-Ross who, like Christopher Isherwood, frequently encourages readers to identify him with his narrators. Not only does the narrator share his profession and christian name, but he also mixes in the same circles and visits the same places, the true identities of which are barely disguised. 'Adam Stroud' is, for instance, a pseudonym for Donald Taylor, Maclaren-Ross's boss at Strand, the documentary film company where he worked alongside Dylan Thomas. And 'the Scotsman' pub is obviously the Highlander on Dean Street, once a favoured movie industry haunt, these days known as the Nellie Dean.

Such links between life and art are common in most literary fiction. The balance between reportage and imagination in Maclaren-Ross's stories seems to be tilted towards the former, yet witnesses to the events on which his stories were based generally recall how they weren't straightforward transcriptions of reality. The facts would be streamlined and distorted to meet the demands of the narrative. Many of his stories began as bar-room anecdotes that he'd declaim again and again, each time editing and revising the contents, their oral source reflected in their conversational flavour. Revitalised by an eye-popping dose of amphetamines, he'd spend the hours after pub closing-time writing down the final draft in his creepy, pathologically neat script. Anyone who has seen his handwriting won't be surprised to learn that he was an obsessive, his obsessions—not least an erotic fixation with George Orwell's widow—pushing him to the brink of insanity, and in the process compounding his many other problems.

Hounded by creditors and bailiffs, repeated changes of address temporarily enabling him to dodge court summonses, he was imprisoned in 1957. Always keen to transmute his experiences into a remunerative literary form, he wrote about his brief spell in prison soon afterwards. The result was *Inside Story*, first published in *Punch*, a magazine to which he had been a regular contributor. *Inside Story* offers a rare—notably sympathetic—portrayal of a black immigrant in the British fiction of that period. Through its depiction of 'Hooper', Maclaren-Ross's alter ego, who shares a cell with the unnamed West Indian, this previously uncollected story conveys a strong sense of its creator's exceptional resilience.

Undaunted by all the obstacles confronting him, many of them self-imposed, Maclaren-Ross produced some important work that merits a place in the top rank of twentieth-century fiction. Part of its significance derives from his innovative fusion of American and English influences to create a chatty, informal brand of writing that anticipates so much contemporary British fiction and journalism. *Selected Stories* showcases the stylistic range, the exuberance, and the lightness of touch that make him such an entertaining and accessible writer. Reading these stories, written between about 1938 and 1957-58, it's easy to understand why he has attracted a devoted cult following, and why so many of his peers, ranging from Anthony Powell to Graham Greene, rated him so highly. It is, however, much harder to comprehend why he isn't more widely appreciated.

Paul Willetts

Do I remember that night? God, I should say I do. We had the hell of a bloody time. That was when the Simon Commission first came out to India, in 1927 or thereabouts, and there was a lot of ill-feeling against the Europeans. All the native shops in Madras were closed down, every damn one of them; a *hartal*, they call it, a strike of shopkeepers, as a political protest.

There was no actual rioting, but all day long cars kept on pouring in for repair, some with their windscreens smashed or darn great holes in the doors, where bricks had been thrown at them.

At that time I hadn't been out East very long; I was in the works, sweltering under corrugated iron in 105 degrees of damp heat. You can't imagine what that's like until you've been there. We used to knock off about six in the evening.

Well the night I'm telling you about, we were at a loose end and old Sturgess, who was coach-works manager, said to me, 'Adams old boy,' he said, 'what about going along to George Town tonight and seeing the fun? There's bound to be something doing out there.'

'All right,' I said. 'We might have a drink at Harrison's.'

George Town is the native quarter of Madras and Harrison's is a damned awful place, full of Eurasian tarts and so on, where no decent European would be seen dead, in the normal course of events. Though I've been there a good few times, I don't mind telling you.

'That's an idea,' Sturgess said, 'we'll do that.'

He was the hell of a fellow, old Sturgess. Drink? God! Fish wasn't in it with him. He was the hell of a lad. Yet he never got the push—how he kept his job, God only knows. I don't. He's probably a director by now.

Well we had a lot of whisky first and I don't mind telling you we were pretty well stewed by the time we started off, about half-past seven.

Sturgess had a new motor-bike, an Enfield, a damn good machine. I climbed in the sidecar and we got going.

Halfway along we heard a shout and blowed if it wasn't Fred Logan, an American, fellow we knew pretty well. He was on a motor-bike too, a bloody awful thing he'd had for donkey's years. I remember the exhaust-pipe used to come off at times and he'd tie it on again with his handkerchief.

Logan had another chap in the sidecar, bloke called Brady, a reporter on the *Madras Mail.*

'Where you guys going?' Logan shouted to us.

'We're going to have a drink at Harrison's,' Sturgess shouted back. 'Coming?'

'Okay,' Logan said; he was ready for anything. 'How about you, Dan?' he asked Brady.

'I'm on,' Brady said.

'Okay,' Logan said. 'Let's go.'

It was when we got down to Broadway that the fun started. There they were, milling and shouting, Muslims and Hindus all mixed up together, some of 'em wearing Gandhi caps. The police were holding them back one side of the esplanade. When they saw us, four Europeans together, they raised the hell of a row. As I say, feeling was pretty rife at that time.

The inspector in charge came over to us. He was a European too. He said: 'And where do you think you're going?'

'We're off to have a drink at Harrison's,' Sturgess said.

'That's right,' Logan said.

Brady and I nodded.

'Now listen,' the inspector said. 'You're going right back the way you came.'

'Oh, no we're not,' Sturgess said. 'You're quite mistaken inspector.'

'I'll say you are,' Logan said.

'We're going down to George Town,' I said.

'I'm a reporter,' Brady said. 'I'm gonna write it up for the *Mail.*'

'After we've had a drink at Harrison's,' Sturgess said.

'That's right,' Logan said. 'We wanna see the fun.'

'You'll see all the bloody fun you want if you go down there tonight,' the inspector said. 'And a bit more.'

'That's all right with me,' Logan said.

The crowd was pretty het up by this time, yelling and bawling, with the police keeping them back. They were beginning to sound ugly.

'Don't be damn fools,' the inspector said. 'Go on home while you're still in one piece.'

'No bloody fear,' Sturgess said.

'Not a chance,' Logan said.

'All right,' the inspector said. 'Don't say I didn't warn you.'

'Okay, sarge,' Logan said. 'Come on, you guys. Let's get going.'

We started off down the esplanade. The mob yelled and booed at us, sounding fierce. Something whizzed through the air by my head. 'God,' Sturgess said. 'The swine. They're throwing bricks.'

He drove on full speed. Suddenly there was a shout behind us from Logan. I looked back and saw Brady had been hit. He was lying back in the sidecar with blood running down his face.

'Don't stop,' I shouted to Logan, 'for Christ's sake don't stop.'

I knew if he did, with that bloody old bus of his, he'd never get her started again and then we'd be for it. The crowd was getting out of hand; bricks flew thick and fast. The police were having a time—they weren't allowed to use their batons.

I crouched down in the sidecar, dodging the bricks. Logan kept calling out behind us. We'd given up the idea of getting to George Town by this time. We thought we'd get away along the Marina, once we were clear of the crowd. I looked back and saw Brady slumped down in Logan's sidecar. He'd been knocked cold.

At the Marina a military picket picked us up.

'Where the hell are you going?' the officer in charge asked us.

Sturgess said: 'Along the Marina.'

'You're bloody well not,' the officer said. 'Why God Almighty you'd be killed. Go back the way you came.'

'We can't do that,' I said. 'They're throwing bricks. This bloke's been hit by one. We can't take him back there.'

Logan had stopped and we all had a look at Brady. He was out all right, with a whacking great gash in his forehead and blood all over him.

'By Christ,' the officer said, 'he's caught a packet he has.'

'What the hell we gonna do?' Logan said.

I was sweating like a bullock. We were all near sober by this time and I don't mind telling you I had the proper wind-up, because I'd just remembered Brady was a delicate sort of chap, who had a weak heart and was likely to conk out anytime.

'Best thing is to go down the harbour,' the officer said. 'If you went on the Marina they'd spill your guts for sure. We couldn't help either—before we could draw a bloody bayonet we'd have to get written permission from the fort. We've no orders to use violence. I can't think what the devil you're doing down here at all.'

Sturgess said: 'We were going to have a drink at Harrison's.'

'Christ,' the officer said, 'you must be crazy.'

Well, we went down the harbour and it was quite calm down there. We went on board the first B.I. boat we saw and had the doctor look at Brady. The cut turned out to be nothing much after all. The doc brought him to and he had a few whiskies with us in the bar and felt fine again, except he was fed up because of the blood on his suit. He was always a natty sort of bloke, old Brady.

We came back along the Marina about eleven and it was all quiet, not a native to be seen for miles, but down by the iron bridge there were three cars piled up, pretty badly smashed. God knows what happened to the people in them.

I saw Brady next day and he felt none the worst; he'd written a piece about it in the *Mail* and was feeling pretty bucked, all told. Matter of fact, though, he did die a few weeks later. He was out on a binge and his heart went back on him, poor bastard.

Yes, I remember that night quite well. We never got our drink at Harrison's, but by God we certainly had the hell of a time.

A Bit of a Smash in Madras

I

Absolute fact, I knew damn all about it; I'd been on a blind in Fenner's with some of the boys and I was on my way back when a blasted pi dog ran out in the road and I swerved the car a bit to avoid it. I don't remember the crash or anything, I must have hit into them and driven straight on to the bungalow without stopping. I was so damn tight I don't remember anything, but these fellows were coming out of Fenner's, the two of 'em, and they saw it all right and this bastard Krishnaswami recognized me: I'd a big open Vauxhall in those days and I was driving with the hood down.

The night watchman from Spinner's saw it too and he came across and there were these coolies pretty badly smashed about, one of them had a broken leg and God knows what, and Krishnaswami was shouting that he'd seen me and knew who I was. Mind you, he was properly sewn-up himself, and the other bloke with him was so bad that the station inspector refused to accept his evidence. But Krishnaswami had got the number of my car, so after they'd carted the two coolies off to hospital, the inspector came down to the bungalow to see me.

At that time I shared quarters with a chap called Stanton, he was with the company too, a damn decent chap, and when the peon told him this inspector was out there asking for me, he came into my room and there I was, of course, dead to the world. So Stanton went out and told the inspector I was asleep and could he come back later and the inspector said all right. When he'd gone, Stanton woke me up and told me about it. Honest, it came like a bolt from the ruddy blue: I couldn't remember a thing.

'Accident?' I said. 'What the hell are you talking about? I haven't had an accident.'

'One of the coolies may die,' Stanton said.

'But it's nothing to do with me.'

'The inspector says he's got your number.'

'Holy smoke,' I said.

'You'd better snap out of it,' Stanton said. 'He's coming back presently,' so I got up and bawled for the peon to get my bath ready. This was five in the morning, mind you, and I felt foul. I'd an awful head and a mouth like a sewer from smoking. I couldn't understand what it was all about; I thought they'd got me mixed up with someone else.

After my bath I felt better, but I was still pretty bad. I kept drinking socking great cups of black tea, and about seven the inspector came back. He was a native, but quite a nice chap; I've forgotten his name. He brought two other men with him, and these stayed outside taking photographs of my car, which had a mudguard buckled and one of the headlamps knocked back. I'd already had a look at it, and it certainly seemed I had been in a smash, though I still couldn't remember anything.

Of course, directly these fellows started taking photos, I saw the red light, so when the inspector asked me if I'd make a statement, I said no, not without seeing a lawyer first.

'Very well,' the inspector said, 'but I'm afraid I shall have to ask you to accompany me to the station.'

'Is this necessary?' I said.

'I'm afraid so, sir,' he said. 'Purely a matter of form, you know,' so I said all right but could I call my solicitor's on our way down. The inspector said certainly and who was my solicitor?'

'Mr Shankran,' I said.

Of course the inspector knew Shankran; everyone in Madras did. I'd never had to employ him myself, but we'd always been good pals and I knew he'd always be ready to help me out of a hot spot. Besides, he was a damn smart lawyer: look what he did for Cornford that time he crashed into a Mohammedan funeral and killed five. Why, Cornford would have got life if it hadn't been for Shankran; as it was he got off with three years, and on top of that Shankran raised such an awful stink everyone was scared stiff of him; he had several officials sacked, two police sergeants reduced to the ranks, and even got the magistrate reprimanded—all through pull. I tell you, if Shankran couldn't get me off, nobody could.

But on the way to the station, I remembered that I didn't know his address, so I asked the inspector to pull up at Fenner's, which he did.

'By God, Adams old boy,' Fenner said when he saw me, 'you're in a mess this time.'

'I seem to be,' I said: luckily the inspector had stayed outside in the car.

'By God you are,' Fenner said. 'I've had the police round wanting to know all about you, what state you were in when you left, if you were sober, and God knows what. Course they got no change out of me.'

'Did they ask to see the bar chits?'

'Not yet. But you needn't worry: I've fixed those.'

'Thanks, old boy,' I said.

'Anything to oblige,' Fenner said, winking.

'Did you see the accident?' I asked him.

'No, but it sounds pretty serious from what I hear.'

'I'm just off to the station now.'

'Seen a lawyer yet?'

'No. I'm going to get Shankran.'

'Couldn't do better, old boy.'

'Matter of fact, that's what I came to ask you for—his address.'

So Fenner told me and I went back to the inspector and he drove me round to Shankran's bungalow. He was just having *chota hazri* when his boy announced us and he jumped up from the table as we came in, holding out his hand. He was a Brahmin, small and wearing gold-rimmed glasses, and you couldn't tell his age from his looks.

'Hullo, hullo, hullo,' he said. 'Adams, eh? How are you keeping? Sit down, sit down. Boy, bring some gin! Sit down, Adams, don't look so worried!'

He seemed a bit surprised to see the inspector, but he said hullo to him too, and spoke a few words in Tamil, and the inspector smiled.

'Look here, Shankran,' I said, 'I'd like your advice. It seems I had a bit of a smash last night.'

'Oh? Well, well. Not a bad one, I hope? Ah, here's the gin. That's right, put it on the table. Help yourself, Adams, Inspector?'

The inspector said he wouldn't, being on duty. I felt better after I'd swallowed some gin.

'Now tell me all about it,' Shankran said. He spoke to the inspector in Tamil and the inspector went out on the veranda, leaving us together. I told Shankran what I knew, while he walked up and down saying 'Yes.

Yes. Yes,' sucking at a cigarette without touching it to his lips, the way Brahmins do.

'Yes. Yes,' he said. 'Of course I'll do my best for you. Trust me. Yes. Inspector!'

The inspector came in.

'How badly are these coolies hurt?' Shankran asked him.

'One of them is not expected to live, sir.'

'H'm. H'm. That's bad. Yes.' Shankran turned to me. 'Pity you couldn't come here at once, directly it happened. There'd have been no case, I would have squashed it from the start. Now, of course—h'm.' He sucked at his cigarette, thinking. Then suddenly he turned to me again, holding out his hand. 'All right,' he said. 'Don't you worry. I'll see you through. Make no statements to anyone. Keep mum and meet me in Fenner's tonight, nine o'clock.'

He came to the door with us, telling me again not to worry, and we drove off. He was a damn good scout, Shankran, and except for his skin a good deal whiter than some of those swine that swank about the club thinking they're sahibs. I felt better now the case was in his hands.

We got down to the station and went in and there were a few native police standing about in boots and puttees, but nobody else. The inspector sat down at his desk and was starting to ask me a few questions when suddenly there were voices raised outside and that swine Holt, the Assistant Commissioner, came storming in.

'Arrest that man!' he shouted as soon as he saw me. 'Put him under arrest!'

'But Mr Holt—' I started to say.

'Be silent,' he shouted, and to the inspector: 'Detain him, don't let him get away. He's a dangerous man!'

Of course this was damn ridiculous and unprecedented to boot, treating a European that way. Truth was, I'd had a bit of trouble with Holt over the licensing of buses: he was Traffic Commissioner as well and he didn't like me. He was only doing this to get his own back.

'Can I have bail, sir?' I said.

'Bail? Yes. A thousand rupees,' and with that he stamped out of the station. Well, of course the inspector didn't put me in a cell; I was simply shut in a room on my own. I'd just thought I should be phoning the office, when who should roll in but old Major Brant: he'd been with me the night before and had heard about the accident from Fenner.

'Well, Adams, old boy,' he said, 'in a jam again.'

'By God I am. It's that bastard Holt. He put me under arrest.'

'Won't they let you have bail?'

'A thousand chips.'

'That's all right, old boy. I'll fix it for you.'

So he went bail for me and the inspector let us out. We went down to Fenner's and Brant said: 'Boy, bring Master a large brandy.' So I drank three large brandies altogether and Brant said he'd testify I was sober the night before, because a short time before I left I'd been playing the big drum in the dance band and it's difficult to keep time when you're tight— although I had done it apparently. What's more, Brant said, I had been dancing with his wife earlier on, and he certainly wouldn't let his wife dance with a drunken man. He winked at me and I thanked him and got off to the office. When I came in there the secretary had a message the Old Man wanted to see me.

'What's the meaning of all this, Adams?' Sir Alec said.

'Well, sir, I had a bit of a smash last night.'

'So you said last time you drove your car into a tree and smashed it up completely. Were you drunk?'

'No, sir.'

'Why didn't you stop then?'

'I must have lost my nerve.'

'Humph!' Sir Alec said. 'Well, this is Dr Menon, the company solicitor, who will act for you.'

Dr Menon came forward and shook hands. He was a Hindu, Oxford degree, BBC accent, and all in European dress, even to the green felt hat lying on the desk: people don't wear topees the whole time out East the way you read about in books. I knew Menon slightly: he was a slimy skite and I wouldn't trust him an inch. I didn't let on I'd already been to Shankran.

Menon suggested we should go down to the scene of the accident, and I said all right, without telling him I didn't know where it was. I knew it was somewhere near Fenner's because the inspector had told me so, and we drove down there. Of course all traces had gone by this time, and Menon said he could do nothing more at the moment.

'It all depends on the condition of the coolies,' he said. 'I will inquire at the hospital and let you know later.'

'Righto,' I said.

II

That night I went into Fenner's to wait for Shankran. I was sitting outside drinking a double scotch when a chap came up to me called Turpin, awful little squirt he was, supposed to be a jockey, though he never seemed to do any riding. Matter of fact, I found out afterwards he'd been warned off.

'Evening, Mr Adams,' this chap said to me.

'Evening,' I said. I'd never spoken to the little bastard before and wondered what in hell he wanted.

'Sorry to hear about your smash last night,' he said. 'It was a bad break.'

'Yes.'

'Nasty thing to happen.'

'Yes.'

'Suppose this coolie croaks. You'll be in the cart.'

'Yes.'

'But maybe I can help.'

'How?' I said.

He looked round to see no one was listening, then leant across the table. I moved back a bit: the little bleeder stank of booze.

'Look here,' he said. 'It happens I know the bloke that's making all the bother. Name of Krishnaswami. He's the bloke you want to look out for.'

'How d'you mean?' I said: I hadn't heard of Krishnaswami until now.

'He's the bloke that saw it all. Took your number. Told the police.'

'I see. I didn't know they had a witness.'

'You bet they have. He's the star turn.'

'Well, what about it?'

'He might be fixed,' Turpin said, looking at me and putting a finger alongside his nose.

'But if he's given his evidence?'

'He could slip out of that easy enough. He's got pull, see? His dad's

Trade Commissioner back home. A big bug. He could pull strings.'

'Ah.' I began to see daylight. Turpin and Krishnaswami were in cahoots, and Turpin was the pilot-fish. But I didn't let on I'd spotted their little game, and simply nodded to what he'd said.

'Suppose you talked to Krishnaswami, see? Just a friendly chat. It wouldn't hurt you.'

'Where can I meet him?'

'He'll be here in a tick. He said he was coming at eight.'

'All right.'

'I'll get along then. If Krishnaswami comes in, shall I send him over?'

'Yes, do.'

'Right you are.'

He went out, and I guessed he'd gone to fetch Krishnaswami. Sure enough in about five minutes, this bloke blew in, complete with white bum-freezer and smoking a cheroot. I'd often seen him about, without knowing who he was. He always seemed to have plenty of cash to sling about. He was a thick-set chap with a little moustache and a brown spot on the white of his right eye. He looked sly, and he was, as things turned out.

'Excuse me,' he said, 'but am I addressing Mr. Adams?'

'You are.'

'May I sit down?'

'Certainly.'

He gave a little bow and sat down opposite me. 'What'll you have?' I said.

'A brandy, if I may.'

He sat there smiling and looking smug until the boy brought his brandy. Then he said: 'Mr Adams,' and stopped.

'Yes?' I said.

'It seems that my action in giving evidence last night has caused you much inconvenience,' Krishnaswami said. 'I should like to apologize for the trouble to which you have been put.' He spread his hands and smiled. 'Believe me, I am sincerely sorry.'

'That's all right,' I said.

'You are very kind. But perhaps if you would allow me to explain, you will understand the motives actuating my conduct. I feel sure you will understand.'

'Carry on.'

'Mr Adams, I am an Indian! Those coolies whom your car injured are Indians also—my own people. I am an enlightened Indian, a democrat. I do not believe in the caste system. It is barbarous and should be abolished. To me, all men are brothers. Those coolies are human beings like ourselves, are they not?'

'Oh, absolutely,' I said.

'Imagine, then, my feelings when on emerging from Fenner's, I saw these men struck down by your car and left bleeding and mangled in the roadway, while you yourself drove on without heed. Indians, Mr Adams, my own people! Natives, it is true, but not animals, to be slaughtered like cattle. I knelt down beside them, I was bathed in their blood. One had sustained terrible injuries to his head, it seemed as though he might die there in my arms. You can understand my anger, Mr Adams, and why, having noted the number of your car, I immediately denounced you to the police. Also, I must admit, I was at the time slightly intoxicated. Under the influence of liquor. It had gone to my head. Had I but reflected, I should not have taken the course which I did. But I acted on impulse. Upon the spur of the moment. Now I realize that I was wrong, that if you drove on it was from some other reason than callousness, and I am prepared, so far as I am able, to make amends. I cannot, alas, retract my statement to the police, but there are ways and means by which its effect may be softened.' He pulled a handkerchief out of his sleeve and started to mop his forehead. He'd got very heated talking about the coolies. He drank some brandy and went on. 'If for instance you were to offer some compensation to the family of the injured man—'

'Would that do any good?'

'In my opinion, yes. It would be a point in your favour when the case is brought to court.'

'How much money should I offer?'

'Something in the nature of five hundred rupees.' He looked at me sideways out of the eye that had the brown spot in it. 'If you were to give some such sum into my hands, I would see that it was distributed to the best advantage and in a manner which would rebound to your credit.'

'Oughtn't I to give it them myself?'

'No, I think perhaps it would come better through me—one of their own people, you know. I should of course make it quite clear that you were the donor, and that I was merely acting as intermediary.'

'Well, I tell you what. I'll sleep on it and let you know. How's that?'

'Admirable. I am staying at the Laburnum, just round the corner. Here is my card. You can always get in touch with me there.'

'Right.'

'And with regard to my evidence, I think we might achieve some compromise. My father, as you are doubtless aware, is Trade Commissioner in England at the moment. He would gladly exert his influence on your behalf.'

'Thanks.'

'I am pleased to be of service,' Krishnaswami said. 'Will you join me in a drink?'

'No, I won't have another now, thanks.'

'Just to show there is no ill-feeling.'

'No really, thanks. Not now.'

'As you wish,' Krishnaswami said. 'But I see you are a good sport, you do not bear malice. And perhaps you are wise not to drink too much. The police have an unworthy suspicion that you are a man of intemperate habits. Mr Holt, the commissioner, is your enemy. Beware of his spies. You are being watched at this very moment!'

'How d'you know all this?'

Krishnaswami smiled, smoking his cheroot. 'We natives have many systems of communication unknown to the European. Besides, news travels fast in the East. If you observe that table behind you, you will see that I am speaking the truth.'

I looked behind me. There was an awful crowd of Mohammedan sods sitting at that table: they looked more like cut-throats than detectives, but they were watching me right enough.

'Agents of Mr Holt,' Krishnaswami said. He got up from the table and bowed. 'Till our next meeting, Mr Adams.'

'So long,' I said, and watched him walk out, strutting, with the cheroot cocked up at a jaunty angle in his mouth. I looked at the card he'd given me. H. B. KRISHNASWAMI, it said, BACHELOR OF ARTS, OXON, and written underneath, 'Laburnum Hotel, Madras.' I took another look at those Mohammedans. Detectives be damned. More likely some of

Krishnaswami's pals, keeping an eye on me. It'd take more than them to stop me drinking. 'Boy,' I called, 'bring another whisky. A large one.'

Soon after this Shankran rolled in, all smiles as usual.

'Well, well, well! How's it going?'

'Not too good,' I told him.

'Now, now, don't get downhearted. Never say die, you know. This case isn't as bad as it seems, I've been making inquiries. It appears the police have a witness. A man named Krishnaswami.'

'I know. I've just been talking to him.'

'What!'

I told him what Krishnaswami had said to me. Shankran listened, holding a cigarette with his hand cupped round it, sucking up smoke from time to time. 'Yes. Yes. Yes,' he said, and when I'd finished: 'It's as you thought. This Krishnaswami is a crook. I have him taped, I've been on his track for some time. That's why I was pleased when I came in just now. If Krishnaswami appears in court I shall unmask him as an impostor. His evidence will be discredited.'

'But isn't he the son of Sir Somebody Krishnaswami then?'

'No, no. That's all bunk. Absolute nonsense. He's an imposter.'

'He said I was being watched by detectives. At the table behind.'

'What? Those ruffians. Bunk, my boy, bunk. Krishnaswami's after your cash.'

'That's what I thought.'

'You were right. But don't worry, we can circumvent him. He doesn't present a serious obstacle. No. The main thing is that coolie. If he dies, Holt will make it hot for you.'

'He put me under arrest this morning.'

'I know, I know. And Major Brant bailed you out.'

'News travels fast in the East,' I said.

Shankran said: 'I got it from the inspector. He and I are good friends. He will keep me posted with all details and developments as to police work.' Suddenly he looked very serious. 'But if that coolie dies…' He shook his head.

'What about the other one?' I asked.

'Oh, he's all right. A broken leg, that's all. We needn't worry about him.' Shankran tapped on the table. 'And listen, on no account give

Krishnaswami any money. Stall him, you understand. Procrastinate. But give him nothing. Take no one's advice but mine.'

'Sir Alec has called in Dr Menon, for the company.'

'Menon? I know him. One of these kid-glove lawyers. No pep. Not the man for this case. Pay no attention to him.'

'All right.'

'I'll deal with Krishnaswami. For the rest, pray to God that coolie doesn't die. Pray to God. I will pray for you myself tonight.' He was serious.

'Holy smoke!' I said.

'Boy, bring some gin!' Shankran said.

III

There were two mosquitoes had got in my net that night, and I couldn't sleep. Every time I dozed off, one of the bastards'd come singing round and sting me, and at last I had to get up and swat them. Even so I couldn't sleep for thinking of that coolie. It was bloody hot and I was sweating and I thought, suppose he does die? I didn't want to get three years like Cornford. I don't mind telling you I did pray that night, I was in an awful state. At last I managed to sleep, and woke late in the morning feeling lousy. I fined the blasted boy an anna for each of those mosquitoes and got off to the office. I hadn't been there long before the Old Man sent for me. I went up and he had Dr Menon with him, who looked serious.

'About this accident of yours, Adams,' Sir Alec said. 'Did you know the police have a witness?'

'Yes, sir,' I said. 'I've spoken to him.'

'Is it true he is the son of the Trade Commissioner in England?' Dr Menon said.

'He told me he was.'

Menon nodded. I could see he was impressed.

'What did he speak to you about?' Sir Alec said.

'He suggested that I should offer compensation to the injured man's family sir.'

'Humph! How much?'

'Five hundred chips.'

'Humph. What d'you think, Menon?'

'It wouldn't do any harm to parley with them sir,' Menon said. 'Have you got his address, Mr Adams?'

'Yes. Here's his card.'

'Well, we might go round there and see him this evening, eh?' He looked at Sir Alec, who grunted 'Good idea,' so I agreed.

That evening Menon and I went round to Krishnaswami's hotel, back of Mount Road. He was in right enough, very smooth and pleased to see us. It was a bloody sight to see those two, Menon and him, both talking Oxford English and trying to outdo each other at it. By God, you should have heard them. Krishnaswami let off a little bit about his father and I could see Menon believed him. He swallowed it whole. At last, after a lot of this, we got down to brass tacks. Krishnaswami still stuck out for five hundred chips and Menon seemed to think it'd be a good thing if I shelled out.

'But look here,' I said. 'The police are prosecuting me, not this fellow's family at all. How will it help to give them five hundred?'

'It would make a good impression on the court,' Menon said.

'But in any case the sum seems a bit stiff,' I said, and so it was. Why, what the hell, five hundred chips was pretty near a whole month's screw.

'Oh come, Mr Adams,' Krishnaswami said. 'When I think of that poor coolie, with his blood and brains bespattering the roadway, when I think of his poor family, of the terrible worry and uncertainty which they must be undergoing, I sometimes wonder whether any sum of money, however large, could be adjudged sufficient compensation.'

'Well anyhow,' I said, 'he's not dead yet, because I phoned up the hospital this afternoon and they say he's getting along nicely.'

I'd been keeping this up my sleeve as a trump card, and I could see it was a setback for Krishnaswami: he didn't like it at all. Then Menon came in with another one.

'Well,' he said, 'we will consider your proposal, Mr Krishnaswami. I personally am in favour of it. If Mr Adams will appoint some responsible person to distribute this sum among the man's family, I have no doubt that such an action would influence the court favourably.'

Krishnaswami didn't like that either. He'd counted on getting hold of the dough himself. He bowed and showed his teeth, but it wasn't a smile.

He said: 'Perhaps Mr Adams would prefer to consult his other lawyer, Mr Shankran, before committing himself to any course?'

'Mr Shankran?' Menon said. He frowned.

'I think I am correct, Mr Adams, am I not?' Krishnaswami said. 'Mr Shankran is acting for you also?'

'Yes,' I said.

I wondered for a moment how the hell he knew, and then I remembered those Mohammedans.

'News travels fast in the East,' I said.

Krishnaswami smiled and bowed. He knew I'd caught on, but he didn't care. He saw the game was up. Menon was still frowning. He didn't say anything more about Shankran, but he was upset all the same. Going downstairs, I tried to explain to him how it was, but he turned away and said: 'It is most unprofessional having two solicitors. You should have informed me before now.'

In the car he'd evidently thought up something, because he said: 'I wonder if it would be possible to see Mr Shankran this evening. Since this state of affairs has been allowed to transpire, perhaps it can be turned to advantage. Mr Shankran and I should compare notes as soon as possible.'

'We can see if he's in,' I said.

He was. We found him sitting at a table covered with briefs, busy on a big case, he told us.

'Dr Menon and I have just seen Krishnaswami,' I said.

'Oh, yes? What happened?'

Menon, still upstage and on his dignity, said: 'Apparently Mr Adams consulted you first, before Sir Alec called me in. I think therefore that we should pool our knowledge and work together as far as possible from now on.'

'Yes, yes. Quite. A pleasure, Dr Menon. What did Krishnaswami say?'

Menon told him.

'Are you satisfied that this man has no ulterior motive in suggesting compensation?' Shankran said.

'For my part, I am perfectly satisfied,' Menon said. They argued about it for some time, but Shankran wouldn't agree; he still didn't like the idea. At last Menon got up to go. He'd said good-bye and was at the door, when he turned round again as if he'd remembered something.

'Oh, yes. One moment, Mr Shankran.' He turned to me. 'I am sure you will excuse us, Mr Adams. Just a technical point.'

'Sure,' I said, 'don't mind me,' so they went out on the veranda together while I mixed myself another whisky and soda and as I was drinking it I could hear them out there talking away in Tamil. Presently they came back, both smiling, and Menon seemed in a better temper.

'That's settled then,' he said. 'If you should decide in favour of compensation, will you let me know, Mr Shankran?' and Shankran said he would, and Menon went out. He didn't shake hands with me, just said 'Good-bye,' and I think he was still a bit put out. Directly he'd gone, Shankran stopped smiling and turned round on me.

'The dirty bainchut,' he said. 'D'you know what he told me outside?'

'I've no idea.'

'Don't worry, Shankran,' he said, 'Get as much out of him as you can. I'm paid by the company, I won't ask you for a cut.' You see? The corrupt bainchut. They're all the same out here: squeeze you for your last anna. By God, Adams, you can thank your stars I'm straight!' He tapped on the table again. 'As for Krishnaswami, if he comes near that court I'll smash him. But he won't, depend upon it. Those five hundred rupees, he wants them for his hotel bill. It's the amount he owes the proprietor!'

'What!' I said. 'How do you know?'

'I found it out,' Shankran said. 'It's my business to find out things. Krishnaswami's up to his nose in debt. He's a twister!'

He took off his glasses and wiped them. He was so furious he started sweating hard, and the sweat ran down his nose on to his glasses so that he couldn't see. He wiped the glasses and said: 'However, he won't appear in court. He knows I'm after him!'

'You don't think Menon's working with Krishnaswami, do you?' I said.

'Menon? Oh, no. He's a twister too, but not that kind. Hasn't got the guts.'

'You don't think so?'

'I'm sure of it, my boy, sure of it. No. You needn't worry about that. As for the case, it'll go off all right if that coolie recovers.'

'He's doing well so far. I'm going up to see him at the hospital tomorrow.'

'That's fine,' Shankran said. 'But remember, don't give him any money. I'll tell you when the time comes to pay out.'

'Righto,' I said.

IV

I got up to the hospital next day and there was this coolie with his head and face bound up in bandages and all his family weeping and wailing round the bedside. The other coolie who had a broken leg was there too, but he didn't seem to have any family, or at least I didn't see them anyway.

The mother of the broken-headed coolie came across and, spoke to me. Of course it was all in Tamil and I couldn't understand the half of it, but I told her in English how sorry I was, and I think she understood, because she made a salaam and pointed to her boy and said a piece more, weeping all the time. I felt awful. The old woman didn't sound angry, only very sad, but she couldn't stop crying. I bloody near wept myself, I don't mind telling you. I spoke to the coolie, but he didn't answer: he was lying back with his eyes closed where you could see them through the bandages, and he looked pretty bad to me. I felt terrible. I spoke to the other coolie and he grinned up at me and seemed quite cheerful, so I said a bit more to the old mother who salaamed again, still sobbing, and the rest of the family crowded round all chattering and some of them salaamed too. They could tell I was sorry. Then I got out and told the matron to give the coolies anything extra they wanted and charge it up to me.

'That's very good of you, Mr Adams,' she said, 'but I think they are quite comfortable. They have all they want.'

'The one with the broken head looks bad. Will he live?'

'Certainly. He's quite out of danger now,' she said, so I thanked her and went out. Driving back to the bungalow I still felt awful about it though.

A week went by and I heard nothing more, except I had a summons from the police saying I was to appear on various charges in three days time. Then one morning Sir Alec sent for me.

'Adams,' he said, Dr Menon was here yesterday. He says he wants to give up the case as you already have a solicitor acting for you. Is that so?'

'Yes, sir,' I said.

'Who is he? A good man?'

'Yes, sir. Mr Shankran.'

'Humph! I've heard of him. Sails a bit near the wind sometimes, doesn't he?'

'He's a smart lawyer, sir.'

'Humph. Didn't he act for Cornford?'

'Yes, sir.'

'Think he'll get you off?'

'He seems pretty certain of it.'

'I'm glad of that. Sure you don't need Menon then?'

'No, sir.'

'Very well,' Sir Alec said, 'if you're satisfied.'

V

I couldn't find Shankran anywhere. He'd gone off on a case and nobody seemed to know where he was. I was due to appear next day and didn't know what the hell to do. I sat in Fenner's sopping up straight Scotch and feeling awful. Then suddenly, towards the end of the evening, Shankran came in. By God I was never so glad to see anyone in my life.

'Hullo, hullo, hullo,' he said. 'How are you? I've just come back from the hills. Been chasing a witness. Boy, bring some gin!'

'Listen,' I said. 'My case comes off tomorrow at twelve. Have you got everything fixed?'

'Tomorrow? I can't appear for you tomorrow. I'm up to my eyes. Rape. A very difficult case. I've bribed the chief witness but there are still two I've got to get at. Tomorrow's impossible. I shan't be here.'

'Well, what the hell's going to happen?'

'Don't worry. You won't appear either.'

'But I've had the summons!'

Shankran shook his head. 'You won't appear. You're ill. You can't appear if you're ill.'

'What d'you mean—ill?'

'You're sick. You've got dysentery.'

'I haven't at all.'

'Of course you have. Don't be silly. We'll get the case postponed. Meet me tomorrow morning and I'll fix it for you.'

So I met him next morning and he drove me right down to George Town, through the bazaar and a lot of stinking little streets and stopped at a chemist's shop that had posters up on the walls outside, advertising cures for siph.

'Up here,' Shankran said, so we went up some awful filthy stairs and into a doctor's waiting room full of natives covered in sores. Shankran sent in his card and the doctor saw us straightaway. He was a Hindu with a big black beard.

'Ah, yes. Mr Adams. How do you do? Dysentery, isn't it? I'll make the certificate out at once.'

He sat down and wrote a certificate saying I was suffering from dysentery and we thanked him and went.

'That's settled,' Shankran said. 'Drop me at the court as we go by, I'll just file the certificate. Don't be alarmed if you don't hear from me for a while, I've got to get after those witnesses. Curse the corrupt bainchuts. Baksheesh, that's all they think about in this country.'

VI

Fenner said to me one night: 'Seen Krishnaswami lately?'

'No,' I said.

'Well, you won't either. He's shot the moon. Blown off to Bangalore.'

'By God. Is that so?'

'It bloody well is. He owes that fellow at the Laburnum five hundred chips.'

'By God. Does he owe you anything?'

'No. But that little blighter Turpin does, and he's gone too. They've done a bunk together.'

'By God,' I said. 'Have another drink?'

VII

Well at last the case came off. I met Shankran the night before and he gave me a whacking long list of answers I had to make in court.

'Better memorize those,' he said. 'Learn them off by heart. You won't have much trouble, I know the magistrate. He's a gentleman. You won't have to go in the box. As for witnesses, Krishnaswami's gone. He got out when I threatened him with exposure. The night watchman from Spinner's saw the smash but I've fixed him all right. Major Brant will of course speak for you. The inspector's on our side as well. You'll have to give him three hundred chips by the way, when it's all over.'

'D'you think we'll win?'

'Of course we shall. Without Krishnaswami they've got no case at all. It'll be a walkover.'

The court was very hot and crowded, with bags of natives sprawling about the corridors, all chattering to beat the band, gobbing and chewing betel nut, and peons with red sashes and great brass plates on their chests strutting up and down bawling for silence and making more row than all the rest put together.

Inside, some native police were keeping order and it looked pretty much like the American courts on the cinema, with benches all the way down and a high dais for the magistrate to sit at. I saw old Brant and several of the boys, but no sign of Krishnaswami. Holt wasn't there, of course, being commissioner, but all the coolie's family were, and soon after an ambulance rolled up and the coolies themselves were carried in on stretchers.

'Have you got the answers off pat?' Shankran asked me.

'Yes,' I said.

Then the magistrate came in and we all stood up. He was a Mohammedan and Shankran knew him well. He rapped with the gavel and we all sat down again. Mine was the first case called. The inspector gave his evidence first, for the prosecution, then Shankran called Major Brant, for the defence.

After he had spoken, Krishnaswami's name was called. No answer. The usher walked up and down shouting 'Mr Krishnaswami!' but Krishnaswami didn't show up. The inspector was called back to the box.

He read out the statement made by Krishnaswami, to the effect that I had caused the accident and furthermore had callously driven on, being at the time under the influence of drink.

Shankran jumped up. He was sweating hard. He wiped his glasses and the back of his neck and shouted: 'Do you deny that this witness was himself intoxicated at the time of giving his evidence, and that moreover one of his companions was in such an unseemly condition that you refused to accept his statement?'

The inspector didn't deny it.

'Therefore the case for the prosecution rests solely upon the evidence of two men who were themselves in a state of intoxication, and who have since left the city,' Shankran said. 'Thank you, that is all.' He sat down again.

'You say these witnesses cannot be found?' the magistrate said.

'No, your worship,' the inspector said. 'Their present whereabouts are unknown.'

'H'm. Does the defendant plead guilty or not guilty?'

'Guilty, your worship,' Shankran said, 'on the charge of causing the accident; not guilty on the charge of intoxication.'

'Will the defendant please approach?'

Shankran nudged me, and I went forward and stood in front of the dais.

'You plead guilty to the charges against you?'

'Except to that of intoxication, your worship,' I said.

'What caused your car to collide with these men?'

'A pariah dog, your worship. It ran out in the road, and in my efforts to avoid it, caused the accident.'

'Why did you drive on, instead of stopping to assist the men you had injured?'

'I lost my nerve, your worship.'

'Why didn't you report to the police?'

'Same reason, your worship.'

'H'm. Well, in the absence of further witnesses, the case will have to be adjourned in order that the question of compensation be discussed among the parties concerned.'

Shankran jumped up again, wiping his glasses like mad.

'Your worship!' he said. 'Cannot the question of compensation be discussed without delay? My client has suffered considerable inconvenience as a result of this case and we would sooner proceed to its conclusion without further postponement.'

'Very well,' the magistrate said. He looked over at the coolies. The one with the broken leg had it done up in plaster of Paris and the other one had some of the bandages taken off his face and looked a bit better.

'Let us say then,' the magistrate stroked his chin, 'the sum of three hundred and fifty rupees.'

He repeated it in Tamil and looked at the coolies and at the old mother who was sitting with the family on the front bench. She nodded and started to cry again and the rest of the family began to argue and talk in Tamil.

The magistrate rapped for order and said: 'You are also fined one hundred and fifty rupees for driving an automobile to the common danger and fifty rupees for failing to report an accident to the police. These sums should be paid to the clerk of the court. Case dismissed,' so it cost me eight hundred and fifty chips altogether, including three hundred for the inspector, and on top of that came Shankran's fee. By God, it was worth it though. I went on the binge for a bloody month afterwards, I was so relieved at getting off. In fact that's what got me the sack eventually, not the accident at all. Sir Alec was damn decent about it on the whole, he said he couldn't keep me in the circumstances, but he gave me a damned good reference just the same. That's how I come to be home again.

Don't know of any good jobs going, do you?

Welsh Rabbit of Soap: A Romance

'You may find something new in a new face, you may be surprised by a different kind of a face, you may even be shocked by a different kind of a face, you may like or not like a new kind of a face, but you cannot refuse a new face. You must accept a face as a face.' Gertrude Stein (*Lectures in America*)

You know The Scotsman, off Soho Square? That's where I met her. I was pinned in a corner between the fireplace and the door of the Gents, and before I could escape Hester Hewart had introduced us. Her name was Vicky Baker.

I'd barely time to take in her beret and brown corduroy slacks when she said bang off: 'I don't like what you write. At least I like the style, but not the things you write about.' And she added: 'You see I'm a Conservative.'

Well naturally neither of these statements could be calculated to please me. But it wasn't only what she said: it was the way she looked.

She'd the blankest face I'd ever seen on a girl. Its utter lack of expression made it at first sight seem startling. It was a plump face and powdered dead white. A bell of smooth straight reddish-gold hair enclosed it. Her eye-lashes were stiff with make-up and she used orange lipstick.

Nor was this all. To make matters worse, she was clinging to the arm of a young man I particularly loathed: an R.A.F. Corporal called Dickie Galbraith. This person, tall, drooping, with corrugations of blond hair and a pink-and-white complexion, now greeted me as a long-lost pal and pressed a bitter into my hand. I was trapped. Over my head hung a sign saying that Betting Slips must not be passed in the pub. On my left was Hester Hewart holding forth on the Marxist interpretation of poetry. She broke off on seeing Galbraith to say in a loud voice how beautiful she thought he was. She and Vicky discussed his beauty enthusiastically for a bit while Galbraith himself simpered into his pint.

Then Vicky returned to the attack, saying 'Why don't you write about something else? It seems silly to spend all one's time slanging the army.'

I said: 'Perhaps if you'd been in the army you might feel like slanging it too.'

'Oh but I have,' she said. 'Two years in the ATS. I enjoyed every moment of it.'

'Pity you didn't remain in, then,' I told her.

Soon after this a stupid argument started. Hester Hewart, who was in her end-of-the-evening mood and becoming bellicose, began saying that the poet should be integrated with society. In opposition to this theory I cited Baudelaire, Verlaine, Dylan Thomas. She said: 'Look at Mayakovsky.'

I said: 'Mayakovsky was so integrated he committed suicide to prove it.' Then suddenly I couldn't stand them any more, and thrust my way out. It was nearly closing time, anyway.

Next time I saw Vicky she was again with Galbraith and they were holding hands. It was in another pub, the Burglars' Rest behind Charlotte Street, and they stood by the stairs, she leaning her head against his shoulder. Both had foolish smiles on their faces and glasses of bitter in their disengaged hands.

Three nights later, same pub, she bobbed up beside me at the bar and Galbraith was nowhere in sight. She opened fire immediately by saying: 'You know I'm not really a Conservative.'

'What!' I said; 'Changed your Party already?'

'No, no. You see I was never really one at all. I just said that for something to say.'

'You must be awfully hard up for topics of conversation,' I told her.

She pushed her half-pint round and round on the counter so that the bottom of it made circles of wet on the wood.

'You don't like me,' she said, 'do you?'

I saw no reason to be untruthful. I said: 'Not a lot.'

'Was it because of what I said about your work? Because I hadn't really read any of it then. I'd only read reviews.'

'And what have you read now?'

'I bought your book. I liked it awfully, especially the parts taking off the army.'

'But I thought you liked the army.'

'No,' she said, 'I hated it. You see I get nervous, and then I just say anything that comes into my head.'

At this, as though it had been his cue, a bald man with an ex-service badge in his lapel and strips of sticking-plaster across his forehead, staggered between us and said: 'D'you know what I'd do with the dead?'

'Bury them,' I suggested.

'That's it,' he said. 'Bury them. And over each grave I'd just put a simple wooden cross. What d'you say to that now?'

'Sound idea,' I said.

'No inscription, nothing. Just a simple wooden cross. That's all the lads ask for, eh? Have a drink.'

'I've got one, thanks.'

'That, sir,' the bald man said, 'is an inadequate reply to my question. I repeat: 'what're you drinking? As one ex-serviceman to another, I insist.'

'All right then, a Scotch ale.'

The bald man swivelled round, pointing an accusing finger at Vicky. 'And the lady?' he asked.

Vicky said: 'A bitter, please.'

I said 'This is Vicky. An ex-serviceman too. I didn't get your name.'

'Bob,' the bald man said. 'just plain Bob's good enough for me.' He called down the counter for drinks.

Vicky said: 'D'you like me any better now?'

'No,' I said. 'Why should I?'

'I thought you might.'

'I don't.'

'Oh.' Then she said, 'Are you still with Adam Stroud, doing scripts?'

'Alas, no longer.'

'What happened? He was so thrilled to have you with him last year.'

I said: 'He got less and less thrilled as time went on.'

Bob said: 'I used to know a bloke name of Stroud. In the Ninth. Would it be the same one?'

'It wouldn't,' I said. 'This one's a film producer.'

'My mistake,' Bob said. 'Stroud I knew was a postman.' He lifted his glass and said 'Pip.'

I said: 'Cheers,' and to Vicky: 'How d'you come to know Adam Stroud?'

'My husband used to work for him,' she said. 'Cutting room.'

'Your husband? I didn't know you were married.'

'I'm not any longer. I've just divorced him. Queer as a coot.'

'You must have married very young.'

'Last year. I'm twenty-two. We only stayed together three months.'

'I stayed with my wife six months. That's better.'

'And are you divorced now?'

'Definitely.'

'I've been married too,' Bob told us.

'How long did *you* stay married?' I asked him.

'I'm still married,' he said. 'More's the pity.'

'I liked being married,' Vicky said. 'At least I liked the idea. I shall marry again as soon as I can.'

'Who've you got marked down?' I asked her. 'Boy beautiful?'

'D'you mean Dickie?' She looked at me with a hurt expression in her enormous dark eyes, almost all pupil and the colour of toffee. 'Now you're being horrid,' she said.

'Horrid?' I said. 'How come?'

'Well, didn't you know? He's left me. Gone back to his wife.'

'Oh he's married too, is he?'

'Everyone seems married round here,' Bob said, staring gloomily into his glass.

'Vicky's not,' I said. 'She's divorced. We're both of us divorced.'

'Wish I was,' Bob said. 'How 'bout another wet?'

I said: 'Two Scotch ales and a bitter,' and to Vicky: 'What's Galbraith's wife like?'

'Possessive. Terribly possessive.'

'Let's get off the subject of wives,' Bob said. 'Sore point somehow.'

'Of course he's frightfully weak, poor darling,' Vicky said. 'He does just whatever she tells him to. D'you know, he was going to get a divorce and marry me, and she simply wouldn't let him.'

'You could hardly expect her to welcome the idea,' I said. 'Although I would in her place.'

'Now you're being horrid again.'

'Nonsense. I think you're well rid of him.'

'I know. But I just can't get him out of my mind. He's got such a beautiful face.'

'Drink this and don't be absurd,' I told her.

She drank it with several more to follow. She was evidently drinking to drown her sorrow. The pub began to fill up and Bob rapidly became inarticulate. He staggered about expounding his views on the disposal of the dead to everyone who came in. I took a trip aloft. When I got down Bob was still there, arguing with an American, but Vicky had vanished. I peered about for her; the atmosphere was now so thick the hanging lamps seemed to diffuse smoke downwards. Through the fog, at its thickest where the Public Bar was partitioned off, I could distinguish, leaning against the glass and wood, a group of young men swathed in scarves and smoking curved pipes, technically known to me as the Slithy Toves. To my dismay I suddenly caught sight of Vicky in their midst. A Tove with even more scarves on than the rest and wearing a polo sweater to boot, swayed in front of her, talking nineteen to the dozen. She saw me at the same time and waved wildly, calling out: 'Julian! Come and meet Walter.'

I looked round for my drink. It had disappeared, probably drunk by Bob. In a very bad temper I forced my way towards Vicky.

She said: 'Julian, this is Walter. We were up at Cambridge together.'

In an instant I was shaking hands with every Tove in sight. 'You can't all have been at Cambridge,' I said.

'No, I was at Oxford,' a Tove with an orange beard told me. 'I edited a magazine there. Are you an editor?'

'God forbid,' I said.

'Pity, because if you were, I'd some poems here I'd like to show you. D'you know Tambi by any chance?'

I was saved from replying to this by a nudge in the ribs from behind. I turned and saw Sheila Parsons, wrapped in fur and smiling at me over the top of a gin which she held in both hands, to safeguard it.

'Just thought I'd say hullo,' she said, and nodding towards the group: 'Your latest?'

'The orange beard?' I said. 'Really, Sheila!'

'No, silly. The little girl in trousers. *You know quite well who I mean.*'

'Really, Sheila,' I began again, and then stopped. There in front of me was Vicky's hair; she hadn't her beret on, she was shaking it back; smooth straight reddish-gold hair, worn in a bell: exactly the sort of hair I hate most. And I suddenly realised that what I wanted to do most was to stroke it.

I took a step back; it was an awful moment. This outcome to the evening had honestly not occurred to me. I glanced round for a way of escape, but the Toves were between me and the door; beyond them was Bob, and at my side was Sheila, grinning at me over her gin-and-lime.

'Well,' she said, 'I'll leave you to it. Good hunting,' and with that she started to sidle away in the crowd. I tried desperately to call her back, but she was gone: swallowed up. This was shocking; I hadn't even a drink. The landlord was engaged down the other end of the counter. There was nothing for it; I reached out and tapped Vicky on the shoulder. She turned instantly and ducked in under my arm; her head came exactly level with my chin.

'Let's get out and go elsewhere,' I said to her.

She shook her hair back and smiled. 'You do like me better now, don't you?'

'No, I don't.'

'Yes you do, or you wouldn't want me to come with you.'

'All right,' I said, 'but let's go.'

At once all the Toves surrounded us with cries of protest. They saw Vicky slipping through their fingers. The orange-bearded Tove even offered to show me his poems on the spot if only we'd remain. I resisted this tempting offer and, holding Vicky by the arm, steered for the exit. Bob suddenly staggered in front of us but I swept him aside.

At last we were out in the street, heading for The Scotsman. Vicky swayed a little as the cold air hit her. She said: 'You know, I think I'm a tiny bit tight.'

'Wouldn't surprise me at all.'

'I'm not much good at drinking,' she said. 'I'm more cut out for a domestic life. Darning socks and so on.'

'Slippers by the hearth,' I said.

'That's it. I'd make someone an awfully good wife.'

'Well,' I said, 'why not marry me?'

'Instead of Dickie?'

'A much better idea.'

'But you don't like me.'

We were crossing Oxford Street.

'I might in time,' I said.

'You really think so?'

The lighted windows of The Scotsman loomed up ahead of us.

I said: 'It's possible.'

'All right,' she said. 'Then I can darn your socks.'

'They've got big holes,' I told her.

There weren't many people in the pub: no one we knew. I got a couple of gins and said: 'Let's drink to our forthcoming marriage.'

'All right.' So we drank. Then she said: 'You are serious about this, aren't you? You do mean it?'

'Of course.' And the funny part was that I did mean it. Every word. When I realized this I got a little nervous, and said: 'What about you? Are you serious, or just tight?'

'No,' she said. 'I'm not tight any more. Mixing them must have sobered me up.'

'Good. Then we'll get married.'

'Yes, when?'

'Soon as I find a flat. We'll start looking round tomorrow.'

'We're bound to find something,' Vicky said. 'Now let's play pin-table.'

So we did. It was a disappointing pin-table; it was supposed to light up but it didn't. Vicky was much better at it than I; she got huge scores and danced about delighted.

'I'll kiss you when we get outside,' I told her.

'Of course you will,' she said. 'Look, 5,000!'

The steel balls ran down grooves in the board; bells rang up the score; the machine should have been lit like a Christmas tree. Vicky said: '12,500,' shaking back her hair triumphantly.

'I don't believe you're the least bit interested,' I said.

'In what?'

'In my kissing you.'

'But darling of course I am.' She took hold of my hand and squeezed it hard. 'I wanted you to kiss me ever since we first met.'

'What rot!'

'It isn't rot. That's what made me so nervous.'

The door burst open and everyone came in: the complete cast from the other pub; all the Toves and Bob in the background, by now speechless with drink. Vicky let go of my hand and said: 'Look, there's darling Walter! Toves surrounded us immediately on every side; I cursed quietly to myself. It was clear that with this crowd I'd never succeed in getting more gin; the bar was blocked from sight; it would also be difficult to pry Vicky loose from the Toves, who had backed her away from me into a corner.

Luckily at this moment a fight started up in the centre of the floor. I swiftly downed my drink, thrust Walter aside, and got Vicky by the arm. We edged round the fringe of the fight; a huge Guardsman was good-naturedly holding apart the combatants, both small men, who were spitting and snarling at each other in his grasp. One managed to get an arm loose and throw his beer, which missed and went over Bob, who was offering inarticulate advice to the man the beer was intended for. I pushed Vicky through the door into the street: we heard a crash of glass as it closed behind us.

I said: 'Let's get clear before the police come.'

We walked rapidly down the street, dark and quiet with no one about. By the pillar-box we both stopped and Vicky said: 'My lipstick doesn't smear.'

Her mouth felt large and dry at first, the lips a little rough; then as they opened, cool and wet with a taste of violets on her tongue. Her hair fell against my cheek and I stroked it back, smooth and silky under my hand.

'Darling,' I said, and she murmured back Darling; 'You really will marry me?'

'Whenever you like.'

We kissed again; it lasted a long time; her fingers convulsed on my shoulder and she went limp within my encircling arm. Then from the direction of The Scotsman a shout, stumbling footsteps, the sound of someone falling, made us draw apart.

'Damn,' I said.

Vicky said: 'I think I'm going to fall in love with you.'

'Well that's natural, since we're engaged.'

Behind us the fight seemed to have extended into the street; by the sound of it more people were being slung out, and I said to Vicky: 'Come on'—up an alleyway, out into Charing Cross Road.

Vicky said: 'Where to now?'

'Eat,' I said; 'St. Giles' High.'

'Good, I'm starving.'

A red neon sign said OPEN and we walked into a restaurant full of Americans and tarts chewing gum. Over spam and chips I said: 'Will you meet me for lunch tomorrow? Back bar, Café Royal?'

'Of course. My time's yours from now on.'

I said: 'She promised him all her days, as though they had been dances.'

'That's sweet,' she said. 'Quotation?'

'I can't remember from whom.'

She put on her serious look and said: 'You know I'm monogamous. You won't mind, will you?'

'You mean you'll always be in love with Galbraith?'

'No, with you, of course. How stupid you are. I'd forgotten all about Dickie.'

'Keep on forgetting.'

'I'll have amnesia,' she said, and giggled into her coffee-cup.

'Closing now, please,' a waitress with a scar on her cheek told us.

'God, the last tube,' Vicky said springing up. 'It goes at twelve.'

Outside in the dark, among the dustbins and milk churns, we kissed goodnight, but not for as long as I'd have liked because of the tube. Another quick kiss at the foot of the escalator, and I watched Vicky run helter-skelter through an arch with NO ENTRY written across the top of it.

She lived, so she'd told me, near Baker Street; I was staying with friends at Hyde Park Corner. Change at Leicester Square; Gillette Blades; Nestlés Milk; Barclays Lager; a guardsman in a bearskin, advertising Greys Cigarettes, stared at me sternly down from the wall.

I thought about flats; in the Piccadilly train a woman in a white fur coat, with a lilac scarf tied round her head and holding her ticket between her teeth, was reading the *Complete Works of Oscar Wilde* through horn-rimmed spectacles.

When I came back into the bar at one o'clock next day, Saturday, Vicky wasn't there. At first this didn't worry me; I ordered a gin and leant back against the rail to wait for her.

I was in a very good mood and still surprised about it. I'd fully expected to wake with a hangover and the sense of doom attendant, in days gone by, upon the realization that once again I had become engaged to be married.

Ten minutes passed; a quarter of an hour. I began to get anxious. I suddenly thought: suppose she doesn't turn up at all? Suppose she's thought it all over and decided not to come. I drank two more gins, glanced round at the door each time it opened: a naval officer, a war correspondent: still no Vicky. At last, just as I had begun to despair and to order doubles, in she bounced: plaid raincoat, corduroy slacks and all, but minus her beret.

'Am I late?'

'No, no. Another large gin, please, Frank.'

Vicky said: 'D'you think we could sit down? I feel awfully conspicuous dressed like this in here.'

'Nonsense. You look lovely.'

'I feel like death.'

This did not sound a promising start, and as we sat down I searched her face for signs that she was preparing to say she'd changed her mind or that we should regard the night before as a drunken interlude much better forgotten by both of us. Her face, being as usual completely blank, gave nothing away, but she seemed at the same time a bit jumpy, drinking half her gin at a gulp, glancing furtively from side to side, and shaking her hair back far too often. I decided to put matters to the test, and said 'Darling, do you still feel the same?'

Vicky said: 'Of course, darling,' with a quick scared smile: 'Do you?'

'Of course.'

'I'm so glad!' she said, and her smile became radiant.

'I was terribly afraid you wouldn't. All the way here I kept saying to myself, "He won't feel the same. I know he won't feel the same." And now you do and everything's marvellous. We both feel the same, don't we, darling? About everything?'

'About everything.'

'I'm so glad. Look, I brought *Dalton's Weekly* with me. We'll go through it over lunch, line by line.'

'Flat by flat.'

She squeezed my hand. But the sight of a girl in a mink coat, with orange hair and green spectacles, moving to the bar attended by a white poodle, plainly intimidated her, and she said: 'Could we go and have lunch, darling? I feel terrible in these clothes with everyone else so smart.'

Nothing I could say would make her feel any better, so we went out. On the way upstairs she explained all about her clothes; they were locked up in a bungalow she had near Southend; she had sublet this to a man who'd suddenly gone abroad on a ministry job and taken the key with him; now, until his return, she had only the things she stood up in.

We got to the balcony. There was a table reserved for someone called Ross, but he was an admiral and the table was for seven. 'Try the next floor, sir.' We did; there was one table vacant: it was set in the middle of a room occupied by people even smarter than those in the back bar. I feared that this would further embarrass Vicky, but she was by now determined to brazen it out. She did, however, remove her plaid raincoat, in design curiously like a bath-robe, and was revealed to be wearing underneath a white silk blouse with short sleeves. Her arms were plump and round and freckled. She propped her elbows defiantly on the table and handed me the menu, saying: 'You choose.'

Later, while we ate pâté maison, she said: 'You know, I had a visitor this morning. Guess who. Dickie!'

'I thought he'd gone back to his wife.'

'He had, but you see his leave's up. He's back in town, stationed not far from my flat. This morning he popped round before going on duty. It was horribly early, not even daylight. I woke up and there he was, standing by the bed reciting *Finnegans Wake*. I nearly passed out, he was the last person I expected to see.'

'But how the hell did he get in?'

'I'd left my key on the outside last night. I often do. I never can remember things like that. So Dickie walked calmly in and made himself a cup of tea, just like he used to in the old days before we agreed to split. I thought he had a nerve, I must say.'

'What'd you do?'

'Well, at first I didn't think I could face up to a scene that early, I was still only half-conscious. But by the time the tea was made and he'd stopped reciting I'd woken up enough to tell him where he got off. I told him it was all over and anyway I was going to marry someone else, but I don't think he took any of it in; at any rate he pretended not to. He just recited another long piece of *Finnegans Wake* and then he drank the tea and went off to duty and I went back to sleep again.'

'Did you tell him not to come back?'

'Of course, darling. But anyway I'll remember to lock the door at night and then he just can't get in at all. Simple,' and she smiled radiantly at me.

'What's all this *Finnegans Wake*?' I asked her.

'Poor sweet, it's his one parlour trick. The only thing he *can* do, really. He does it beautifully, word for word. You really ought to hear him.'

'I don't want to hear him and I've read *Finnegans Wake*.'

'Now you're jealous.'

'Yes.'

'You don't have to be, darling. He doesn't mean a thing to me any more.'

'I don't like him hanging around.'

'He won't hang around. If he does I'll tick him off.'

I was afraid all this talk about Galbraith, and the morning visit, would have brought back memories which I'd no wish to have rekindled in her, but she seemed to speak of him quite impersonally, and for the moment I was reassured.

Over the escalope de venaison she changed the subject herself to a long account of how she got chucked out of the C.P.

I said: 'I didn't know you were ever a Communist. I thought you were a Conservative.'

'Now darling you mustn't tease me. I was a terrific Communist once upon a time. My husband was a Communist too, so there.'

'Did he get chucked out as well?'

'No, only me.'

'And what are your politics now?'

'No politics, only you.'

'Darling,' I said. 'Let's look out some flats.' So we spread *Dalton's Weekly* open on the table, but the only flat that seemed remotely possible was in Percy Street, seven rooms and six guineas a week.

'Too big and too expensive,' Vicky said. 'Unless you've got a lot of money, darling.'

'No.'

'*I* haven't any. My papa allows me two-ten a week, that's all. Of course I could always get a job, couldn't I?'

'No.'

'I've had lots of jobs,' Vicky said. 'I was a reporter once on a paper in Liverpool and then I acted in Rep, then there was the ATS, I did mess orderly and signals, and then I worked in a shop selling gramophone records. I asked Adam Stroud for a job once. I'd done cutting in the Cambridge Film Society you see, so I had experience. But he wouldn't take me on.'

'What'd he say.'

'I talked to him like mad for two hours, all about angles and montage and crane-shots and *Citizen Kane*, and all he did in the end was laugh and say come back in two years time. The two years is just about up, come to think of it.'

'No, you stick to darning my socks.'

'All right, darling. Will you look after my allowance for me when we're married? I'll turn it all over to you.'

'No.'

'As you like, darling. Have you got a comb? I lost mine last night. Damn nuisance.'

I lent her my comb and she began on her hair in bravado, glaring across the restaurant at a woman in a leopard-skin hat. After she'd finishing combing and we'd had coffee, I said: 'What d'you want to do now?'

'A flick.' So we had a last gin in the upstairs bar among the red tabs and came out into Glasshouse Street where rain had begun to fall quite fast. Because of Vicky's hair we sheltered in a doorway in Brewer Street. I leant over and kissed her quickly on the mouth; a tart from an upstairs window opposite made rude noises at us and we broke away; the rain began to pour down in a torrent; a party of drunken sailors came reeling up the road and, undeterred by weather conditions, began to call on the woman to come down.

We ran for it through the rain to a doorway lower down and Vicky suddenly said: 'Damn, I'd forgotten. Darling, I *must* get a job.'

'Why "must"?'

'It won't be for long, only about a week. You see I must have £7 to buy myself some new clothes.'

'I'll give you £7.'

'No, that wouldn't be right, darling. I promised myself I'd earn the money. It wouldn't be honest to take it from you.'

We argued about this for some time; the sky had cleared meanwhile and the rain degenerated into a drizzle; the sailors had staggered off and could be heard shouting 'Taxi' in the distance. In the end Vicky agreed to accept the £7 as a wedding present, but not until we were actually married. 'Now I must spend my points,' she said. 'I've just remembered it's the last day.'

We went to a store called Wales, where Vicky was found to have enough points to buy a tin of beans. As we came out she said: 'Look, a rainbow!' and there it was: an enormous one, arching across the sky above the tall grimy houses, the stalls selling vegetables, the cabbage leaves stamped flat on the wet pavement, as the sun came out and the rain ceased altogether as though turned off from a tap.

'That's for us, darling,' Vicky said. 'A good omen. I'll always remember that,' while the stallholders shouted and a fat Frenchwoman argued the price of apples.

Cutting through an alleyway off Wardour Street we came upon a man being beaten up. An American soldier was doing it, while his pals stood by to lend a hand if necessary. The first blow had already been struck and the seedy man in the bowler hat who'd received it was leaning dazed against the wall with blood trickling down his chin. He made no attempt to defend himself; his hands hung limply at his sides; a pencil had just fallen from between his fingers, but it seemed unlikely from the look of him that he was an artist or that he had been using the pencil to make a sketch.

I wanted to interfere but Vicky hurried me on. She said: 'I hate fights, I can't stand the sight of blood. It makes my stomach go all funny.' She had hold of my arm tight; the incident had clearly upset her, but next moment she seemed to have forgotten it, saying: 'Let's see if *Horizon*'s out, darling.' In the shop she bumped into a boy she knew called Derek. He was a typical Tove: pale and small and spotted, wearing a dark blue shirt and a pink tie. Before I knew what was happening, we were invited to supper with him on Monday and Vicky had accepted for both of us. I thought this a bit thick, and outside I said so. Vicky said: 'But darling, he's a Quaker.'

'What's that got to do with it?'

'Well, I'm a Quaker too.'

This shook me. A Conservative, a Communist, a Quaker—what would she turn out to be next? I said: 'Does that mean I have to have supper with every member of the Society of Friends?'

'All right,' Vicky said. 'Don't come if you don't want to.'

'I won't.' We walked on towards Leicester Square in silence for a bit, then she slipped her hand into mine. 'Don't be angry, darling.'

'All right my pet.' But I decided that when we were married people like Derek would have no part in our existence.

The sight of a chemist's shop recalled to Vicky the loss of her comb. The search for one to replace it now started up in earnest. This was wholly unsuccessful, and I began to fear it might go on all day. 'Here,' I said, 'take mine, and let's go to the cinema.'

'Darling you are sweet. Can you spare it?'

'I've got another. Now what d'you want to see?'

To my surprise she chose, not Carmen Miranda or Maria Montez, but *The Mask of Dimitrios.* Posters outside promised us Bigger and Better Murders, and depicted Sidney Greenstreet in a dressing-gown, pointing a pistol at the queue, with Peter Lorre in the background.

Dimitrios was just starting when we took our seats: the ragged children scampered shrieking away from the swollen corpse on the Bosphorus shore and Vicky felt for my hand. It'd been my intention to make love to her in the dark of the cinema, but the film was too good for that; except for an occasional comment designed to display her knowledge of cine-technique, Vicky also became immersed in the intrigue and action. The film drew to a close: the *mille* notes fluttered down the stairwell and Greenstreet called sadly back: 'There's too little kindness in the world' from between the escorting agents; we rose and made for the exit.

Outside it was quite dark and seven o'clock. Vicky hummed happily to herself the tango from the night club scene: 'That'll be our tune, darling,' she said. 'Whenever I hear it played I'll think of you.'

It was not until we had neared Piccadilly that she remembered leaving her tin of beans under the seat in the cinema. She immediately wanted to return and look for it, but I managed to dissuade her from doing this.

'Anyway,' she said, 'I couldn't care less. I hate beans. Where are we going now?'

'Café Royal.'

We had dinner in the downstairs café, where Vicky felt less uncomfortable. The meal was not without interruption; a young actor with a silver chain round his wrist came over to our table and tried to date Vicky up; shortly afterwards she wanted to go across and ask James Agate for his autograph; but it was not until coffee had been cleared away and we'd settled down to drink that the real trouble started.

Vicky suddenly said: 'My God, it's after nine. I've got to go up to The Scotsman.'

'What for? The Scotsman's hell on Saturday night.'

'I've got to go there, that's all.'

'But you must have a reason.'

Vicky at this became very vague. She began a long incoherent explanation: a strawberry blonde and a message that had to be given her came into it somehow. I got angry. It seemed that our life together was to be lived entirely on the borders of Soho, subject to constant intrusion from Toves and Quakers and strawberry blondes. This wasn't my plan at all, and I told her so. Vicky's mouth began to droop dejectedly at the corners as I talked on. At last she said in a wretched voice, 'Then you have changed your mind after all.'

'I haven't in the least. But don't you see, I want to marry you, not the whole of the Burglar's Rest.'

'You're not just making this an excuse to get rid of me?'

'No.'

'Certain?'

'Absolutely.'

She blinked her eyelashes at me and her smile came slowly back. 'Oh darling, I'm so glad. I was afraid you'd got bored with me already.' She said: 'You see I've no self-confidence at all.'

'Don't sound so miserable, darling,' I said.

'It upsets me when we quarrel.'

'Me too. Let's have another drink.'

'And I won't go to The Scotsman if you don't want me to.'

Later, while we were drinking gin, she said: 'You know, I lied to you just now. About the strawberry blonde.'

'Did you?'

'I was meeting Dickie. I promised him I would this morning.'

'But why? I thought you'd told him it was all over.'

'So I did, but he looked so helpless, poor darling, I agreed to have a final talk tonight.'

'To hell with him. He can go and recite *Finnegans Wake*.'

'All right, darling. Let's talk about us. You do love me?'

'I've told you so. I usually tell the truth.'

'I don't.'

'I've noticed that.'

She giggled. 'Now don't be nasty, darling. When do we get married?'

'First a flat. Then special licence.'

'Oughtn't we really to think it over first,' she said with her serious look. 'We're not being awfully practical, are we?'

'I don't want to be practical and I don't need to think it over. Do you?'

'No, darling. Not in the least.'

It was finally decided we ought to be married by Wednesday. Vicky remembered a friend of hers who was moving out of her flat on Monday, it was three-ten a week and sounded ideal; we'd ring her first thing in the morning. On this note of hope the lights in the café went down and we got up to go.

Outside I slipped my arm round Vicky and drew her into a doorway. After a moment she jerked free so suddenly I hit my head a whack on the wall. 'What's wrong?' I said crossly.

'I'm not sure I like being kissed like that.'

'You didn't seem to mind it last night.'

'Don't be vulgar, darling.'

'Ah, to hell,' I said. The bump on my head hurt and Vicky suddenly seemed impossible: just another tiresome little girl who wasn't worth the trouble one took. I turned to walk away from her, but two paces along the street she caught me up. 'Please, darling, don't be furious. It wasn't that really.'

'Wasn't what?'

'That I didn't like being kissed. It's that I've got a burn on my lip that hurts. Honest. I burnt it with a cigarette this morning. Look, you can see.' She drew me under a gaslamp and pointed to her lower lip, but by the dim jet I could see nothing. 'The light's too bad,' I said.

On the escalator at Piccadilly she again tried to show me the burn; her lip was a little swollen, but I still couldn't see anything else. 'I'll take your word for it,' I said.

'You're still cross. Please, darling, don't be. Look, I'll come with you to your train.'

Down in the corridor, with people clattering past, she suddenly threw her arms around my neck. The burn didn't seem to prevent her from kissing this time. We stood firmly embraced until someone behind shouted: 'Mind yer backs!'

'Damn,' Vicky said, smoothing her hair. 'I do wish we were married.'

'So do I.' Hand-in-hand and at peace once more, we came out on to the platform. My train was in and I jumped aboard. Vicky called out: 'What about tomorrow? Where?'

'Burglars,' I called back, 'Lunchtime'—the glass doors slid-to, cutting us off one from the other; I was carried away in the Tube with a lump on my skull and an orange stain of lipstick round my mouth to commemorate our second day together.

In the morning the bump had gone down, but the day started with a disappointment. Vicky's friend had already let her flat.

'So we're back where we started,' I said, watching Vicky wind spaghetti round her fork in the Frith Street restaurant where we went after the pubs shut down on us.

Vicky said: 'We'll try the agents tomorrow. In the end there's always that flat in Percy Street. Between us we might manage it.'

'Yes, there's always Percy Street.'

And that was where we later found ourselves, after an interlude during which we looked in shop windows in Oxford Street. 'I love looking in shops,' Vicky said. 'Sunday's the only day you can do it without being crushed to death by crowds.'

We stared through plate glass at a scarlet hat on a chromium stalk. Then into a static water tank, at the houses reflected, rippling, upside down in it. Then we wandered up into Percy Street to look at the outside of the flat. The house was painted white and above a restaurant. We rang the bell but no one answered. We stood on the sidewalk debating what to do with our day; we'd both seen the French film at the Carlton; the bigger cinemas were sure to be full up; Turkish coffee in

Tony's seemed to impend like a threat.

'What about your place?'

'No good. What about yours?'

'Too sordid,' Vicky said. I could imagine it: the unwashed dishes, unmade bed, perhaps a brassiere crumpled up in a corner of the room. 'Never mind. This time next week we'll be married.'

Arm in arm, hugged closely together, we walked along Charlotte Street, stretching emptily ahead in the Sunday afternoon silence. Then I had a brainwave. 'Let's see if Sheila Parsons is in.'

'I don't think I know her.'

'I'll introduce you.'

Sheila was in: she popped her head out of the third-floor window, she waved and threw down the key. Vicky at once became worried, patted her hair, examined her mouth in a hand-mirror halfway up the stairs. 'It makes me nervous meeting your friends.' But by the time Sheila opened the door she'd put on a false front of self-assurance, talking a little louder than usual, moving immediately to the gas-fire and sitting beside it on the floor, while Sheila fetched in the coffee and the cake.

I could see straightaway that things were not going to go well. Sheila's air of great sweetness, her wide ingenuous eyes whenever she addressed Vicky, told me that from the start. They soon discovered mutual friends and settled down to the discussion of someone called Sammy, who sounded hell. They talked about his taste in wine. Actors came next, after Sammy was exhausted; this led Vicky to a description of how she had played Sadie Thompson in Rep.

'I'm sure you were frightfully suited to the part,' Sheila said, with her most innocent flattering stare. I wasn't going to stand for this; I sidetracked Sheila, by a quick mention of Budapest, on to a train of reminiscence: girlhood in Hungary, parties at which she'd become Cleopatra. Unfortunately her marriage cropped up midway; Vicky, not content to let well alone, blundered in with an account of her own wedding, and Sheila's eyes narrowed instantly to slits. 'Now let me see. What did you say your husband's name was?'

Vicky's husband turned out to have two names and to be Irish; Sheila innocently disclaimed any knowledge of his family: had he lived in America? Ah yes, that explained it, he was possibly an Irishman whose parents had emigrated. I chipped in with a request for more coffee; Sheila, pouring out, became at once the perfect hostess; Vicky complimented her on the beauty of her flat.

'I'm a believer in gracious living,' she said several times—far too often. I could see Sheila storing up this phrase as a stick to beat me with in time to come. The gas-fire glowed and hummed; dusk had long since darkened the windowpanes; as we got up to go I couldn't resist dropping my bombshell.

'You know, Sheila, Vicky and I are going to be married some time this week.'

'On Wednesday,' Vicky cut in. 'Wednesday at the latest.'

There was a moment of silence. Then Sheila said: 'Married?'

'That's it. Married on Wednesday. Aren't you going to wish us luck?'

Sheila put down the coffee cup she was holding in her hand. She stared at us both in an effort to decide whether we were joking or just drunk. Then after another pause she managed to say she hoped we'd be happy. Her voice sounded quite dazed and she forgot to come with us to the door.

Out again in Charlotte Street, heading for dinner in Bertorelli's, Vicky said: 'But, darling, you didn't ask her to the wedding.'

'Nobody's being asked to the wedding,' I told her.

All down the street she prattled on about how much she liked Sheila; she firmly believed she'd been a success; I did nothing to disillusion her, beyond a mental note that Mrs. Parsons was to be avoided in future.

Pubs opened at seven: the Burglars, owing to beer-shortage, at eight. By the time we entered the saloon-bar it was already crowded; a man with a waxed moustache was going round with a hat collecting bail for Bob, run-in on Friday night after the fight in The Scotsman.

Suddenly Vicky pulled at my coat-sleeve; she'd gone quite pale. 'Here's Dickie. He's just come in.'

'What of it?' I said.

'Don't let him see me, that's all.'

I looked along the counter and saw Galbraith, in civvies, buying himself a pint of bitter. He was wearing a brown suit and a bright blue shirt and looked, in this combination of colours, with his fair flushed face, like a farm-hand in his Sunday best. He made no attempt to approach Vicky: walked over and stood with his back to the fireplace, glass in hand, looking over the heads of the crowd with his tired self-conscious simper.

But his presence plainly made Vicky uncomfortable, she shook back her hair, fidgeted with her gloves, spilled her beer, and finally said: 'I'd better go over and speak to him, darling. Do you mind?'

'Go ahead,' I told her. I leaned on the counter, not looking at them; the man with the waxed moustache came past again with the hat; he'd bought a round of drinks with the proceeds of his first collection; I didn't fancy Bob's chances of being bailed out at this rate.

Vicky bobbed up again at my side. 'Well, that's done, darling. Buy me a gin.'

But later she said: 'Darling, I've got to speak to Dickie again. I've just remembered he's got a book of mine I want back.'

'Carry on,' I said.

So over she went and said something to him; his expression did not alter when she spoke, he nodded and she sat down again beside me. The pub was filled to bursting, one's eyes smarted from the smoke, Scotch ale ran out and left only bitter: the man with the waxed moustache was buying another round. The original purpose of his collection seemed by now to have completely faded from his memory.

It was when Vicky decided for the third time that she must speak to Galbraith that my patience began to wear a little thin. I said 'No.'

'Darling, I *must*. I promise this'll be the last.'

'Look,' I said. 'There's no sense in telling a man you're all washed up with him if every five seconds you've got to run over for another little chat. You just leave the fellow alone.'

'I've got to talk to him. Please.'

'All right,' I said. 'Then I'm off.'

'Don't be silly, darling. I'll be right back.'

'You won't find me waiting.'

She evidently didn't take me at my word, so I thought I'd teach her a lesson. While she had her back turned talking to Galbraith, I pushed my way through to the door. But by the time I'd reached the street corner my anger had abated, and I paused. I half expected her to come running after me, but she didn't. At the same time I was damned if I'd go back there. It was nearly ten; the pub'd be closing soon; I thought I'd wait for her in the Tube.

But after twenty minutes it was plain she wasn't coming. Perhaps she'd taken a bus, or meant to walk. I thought I'd wait for her outside her flat.

Then I realized I didn't even know where she lived. Oh well, there was always tomorrow. She was bound to turn up somewhere in the neighbourhood. I set out along Oxford Street with the idea of encountering her perhaps on the way. I didn't. I turned down a side-turning off Regent Street, thinking perhaps she'd ring me when I got home. 'Tu viens, mon petit?' asked a Frenchwoman in furs, appearing out of a doorway and flashing a torch in my face.

'Ah non, madame, c'est impossible.'

She showed no surprise at being answered in French: the sound of her own language merely made her more difficult to shake off.

'Impossible, pourquoi? T'es malade?'

'Pas du tout.'

'Fauché?'

'Non. Suis marié.'

'Ah, moi aussi. Mais faut bien s'amuser quelquefois, hein?'

'Madame vous êtes bien aimable. Mais pas ce soir.'

'Une livre, c'est tout-ce que j'demande. C'est bon marché.'

'Peut-être une autre fois.'

'Comme tu voudras, alors. C'est bien dommage.'

'Bonsoir, madame.'

'Soir, mon petit.'

Vicky didn't ring me when I got home Sunday night. She didn't ring on Monday morning either. I lunched at Bertorelli's, her favourite restaurant, in the hope of seeing her. She wasn't there: nor did she come into the Burglars' or The Scotsman. When the pubs closed I was stumped. I'd no idea what she normally did in the afternoon or where she was likely to be. I rang Hester at her Ministry in the hope of finding out Vicky's address, only to be told that Miss Hewart was taking a couple of days' leave in the country.

I wandered down Charing Cross Road thinking she might be in one of the bookshops, but no. Still, I thought, she's sure to come round this evening, if only to collect me for the Quaker supper. On the other hand she might easily go there direct, and I'd completely forgotten where it was to take place. Bermondsey? Brixton? I couldn't for the life of me remember.

At 5.30 I went into the Café Royal: no Vicky; I trekked up to The

Scotsman: same result I looked in the Fitzroy, the Marquis, Bertorelli's again: not a sign of her. Then I settled down to wait in the Burglars'. Every time the door opened my heart gave a hop, but by half-past nine I'd abandoned hope. She was surely supping with the Quakers by now.

Krishna came in. 'Hallo, Julian. All alone?'

'D'you know a girl called Vicky Baker?'

'Long hair, Bloomsbury type, goes about with Galbraith?'

'That's her. Seen her anywhere about.'

'Not tonight, last night. She was having supper in Tony's.'

'Galbraith there?'

'I think so, I don't remember. She was with a whole crowd.'

So, I thought. Perhaps they've made it up. But a few minutes later Galbraith himself blew in, back in uniform again, and ordered himself a bitter. 'Seen Vicky?' he asked me.

'Not all day. Have you?'

'No. I expect she's disappeared again. It's a habit of hers.'

'I see.'

I wasn't going to discuss her habits with him. At any rate they hadn't made it up: that was something. Probably she'd roll up next day. I had a look in at Tony's on my way home, just in case, but it was empty except for a Cypriot eating Kebab.

The 'phone didn't ring that night or next morning; I repeated the movements of the day before, without success. Sheila, whom I consulted, was unsympathetic.

'Well, all I can say, darling, you're well rid of her. She's *quite* the worst you've trotted out yet, all that awful gush about gracious living; and as for marrying her, well you must be out of your mind.'

So we had a quarrel and I later got drunk on gin.

Wednesday was the day we were to have been married. I had high hopes of Wednesday. They were unfulfilled. The 'phone remained silent: the pubs, the restaurants, the Soho streets, empty of her presence. Nobody seemed to have seen her; I even asked Walter and the Toves. I began to imagine a fatal accident: a slip under a bus, blast from a doodle-bug, a dose of 'flu. Surely something must have happened to her.

Supper at the Scala, coffee in Tony's; at midnight I paced the Tube platform waiting for the last train home. I stared at a poster on the wall which seemed to advertise V.D. Then a voice behind me said 'Julian', and there was Galbraith.

'I thought you'd like to know,' he said. 'I'd a 'phone-call from Vicky this afternoon.'

'Oh?' I said, making my voice casual. 'What'd she have to say?'

'Just goodbye. She's gone away you know. She often does that when things get a bit too much for her. I can't say I'm sorry, it was all getting too much for me too. I've no doubt you felt the same.'

'But where's she gone?' I said.

'The Scilly Isles, I think. Somewhere like that. She's got an aunt tucked away that she puts up with whenever she wants to go into hiding.'

I stood stupified: the train clattered past us out of the tunnel, stopped alongside as the doors flew open; Galbraith took a step towards them. 'Coming? It's the last one, you know.'

'I think I'll walk.'

'As you like. So long.'

Doors clashed shut on him and the train drew out along the platform. I watched for a moment its red tail-light receding; it vanished into the tunnel; a dry wind whistled in its wake and the sleepers turned restlessly on their bunks.

So she was gone and I'd lost her. Walking furiously along outside, I cursed everyone connected with the affair: Vicky and Galbraith and Galbraith's wife and Vicky's aunt in the Scilly Isles or wherever it was— and, most of all, myself. But cursing, even out loud, didn't seem to change the situation, and I realized I was walking in the wrong direction. I retraced my steps, passing a soldier and his girl kissing in a doorway. Yes, she was gone, and what had I to remember her by: a rainbow over Brewer Street, the man in a bowler hat bleeding by the wall, music from *The Mask of Dimetrios*? All the way down the long perspective of Oxford Street the traffic lights changed colour under an empty sky; my footsteps rang hollow on the empty pavement and the last buses, unlighted and without passengers inside, rumbled along from Marble Arch.

But in Regent Street there was noise and life: a nightclub disgorged a load of drunks and the headlamps of cars flashed back off plate-glass: the Americans stood shouting for transport on the kerb. I hesitated, undecided what to do. Then the sight of a 'phone-box islanded in the middle of the road reminded me of Hester Hewart, and on an impulse I stepped inside. She was back at her flat and just about to have a bath.

'What d'you know about Vicky Baker?' I asked her.

'Oh dear, oh dear. Don't tell me you've got involved with *her*?'

'Well yes, I have in a way.'

'She didn't want to *marry* you by any chance?'

'She said she did.'

'Yes she always does. That's her Thing, you know; she tries it on everyone. She was going to marry poor Dickie Galbraith only a week ago, if it hadn't been for his pangs of Conscience, my dear. She's absolutely mad on the idea of getting married. I'm rather surprised you took her seriously, though, I must say.'

'Why? She's very attractive.'

'Yes I know, she's a perfect poppet, but the point is she can't marry anyone at all: at least not just yet.'

'Why can't she?'

'Well, didn't you know, her decree isn't even through, months more to wait. How can she marry again when she isn't even divorced?'

'Good God,' I said. 'We were to be married by special licence today.'

'There you are, she'd have been in clink for bigamy first thing you knew. I tell you the poor sweet's quite, quite crazy. She'll get herself in terrible trouble one of these days.'

'But this is a frightful story. The girl must be completely irresponsible.'

'Of *course* she is. *Nuts*, my dear: absolute nuts. Very odd you didn't find it out, though I admit she seems perfectly plausible if you don't knew her well.'

'Now she's gone racing off to the Scilly Isles or somewhere.'

'Yes, that's another of her tricks: disappearing for months at a stretch. Nearly drives her poor Papa frantic with worry, he's never certain she hasn't been murdered or else committed suicide. Mark my words, she'll bob up in a few months, large as life and engaged to someone completely new.'

'Just another neurotic,' I said bitterly.

'Yes, poor darling, you do seem to collect them, don't you? One'd think you did it on purpose. Still it's a good thing for you she's gone away.'

'I'm beginning to think so too.'

'I'm sure of it... well, darling, I must dash: I can hear my bath boiling over, the whole place'll be flooded if I don't turn it off quick. See you soon, sweet.'

'On the barricades,' I said.

So that was that; just another neurotic: neurosis followed me out of the 'phone-box into the violent noisy night—drunks singing, shouts of TAXI, the rumble of a rocket exploding in the suburbs; neurosis, not happiness, lay in wait round the corner: my own neurosis, augmented by a succession of psychopathic girls, transmitted through the mind and through the blood, playing hide-and-seek, now dodging ahead, now pacing a step behind, waiting its chance to catch up: the hooded stranger, the shadowy third, of T. S. Eliot and the arctic wastes.

As I turned off Regent Street—towards the Frenchwoman in furs—I remembered a story Vicky had once told me against herself: how, waking one morning after a thick night, she had made herself a Welsh rabbit for breakfast. She ate it and noticed nothing wrong: until, going to the kitchen sink to wash her hands, she found that the soap was gone.

So then she washed with the cheese.

I hadn't been in the army long at the time. About a week, not more. We were marching round the square one afternoon and I couldn't keep in step. The corporal kept calling out 'Left, left,' but it didn't do any good. In the end the corporal told me to fall out. The platoon sergeant came rushing up and said, 'What the hell's wrong with you, man? Why can't you hold the step?'

I didn't know, I couldn't tell him. There was an officer on the square, and the sergeant-major, and they were both watching us.

'Got anything wrong with your leg?' the sergeant said.

'Your left leg?'

'I've got a scar on it Sergeant,' I told him.

'Dekko,' the sergeant said.

So I rolled up my trouser leg and showed him the scar on my knee. The sergeant looked at it and shook his head. 'That don't look too good, lad,' he said. 'How'd you come to get it?'

'I was knocked down by a bike. Years ago.'

By this time the sergeant-major had come up and he looked at the scar too. 'What's your category, lad?' he asked me. 'A1?'

'Yes sir.'

'Well you go sick tomorrow morning and let the MO have a look at that leg. Meantime sit in that shed over there till it's time to fall out.'

There was a Bren Gun lesson going on in the shed when I got there. My arrival interrupted it. 'Who the hell are you?' the NCO taking the lesson asked me. 'What d'you want?'

'I've been sent over here to sit down Corporal.'

'To sit down?'

'Sergeant-major sent me.'

'Oh well if he sent you that's all right. But don't go opening your trap, see? Keep mum and don't say nothing.'

'Very good Corporal.'

'Not so much of it,' the corporal said.

The lesson went on. I listened but couldn't understand what it was all about. I'd never seen a Bren Gun before. And then the corporal's pronunciation didn't help matters. I sat there in the shed until everyone else had fallen out. Then the sergeant-major came over to me.

'Fall out,' he said. 'What're you waiting for. Parade's over for the day, you're dismissed. And don't forget—you go sick tomorrow morning,' he shouted after me.

'How do I go sick?' I asked the other fellows, back in the barrack-room.

They didn't know, none of them had ever been sick. 'Ask the Sarnt,' they said.

But I couldn't find the sergeant, or the corporal either. They'd gone off to a dance in the town. So I went down to the cookhouse and there was an old sweat sitting on a bucket outside, peeling spuds. You could see he was an old sweat because he was in shirt sleeves and his arms were tattooed all over. So I asked him how to go sick and he said 'Ah, swinging the lead, eh? MO'll mark you down in red ink, likely.'

'What happens if he does that?'

'CB for a cert. Scrubbing, or mebbe a spot of spud bashing. You won't get less than seven days, anyhow.'

'What, seven days CB for going sick?'

'Sure, if you're swinging the lead. Stands to reason. There ain't nothing wrong with you now is there? A1, aintcher?'

'Yes.'

'There you are then. You'll get seven all right,' said the sweat. 'What d'you expect. All you lads are alike. Bleeding lead swingers the lot of you.'

He spat on the ground and went on peeling spuds. I could see he wasn't going to say any more so I walked on. Further along I stopped by another old sweat. This second sweat was even older and more tattooed than the first one. And he hadn't any teeth.

'Excuse me,' I said, 'Can you tell me how to go sick?'

'Go sick?' said this second, toothless sweat. 'You don't want to do that.'

'Why not?' I said.

'Well look at me. Went sick I did with a pain in the guts, and what's the MO do? Silly bleeder sent me down the Dental Centre and had them take all me teeth out. I ask you, do it make sense? Course it don't. You got the guts-ache and they pull out all your teeth. Bleeding silly. And they ain't given me no new teeth neither and here I been waiting six munce. No,' said the sweat, 'You don't want to go sick. Take my tip, lad: keep away from that there MO long as you can.'

'But I've got to go sick. I've been ordered to.'

'Who by?'

'Sergeant-major.'

'What's wrong with you?'

'My leg, so they say.'

'Your leg? Then mebbe they'll take your teeth out too. Ain't no knowing what they'll do once they start on you. I'm bleeding browned-off with the bleeding sick I am.'

'Well how do I go about it?'

'On the door of the orderly sergeant's bunk it said KNOCK AND WAIT. I did both and a voice shouted 'Come in, come in. Don't need to bash the bleeding door down.'

There was a corporal sitting at a table covered with a blanket writing laboriously on a sheet of paper.

'Yes?' he said, looking up. 'What d'you want?'

'I was looking for the Orderly Sergeant,' I said.

'I'm the Orderly Sergeant,' said the corporal. 'State your business and be quick about it. I ain't got all night.'

'I want to go sick Sergeant. I mean Corporal.'

'Don't you go making no smart cracks here,' said the corporal. 'And stand properly to attention when you speak to an NCO.'

'Sorry Corporal.'

'Ain't no such word in the British army,' the corporal told me. 'Now what's your name? Age? Service? Religion? Medical Category? Okay, you parade outside here 8.30 tomorrow morning. On the dot.'

I went to go out, but the corporal called me back. 'Here, half a mo. How d'you spell Picquet? One K or two?'

'No Ks at all Corporal,' I told him.

'Listen didn't I tell you not to be funny? I'll stick you on a chitty so help me if you ain't careful. How d'you mean, no Ks? How can you spell Picquet without no Ks?'

I explained. The corporal looked suspicious. 'Sure? You ain't trying to be funny?'

'No Corporal. P-i-c-q-u-e-t.'

'Okay.' He wrote it down. 'Need a bleeding dictionary to write this bastard out,' he muttered, and then looking up: 'All right, what're you waiting for. Scram. Gillo! And don't forget: 0830 tomorrow. Bring your small kit in case.'

I didn't like to ask him in case of what. I got out quick before he gave me scrubbing or spud-bashing or tried to take my teeth out maybe.

I didn't sleep too well that night, I can tell you. Next morning at 0830 there I was outside the orderly sergeant's bunk with my small kit: I'd found out from our sergeant what that was. There were quite a lot of other fellows there as well. It's funny how they pass you A1 into the army and then find out you're nothing of the sort. One of these fellows had flat feet, another weak lungs, and a third reckoned he was ruptured.

After a while the corporal came out. 'All right,' he said. 'Get fell in the sick.'

We fell in and were marched down to the MI Room.

'Keep in step, you!' the corporal shouted at me. 'Christ, can't you keep step?'

Down at the MI Room it said on the walls NO SMOKING, NO SPITTING, and we sat around waiting for our names to be called out. At last mine was called and I went in. The MO looked up. 'Yes, what's wrong with you?'

I looked round. There were two fellows standing behind me waiting their turn. A third was putting on his trousers in a corner. More crowded in the doorway behind. I felt silly with all these fellows listening in. I didn't know what to say.

'Come on, out with it,' said the MO. 'Or perhaps it's something you'd rather say in private?'

'Well sir, I would prefer it.'

'Right. Come back at five tonight.'

I went out again.

'What'd you get?' the orderly sergeant asked me.

'He said to come back at five Corporal.'

'What's wrong? Got the clap?'

'No Corporal.'

'Crabs, maybe?'

'No, not crabs.'

'Well what the hell you want to see him in private for, then? Only blokes with VD see him in private as a rule. Unless they've crabs.'

At five I reported back to the MI Room.

'Right,' said the medical corporal. 'This way. Cap off. Don't salute.'

The MO said, 'Ah yes. Sit down and tell me about it.'

I did. He seemed a bit disappointed that I hadn't VD but in the end he examined my leg.

'Does it hurt? No? What about if you kneel on it? H'm, yes, there's something wrong there. You'd better see the specialist. Report here tomorrow at ten.'

The specialist was at a hospital some miles away from the camp. He said 'Try and straighten the leg. What, you can't? All right. Put your trousers on and wait outside.'

Pretty soon an orderly came out with a chitty. 'You're to have treatment twice a week,' he told me. 'Electrical massage. This way.'

I followed him down a lot of corridors and finally out into the grounds and up some steps into a hut with MASSAGE on a board outside it. There I lay down on a table and a nurse strapped some sort of pad on my thigh. After that they gave me a series of shocks from an electric battery. It lasted about half an hour.

'Feeling better?' the nurse asked me when it was over.

'No,' I said.

I could hardly walk.

'That'll wear off by and by,' said the nurse.

I drove in by an ambulance to the MI Room.

'Had your treatment?'

'Yes sir.'

The MO started to write something on a piece of paper. I was a bit nervous in case he used the red ink. But he didn't after all. He used blue ink instead. 'Give this to your orderly sergeant,' he said.

On the piece of paper it said 'Att. C.'

'Attend C!' said the orderly sergeant. 'Cor you got it cushy ain't you?'

'What's it mean Corporal?' I asked.

'Attend C? Excused all duties. Bleeding march coming off tomorrow and all.'

Two days later I went to the hospital again. After a week or two of treatment I'd developed quite a limp. The fellows all said I was swinging the lead. I limped about the camp doing nothing, in the intervals of having more electric shock. Then, after about three weeks, the MO sent for me again.

'Is your leg any better now?'

'No sir,' I said.

'Treatment not doing you any good?'

'No sir.'

'H'm. Well I'd better put you down for a medical board in that case.'

So I didn't even go to the hospital any more. I used to lie on my bed all day long reading a book. But I got tired of that because I only had one book and I wasn't allowed out owing to being on sick. There weren't any other books in the camp. Meanwhile the fellows were marching and drilling and firing on the range, and the man in the next bed to me suddenly developed a stripe. This shook me, so I thought I'd go and see the sergeant-major.

I was a bit nervous when I got to his office. The sergeant-major had an alarming appearance. He looked almost exactly like an ape. Only he'd less hair on him, of course. But he was quite a decent fellow really.

When I came in he was telling two clerks and an ATS girl how he'd nailed a native's hand to his desk during his active service in India. He broke off this recital when he saw me standing there. 'Yes, lad, what d'you want?'

I explained that I was waiting for a medical board and meantime had nothing to do, as I was excused parades.

'But d'you WANT something to do?' the sergeant-major asked. He seemed stupefied.

'Yes sir,' I said. 'I didn't join the army to do nothing all day.'

The two clerks looked up when I said that, and the ATS stared at me with her mouth open. The sergeant-major breathed heavily through his nose. Then he said, 'Can you use a typewriter, lad?'

'Yes sir,' I said.

'Ah!' He jumped up from his table. 'Then sit you down here and show us how to use this ruddy thing. It's only just been sent us, see, and none of us know how to make the bleeder go.'

It was a very old typewriter, an Oliver. I'd used one before, so I didn't find it too difficult. Soon I was typing out long lists of names and other stuff full of initials and abbreviations that I didn't know the meaning of. Sometimes I couldn't read the handwriting, especially if one of the officers had written it, but the ATS used to translate for me.

Then one day the company commander walked in.

'Who's this man?' he said, pointing at me with his stick.

'Sick man, sir,' the sergeant-major said. 'Waiting a medical board.'

'Well he can't wait for it here. We're not allowed any more clerks. You've enough clerks already,' and he walked out again, after hitting my table a whack with his stick.

'All right, fall out,' the sergeant-major said to me. 'Back to your bunk.'

'Now we've no one to work the typewriter,' he said. 'Have to do it all by hand. Hell.'

Next day the orderly sergeant told me to go sick again. I'd got used to it by now. The other fellows called me the MO's right marker.

This time it was a new MO: the other one had been posted elsewhere.

'Well what's wrong with you?' he said.

I explained my case all over again.

'Let's see your leg.' He looked at it for a moment and then said, 'Well there's nothing wrong with that, is there?'

'Isn't there, sir?'

'No.' He poked at the scar, seized hold of my leg, bent it, straightened it a few times and then looked puzzled. 'H'm. There is something wrong after all. You'd better have a medical board.'

'I'm down for one already, sir.'

'What? Well why the devil didn't you say so then? Wasting my time. All right. You can go now.'

In the morning the orderly sergeant came into our hut. 'Get your small kit together,' he said, 'and be down the MI Room in ten minutes. You're for a medical board. It came through just now.'

At the hospital I sat for some time in a waiting room and nobody came near me. It was another hospital, not the one I used to go to for treatment. Then at last an officer came in. I stood up. He was a colonel.

'Carry on, carry on,' he said, and smiled very kindly. 'What's your trouble eh?'

'I'm waiting for a medical board, sir.'

'A medical board? What for?'

'I have trouble with my knee, sir.'

'Oh? What happens? Does it swell up?'

'No sir.'

'What, no swelling? H'm. Well come with me, we'll soon have you fixed up.' I followed this kindly colonel to the reception desk. 'Take this man along to Ward 9,' he told an orderly.

So I went along to Ward 9 and all the beds in it were empty except for one man sitting up in bed doing a jigsaw puzzle.

'Watcher, mate,' this man said. 'What you got? Ulcers, maybe?'

'Ulcers? No,' I said.

Then a nurse came in. 'Ah, you're the new patient. This way to the bathroom. Here are the pyjamas you change into afterwards.'

'Pyjamas?' I said.

'Yes,' said the nurse. 'And directly you've bathed and got your pyjamas on you hop into this bed here,' and she pointed to one next to the man with ulcers.

'But I don't want to go to bed,' I said. 'I'm not a bed patient. There's nothing wrong with me.'

'Then why are you here?'

'Nothing wrong with me like that, I mean. I'm waiting for a medical board.'

'Oh. Wait here a moment, please.' She fetched the orderly.

The orderly said, 'SMO's orders he was to be brought here. Said it hisself. The SMO Ward 9, he said.'

'But this ward is for gastric cases,' the nurse said. 'This man isn't a gastric case.'

'I don't know nothing about that,' the orderly told her.

The nurse said, 'There's some mistake. I'll see about it while you have your bath.'

So I had a bath and when I came out she gave me some clothes and a shirt and a red tie to put on and said I needn't go to bed.

'You'll have to stay here until we get this straightened out,' she said.

'Would you like anything to eat?'

'I would, thank you Nurse.'

'Well there's only milk pudding. This ward's for gastrics you see.'

'You won't get very fat on that, mate,' the man with ulcers said.

He was right. I ate two lots of milk pudding but still felt hungry afterwards. Then later on the MO came round. A lieutenant, he was. Quite young. He looked at my leg and said, 'This man's a surgical case, Nurse. What's he doing in here?'

'SMO's orders, doctor.'

'Oh. Well he'll have to stay here then.'

'How long will it be before I get this medical board, sir?' I said.

'Medical board? Might be months. Meantime you stay here. Yes. you can have chicken. Give him some chicken, Nurse.'

So he went away and I ate the chicken.

'Wish I was you, mate,' said the man with ulcers.

It wasn't so bad being in the hospital except that you only got eight-and-six on pay day. Every morning I used to go down to the massage department. 'Electrical massage's no good for your trouble,' said the MO. 'We'll try ordinary massage.' So I had ordinary massage and then sat on a table with a weight tied to my leg swinging it to-and-fro.

'Now I know what swinging the lead means,' I said.

I used to have to lie down for two hours a day to recover from the treatment. I was limping quite heavily by the time the MO put his head in one morning and said 'You're for a Board today. Twelve o'clock down in my office.'

I waited outside the office nervously. I thought they might order me to have my teeth out. But they didn't. I was called in and there were three medical officers, one a lieutenant-colonel, who asked me a lot of questions and examined my leg, and then I went back to the ward.

'How'd you get on, mate?' asked the ulcers-man. 'What'd they do?'

'I don't know,' I said. 'They didn't tell me.'

But that evening the MO came in and said, 'You've been graded B2.'

'What does that mean, sir?'

'Garrison duties at home and abroad.'

'Can I go back to the camp then, sir?'

'Not till the papers come through.'

A few days later he sent for me. In his office. 'Something's gone wrong,' he said. 'We've slipped up. It seems you should have seen the surgical specialist before having the Board. But you didn't, so these papers aren't valid. You'll have to have another Board now.'

'What'll that be, sir?'

'I don't know. Don't ask me.'

So that afternoon I saw the surgical specialist. He was a major, although he seemed quite young. He was very nice and cheerful and laughed a lot.

'Lie down on the table,' he said. 'That's right. Relax. Now bend the knee. Now straighten it. Hold it. Hold it. Try to hold it steady. Ha ha! You can't, can you? Ha ha! Of course you can't. You've got no tendon in it, that's why. The tendon. It's bust. How long ago did you say the accident...? Sixteen years? Good lord, nothing we can do about it now. You'll have to be awfully careful, though. No running, no jumping. If you were to jump down into a trench your leg'd snap like a twig. Can't understand how they ever passed you A1. Ha ha! Well I'll make my report on you right away. Oughtn't to be in the infantry with a leg like that at all.'

I went back to Ward 9. It was supper time. Junket.

'Can't keep it down,' said the man with ulcers, and he proved this by bringing it up again.

Well then the MO went on leave.

'Now you stay here,' he told me, 'until the next Board comes off. Don't suppose it'll be till I'm back from my seven days. Meantime you stay put.'

'Yes sir,' I said.

But in the morning a new MO came round. He was a captain. With him was the Matron. 'Stand by your beds!' he called out as he came in.

The ward had filled up in the last week or two, but most of the patients were in bed, so they couldn't obey. The five of us who were up came belatedly to attention.

'Bad discipline in this ward Matron,' the captain said. 'Very slack. Who's the senior NCO here?'

There was only one NCO among the lot of us: a lance-corporal. He was up, as it happened, so he came in for an awful chewing-off.

'You've got to keep better order than this, Corporal,' said the captain.

'See that the men pay proper respect to an Officer when he enters the ward. If I've any further cause for complaint I shall hold you responsible. Also the beds aren't properly in line. I'm not satisfied with this ward, not satisfied at all. I hope to see some improvement when I come round tomorrow. Otherwise…'

He walked on round the beds examining the patients in turn. The ward was electrified. He ordered most of the bed patients to get up and those who were up to go to bed. Except the lance-corporal, who had to keep order, and me. As for the man with ulcers, he was ordered out of the ward altogether. I was last on the list, standing by the end bed, when he came up.

'This man is fit to return to his unit Matron,' he said when he'd looked at me.

'But he's awaiting a medical board Doctor,' the matron said.

'Well he can wait for it at his unit. We're not running a home for soldiers awaiting medical boards. I never heard of such a thing.'

'Lieutenant Jackson said…'

'Never mind what he said. I'm in charge here now, and I've just given an order. This man will return to his unit forthwith.'

Then he walked out and the matron went too. Two nurses came in and helped the man with ulcers into a wheel-chair. 'So long, mates,' he said, then they wheeled him away. I don't know what became of him: he just disappeared. After that we straightened the beds and got them all in line.

'Keep order,' said the lance-corporal. 'Why the hell should I keep order. I'm not an NCO no more, they'll revert me soon's I get back. I'm Y listed, see? A bloody private, so why should I bother? Bleeding sauce.'

I wondered when they were going to chuck me out. Forthwith, he'd said, and forthwith turned out to be the next day.

I left about two o'clock. In a lorry. It dropped me at the station and I'd two hours to wait for a train. At last I got back to the camp and it looked all changed somehow, with no one about. Everything seemed shut up. I reported to the sergeant's bunk. Sitting in it was a corporal I'd never seen before.

'Who're you?' he said. 'What d'you want?'

I told him.

'No one told us you was coming,' said this new corporal, scratching his head. 'All the others have cleared off. Jerry been bombing the camp, see? We've been evacuated. Last draft leaves tomorrow.'

'Am I on it?'

'You'll be on it all right.'

'Well where do I sleep? And what about my kit.'

'That'll be in the stores, I suppose. Buggered if I know. I'm from another company, I don't know nothing about you. Wait here, I'll see the storeman.'

But the storeman was out, and the stores were locked up. The corporal came back scratching his head.

'Buggered if I know when he'll be back. Gone on the piss I shouldn't wonder. You better find a place to kip down. Here's a coupla blankets, if that's any use to you.'

Eventually I found a barrack room that wasn't locked: all the other huts were closed up. There were two other blokes in this room, both out of hospital. 'Where're we going to, mate?' they asked me.

'Damned if I know.'

'Nobody bloody well does know, that's the rub.'

At last, after a lot of conjecture, we dossed down for the night. It was autumn by now and turning cold and my two blankets didn't keep me very warm. I slept in all my clothes. Jerry came over during the night but didn't drop any bombs, or if he did we didn't hear them.

Then in the morning the corporal appeared. 'I've found some of your kit left.' Most of it had been pinched. My overcoat was gone and another one, much too small, left in its place.

'I don't know nothing about it,' said the storeman.

'You better get some breakfast,' the corporal said. 'I'll sort this lot out for you.'

Breakfast was a bacon sandwich, all the cookhouse fires had been let out.

'Bloody lark this is, ain't it?' said the cooks.

'You're telling us,' we said.

Then we paraded on the square, about forty of us. Don't know where all the others came from. Other companies I suppose. A lieutenant was in charge of us.

'Where's your equipment?' he asked me.

'I've never been issued with it, sir,' I said.

'Never been issued with equipment!'

'No sir. I was excused parades. And then I've just got out of hospital. I have the papers here, sir, that they gave me.'

'Oh all right. I'll take charge of them.' He took the long envelope from me. Then a sergeant turned up and shouted, 'Shun! By the left, quick—MARCH!'

We started off.

'Keep in step, there!' the sergeant shouted at me. 'Can't you keep in step? What the hell's the matter with yer!'

'I'm excused marching, Sergeant,' I said. 'I've just come from hospital.'

'Oh. All right lad. Fall out. Wait here.' He went up to the officer and saluted. 'Scuse me, sir, there's a man here excused marching, sir.'

'What's that? Excused marching? Well he'll have to bloody well march. This isn't a convalescent home.'

'It's five miles to the station, sir.'

'Oh well, damn it, what d'you want done? Shove him on a truck or something. Can't march, indeed. He'd march soon enough if Jerry was after him.'

So the sergeant told a truck to stop and helped me to board it. It was full of kits and very uncomfortable, I nearly fell off twice. I felt a mass of bruises when we got to the station, and my leg had begun to ache. I sat down on a trolley and waited for the train to come in. It didn't come in for an hour, and the men who'd marched up meantime stood around and argued about where we were going. Some said Egypt, but others said no because we weren't in tropical kit. So then they said Scotland and *then* Egypt. I personally didn't care where we were going. I was fed-up with the whole business, and my leg ached badly: I'd hit my bad knee getting down from the truck.

Then the train came in and it turned out to be full of recruits from another regiment going to wherever we were going, a new camp somewhere or other, and so we'd nowhere to sit. We stood for a long time in the corridor and then I tried sitting on my kit but that wasn't a success because fellows kept falling over me and one of them kicked my bad leg. I was pretty browned-off by this time, so I got up and was going to sock him, but another chap got in front of me and said, 'You can't hit a sick man.'

'Who's a sick man?' I said. 'I'm a sick man.'

'So am I,' said the man I wanted to sock. 'I'm sick too. Hell I got a hernia so bad they daren't operate. I'm waiting my ticket.'

'Sorry, mate,' I said, 'I didn't know.'

'That's okay,' he said so we shook hands and he gave me some chocolate out of his haversack: we'd got bloody hungry by now.

'What about some grub?' everyone was saying. 'Where's the grub?'

By and by it came round in tins. A sergeant brought it.

'What's this?' we said.

'Beans. Take one.'

'Where's the meat?'

'You've had it,' said the sergeant. Everyone cursed. Then an officer came round, a captain. 'Any complaints?'

'What about some more food, sir,' we said.

'There isn't any. I've had none myself,' he said. 'Mistake somewhere.'

'You're telling us,' we said, but not to him.

It was dark when we got to this other town and the searchlights were up overhead. We formed up outside the station. Our sergeant appeared and recognized me. 'I'll see to you in a minute,' he said. But he couldn't, because all the transport had already gone. So I had to march after all. It was three miles, and after all that standing about I felt done in when we got to the new camp. We had a hot meal and I'd have slept like the dead if Jerry hadn't dropped a bomb somewhere near the barracks and woken me up.

'Bugger it,' I said. 'Now we'll have to go to the trenches.'

But they didn't blow the alarm after all, so we went off to sleep again.

In the morning I was down for sick, but the MO at this camp proved to be a much tougher proposition than any I'd yet encountered.

He said, 'What d'you mean, you've had a medical board? How can you have had a medical board? Where're your papers?'

'I gave them to the officer in charge of the draft, sir.' I said.

'Well I haven't got them. What was the officer's name?'

'I don't know, sir.'

'You don't know. My God you give your papers to an officer and you don't even know his name.' The MO held his head in his hands. 'God deliver me,' he said, 'from such idiocy.'

'I don't think I'm especially idiotic, sir,' I said.

'Your opinion of yourself is entirely irrelevant,' said the MO. 'And you must remember who you're talking to.'

'Yes sir,' I said.

'Silence!' said the medical corporal, who'd come up at this.

The MO said, 'Now what's all this nonsense about a medical board? What happened? Were you re-graded?'

'Yes sir. B2.'

'Let's see your pay-book. Corporal, get his AB64 Part I.'

I produced my pay-book.

'Not in it, sir,' said the corporal. 'A1 it says here.'

'I know,' I said, 'but . . .'

'Silence!' said the corporal. 'Speak only when you're spoken to.'

The MO had his head in his hands again. 'All this shouting,' he said. 'If that man gives any more trouble you'll have to charge him, corporal.'

'Yes sir,' said the corporal.

'Now listen,' the MO said to me, speaking very quietly. 'You say you've had a medical board. You say you've been re-graded. Well you haven't. It's not in your pay-book. Therefore you've not been re-graded at all. You're lucky not to be charged with stating a falsehood, understand? Now don't come here again with any more nonsensical stories or you'll find yourself in trouble. Corporal, march this man out.'

'But sir…,' I said.

'Come on, you!' the corporal said. So I went. Two days later we started training, and the new sergeant found out I couldn't march and sent me sick again. It was another MO this time and he had my papers, they'd turned up again, and he said I've got to have another medical board.

That was a month ago, and I'm still waiting. I've not done much training so far, and I've had to pay for all the kit I had pinched at the other camp, and all I hope is this: that when they give me the Board, I don't have to go sick any more afterwards. I don't care if they grade me Z2 or keep me A1, so long as I don't have to go sick. I've had enough of it. I'm fed-up.

I'm Not Asking You To Buy

She wasn't called Mrs. Prospect, naturally; her name, according to my notebook, was Mrs. Crick. I'd fixed a demonstration at her bungalow for 10.30am one Tuesday. I arrived punctually on time; it was hot and I was sweating.

I set down the heavy boxes containing the cleaner with a sigh of relief. I rang the bell and waited, mopping my forehead.

A furious barking began immediately inside the house, and I could hear a dog pattering about: it barked again, quite close to the door.

A woman's voice called 'Quiet, Dinkie!' and the door was opened cautiously a crack.

'Good morning, Mrs. Crick,' I said, stepping forward with a smile. 'I've called with the cleaner.'

'Oh, nothing today, thank you.' The door started to close again.

'But I thought you wanted a demonstration,' I said desperately. 'Don't you remember? I called yesterday morning.'

'A demonstration?' Mrs. Crick repeated, peering round the door at me. 'Oh, you mean the vacuum cleaner. Of course; come in.'

Picking up the boxes again, I entered the house; a small fluffy black dog receded at my approach, but continued to bark furiously, making a surprisingly loud noise for so small an animal.

'Be quiet, Dinkie!'

She said to me: 'I thought at first you'd called about my fur coat again. The cleaners kept bothering me for 4s.6d. Silly, isn't it?'

She led the way into the drawing-room; I negotiated the entrance awkwardly, and the long box containing the handle became wedged between the doorposts; while I struggled to disengage it the dog yapped angrily around my heels.

'Down, Dinkie, down!' Mrs. Crick said to me: 'That's Dinkie, my dog. He has fits sometimes. What d'you think I should do about it?'

'Well, have you taken him to the vet?'

'No. Do you think I should?'

'It depends. How old is he?'

'He's getting on. Twelve next birthday.'

'That's pretty old.'

'I've had him since a pup.'

Dinkie had stopped barking and now began to cough. I dropped on one knee and started to unpack my boxes.

'Have you seen one of our machines before?'

'Not for some time.'

'This is the latest model. Streamlined. Dustproof bag. Special rubber grip handle. Fifteen feet of unkinkable, unfrayable, heavily insulated flex. Pins to fit any plug.'

'It's a lovely machine.'

'As efficient as it is attractive.' I plugged in the adaptor, clicked the switch, and the machine began to hum and whirr; the bag inflated, filled with air. Dinkie jumped back with a growl. He eyed the cleaner suspiciously as I pushed it to and fro across the carpet.

'Poor darling, did it make you jump, then?' Mrs. Crick said. She explained to me, 'Dinkie doesn't like the noise.'

'You can only silence these machines at the cost of their efficiency,' I told her, raising my voice above the hum of the motor. 'Notice the two speeds on the switch in the handle. Another new feature: this light. It guides the way into dark corners where the dirt...'

'Have you got a cigarette?' Mrs. Crick interrupted me.

'Certainly.' I switched off the machine and offered my case. In the case were my last five cigarettes. Mrs. Crick said: 'Do you mind if I take two?'

'Not at all.'

Mrs. Crick took two. She said: 'I'm a slave to smoking. An absolute slave. I know it's silly, and yet I can't get on without it. Just like a drug. My husband's always telling me.'

A heavy knock sounded at the back door.

'Quick!' Mrs. Crick told me; 'switch on the cleaner!' She explained: 'It's the baker. He's called with his bill. If you switch on he'll think we can't hear him because of the noise.'

I obeyed. I pushed the cleaner up and down over the carpet and the bag began to fill with dirt.

'These tradesmen,' Mrs. Crick said. 'They'll be the death of me. Always wanting money. They think of nothing else. Such a nuisance.'

She puffed at her cigarette nervously. Finding that no attention was paid to him, Dinkie retreated to a cushion in the corner, where he lay curled up, coughing from time to time. The blow on the back door continued, like the knocking in *Macbeth*.

'They'll drive me crazy, these tradesmen,' Mrs. Crick said. 'Sometimes I feel I shall go mad. I daresay it's only a form of nerves.'

'Undoubtedly,' I said. 'My wife suffers very badly with nerves.'

I had no wife, but it was always best to identify oneself with the prospect's troubles; they'd taught me that at the school.

Mrs. Crick said: 'My nerves are very bad. I expect it's too much smoking. D'you think smoking is bad for the nerves?'

'It all depends.'

The knocking ceased; evidently the baker had retired in disgust.

'Thank goodness he's gone,' Mrs. Crick said, stabbing out her second cigarette. 'You can switch off now.'

'Let's see what's in the bag.'

'I know the house is filthy,' Mrs. Crick said. 'I haven't swept it for three days. I just don't seem to have the energy.'

'That's why you need one of these machines. Think of the work it would save you. Your cleaning done in half the time.' I started to empty the bag, shaking it from side to side and exclaiming in simulated surprise at each pile of dirt.

I took a screwdriver from my tool-kit and rubbed it through the dirt. 'See this: grit! Dangerous, destructive, germ-laden grit,' I told her. 'It cuts the pile, destroys the life of your carpet.'

'I know. But what can I do?'

'Very simple, Mrs. Crick,' and out came the order-form. 'You just sign here.'

'I could never afford it.'

'Five shillings a week. Eightpence a day. The price of a seat at the cinema, or a nice tablet of soap.'

'I know. I'd like one very much, only my husband would never allow it.'

'Not even when it would save you work?'

'He'd object. We've a lot of worries already. Debts. Unpaid bills. My fur coat. The baker.'

Dinkie came over and sniffed at the dirt. He drew back, sneezing.

Mrs. Crick said: 'Life's such a bore. Sometimes I feel I could just go out and walk into the sea. Commit suicide.'

'Oh, I shouldn't do that, you know.'

'No? Well, perhaps not. Besides, I can swim.' She looked at me closely. 'You seem quite a nice young man. How is it you're doing this job?'

'Well, I lost all my money.'

'The slump?'

'Absolutely.'

'Sold any of these things yet?'

'Unfortunately, no.'

'I'd like to be able to help you. If things were better...' She broke off. 'Oh, Dinkie, you've walked in the dirt!'

'That's all right, Mrs. Crick.' I touched the switch, the motor hummed, the dirt scattered by Dinkie vanished into the bag. 'You see? No trouble at all.'

I continued to clean the carpet. It was my second week and I was still conscientious; she didn't sound too good a prospect, but you could never tell.

I went through the twenty-eight steps of the Show More Dirt Demonstration. I cleaned curtains and picture-rails and upholstery; I dug dirt from chairs and couches and settees until the room was littered with little heaps of dust and linen squares to mark my progress, like a paper chase. At last I paused, out of breath.

'Well, what do you say? Have you decided?'

'I'd like one very much, but...'

I pushed the order-form towards her. 'You sign here, please. A pound down and a pound a month.'

'I haven't a pound in the house.'

'You needn't worry about that. You can pay when the machine is delivered.'

'And another thing. I've had one of your cleaners before. Two years ago. I didn't like it. So much fuss. Turning it upside down to fit on the tools.'

'You don't have to do that with the new model.'

'No, I see, it's a great improvement. Well...'

I unscrewed the cap of my fountain-pen and handed it to her. She took it with a sigh. 'I don't believe I should, really. My husband'll be furious.'

She signed Bertha Crick across the order-form. 'But I'll get round him somehow.'

'By the way,' she said. 'Before I forget. I wonder if you'd be awfully kind. My husband's gone out and forgotten to leave me any money for the shopping. If you could lend me half-a-crown...'

'Certainly.' I had two half-crowns in my pocket. They had to last me until pay-day, but having made a sale it was worth it. I took one out and handed it to Mrs. Crick.

'Thank you *so* much. When can I pay this back?' Without waiting for an answer, 'When I can? *Thank you.*' And she added: 'Oh, and another cigarette before you go.'

'With pleasure.' I left the house walking on air. I'd left the machine behind with the dirt, to show Mr. Crick when he came home from the office. I looked at my notebook: the next dem was for twelve noon. I'd time to tell the Boys.

They were all in the shed behind the shop when I got there: Ritchie and Barrington, Finklebaum and Hull. The air was thick with cigarette smoke, despite the sign which hung on the wall. NO SMOKING ALLOWED IN THIS SHED.

'Any luck, old boy?'

'Not so bad. I made a sale.'

'WHAT?' The Boys fell back in surprise.

'A big model?' Finklebaum, the supervisor, said.

'The latest. Three guineas commission.'

'Let's see the order-form,' Finklebaum said. He pushed his hat back on his head and read the details slowly, squinting against the cigarette smoke.

Ritchie said: 'What sort of a prospect?'

'Batty as hell. She borrowed half-a-dollar.'

Finklebaum looked up suddenly from the order-form. He said: 'Mrs. Crick? Elderly? Grey hair? Smokes a lot?'

'She smoked my last cigarette. Why? Is anything wrong?'

'I should say. Why, we had a debit on that woman. Two years ago. I sold her the machine myself, before I was supervisor.'

'You mean it's no good?'

'No ruddy good at all. She's blacklisted. Didn't keep up the payments. We'd the devil's own difficulty getting the machine back.'

Ritchie began to roar with laughter. 'I'm afraid you've been done, old boy.'

I said: 'She borrowed half-a-crown. The old so-and-so.'

'You'll never see that again,' Finklebaum said. 'Did she give you the deposit? No, I thought not. Well, you better go and fetch the cleaner from her. You'll need it for your next dem.'

Barrington said: 'And she smoked your last cigarette! Not so batty, eh?'

I could still hear them laughing in the shed behind me as I went out. I thought of what I'd say to Mrs. Crick when I saw her, but walking along my anger evaporated and I began to laugh.

After all, the old girl'd been pretty smart. She deserved to get away with it. Things weren't so bad: I had three more dems that day, and one of them might turn out a sale.

In those days I was an optimist.

The Tape

We'd been together from the start, old Phil and me. Joined up same day, done all our training together. We was both in B Company, 8 Platoon, under Sarnt Oakes, and we both slept in No. 10 Hut, next each other. We used to fix it to do picquets together too. Sarnt Oakes was a pretty good bloke, one of the best, and he usually put us on same time.

It's funny we got on so well, 'cause Phil was such a differen't kind of feller. I'm just an ordinary kind of a bloke meself, but Phil was educated. Been to college and everything. He talked pound-noteish, but not in a way to get on your wick, like Weston, who was in for a commission and treated you like you didn't even exist. Old Phil weren't like that. Mucked in same as the rest of us. He was a socialist, see? That's why he wouldn't put in for a pip. He'd have passed all right mind you, 'cause he was smart enough on drill and all that stuff on Gas and the Bren he could give you right off the reel, without having to read it up in a book like Corp Draper did. Yeah I reckon he'd have made a good officer too. Only he wouldn't put in. His girl was always on about it in her letters to him. Why didn't he try for OCTU and so on and so forth? Reckon she didn't like the idea of walking out with a private's uniform when he came home on leave. Still he could always change into civvies, couldn't he? I dunno what she had to beef about, honest I don't. He was one of the best was old Phil and she was lucky to hook a bloke like him, believe me. Smashing tart she was, though. He shown me a snap of her once.

Well the morning I'm telling you about we was on Drill, freezing it was, snow on the ground and your hands that cold you couldn't hardly hold your rifle. They wouldn't let us wear gloves. Not on drill.

Sarnt Oakes had mucked off somewhere and Corp Draper was on Dental, so L/C Bax was taking the drill. Ignorant bar-stud he was. Peacetime bloke. Regimental as muck. Ask anyone down at Depot if they remember him. They'll tell you soon enough.

'Toon! Toon—SHUN!' he give us suddenly. 'Stand at ease! SHUN! Stand at ease!'

He kept that up about ten minutes without a break 'cause we'd not done it smart enough the first time. I tell you it was that cold you couldn't hardly feel your feet inside your boots.

'Slope—HUP!' he bawled at us. 'Order—HUP!' He bawled out: 'Wake up you—Ford!' That was me. 'Where d'you reckon you are? Back in ruddy kip? Brass your ideas up, you're in the army now!'

Didn't I know it. Bloke talk to you like that in civvy-street you'd bash him on the bleeding earhole. Bax always had it in for me, I dunno why. I never done nothing to him. He nigh had me on jankers once, for coming in one minute late when he was Ordy Corp. He'd got it in for me proper. Phil reckoned it was 'cause I was a big bloke and he was only a short-arsed little bugger. With his tin hat on you'd take him for an air-raid shelter. Phil reckoned that had something to do with it. A complex Phil called it. I reckon Bax had a complex all right. I'd have given him a ruddy complex if he hadn't of had that stripe on his arm. But he knew that with the tape on I couldn't do nothing.

He kept after me right through the parade. Once, marching, I slipped and fell down bump, it was ice had got clogged under my heel. Then Bax said I oughter be ashamed, it was time a great big mucker like me learned to walk without falling down.

Well after that was our break. I said to Phil, 'Come on, let's get a cup o' char,' and we doubled back to park our rifles, the Naffy was just behind our hut. But then Sarnt come in, who'd been down with the Old Man someone said, and he told Phil he wanted a word with him. So I went off on me own and got two teas and a couple o' wads and waited for Phil to show up, it was warm in the Naffy anyroad. I got us seats by the stove but it was some time afore he come in. I said, 'Where've you been Phil, your char's got cold,' and he said it wasn't nothing. Then he said Sarn't had wanted to see him about having a tape, we'd done two months and he had to make some of the fellers up, but Phil'd told him No.

'Go on,' I said 'You take it Phil,' I told him, 'Don't you be silly,' but Phil said No he didn't believe in authority he said one man didn't ought to have authority over another. 'That's all very well,' I told him 'but in the army someone's got to have it, if it ain't you it'll be another, and think how pleased your girl'll be.'

But he still held out he wouldn't and I told him again he was silly and he said Maybe. Then Break was up and we had to get back, but next two periods was Bren and that wasn't so bad, we had it in the hut and one of the stoves was lit that we weren't supposed to have only Sarnt turned a blind eye, like Nelson he said.

Well after Bren he took Phil aside and asked him was he still of the same mind. He had to give the Old Man the names after dinner. Well they argued a bit and in the end Phil said okay. Sarnt slapped him on the back and I did and all the other blokes did too, they all liked Phil even if he did talk different which weren't his fault. Then Sarnt said he better get his tapes sewn on and all the blokes took it out of him a bit but friendly-like and Phil laughed, he didn't mind. I went down the Naffy with him after and we was having a supper there when up come Weston with his fag-holder and a tape on his arm as well and he said to Phil in that way of his that got me down, 'Congratulations' he said and Phil said Thanks and then Weston said Wasn't it against Phil's principles though to take authority, and Phil flushed up and I said 'Well anyroad he got his tape 'cause he deserved it and not 'cause he's in for a bleeding pip,' which was true of Weston and he didn't like it and went off then. I said, 'Whyn't you sock him?' but Phil said Why bother, it didn't matter. But I could see he was worried about it though, and he didn't say much more that evening.

Well it come up on Detail that night that all NCOs newly made-up was to parade for C.O.'s lecture in morning, and the camp was crowded with 'em all walking down with their stripes sewn on white and new. Two blokes had been made up in each Platoon. The other bloke in our squad was called Tasker, he'd been in the army before so it was only natural. I never thought much to him though.

This lecture was at eleven and the rest of us was on Vision Training out on the field and it was still freezing cold. I asked Phil how he got on after and he said it was just a lot of bull: discipline, what an NCO shouldn't do and so forth, like walking out with a private, and he'd got real angry with it, how they tried to keep you separate from your mates once you'd been made up and he was damned if he'd pay any attention. Then Tasker chipped in and said you couldn't keep discipline if NCOs didn't keep theirselves to theirselves, stands to reason, and Phil said what about democracy and what the hell were we fighting for? Then Tasker said you couldn't have democracy in the army and Phil said he'd got just the kind of slave-mind the army wanted and they nigh come to blows only Corp Draper told 'em to turn it up, he was feeling bad through having his teeth out.

Well Phil was still pretty mad and he said to me the system was all wrong and I said never mind, come over to the Naffy. He said okay but when we got there of course we'd forgotten he couldn't come in with me. He had to go in the Corporals' Mess, any NCO caught in the Privates' got put on a fizzer.

'You see?' Phil said, 'That's how they get you,' but I said No matter, we could go over to the Salvation, they'd a canteen other side of camp. So we went there instead and it was full of these new NCOs with their mates that was still privates and everything was okay. But somebody got wise to this and it went up on Detail that night the Salvation was out of bounds to all NCOs from that date onwards.

Phil was furious and he said all right, we'd go downtown nights, instead. But we couldn't take our break together anymore, they had us there. Another thing we couldn't do together was picquets. I was on Fire Point next night but Phil wasn't and Sarnt said he was sorry, an NCO couldn't do picquet unless he was in charge and Corp' Ames was in charge of this one. So that was that and there wasn't nothing we could do about it. We still saw one another a good bit though and we used to go off downtown together of an evening.

And then Phil's girl come down. He'd written to her naturally about how he'd been made up, and she was that thrilled she come all the way down from London to see him. Old Phil wanted me to come out and meet her but I said not bleeding likely. 'Two's company' I told him, 'and three's none.'

I saw 'em out together in the town though, her all dolled up in bleeding furs and holding onto his arm that had the stripe on it as proud as proud. She stayed a weekend. The Monday she went back Phil acted like he'd something on his mind. I reckon she'd been on at him again about OCTU. He didn't say so right out but I guessed as much from what he did say. Well that night I said as usual for us to go out and he said okay but he didn't seem too keen. Said he was feeling a bit tired. 'And no wonder with that dame of yours down,' one of the blokes told him, and he laughed but not like it come natural to him.

Anyroad we went out and he said 'How about a beer?' which wasn't like him because he didn't do much drinking as a rule. So we went in boozer, The Feathers it was we went in, and Phil kept ordering pints and wouldn't let me pay. I was kind of worried 'cause it weren't like him to go on the beer as I say. He kept saying 'Come on, drink up, have another,' and laughing a lot and then he got silent and didn't say nothing and I asked him what was up. Course then it come out. He'd had a split with his girl about this commission business and she'd gone off in a huff and he didn't know what to do, he was proper miserable. I told him not to mind, it'd all come right in the end, and then he said what the hell, why worry, have another.

I said: 'We'll have to look slippy, it's nigh time we was back,' and Phil said what the hell, he didn't care what time he got back. I said Don't be a fool, you don't want to get busted I said and we was arguing when door opened and in come Mr Burns, that was one of our officers and pretty regimental. He saw us same time and give Phil a pretty dirty look but he didn't say nothing and went on up to the bar. Old Phil went white as bleeding chalk. He got up then and said okay we'd best be getting back.

He didn't say nothing on the way to camp and what with the black-out and one thing and another we only just made it. Bugle blowing Last Post as we come in the gate and when we got in the hut there was all the blokes lined up by their beds and Bax with a paper in his hand waiting for us, I'd forgot he was Ordy Corp that week.

'Know the time?' he snapped out at us.

'Two minutes past ten,' Phil told him looking at his watch.

'Ain't I got a rank?' Bax asked him then.

'Yes *Corporal.*'

'Well whyn't you use it, hey? And stand to attention when you talk to a senior NCO,' he bawled out suddenly and old Phil come up right smart, he was red in the face though.

'You may've just been made up,' Bax told him then, 'but to me you're just a private same's anyone else, see? And a private you'll be again soon enough if you ain't bloody careful,' he said. 'What time you supposed to be in?'

'2200 hours Corporal,' Phil told him.

'Right. Next time you're late you'll find yourself on report, See? I'm minded to stick you on as it is. Both of you,' and then he seen it was me with Phil and he said 'What you doing walking out with a private soldier hey?'

'We met on the way up Corporal,' I cut in quick.

'And who's talking to you?' Bax bawled out rounding on me, 'Speak when you're spoken to! You ain't answered my question Corporal,' he said then to Phil, and Phil said 'Well if I rank as a private as you've just said, Corporal, there's no reason why I shouldn't walk out with one,' and Bax bawled out 'Don't answer me back.' He bawled but he knew Phil had him knackered there, that's what made him so wild.

Out he went then and banged the door after him and all the blokes come up and slapped old Phil on the back and all said he'd got the better of that one, he had old Bax bolloxed that time, the regimental bastard. But Phil he didn't say nothing and they helped us make our beds then, we got 'em done just before lights out blew. Well in orders next night there was a bit that said any NCO seen frequenting public-houses with private soldiers would forthwith have disciplinary action taken against him, and we knew that was aimed at us on account of Mr Burns seen us in The Feathers and I said to Phil it looks like we better not go round together no more and he said no Fordy, he said, we can't let them get us down like that, I'll chuck in my stripe that's all, but I argued him out of that, I said we could still meet downtown in the Y.M. so long's we walked down different ways, and for a time we did that and it was okay. But old Phil weren't the same, this bust-up he'd had with his girl had worked on him proper, and one day he come up to me and he said 'Fordy it's no good, I've got to put in for this blasted commission,' he said, 'I can't help myself,' and I said That's the stuff Phil, I'd do the same in your place, I told him.

'I'm sorry Fordy,' he said and he looked proper down in the mouth, 'but we won't let it make any difference to us,' he said and I said 'No, course not,' though I knew it would.

Well he wrote in to the Old Man, and then he come up before a Board, and that passed him, and then he had to come up before the C.O.. His girl was all over him now in her letters of course, you could tell that by the way he looked when he was reading 'em. He seemed a good deal happier too now he'd done it, but I didn't see so much of him 'cause he used to stay in a good bit swotting up them pamphlets he got give him.

Then one morning we had a bust-up. We was on P.T., see, and Sarnt put Tasker on to march us down to Gym, Bax and Corp' Draper was off on some lecture. Well we was late changing on account of it being so cold and when we got on the road Tasker bawled out to us to double. We started off doubling but road was that slippery with ice you couldn't run even with slippers on and one bloke fell down twice and cut his leg and then he said he wouldn't double no more. Tasker bawled out 'I said DOUBLE!' and this bloke come back 'BOLLOX.' Well Tasker said he'd have him on a thickun and this bloke said he could do what he bleeding liked. Anyroad Tasker made him fall in and he didn't give us double no more, but when we got down the Gym, P.T. Sarnt asked why we was late and give Tasker a bollocking and when we come back Tasker shoved this bloke that'd fallen down on a chitty and he come up before the Old Man and got seven days, the Old Man never give less than seven.

Afterwards in the hut we was talking about it and I reckoned Tasker was getting too big for his bleeding boots and then Phil said 'Well he was in his rights you know.' I said what'd he mean, I was proper staggered hearing Phil stick up for a thing like that, and Phil said Well after all the bloke had disobeyed an order and got Tasker chewed up about it and what else could Tasker do but peg him?

I said 'You've changed a bit, ain't you Phil?' and Phil jumped up white in the face and said 'What the hell d'you mean, changed?' and I said 'What I say.'

Then we had a proper row and one or two of the other blokes joined in and anyroad Phil never said a word to me for about three days after that and he was going about with Weston and them other OCTU wallahs now and I never saw much of him.

Then we got moved, the lot of us, into other huts and Phil was in Hut 20 and I was in 19 and we didn't make no move to change over, although we talked to each other now when we met. Still it wasn't the same and I felt kind of lost without him at first. I couldn't find nothing to do with meself somehow. I used to go a lot in boozer, that I never done before 'cause as I say Phil didn't use to do a lot of drinking.

Well one night I was in there and I met up with a lot of jocks that was stationed other end of town and we started putting back pints and I got proper pissed, it was pay-day. When I come out the pub was closing and

I got back to camp after lights out and Bax was NCO in charge of our hut and he was waiting up for me.

'Where you been Ford?' he said, 'You got a pass?' and I said 'No I ain't,' I was that puddled I didn't give a bollock what happened.

Then Bax said 'Consider yourself an accused soldier,' he said, 'You been drinking too, that makes two charges,' and I said, he'd made me right mad, 'Okay,' I said, 'Well here's another, socking an NCO' I said and with that I give it him bang in the jaw, lifted him clean off the floor it did, and he come down flat out and lay there not moving even when one of the lads sloshed a bucket of water over him to make him come round.

Well course they turned up the lights and come tumbling out of kip and there was such a bleeding row going on Corp' Draper come in from other hut to see what was up.

'All right' he said when he seen Bax laying there, 'Fall in two men,' and I didn't blame him, he couldn't do no other.

They marched me down to guardroom and I come up before the C.O. and in due course they give me 156 days Aldershot for it, that's the glasshouse. Do everything at the double there. Full pack and all. It was worth it to have socked Bax like that though. I'd do it again, buggered if I wouldn't.

Well when I come out of there and got sent back to depot, I was walking up by Company Office with all my kit on when who should be coming along but Phil, whose stripe had got dirty by this time and didn't show up no longer on his sleeve, and I said 'Wotcher, Phil,' and he stopped to say Hullo but by the way he was looking round I knew he didn't want to be seen talking to me, you could tell I was just out of glasshouse by my haircut and the way my tin hat was painted.

'Well,' I said, 'I'd best be getting along I reckon. You doing all right Phil?' and he said 'Oh yes, thanks, I'm in C Company now,' he said, 'I go up to OCTU next week,' and I said So long, all the best, and that's the last I seen of him.

This Mortal Coil

I was on picquet that night, I'd just come off the door. It was about ten o'clock and when I came in the guard-room I expected to find them all dossed down for the night. But instead they were up, fire-watchers and all, some standing about, some sitting on benches by the table, and Corporal Weemes, the Picquet Commander, sat on the table itself. All looked so expectant that I said: 'What's up? Scheme on or something,'

'No, no,' they said. 'It's Kelly.'

'Kelly?'

They pointed to a corner of the room, by the telephone table. What I had taken for a heap of blankets lay there. But these evidently concealed a man of some sort, because as I looked at them they began to heave and writhe about: at the same time a series of grunts came from underneath them. The fellows bounced up and down on the bench, some clapped their hands in glee.

'He's starting,' they said. 'He's got started.'

Corporal Weemes looked at his watch. 'Ten o'clock,' he said. 'On the dot. He always starts off at ten.'

The grunts were succeeded by an awful, unearthly sound, like a wolf howling. At first it was muffled by the blankets, but as these fell off and a head emerged, it positively filled the room with its volume.

'What's wrong with him?' I said. 'Is he sick?'

'Ssh!' they said. 'Just wait till he gets properly going.'

'Regular circus,' Corporal Weemes said.

The howl died down and became split up into words. These, unintelligible at first, clarified suddenly into a shout: 'The rotten bastards!'

'He's off,' they said, shaking with laughter.

'Rotten bastards!' came the shout. 'I'll learn you, you rotten sods!'

'That's right, Kelly,' someone shouted from the bench. 'Brass the buggers up.'

'Company, shun!' came from under the blanket. 'Or-der-HUP! As you were!' He'd a good word of command, anyhow. 'Company will advance. Right-turn!'

'But is he asleep?' I said.

'Sure he's asleep,' Corporal Weemes said. 'He's dreaming, see?'

'Ab-out TURN!' Kelly shouted in his sleep. 'Pick up that step, you sods!'

'Proper sarmajor, ain't he?' they said in admiration.

'Look out, Kelly!' someone shouted. 'Here comes the R.S.M.'

'Fuck the R.S.M.' came back from Kelly. The fellows rocked with laughter, one nearly fell off the bench. 'That's right, Kelly boy,' they shouted. 'You size him up!'

'Where's Joan?' they asked him next. 'She's looking for you, Kelly. Joan! Wake up! Joan's his girl,' they explained to me.

'Joan?' Kelly mumbled. He was puzzled. The transition from parade ground to girl was too much for him to accomplish at a moment's notice.

'Yes, Joan!' they shouted, hopping about from foot to foot. 'She wants you, Kelly boy!'

Kelly kicked off all his blankets. One got entangled with his boots, but he got rid of it at last, muttering 'Rotten bastard'. But the idea of Joan was evidently uppermost in his mind, and he murmured at the same time 'Darling'.

Sitting up, still asleep, with all his equipment on, he was revealed to be a small, dark lad about twenty. 'Joan,' he murmured, 'my sweet darling,' and kissed his haversack. The fellows were delighted. 'Go it, Kelly!' they screamed. 'Give her the works!'

Thus encouraged, Kelly became passionate. He embraced the haversack and, holding it tightly, climbed on top of it. He fell off and rolled over, hitting his head a whack on the door. But the blow did not fetch him to; he lay on his back murmuring 'Dearest love', and feeling for the haversack.

L/C Staines, N.C.O. i/c firewatching, came dashing in. 'Have I missed anything?' he asked. 'How long's he been started?'

'You're in time, Corp. Only got to Joan so far.'

'That's all right, then.' L/C Staines sat down by the telephone table, quite close to Kelly. He had a ringside seat. The boxing metaphor is justified because the haversack, formerly representing his girl, now apparently became identified in Kelly's dream with some mortal enemy. He clinched with it and delivered a short-arm jab to the straps.

'Go it, Kelly!' the chaps shouted, 'You got him groggy. You got him on the ropes. Go in and K.O. him, Kelly boy!'

Kelly did his best. He abandoned boxing for all-in wrestling and took a large bite of Blanco from the flap of the haversack. But the haversack in his mind had evidently hit back: he rocked sideways and slipped down by the wall, shaking his head. One of the blokes began slowly to count him out. 'One—two—three—four—.'

'Can't get up,' Kelly mumbled in a bemused voice, punch-drunk. He took a swing at the air and missed. He hit the door instead and laid his hand open.

'Surely that'll wake him?' I said.

'Don't you believe it,' one of the blokes said. 'Hammond hit him on the nut with an entrenching tool once and *that* didn't wake him. Nothing'll wake him once he starts on this stunt. He don't feel nothing, see,'

'What does he do when he's not asleep? Is he a boxer?'

'Not likely. Look at him daytime you wouldn't think butter'd melt in his mouth. Don't swear neither not unless he's dreaming.'

A stream of obscenity began to pour from Kelly as though released by these words. He'd been counted out and was now standing on his head in a kneeling position, as if about to perform a somersault. In this posture he appeared so funny that everybody again burst out laughing. But Kelly himself continued to swear, with his face close to the floorboards. It soon became apparent that his epithets were addressed not to anyone in particular but to the army in general.

'Doesn't he like the army?' I said.

'Dunno,' Corporal Weemes said. 'We have to chase him about sometimes. Bit of a dodger in his way. Lazy. Ain't a bad lad, not really, though.'

'Done any defaulters?'

'He done plenty of *them*. Just come off, matter of fact. Come off last night.'

'Fuck the army!' Kelly was shouting in his sleep. 'Fuck the jankers. Fuck 'em all! Give me my civvy clothes,' he began to sing in a horrible toneless voice. 'Give me my civvy... clothes,' and the fellows slapped their knees and danced around him in delight. Then he went back to saying, 'Bugger the army!' in a tone of such stridency that L/C Staines leaped up off his chair. Either his sense of discipline was outraged or else he was afraid the duty officer would overhear.

'Come on, Kelly,' he said in a voice of command. 'That's enough, lad. Come on, wake up!'

He grasped Kelly by the braces and swung him upright. With his other hand he administered a smart cuff on the ear. While delivered smartly it was still heavy enough to rock Kelly's head on his shoulders. But Kelly's eyes remained obstinately closed, and as if it were a reflex action his boot shot out at Staines's kneecap. Staines, an expert in unarmed combat, dodged nimbly back, releasing Kelly, but at the same time jerking his bayonet from its scabbard and tossing it on the telephone table. Kelly fell on his face and lay there, with blood dripping on the blankets from his cut hand.

'That's got it,' Staines said.

'The bayonet?'

'Yeh. He can be awkward sometimes. Remember that time, Wilhams, when he walked in his sleep? In Don Company?'

'Cor, don't I!' Williarns said. 'I won't forget that not in a hurry. Fixed bayonet, all in his sleep, and come charging down the hut. We was all scared stiff. Then he come charging back again.'

'What'd you do?' I asked.

'We all got out right sharp and shut the door. After 'bout a quarter hour we looks in again and there he was sleeping sound, bayonet back in scabbard and all. Bloody rum bloke Kelly is, no error.'

'He's getting married next week,' another man said. 'Joan. His tart. Cor,' he chortled, 'I reckon she won't half get a surprise the first night, eh?'

'Getting married?' I said.

'Ah. Put in for leave today. Pass signed and all. He seen the Padre.'

'But damn it all he oughtn't to get married when he gets these fits. He ought to see the M.O., or the psychiatrist.'

'Psychiatrist? Ain't that the bloke what they took Wiggs to, that they said was loopy?'

'Ah. Got his ticket and all, Wiggs did.'

'Reckon old Kelly'd get his ticket?'

'Nah, he ain't loopy. He's all right. Won't remember nothing about it when he wakes up.'

'Why don't you send him sick,' I asked Corporal Weemes.

'Wouldn't do no good,' Weemes said. 'He don't believe he does it, see? Thinks we're kidding when we tell him.'

Meanwhile one of the fellows had got hold of a broom and was dancing round Kelly jabbing him in the ribs with it, while Kelly, flat on the floor, made feeble efforts to snatch the broom away. But this comic relief roused a storm of protest from the others.

'Nah, let him be! Put the broom down!'

'It ain't fair poking him like that. Not with the broom.'

So the broom was abandoned. But Kelly now began to cry. 'They got me again,' he sobbed. 'They got me on another charge and I ain't done nothing! I ain't done nothing to nobody!' His body shook with sobs.

Immediately the fellows gathered round him. 'It's all right, Kelly boy. You ain't on no charge, mate. You don't have to take on,' and gradually Kelly was convinced. His sobs subsided and briefly he went through his whole repertoire, 'Sweet darling, rotten bastards, Company shun,' finishing up with a decisive 'Fuck the army!'

Then his head fell peacefully back, and he at once began to snore. Two fellows came forward and covered him with his blankets again. The performance was evidently at an end.

'Will he be all right now?' I asked.

'Right as rain. Won't wake till reveille. Unless the alarm goes.'

Corporal Weenies looked at his watch. 'Okay, lads. Ten forty-five. Pack it in now. Kip down.'

L/C Staines stood up and said in his parade ground voice: 'Come on. Next man on firewatching. Quick march!'

A steel helmet was clapped on, rifle snatched up, the door banged behind them. We all moved towards the beds and fairly soon we were sound asleep: even Kelly, dreamless now, huddled in his blankets with the blood drying on his cut hand, snoring quite happily to himself.

Only Corporal Weemes stayed awake, sitting up on the bench with a sixpenny thriller, because a Picquet Commander must not sleep on duty.

The Café, a converted cellar, was full of cigarette smoke and very hot; there were no fans to blow the smoke away. It was uncomfortable and the quality of the liquor poor, but despite its drawbacks most of the Russians in Nice went there every evening because they found difficulty in obtaining credit elsewhere.

Outside it was also very hot, the middle of July, and the whole town seemed to smell of tar. Even walking along the promenade it was not easy to escape from the smell.

When Sergey came downstairs there were already three Russsians in the bar, drinking beer and beating time to the gramophone. Sergey came over to their table and sat down.

'Did you see Haines?' Stepan Silensky asked him.

'Yes,' Sergey said. 'He was at the dance marathon.'

'Any luck?'

'I tapped him for twenty.'

'By God, that's the stuff,' Stepan said.

'It certainly is,' Pavel Chernikov said.

Boris Silensky, Stepan's brother, did not say anything. He just jerked his head and went on looking gloomy.

'He's a good fellow, Haines,' Sergey said.

'He's an American,' Chernikov said. 'He can afford to be generous, with all his dollars.'

'He is only half American,' Sergey said.

'It is enough,' Stepan said. 'He is rich enough already without being entirely American.'

'All Americans are not rich,' Sergey said.

'Most of them are,' Chernikov said.

'All of them,' Stepan said. 'They are lousy with it.'

'No,' Sergey said. 'Not all of them.'

'Have you ever known an American who was not?'

'I have never known one myself, no,' Sergey said. 'But Haines told me that in America there are many like us. Fellows without money.

'Bums' they are called over there.'

'Bum is slang-English for bottom,' Chernikov said. He had been to school in England and knew the language.

'In America it's the name they give to a tramp,' Sergey said. 'Haines told me there are many such.'

'Perhaps,' Stepan said. 'Perhaps that is true. But they do not come here to the Côte.'

'No,' Sergey said. 'They have not got the money.'

'Exactly,' Stepan said. 'All those that come here are rich, therefore. You cannot deny that.'

'No,' Sergey said.

'Then I am right,' Stepan said.

'Not entirely.'

'How do you mean "not entirely"?'

'Let's not argue,' Chernikov said, 'Sergey has got the money, that is the most important.'

'As you say.'

The gramophone stopped playing and Henri, the owner of the café and also the only waiter, came out from behind the bar and approached the table.

'What are you drinking?' Sergey said. 'Have what you like, I can afford it.'

'It all goes on the slate anyway,' Stepan said.

'That's true,' Sergey said.

Henri came up to the table and stood smirking at them.

'I will have a vieux marc,' Sergey said. 'And you others?'

'I'll stick to beer,' Stepan said.

'Me also,' Chernikov said.

'I'll have a panaché,' Boris said broodingly. He mopped his forehead. 'It's bloody hot in here.'

'Hotter in hell,' Henri told him.

'You ever been there?' Boris asked.

'No,' Henri said, 'but I know.'

'You can't know if you haven't been there. You ought to go and find out for yourself.'

'We will meet there one day,' Henri said, 'and exchange views.'

He walked away, whistling cheerfully.

'Blasted little runt,' Boris growled. 'I'd like to pull his nose.'

'Don't for the love of Christ,' Chernikov said, 'or he'll cut off our credit.'

'You must control your atavistic instincts, Boris,' Stepan told his brother. He said to Sergey: 'Boris is angry because his boss hasn't paid him for a month.'

'Why don't you ditch the job if you don't get paid?' Sergey asked Boris.

'I'd never get paid at all if I did, whereas if I stick on there's always a chance.'

'That's true.'

'Give me a cigarette,' Boris said.

'I've only got blues.'

'They'll do.'

Sergey took out the pack of Gauloises and gave Boris one. The gramophone started up again very loudly and Henri returned with the drinks on a tray.

'Write them down to me,' Sergey said.

'Okay,' Henri said, and to display his knowledge of Russian, added: 'Da da, harosho.'

'Wait a moment,' Sergey said. 'I want a packet of Chesterfield.'

'No tick for cigarettes,' Henri told him.

'I can pay cash,' Sergey said.

'Let's see it then,' Henri said.

Sergey pulled out a ten franc note, which he handed to Henri.

'Spossibo,' Henri said.

'Sergey is a rich man,' Stepan said, 'he has just made a touch.'

'Ah,' Henri said. He winked at Sergey and hurried back to the bar.

'Let us drink to the health of Haines,' Sergey said, lifting his glass.

'To Haines,' the others chorused.

'He's a jolly good fellow,' Sergey said.

'Yes,' Stepan said, 'but as I remarked before, he can afford to be. He is rich enough.'

'Nevertheless he is not forced to lend,' Sergey said. 'Many rich men are mean.'

'Ah, you know how to manage him,' Stepan said. 'You are a prince, that gives you a pull. These Americans worship the nobility. They have none of their own, that is why.'

'They are snobs,' Chernikov said.

'Look how many of their women marry titles,' Stepan said. 'I have always dreamt of that myself. To marry a rich American woman, it has always been my dream.'

'Why don't you do it?' Sergey asked him.

'I am not a prince, unfortunately. I have no title.'

'You could pretend you had.'

'No use, they would find out. These Americans are not fools.'

'True,' Sergey said.

'You could do it though. You are a genuine prince.'

'I have no wish to marry,' Sergey said.

'This panaché tastes like horse's piss,' Boris said, putting down his glass.

'The beer is very bad too,' Chernikov said.

Henri came up with the cigarettes.

'Here you are,' he said to Sergey. 'I've put the rest of the change to your account. Now you only owe me ten francs.'

'Bloodsucker,' Sergey said.

'I've got to live,' Henri said. 'I cannot, like you others, exist on credit alone.'

'Listen,' Boris said to him, 'this panaché tastes like horse's piss.'

'Ever drunk horse's piss?' Henri said.

'No,' Boris said, 'to drink this is bad enough.'

'You should try the genuine article,' Henri said. 'Then you would appreciate the difference.'

He walked off whistling.

'Dirty little squirt,' Boris growled.

Sergey tore the cellophane from his Chesterfield packet and offered it to the others. 'Have an American cigarette,' he said.

'Paid for with American money,' Stepan said, taking one.

'Thank you,' Chernikov said, doing likewise.

'These are good, they satisfy. It says so on the packet.'

'How was the marathon?' Stepan asked Sergey.

'Still going strong,' Sergey said.

'Jackie still in it?'

'Sure.'

'How does she look?'

'A bit bowlegged,' Sergey said.

'She'll knock herself up,' Chernikov said.

'Not she,' Stepan said. 'She's strong as a horse.'

'Women have more stamina than men,' Sergey said. 'Look at childbirth.'

'There's something in that,' Chernikov said. 'D'you think the marathon will stop soon?' Stepan said.

'No,' Sergey said. 'I see no reason why it should ever stop.'

'It must stop sometime,' Chernikov said.

'Yes, when all the dancers are dead.'

'Have any of them died yet?'

'No, I don't think so.'

'I like the marathon,' Stepan said. 'If I had the money I would go there every night to watch.'

'It is a morbid spectacle,' Chernikov said.

'I am morbid too,' Stepan said.

'We are all morbid,' Sergey said. 'We all lead morbid lives.'

'Give me a Chesterfield,' Boris said.

'Here you are,' Sergey said.

'It will satisfy you,' Chernikov said.

'Why don't you enter the marathon yourself?' Stepan asked Sergey.

'I haven't the stamina,' Sergey said. 'Why don't you?'

'I haven't the stamina either. I should collapse.'

'That would be excellent,' Chernikov said. 'They would take you to the hospital and I would bring flowers to you every day.'

'Thanks,' Stepan said, 'but I prefer not. There are other ways of earning money.'

'Like Reggie Kahn?' Chernikov said.

'I hear Reggie has become a professional pansy,' Sergey said. 'Is it true?'

'I believe so,' Chernikov said.

'Why don't you do the same?' Sergey asked Stepan.

'No,' Stepan said, 'it doesn't appeal to me. It is one of those professions where you have to start at the bottom and work upwards.'

Boris smiled grimly, smoking his Chesterfield. The others laughed.

'Talking of hospitals,' Chernikov said then, 'I met Vaska yesterday. He'd just come out.'

'I hate Vaska,' Stepan said. 'He is a common thug. A lowdown ruffian, no less.'

'What was he doing in hospital?' Sergey said.

'He got in a rough-house,' Chernikov said. 'It seems one night he went down the old town and met up with a bunch of Niçois. Vaska started acting tough and they knocked him down and kicked him in the belly.'

'Good job too,' Stepan said. 'It's time someone gave him a beating.'

'He says it took six of them to do it,' Chernikov said.

'It'll be ten next time he tells the story,' Stepan said.

'Well anyhow,' Chernikov said, 'they knocked him out and left him lying in the gutter. When he came to, he started vomiting blood. He went to a doctor and the doctor sent him straight to hospital. It seems the kicks had split open something inside of him. He lived on rice for a month.'

'By god, these old town fellows are tough,' Sergey said. 'Is Vaska all right again now?'

'He doesn't look well.'

'It serves him right,' Stepan said. 'A dose of his own medicine will do him good.'

'Give me another Chesterfield,' Boris said.

'Hasn't that one satisfied you?' Chernikov said.

'No,' Boris said.

'Impossible,' Chernikov said. 'The packet can't be wrong.'

Sergey gave Boris a Chesterfield.

'Did you hear what Vaska and Konstantin did to Laskov one night?' he said.

'No, what was that? I haven't heard.'

'Laskov was playing at the jetée,' Sergey said, 'and he'd made a big killing. He must have won about five thousand francs. He was walking home in high spirits when Vaska and Konstantin accosted him. They were broke as usual and asked him for a loan. "Certainly," Laskov said, producing his pocketbook and starting to open it.

"Don't worry," Vaska told him, "we'll take the lot."

"You won't," Laskov said.

"Won't we?" Vaska said. He struck Laskov a blow in the jaw and snatched the pocketbook. Poor old Laskov tried to fight back and they pasted him all over the place. He had two teeth knocked out and both his eyes blacked. He was in an awful state next day; his face resembled *rosbif.* Of course Vaska and Konstantin walked off with the money.'

'I tell you,' Stepan said, 'Vaska is a ruffian. As for Konstantin, he is a Greek and what can you expect from a Greek?'

'Did Laskov go to hospital?' Chernikov asked.

'No,' Sergey said, 'he went to the police. Next day Vaska and Konstantin were arrested. I went down to the police-court to watch the case tried. They put Laskov in the box with his head all bandaged and asked him to identify the two men in the dock. Vaska and Konstantin didn't say anything, they just looked at Laskov and in the end he said no, these were not the two who had assaulted him. He was sorry, he had made a mistake in accusing them. At this, the magistrate got angry. "Throw them out," he said. "These darn fool Russians. They waste my time for nothing."'

'But I don't understand,' Chernikov said. 'Why didn't Laskov give them away?'

'He knew they'd get him when they came out, that's why. Outside the court they came up to him and Vaska said, "Laskov, you behave like a sportsman. If you had sent us to jail we should have beaten you when we came out. As it is, you behaved well and we should like to be friends. Here is your money back." He held out Laskov's pocketbook, but Laskov wouldn't take it. "Get out of my way, curse you," he said and walked away.'

'He must have been very angry not to take the money,' Stepan said. 'I should have taken it in his place.'

'So should I,' Chernikov said.

'He was very angry,' Sergey said. 'Who wouldn't have been?'

'I should have been angry also,' Stepan said, 'but not too angry to take the money.'

'There's a sequel to that story,' Sergey said.

'Let's hear it,' Stepan said.

'Wait,' Sergey said, 'I will order some more drinks first. Henri! Henri!'

'Monsieur?'

'Same again for all of us.'

'Except me,' Boris said. 'I'll have plain beer this time. It may taste better.'

'You're never satisfied,' Chernikov said.

'Not in this café,' Boris said.

'Why do you come here then?' Henri asked him.

'God only knows.'

'I will tell you,' Henri said, 'although I am not God. You come here because the other cafés will not allow you credit. Isn't that so?'

'I expect you're right,' Boris said.

'Get the drinks, Henri and don't talk so much,' Sergey said.

'I'll get them,' Henri said, 'I'll get them.'

'What was the sequel to your story, Sergey? ' Chernikov asked.

'Ah, yes,' Sergey said. 'When Laskov was in Marseille working as a professional dancer, Konstantin came into the casino where he was employed, and Laskov was so glad to see someone from the Côte that he forgot all about their quarrel and almost embraced Konstantin. They ended up in a whore-house somewhere and have been firm friends ever since.'

'Good God,' Stepan said, 'what a farce.'

'Laskov doesn't know his own mind,' Chernikov said.

'I should not care to embrace Konstantin either,' Stepan said. 'Would you, Sergey?'

'No,' Sergey said.

The gramophone started playing a rumba very loudly.

'Give us another Chesterfield,' Boris said to Sergey.

'You're never satisfied,' Chernikov told him.

One of the boys in our battalion died the other day. He got drowned.

Nothing dramatic: he went bathing in the river one Sunday and never came back. Two of his mates were with him, fellows from the signal section; they told me about it in the evening.

'Heard about old Lennox?'

'Lennox,' I said; 'Who's Lennox?'

'You know, Lennox. In our lot. Fairhaired kiddy from Cambridge. He got drowned today.'

'Drowned?'

'They ain't found the body yet.'

'Good lord. How'd it happen?'

They told me. They didn't even notice he was gone, at first; he must have sunk quite suddenly, like a stone. Weeds, the current, cramp; might have been any of them. Down he went, not a trace. Gone.

'Fair shook me, it did,' one of the signallers said, and: 'You hear about this bloke that got drowned?' the orderly sergeant asked me back in the office. 'One of the signals. Went out bathing, drowned himself in the river. Current got him, I reckon. He didn't ought to've done no bathing in there: it's too bleeding deep.'

'Well,' I said, 'it's too late to stop him now.'

'Too bleeding true it is,' the orderly sergeant said.

'Lennox,' I said. 'What was he like?'

'Blowed if I remember.'

'Neither do I.'

And it worried me, not being able to remember. Working in the army Office I must have seen him scores of times on telephone duty; the signallers had charge of the 'phone.

Lennox, Lennox—I knew the name from typing out nominal rolls, but I couldn't fit it to any face. There were several 'fair-haired kiddies' in the Signal Section, and any of them might have come from Cambridge. Was Lennox the blond, rather tough-looking boy whom I'd last seen at the baths, sitting on a bucket talking about his tart; or was he the other short, cissy-looking one with curly hair, who'd been a barber in civvy street?

Next day the body still hadn't turned up, but a telegram was sent off to Lennox's father, and then, as Company Clerk, I had to compose a letter of condolence, which the Company Commander signed. That night it appeared in orders: 'The Commanding Officer regrets to announce the death...' and underneath: 'A Court of Enquiry will assemble as under to determine the cause of death of 6526854...'

The notice announcing the death had a black border typed in around it. I could imagine the orderly room clerk cursing when he had to take out the stencil and re-insert it twice to get the black line level on either side. With wax costing sixpence a sheet you had to be careful not to make a muck of it; it's quite an undertaking. A death gives a lot of trouble, one way and another, in a battalion. Luckily we don't have many; only three in the last year or so. The sergeant who set fire to his tent, the batman who shot himself cleaning a revolver, the bloke who broke his neck on P.T..

The colour sergeant came in with a sack. 'More work,' he said. 'Lennox's personal kit. Give us a hand to sort it out, will you?'—a suit of service dress, civvy shoes, a pack of cards, an old cigarette case with a broken clasp, two photos of naked girls torn from a six-penny magazine, a bundle of letters, a book: *What a Young Husband Ought to Know.*

'Was he getting hitched?'

'Not that I know of.'

'Here's a letter, from his girl'. S.W.A.L.K. on the back of the envelope: *'Dear Dick, why have you not wrote lately. I haven't heard nothing of you for a fortnight now.'*

'Not much good sending 'em that,' the colour sergeant said. He threw it in the salvage bag, the pack of cards and the naked girls followed; they were retrieved later by one of the runners.

'What about, this?'

A pencilled scrawl dated Sunday. He must have been writing it on the river bank just before he dived in.

'Dear Mum, thank you for the parcel and the P.O.. I haven't any news, but I owe you a letter, so I am writing this...'

'What d'you think? Send it?'

'No. Only brings things home more, I reckon.'

'Yeh. No sense in that.' And at last the stuff was sorted out in two piles on the floor, ready to send off.

Did his life flash before him as they say it does when you're drowning, and was this it: the greasy cards, 'Dear Mum', the girl's bare breasts, S.W.A.L.K., *What a Young Husband Ought to Know*? ('*I'll* take care of that,' the sergeant-major, said, walking out with the book tucked under his arm.)

'What sort of a fellow was Lennox?' I asked the signal sergeant, who'd just come in.

'Lennox? Smart kid. Knew his stuff backwards. But you seen him, surely? On the phone?'

'No,' I said. 'I don't remember.'

It seemed wrong somehow, not to remember a man who'd died like that. Supposing I died myself, would someone say: 'You know him, big tall bloke, used a fag-holder, half-crown voice,' and would the answer be: 'I don't remember'? It seemed to me quite likely.

Service dress and civvy shoes, a bundle of letters, an annoyance to the orderly room clerk, more work for the colour-sergeant; a man dying ought to leave behind him more than that. And so when Lennox's father arrived the next day I tried hard to find in the small, grey-haired man in the dark suit who stood waiting awkwardly downstairs, a raincoat over his arm, some resemblance to a face I must have seen quite often: in the Naffy, or the cookhouse, or in the office, answering a call from the Adjutant. But there was none: he didn't look like anyone I knew.

'Can I see your Commanding Officer?' he said. 'My name's Lennox.'

'If you'll come this way, please,' I said.

He followed me down the long cold stone corridor of the hotel we were billeted in.

'I was very sorry to hear of your loss, Mr. Lennox,' I said to him. 'We were all very sorry. We all liked him a lot.'

'Oh, yes,' he said; 'Yes,' absently, and then: 'You knew him?' with sudden interest; 'My son?'

'Of course I knew him,' I said. 'He was a great pal of mine. We used to go about together.'

'He got on all right? With the others?'

'He got on well with everyone.'

'Good,' he said, 'Good. I'm glad. He wasn't a bad lad.'

And I said: 'One of the best.'

The C.O. was in his office, standing with his back to the empty fireplace; the other officers sat round the long table with a crimson cloth on it; the Court of Enquiry had just been concluded.

'Come in.'

'Mr. Lennox, sir,' I said, and stood back closing the door as the C.O. came forward with outstretched hand and the correct look of commiseration in his face.

In the Company Office, the signaller on phone duty said: 'That his father?'

'Yes,' I said.

'Poor blighter. They still ain't found the body, y'know.'

And they didn't find it till five days later; it'd floated nearly twenty miles: amazing. The current of that river must have been certainly strong; it's out of bounds to all ranks now.

Then they had the funeral, with all the signallers attending, and the signal corporal and the signal sergeant, and another sergeant to play the Last Post as they lowered the coffin into the grave.

And today I wrote off the last of him, typing a letter and posting a parcel to the Officer i/c Records:

'Late 6526854 Pte. Lennox, R., Personal Effects of, forwarded on receipt from Civil Police:

One black leather diary dated 1941.

One piece of broken mirror.

One comb.

One bronze medallion.

One key.

5s.1d. in cash.'

The six o'clock streets were full of people reading newspapers and slapping one another on the back. ITALY SURRENDERS, headlines seen over their shoulders said. I'd heard the news from my tobacconist hours before it was officially announced, so I didn't bother to buy a paper. Besides, all the papers were sold out.

I was with Cedric; you know: Cedric Sykes. The poet. We'd been celebrating the victory all afternoon in some club that had pictures of sailors painted on the walls. We were both perhaps a little pie-eyed. After all, Italy doesn't surrender every day.

We were on our way to have dinner at Cedric's place. Steak, he said. Well, you don't get your teeth in a steak every day either.

'Nature,' Cedric was saying as we walked along. He was not expatiating on its beauties, as one might expect of a poet; he was explaining that he wanted a pee.

I said: 'Let's go to Krishna's. His bookshop's just round the back. You can have a pee there.'

'He'll want us to have drinks in the Holborn Bar.'

'We can refuse. Anyway, they won't let me in there now. I got thrown out last week.'

'All right,' Cedric said. 'If you're sure he'll let us pee. I can't hold it much longer.'

Krishna rolled his eyes round at us, closing one of them in a discreet wink as we came in the shop. He was trying to sell a poetry anthology to an American officer who'd gone in there to buy a thriller.

'Aw shucks,' the American was saying, 'I guess I can't get along with verse.' But he was weakening. Krishna pressed home his advantage. I inspected the backs of books. Cedric shifted from foot to foot with an agonised expression. Smothered giggles came from the back of the shop. Krishna had a harem complex; his place was always full of women. I wondered who was in there this time.

The American army admitted defeat and left with *Poems of 1943* under its arm. Krishna rang up the till with triumph. He advanced towards us smiling rather sadly and smoothing his hair. He had on a brown suit and a resplendent yellow neckcloth.

'Hullo, Cedric. Hullo, Julian. Come and meet Cora.'

I followed him into the back where the telephone was and the swivel chair that tipped you out on the floor if you attempted to sit in it.

A girl, quite evidently Cora, was standing in front of the mirror contorting herself with a Kirby grip between her teeth. She was a new one on me. Krishna's stock seemed quite inexhaustible.

This had long silken dark hair that swept about her face. She tossed the hair back to smile flashingly at me as we were introduced. She had taken the Kirby grip out of her mouth and now pointed it at me as with her other hand she squeezed my fingers hard.

'You're the bloke that wrote the story in this week's *Tribune*,' she said.

I don't like girls who call me a bloke. I felt she'd be saying chaps next.

'That sounds like an accusation,' I said.

'I didn't like the story,' she said.

'I did,' Krishna said.

'You didn't like it because it was about sex,' I told Cora. 'Krishna liked it for the same reason.'

Cora said: 'I thought it was written by someone quite old who'd never been with a woman in his life.'

Krishna said: 'I'm writing a story under its influence. I've got the MS half finished.'

'What's your story about?' I asked him.

'Sex,' Krishna said.

I said: 'I hate sex.'

Cedric, who'd been snorting in the front of the shop for some time, now appeared in front of us, pale with fury.

'You've led me here under false pretences,' he said.

'Christ, I'd forgotten,' I said. 'I'm sorry, old boy. Krishna will you conduct Cedric to the gents without delay? It's urgent.'

'Pleasure,' Krishna said. He bowed.

'Quick, quick,' Cedric said.

They went out quickly.

Cora contorted herself before the glass. She turned, at bay and with her hair back.

'So you hate sex?' she said.

'I detest it.'

'People like you should be in the army.'

'I'm a conscientious objector,' I said.

'You would be,' Cora said. She shook her hair scornfully.

'I'm frightfully conscientious,' I said. 'I object to absolutely everything.'

'And especially sex?'

'With all my heart.'

'Think what you might be missing,' Cora said. Her hair fell across one eye. She looked at me through its meshes.

'I'm sorry,' I said. 'I have a date tonight. I'm having dinner with Cedric.'

Talk of the devil: at that moment he appeared with Krishna, looking plainly relieved but still a bit put-out.

'Another conchie,' Cora said, 'I suppose.'

Krishna said: 'Conchie? Where?' He looked around.

Cora said: 'Your friends.'

Krishna said: 'What gave you that idea? Julian's just been invalided out of the army. Cedric was a pilot officer until…'

'Julian,' Cedric said, 'I thought we were going to have dinner.'

Cora said, 'I suppose you must have a sense of humour. I can't see it myself.'

'Neither can I,' I said. 'You see I'm a humorous writer. We humorous writers seldom have a sense of humour.'

'*Ca se voit*,' Cora said.

'You're educated,' I said, 'French, too.'

Cedric said: 'If you don't come in three minutes our dinner date's off. That's my last word. An ultimatum.'

'Four minutes,' I said.

'Three and a half.'

'Let's go and have drinks in the Holborn Bar,' Krishna said.

'No, we have to go,' I said.

Cora didn't answer when I said good-bye. Her face was now entirely hidden by hair.

Krishna accompanied us to the door. 'You mustn't mind Cora,' he said. 'She means no harm. You see she's a virgin. It irks her.'

'It irks me too,' I said.

'She cannot help it,' Krishna said. 'She is just a poor little virgin. You must excuse her.'

'Come on for Christ's sake,' Cedric said.

So we went and had dinner. It had turned out an eventful day. Italy surrendering and eating an actual steak. Come to think of it, one doesn't meet a virgin every day either.

I hadn't heard from my wife for six years, so one day I thought I'd better see about getting a divorce.

Being in the Army, I went first to see my company commander. This officer, famous in the unit for his absent-mindedness, blinked up at me in astonishment.

'A divorce? Well, I can't give you one. I'm afraid. You have to see a lawyer about that.'

'Yes, sir,' I said. 'But I understand there's a new scheme by which one can obtain legal aid whilst in the Army. I thought you might be able to help me, sir.'

'Oh yes. Now I come to think of it I did see something...'

'Sergeant-major, what's become of that little red book—*Legal Aid for H.M. Forces*? It was knocking about the office a day or two ago.'

The sergeant-major hadn't seen it. Not a red book, sir. The company clerk hadn't seen it either. The company commander said rubbish, it must be somewhere about.

Everybody joined in looking for the red book. We looked everywhere, even in the salvage sack. The edge of a red pamphlet protruded from the muddle of papers on the company commander's desk, but this when brought to light was called *War*, the only other book in the office was not red and was entitled *What's Wrong With The Army?*

'Oh, well, it's bound to turn up, some time. We'll send for you when it's found.'

Two days later I was on Orders again. The red pamphlet had re-appeared; one of the runners had been reading it. He thought it'd help him to get out of the Army.

This time the interview was in private. For a few moments the company commander pored over the pages of the pamphlet, breathing heavily. Then he looked up.

'But this scheme is only for people who haven't any money,' he said.

'Well, I haven't any money, sir,' I said. 'Not enough to pay for a divorce.'

The company commander was surprised. What was I in civilian life?

I said a writer. He said, you mean an author? Oh, well, then, naturally you've no money. Just fill up this form.

I filled up the form; it was to say I hadn't any money. The company commander was reading, through the red pamphlet again. 'Hm,' he said. 'Bad snag here. You've got to plank down five pounds.'

'Immediately, sir?' I said. He said no, later on. I said I could manage that. He said all right; next thing to do was find out the local Legal Aid Representative.

Finding this out took two months. I didn't mind at first, but then one day I fell in love. It happened while I was on leave. So on my return I asked for another interview with the company commander.

'I've come about my divorce, sir.'

'What divorce? Don't know anything about it; not my department. The Welfare Officer's the one you want.'

'But I came to you two months ago, sir. About legal aid.'

'Oh, yes, so you did. Fancy me forgetting that! Well, I don't know if anything's been done, I'm sure. You'll have to ask the company clerk.'

The company clerk had heard something vaguely; there was a letter about it somewhere in one of the files, but under which heading? Legal Aid? Welfare? Compassionate? Divorce? Hadn't time to go through 'em now; look in tomorrow.

Next day I was down for Orders once more. The legal aid representative had been run to earth; he was stationed half a mile away; they'd written him to arrange an interview; there'd be a reply in due course.

There wasn't any reply. After a fortnight they wrote again; this time a reply did come, but from Manchester. The legal aid representative, now no longer local, had been posted there with his unit.

'Bad luck. Next move's to get in touch with the Command Legal Aid Representative,' the company commander said.

'Will it take long, sir?' I said. 'Because I'm thinking of getting married again.'

'Good gracious, whatever for?'

'I thought I'd like to, sir.'

'But what're you going to marry on if you've no money? Not that it's really business of mine, of course.'

'We thought of getting married in June,' I said.

'Oh, I doubt whether you'll be able to do that, you know. Why, it's December already.'

It was no longer December and well on into January before I was sent for again.

'Things are moving at last. A letter's just come from Command. There's a Legal Aid Representative stationed just round the corner with the Bedlingtons. Extraordinary thing, he's been down here six months, too… funny we never found it out. Still, all's well that ends well! I rang up this Major Trask and fixed an interview for you tonight. Eight o'clock. Parade outside here punctually; the Orderly Sergeant'll take you over.'

On the dot of eight I stood outside company office. The building was completely silent and in darkness. It was pay day and everyone had gone out on the beer. Icy draughts coursed up and down the corridor. I stamped my feet in my best boots to keep warm.

After I'd been waiting ten minutes there came the sound of someone falling up the stairs. At length he reached the landing and stood there rubbing his shins and swearing.

'Advance and be recognized,' I told him. I thought it was the orderly sergeant. It was not the orderly sergeant, it was Driver Smith. He was on divorce too, been waiting a blinking month for this expurgated interview. How long since I seen my missus? He'd seen his last Sunday, give her a black eye, and the bloke she was living with as well.

We stood about in the freezing corridor, puffing at cigarettes; a bicycle lamp, held in the hand of the orderly sergeant, was suddenly flashed on the dress-cap and shining buttons of Driver Smith. 'You the two blokes down for divorce? Right, follow me. We're late already.'

At the foot of the stairs he flashed his lamp on a scrap of paper, a scribbled address: "63, Gainsboro Road. Come on." We fell off the pavement and groped our way across the road through an impenetrable black-out.

The sergeant stopped on a corner. 'This is Gainsboro all right. Question is, where the hell's 63? Let's have a dekko at the numbers on these gates.' But this proved impracticable, because even as the sergeant spoke, the light from his lamp began to fade. Before he could focus it on the nearest gate, it had faded altogether. 'That's done it. Battery's conked out. Either of you got a match?'

'I've got two matches,' came the dispirited voice of Driver Smith.

'I've got a lighter,' I said, 'if it'll work.'

It didn't work, at least not for some time, and when it did the wind blew it out immediately.

We stood irresolute, turning up our coat collars against the wind and the drops of icy rain which had now begun to fall on us from above. 'Try one of your matches, Smith.'

The first one would not strike; he cupped the second in his hands close to a gate. 'You see the number?'

'No number. Only a name.'

'Now we've no matches.'

Then the sergeant had an idea. He'd ask at one of the houses, they'd be sure to know.

It didn't work; everyone seemed to be out; a dog, emerging from its kennel without warning, set upon the sergeant and drove him cursing back to our side. 'No more o' that for me. You think up something.'

Neither of us could; our minds were blank; we advanced at random through the black-out, the frozen rain stinging our faces. Clatter of a rifle butt: 'Halt-who-goes-there.'

'Friend. Know where 63 is?'

'Can't say as I do.'

'What mob you in?'

'Bedlingtons.'

'That's what we're looking for.'

'Ask 'em at the guardroom. Up top. You'll find it.'

He was right. The guardroom was lit up like the Crystal Palace. Light from between the bad black-outs streamed across sandbags stacked round the entrance. The front door was open; we stumbled up steps into the hall; another door on the right: PICQUET-ROOM.

This door opened suddenly and we were confronted by an enormously fat soldier whom at first sight I took to be a padre. This misconception was due to the fact that his neck, above the collar of his tunic, was encircled by something white which proved on closer inspection to be, not a clergyman's collar, but a bandage.

'Know where No. 63 is?'

'This is 63, Sarnt,' the fat bandaged man said.

'This is? Well, why the hell couldn't your sentry tell us then? Said he didn't know where it was.'

The fat man began to shake with silent laughter. Above the bandage his neck swelled up red. So did the face of our sergeant. He didn't feel in a mood to be laughed at.

The fat man explained: 'That was old Dinty Moore. Course he don't know the number. Can't read, see? He don't even know his own blinking number, never mind the number of the billet.'

We now entered the picquet-room, blinking before naked electric bulbs; a fire blazed halfway up the chimney; the picquet sat about with their collars undone; an alarm-clock with a cracked face and a tin pail of tea stood on a table littered with crusts and cheese-rinds.

The picquet sergeant said: 'Major Trask? Yeah, you come to the right shop. Our 2 i/c, he is. You blokes on court martial?'

'No,' we said.

'Oh, coz if you was you couldn't wish for a better defending officer. Lawyer in civvy-street, he was. Can't arf tell the tale. Now, which of you is first I'll take you up to him.'

I was first; Driver Smith, in his blue cap, bowed down with his family troubles, sank on to a pile of blankets in a corner and stared into space, gently grinding his teeth.

Major Trask sat in his office upstairs. He wasn't much older than I, had a blond moustache and spectacles, smoked a pipe. He looked brisk and efficient: a pleasant contrast to the company commander.

He made notes on a message pad: when were we first married, how long since my wife left me, what was the cause of our estrangement.

'Incompatibility of temperament, sir,' I said. 'In other words not enough money.'

'No infidelity on either side?'

'No, sir,' I said.

'Pity. Always easier when there's infidelity. However, I take it the suit won't be contested?'

'Not a chance, sir.' That brought me to what I really wanted to know. How long would it be before the divorce actually came through.

'Well, it's all according. You see, first of all the legal aid unit has to agree to take up your case. If they do, then I must turn you over to a civilian solicitor. After that, there's the question of assizes. And the decree.

The decree might take six months alone.'

'September then,' I said. 'There's a chance of it being through by September?'

Yes, he said if all went well. It seemed a pretty straightforward case. In due course he'd send for me again. Would I tell Smith he was ready for him now as I went down, please.

'Okay, Smith. Up you go,' I said, looking in the picquet-room.

The cracked alarm-clock marked 9.30: canteen'd be closed. I suddenly felt violently hungry. Stumbling back up the road in the black-out I thought of fish and chips.

But back in the barrack-room there wasn't anything to eat and the fire was nearly out. 'Get your divorce all right?' one of the blokes asked me.

'No,' I said. I examined him with thoughts of cannibalism running through my head, but he didn't look really edible. So I sat down on my bed and wrote a letter saying September.

Pretty soon after this my seven days was due. I buckled on my equipment and boarded a train for London.

'Anything happened about the divorce,' she asked when I got there. 'Has anything been actually started?'

'Major Trask has it in hand. Won't be long now.'

'I hope to goodness,' she said.

But when I got back the company commander said: 'Oh, by the way. About this divorce. A serious set-back. Major Trask has been posted.'

'Posted, sir?'

'To the Scilly Isles, or somewhere. Damn nuisance. Now we'll have to start all over again.'

'Right from the beginning, sir?'

'Fraid so. Most unfortunate. I've written off to Command explaining the situation; directly there's any news I'll send for you again.'

He hasn't sent for me so far, though. Of course, on the other hand, another three months aren't up yet.

My girlfriend writes saying it doesn't look as though we're ever going to get married at this rate. I don't agree with her.

Supposing they do take another three months before getting started again. With the divorce proceedings and the decree, that brings us well into next year.

Might be all for the best in the long run. Who knows, the war might be over by then. You never can tell.

The Snows of Yesterday

As we came round the corner in the taxi, Mother said to me, 'Now you're going to see it. The house where you were born,' but Father said, 'No, it's the next road. Not this one.'

'I thought it was this one,' Mother said.

'No,' Father said, 'I saw the name on the corner. It's the next one. They all look alike round here.'

I looked out the window of the taxi at the houses going past and they were all big houses made of red brick most of them, and most of them stood back from the road with big gardens in front. It was very quiet in these streets, with no traffic about and hardly anyone to be seen—not like being in London at all, really. Most of the houses had the window blinds drawn down, because it was summer and the sun was hot on that side of the street.

'Don't lean out of the window, dear,' Mother said to me.

'I'm just looking at the houses, Mother,' I said.

'Richard,' Father said, 'do as your mother tells you.'

I sat back in the taxi next to Mother, and Father sat on the seat opposite with his stick between his knees and one hand on the handle of the stick, and I could tell by the way he was pulling at his beard with the other hand that he was getting impatient.

I was getting impatient too—we'd come a long way in the taxi and I liked riding in it, but I was very excited thinking how I was going to see the house I was born in and wondering what Mrs. Macfarlane would be like. Mrs. Macfarlane had nursed Mother when I was born and we were going to stay the night with her before crossing to France to see my Aunt Jane. I'd never seen Mrs. Macfarlane, but Mother had told me a lot about her and I knew she had a dog called Scraps and a cat called Tommy. I'd seen a picture of the house, with Tommy sitting on the window-sill and a cross marking the room upstairs where I was born.

'Do you think Mrs. Macfarlane will still have Scraps and Tommy?' I asked Mother.

'I don't know, dear. Ten years is a long time and I remember they were quite old then.'

Father said: 'This is the road. Round to the right here,' but the taxi turned left instead. Father put his head out the window and shouted at the taximan, who called 'Sorry, sir,' and started to turn the car round again. Father sat back, pulling at his beard and looking angry. 'These damn taxi-wallahs,' he said, 'you've always got to watch them.'

The taxi drove down the road on the right and Father took out his watch and snapped the top open, looking at the time. He said: 'I'm getting damned hungry. I hope to God the old fool has got some tea for us when we get there.'

'Of course she will have, dear,' Mother said.

'I wouldn't be too sure about that,' Father said. 'She'll be so busy chattering to you that she'll probably forget all about it.'

Father didn't like Mrs. Macfarlane. He didn't like her because she talked too much. She could talk the hind leg off a jackass, Father said. But Mother said she wanted to say goodbye before we went to France and in the end Father said all right, it would save the cost of an hotel anyhow.

Mother leant forward looking at the houses as we drove past. 'Here we are,' she said at last; 'this is the one.'

'About time too,' Father said.

He banged on the glass behind him and the taxi stopped. I opened the door and Mother followed and put out a hand to help Father down, but Father said: 'All right, all right. I can still manage, thank God, even if I am a cripple,' and he got down alone, holding the side of the door.

'There you are, Dicky,' Mother said to me, pointing at the house. It looked the same as it did in the picture, except Tommy wasn't sitting on the window-sill, and there was a garden in front like the other houses in the road. Father said to the taximan: 'Bring the luggage along, don't stand there gaping like a fool,' and he walked across to the gate, leaning heavily on his stick and limping from the wounded leg he'd got in the Boer War.

Mother said, 'There's Mac! Looking out,' and she waved her hand at the window that was marked with a cross in the picture, but when I looked up Mrs. Macfarlane had gone.

As we got to the door a maid opened it, but before she could say anything Mrs. Macfarlane had come downstairs and pushed her out of the way and Mother said 'Mac!' and Mrs. Macfarlane said 'My dear! After all these years,' and they hugged and kissed and Father took off his hat and said 'Well, Mrs. Macfarlane!' in a hearty kind of voice, though I knew he didn't like her really. 'Well, Colonel,' Mrs. Macfarlane said, and they shook hands.

Mrs. Macfarlane was very tall and thin and she had red hair and a long face like a horse. I don't know how old she was, but I'd heard Father say she was a hundred and one, although she didn't look as old as that. She had on a black dress like the one in the pictures of my grandmother.

'This is Dickie,' Mother said. 'Say how d'you do to Mrs. Macfarlane, dear,' and Mrs. Macfarlane said, 'Well, Dicky, you've grown into a fine big boy now,' and she stooped down and kissed me. I didn't like it much— Mrs. Macfarlane smelt funny and anyhow I didn't like being kissed. I wiped my face as soon as I could, without her seeing it.

'Well, well,' Mrs. Macfarlane said, 'you're a nice looking boy. You've got your mother's eyes. I remember you when you were so big,' and she held out her hands a little way apart and I thought I must have been pretty small when I was born if I wasn't any bigger than that.

'Oh, you *were* a teenyweeny thing,' Mrs. Macfarlane said. 'I was the first to hold you in my arms. Why I helped bring you into the world,' and Father coughed and began to fidget, and I could tell he was getting tired of Mrs. Macfarlane already, and wondering about his tea.

The taximan came in with a trunk on his back and said to Father, 'What shall I do with this, sir?'

'How the devil should I know!' Father said, and then he said, 'I beg your pardon, Mrs. Macfarlane.'

'Don't mind me, Colonel,' Mrs. Macfarlane said, 'if you want to swear. Goodness, you should have heard my husband sometimes when he was angry. Lord goodness,' she said and threw her head back and gave a very loud laugh, like a horse neighing. The taximan said to her, 'Shall I take this upstairs, ma'am?' and Mrs. Macfarlane stopped laughing and said to the maid 'Doris, show him the way up.'

'Yes, m'm,' Doris said, and the taximan followed her up the stairs, bent double under the trunk. I looked round the hall. It was long and dark, with doors opening off and a case full of butterflies on the wall and a stuffed owl above the case. There was a smell in the hall rather like Mrs. Macfarlane, a sort of smell like a cave, and the sun didn't come any further than the door. Mrs. Macfarlane was talking to Mother and they were both saying how good it was to see each other again and Father pulled at his beard and muttered something and the taximan came downstairs without the trunk and said to Father 'That's the lot, sir,' so Father paid him off and Mrs. Macfarlane said, 'I expect you'll be hungry after your journey. I've got the tea all ready for you,' and Father looked better pleased when he heard that and said 'It's very good of you, Mrs. Macfarlane, I hope we're not giving you a lot of trouble,' and she said no, it was a pleasure.

She opened one of the doors off the hall and it was a big drawing-room with a piano in it and a painting of a man in a Major's uniform on the wall and long windows looking out onto a lawn behind the house. A big black cat jumped down from a chair as we came in and I said 'There's Tommy!' and Mother said 'Not the same one, surely,' and Mrs. Macfarlane said no, it was another cat with the same name. 'Tommy, Tommy,' I said, but Tommy wouldn't come—he edged along the wall and then shot out the open door like a streak.

'He's shy,' Mrs. Macfarlane said, 'he'll get used to you later on.'

'Have you still got Scraps?' Mother said.

'No, I had him put to sleep years ago,' Mrs. Macfarlane said. 'I've got another one very like him though, he's gone out for a walk with Sonny.'

'Who is Sonny?' Mother said.

'Mr. Krishna,' Mrs. Macfarlane said. 'You remember, I told you all about him in my last letter.'

'Oh, yes,' Mother said.

'Sonny's my pet name for him,' Mrs. Macfarlane said.

I wondered who Mr. Krishna was, I hadn't heard of him till now. I knew Krishna was the name of a god they had out in India because I'd read about it in a book I had at home called *The Eye of Krishna*. It seemed a funny kind of name for a man to have though.

Mrs. Macfarlane said: 'Scraps is very fond of Sonny, he follows him about everywhere. You know it was funny, when Sonny went back to India last year, he had to undergo all sorts of purification rites and so forth because dogs are considered pariahs out there. Poor Sonny had a dreadful time.' She threw her head back and laughed very loudly.

Just then the maid knocked and came in with the tea-tray and Father looked pleased and Mrs. Macfarlane said: 'Doris, where's Miss Gerty?'

'Out at the back, m'm.'

'Call her in,' Mrs. Macfarlane said, 'it's tea time.' She said to Mother: 'Gerty's my little niece. She's staying with me for a fortnight.'

'How old is she?' Mother asked.

'Just nine.'

'Oh, that'll be nice for Dicky,' Mother said. 'You'd like to play with her wouldn't you, Dicky?'

'Yes,' I said, being polite, but I didn't want to play with her really, because I didn't like girls. I thought they were soppy.

'I'll bring her in later,' Mrs. Macfarlane said, 'she's a pretty child.' She said to Father, 'Have you got all you want, Colonel?' and Father said, 'Yes, thank you, Mrs. Macfarlane. Splendid, splendid!' looking at the tea-tray.

'Then I'll be getting along,' Mrs. Macfarlane said. 'I've promised to have tea with Sonny when he comes in. I'll come back presently.' She waved her hand and went out. Father raised his eyebrows and looked at Mother, saying 'What d'you think of that?'

Mother said: 'It's a great pity, isn't it?'

'Pity?' Father said; 'it's a damn disgrace. The wife of a British officer too. God, her husband would turn in his grave if he knew!'

'Is that Major Macfarlane up there in the picture?' I asked.

'Yes,' Father said. He sounded angry.

'Then who is Mr. Krishna? Is he Mrs. Macfarlane's son?'

'Good lord, no!' Father said.

'Mr. Krishna is an Indian gentleman, dear,' Mother said.

'*Gentleman*,' Father said. 'H'm!' he snorted.

'Is he a sinister Hindu, like the one in the story, Mother?' I said. 'Will he wear a turban?'

'No, I shouldn't think so, dear,' Mother said.

'For heaven's sake pour out the tea,' Father said, 'and let's wash the taste of this out of our mouths.'

I could hear Doris calling 'Miss Gerty! Miss Gerty!' outside and then footsteps ran past the door and I could hear Mrs. Macfarlane and a little girl's voice talking and then a door shut and I couldn't hear them anymore.

'That's better,' Father said when he'd finished eating and he sat back in his chair. I looked round the room and at the piano and I wanted to play it, but I knew Father wouldn't let me. He didn't like me playing the piano.

Mother said: 'The house hasn't changed a bit has it?'

'No,' Father said, 'the house hasn't, but *she* has. What does she want to dye her hair for, the old fool?'

'Do you think it's dyed?' Mother said. 'It used to be that colour, you know.'

'Yes, ten years ago,' Father said. 'Of course it's dyed.'

'Hush, dear, she'll hear you.'

'I don't give a damn if she does.'

A door opened somewhere and a dog started to bark and I said, 'There's Scraps' and Mrs. Macfarlane's voice said 'Sonny'.

'Sonny,' Father said and gave a snort.

'Be careful,' Mother said, 'here she comes.'

We could hear Mrs. Macfarlane coming down the hall. She opened the door and came in and there was a little girl with her, smaller than me.

'This is Gerty,' Mrs. Macfarlane said.

'What a sweet little girl,' Mother said and Father smiled and said, 'Come and shake hands, little lady. Don't be frightened,' but Gerty hung back. I think she was scared of Father.

'This is Dicky,' Mrs. Macfarlane said. 'He was born in this house, you know. I hope you're going to be great friends.'

'Hullo,' I said to Gerty.

'Hullo,' she said in a shy sort of voice and looked at me with big round blue eyes. She had curly yellow hair and I suppose she was pretty really, though I didn't often take notice of girls because they were such fools, always crying and saying they didn't like rough games.

'Gerty's a naughty girl,' Mrs. Macfarlane said. 'She's just torn her frock climbing a tree in the garden.'

'Yes,' she said.

'Most girls don't,' I said. 'Most girls are scared to.'

'I'm not scared,' Gerty said.

'Was it a big tree?'

'Yes.'

'I've told her,' Mrs. Macfarlane said, 'she'll break her neck one of these days.'

'No I shan't,' Gerty said. 'Look,' she said to me, 'I'll show you the one I climbed.' She went over to the long windows and pointed at the trees at the bottom of the lawn. 'The middle one,' she said.

'It is a big tree,' I said. 'Did you get to the top?'

'Almost,' Gerty said. 'Do you climb?'

'Yes,' I said.

'Well, you're not going to climb any trees in my garden, young man,' Mrs. Macfarlane said, 'so take that from me.'

She added: 'Take Dicky upstairs and show him where the bathroom is. He may want to wash.'

'Yes, Auntie Mabel,' Gerty said. 'Come on,' she said to me.

I went out with her into the hall and up the stairs.

'Here's the bathroom,' Gerty said. 'Do you want to wash?'

'No.'

'Then I'll show you the room you're going to have tonight.'

'All right.'

We went up to the top landing and she opened a door onto a small room with a sloping roof that faced onto the street.

'Won't you be scared sleeping up here all alone?' she said.

'No,' I said.

'Aren't you scared of the dark?'

'No.'

'Oo, I am.'

'But you're not scared to climb trees?'

'No,' Gerty said, 'but the dark's different. The dark's horrible,' and she gave a shiver, looking at me with her big round eyes.

'Well, I don't care about the dark,' I said. 'It doesn't scare me.'

That wasn't quite true, but I wasn't going to tell Gerty I didn't like the dark.

'You must be very brave,' she said.

'Well, so are you,' I said. 'Braver than most girls, because you climb trees.'

She looked pleased when I said that. 'I think you're awfully nice,' she said.

'Do you?'

'Yes, awfully.'

'I think you're nice too.'

She looked pleased again. 'I was so excited thinking you were coming here today,' she said. 'I hoped you'd be nice and you are. I'm so glad,' and she clapped her hands and then her face looked different and sad all of a sudden and she said: 'But you're going away tomorrow.'

'Yes. I'm going to France.'

'I wish you weren't,' Gerty said. 'I wish you were staying here.' She looked awfully sad.

'Never mind,' I said to cheer her up. 'I'll be coming back again.'

'Will you really?'

'Yes.'

'Oo, that's good. I am glad,' and she clapped her hands and looked happy again and said: 'What will you do in France?'

'I shall see my Aunt Jane.'

'Do you speak French?'

'No, but my aunt does. She married a Frenchman.'

'What's he like?'

'I don't know. I've never seen him. He's an officer in the French Cavalry.'

'Can he speak English?'

'Oh, yes. He was at school in England.'

'Your father's a soldier too, isn't he?'

'Yes, he's a Colonel.'

'Was he in the war?'

'Not the last war. He was in the Boer War. My brother was in the last war. He got killed fighting.'

'Have you got a sister?'

'Yes, but we're not allowed to talk about her at home because she ran away and married a man Father didn't like.'

'Why didn't he like him?'

'He said he was a bounder.'

'What's a bounder?'

'A man that isn't a gentleman.'

'Was he a soldier?'

'No.'

'My uncle was a soldier,' Gerty said. 'He was in the Indian Mutiny. He killed lots and lots of Indians and got a medal.'

'Were they Indians like Mr. Krishna?'

'Some of them were.'

'I haven't seen Mr. Krishna yet. Is he sinister? Are you scared of him?'

'No,' Gerty said. 'He's black, but I don't mind. He gave me a box of chocolates yesterday and an ice cream.'

Mother's voice called 'Dicky!' downstairs and I said 'Perhaps we better go down now.'

'All right,' Gerty said.

When we got to the first landing Father was coming up and Mother was trying to help him, but Father said she wasn't to fuss, it made him nervous.

'Ah, there you are, Dicky,' Mother said.

'Gerty's been showing me my room.'

'Good,' Mother said; 'I'm glad you've made friends,' and Father patted Gerty's head and said we were to go and play downstairs and keep out of mischief and not make too much noise.

'I'm not scared of your father now,' Gerty said. 'I was at first, but now I think he's nice.'

We went into the drawing-room and there was nobody there and I lifted the lid of the piano and touched the keys. They were yellow and looked old.

'Can you play the piano?' Gerty said.

'Yes, but Father doesn't like me to.'

'Why not?'

'He says it's effeminate.'

'What's that?'

'It means girlish. I read it in a book the other day.'

'Well, I'm a girl,' Gerty said, 'but I can't play the piano.

'Playing the piano's easy,' I said. 'Do you read books?'

'Not much.'

'I like reading. I'm going to write a book someday.'

'What will it be about?'

'I don't know yet. My grandfather wrote books. He wrote about big game hunting.'

'What's big game?'

'Lions and tigers and elephants. He used to hunt them. He was a soldier too.'

'Are you going to be a soldier when you grow up?'

'Father says so.'

'How old are you now?'

'Ten and a half.'

'You're older than me.'

'Yes.'

Gerty went across to the long windows and opened them. 'Let's go outside,' she said.

The sun was hot on the back lawn and Tommy was lying down with his fur looking brown in the sun, but when I went towards him he jumped up and ran away into the trees at the bottom of the lawn.

'What shall we do?' I asked Gerty.

'Let's climb that tree.'

'Your aunt said we weren't to.'

'She won't know. Come on.' Gerty took my hand and we ran across the lawn to the tree. 'I'll go first,' Gerty said. She let go my hand and started to climb. She climbed quite easily, more like a boy than a girl. I looked round to see no one was watching, then I went up too. It was a high tree and I had to go careful because I had on my best suit, but pretty soon I was up beside her, sitting in the branches. It was cool up in the tree and the wind came through the branches and made a nice breeze.

Gerty said: 'I like being up here with you.'

'I like it too.'

'You're a nice boy,' Gerty said, and she picked up my hand and kissed it. I was so surprised I nearly fell out of the tree. I didn't know what to do. I knew what she'd done was soppy, but I liked it in a funny sort of way. I didn't say anything and we went on sitting in the tree holding hands. We must have sat there some time when Mrs. Macfarlane came out onto the lawn and shouted for us.

'That's done it,' I said. 'We'll get in a row.'

'Ssh,' Gerty said. 'If we keep still she won't see us.'

'Dicky!' Mrs. Macfarlane called. 'Gerty! Where are you?' She walked about the lawn calling out, but we kept quiet in the branches and soon she went back into the house, Tommy running after her with his tail up.

'We better get down now,' I said, 'before she comes back'

'All right,' Gerty said.

I came down quicker than I went up and stood brushing the leaves off my suit. 'Hurry up,' I told Gerty.

'I am hurrying,' Gerty said. just then the branch she was holding on to broke and she slipped and fell down onto the lawn. She was nearly at the bottom when it happened, so there wasn't far to fall, but she came down quite heavy on one knee as she landed.

'Are you, hurt?' I said, going up to her.

Gerty sat up and rubbed her knee. She didn't cry, but I could see she wanted to really. I looked at her knee. It wasn't cut and there was no blood, but the skin had been rubbed off and it looked sore. I helped her up and brushed the dirt off her dress. She stood there rubbing her knee and trying not to cry. I felt all funny inside, as if I was going to cry myself. I didn't like her being hurt. It was funny because I always used to laugh when other girls hurt themselves. I thought it served them right for being such fools, but I felt different about Gerty somehow.

'Now I'll get in a row with Auntie,' she said.

'She won't notice,' I said.

But she did, soon as we got in. She was in the drawing-room talking to Father and Mother and she looked at Gerty and said 'What have *you* been doing to yourself, young lady?'

'We were playing hide-and-seek in the garden and she fell down,' I said.

Mother said, 'You must have something put on that knee.'

'I'll see to it,' Mrs. Macfarlane said. 'Come on, Gerty.' At the door she turned round. 'Dinner won't be a minute,' she said and went out.

'Thank God for that,' Father said when she'd gone.

'Go up and wash your hands, Dicky,' Mother said. 'And whatever have you done to your suit, you've got green all over it.'

Outside, it was still light when we finished dinner and I wondered if they'd let me go out and play with Gerty again. I was just going to ask them when there was a knock and Mrs. Macfarlane came in. There was a man with her and I knew it was Mr. Krishna because, although he wasn't black like Gerty said, he was pretty dark and looked like the pictures in *The Eye of Krishna*, except he hadn't got a turban on and was dressed in a suit like anyone else. He was smiling and he'd got big white teeth and didn't look at all sinister really.

'This is Sonny,' Mrs. Macfarlane said.

'How do you do,' Mr. Krishna said, and he spoke good English

And Mother said 'How d'you do' too. Father didn't say it out loud, he just made a noise in his throat and sat there pulling at his beard and not looking pleased. Scraps had come in with them, keeping close to Mr. Krishna, He was a fat fox-terrier and looked as if he needed exercise. I didn't like him much. He wouldn't make friends and when I went to pat him, he backed away and growled at me, so after that I left him alone.

Mrs. Macfarlane and Mr. Krishna stayed awhile, talking—at least Mrs. Macfarlane talked and Mr. Krishna just smiled and nodded and didn't say much and Father didn't say much either, and after awhile they went out, taking Scraps with them.

'Well,' Mother said when they'd gone, 'what do you think of Sonny?'

'It's a scandal,' Father said. 'A woman of her age. It's disgusting.'

'She says he's a very clever young man. He's got a B.A. degree.'

'Bah!' Father said, 'India's full of natives with B.A. degrees. Every second Babu you meet has got one.'

'Is Mr. Krishna a Babu, Father?' I asked.

'He would be in his own country,' Father said.

Then there was a knock and Gerty came in with a bandage round her bad knee. 'Please, can Dicky come out and play in the garden with me?' she said.

'I don't know,' Mother said. 'He's got a long day tomorrow... what do you think, dear?'

'Oh, let him go,' Father said.

'All right then. But not for long, mind.'

'Come on,' Gerty said, and we went out on the lawn, Gerty limping a little because of her knee.

'Does it hurt much now?' I said.

'No,' she said. 'The bandage is tight, that's all.'

'Did your aunt scold you about it?'

'Not much.'

'What shall we do?' I said.

'Let's sit down and talk.'

'All right.'

There was a bench at the bottom of the lawn and we sat on that. It was getting dark now.

'What time are you going away tomorrow?' Gerty said.

'In the morning, I think.'

'I wish you could stay.'

'So do I.'

'But you won't be away long? Promise.'

'I promise.'

'Oh,' she said, 'I don't want you to go.'

'I don't want to go either.'

She took my hand. 'Kiss me,' she said.

I bent over and kissed her quickly on the cheek. I'd never done anything soppy like that before and I could feel my face going red. But I didn't care really and I didn't want to go away a bit. I wanted to stay with Gerty. We sat there without talking after that and the door downstairs opened and Mother called 'Dicky!'

'We must go in now,' I said.

We got up and went across the lawn to Mother. 'Is it bedtime yet?' I said.

'Yes,' Mother said; 'you've been up too late as it is.'

'I'll take him up,' Gerty said.

At the door of my room she said: 'I'll see you tomorrow.'

'Yes. And don't be afraid of the dark.'

'I'll try not to be.'

Downstairs a gramophone started playing.

'That's Mr. Krishna's gramophone,' Gerty said. 'He lets me play it sometimes.'

'I've met him. He's not really black.'

'He's pretty black.'

'Not really.'

Mrs. Macfarlane's voice called Gerty up the stairs.

'I'll have to go,' Gerty said. 'Kiss me goodnight.'

I kissed her cheek and she ran downstairs. I went into my room. I felt too tired to wash so I took off my things and got into bed. There was a switch over the bed and I was just going to turn off the light when Mrs. Macfarlane came in. 'Got everything?' she said.

'Yes, thanks.'

'This time tomorrow you'll be in France. You'll be with your Aunt Jane.'

'Yes.'

'Are you looking forward to it?'

'Yes.'

'That's fine,' Mrs. Macfarlane said; 'that's the boy.' She leaned over and kissed me, but I managed to dodge most of it and she said 'Goodnight' and went out, turning off the light at the door. I could hear her going down and the gramophone playing and I felt sad because I didn't want to go away, I didn't want to go to France at all. It was dark in the room, but I didn't mind because I felt so sad I didn't mind anything and then I must have gone to sleep because I woke with the sun shining in the window and Mother came to say it was time to get up because we were leaving after breakfast.

When I got downstairs, Father was eating bacon and eggs and I could tell he was in a good temper. I guessed he was glad to be getting away from Mrs. Macfarlane, but I wasn't glad because it meant leaving Gerty. I didn't see her till we'd finished breakfast and then Mrs. Macfarlane came in and Gerty was with her.

'You can go in the garden if you like,' Mother said, 'only don't be long because the taxi will be here soon.'

So we went out and Gerty took my hand and said, 'Will you write to me while you're away?'

'Yes.'

'A lot? You won't forget about me?'

'No.' I didn't want to say much because I could feel something coming up in my throat like when I was going to cry, and I didn't want to cry in front of Gerty. So we stood there with her holding my hand and Mother called for us to come in, I had to get ready.

The taxi was outside when I came down again and the man was carrying the trunks out. Father shook hands with Mrs. Macfarlane and said 'Thanks very much for putting us up. A most enjoyable stay!' and Mrs. Macfarlane kissed Mother and said she hoped we'd have a pleasant journey. Mr. Krishna was out with Scraps and I didn't see Tommy either. Then Gerty came into the hall and I could see she'd been crying.

'Kiss Dicky goodbye,' Mrs. Macfarlane said; 'aren't you going to kiss goodbye?' but I wasn't going to with them all looking on and so we just shook hands and neither of us said anything. I wanted to tell her I wouldn't forget, but I was scared of blubbing. I think she knew, though.

Then we got in the taxi and Mrs. Macfarlane waved and shouted from the gate, but I couldn't see Gerty; she'd gone inside. It took a long time getting to the station.

Father said: 'Thank God we've got away from there.'

I said: 'Mother, how long shall we be away?' and Mother said, 'I don't know, dear. It depends.'

'Depends on what?'

'It just depends. Why? Don't you want to go to France? Don't you want to see Aunt Jane?'

'No,' I said, and I could feel it in my throat and then suddenly I started to blub.

'God bless my soul!' Father said, 'what's the matter? What's wrong with the boy?' and Mother said 'Don't cry, dear. Don't cry,' but I couldn't stop, I couldn't help it, I couldn't stop.

They Put Me In Charge Of A Squad

We were short of N.C.O.s at the time. One of our corporals had scabies, two were away on escort, and another was at B.H.Q. being court-martialled for slackness.

So one morning as I was walking past Company Office, trying not to slip on the frozen pavement, Corporal Dexter yelled down at me from upstairs: 'Hey, you! Come on up, Gillo! I got a job for you.'

Corporal Dexter was the orderly sergeant. He didn't like me because he thought I'd threatened to do him in the black-out. It was really another bloke who'd threatened to do him, and I was only repeating the story when he heard me, but Dexter wouldn't believe that. So he had his knife in me.

I went upstairs and stood to attention in front of his desk.

'Right!' he said. 'You got to take a fatigue squad up the town this morning 0930 hours. There's some furniture wants shifting from out them billets D Company had. You parade 'em out front 0920 sharp. All right? Any questions?'

'You want me to take a squad up the town, Corporal?'

'Ain't I just said so? Don't I speak plain bloody English?'

'Yes, Corporal. But I'm not an N.C.O. How can I take a squad?'

'You're an O.C.T.U. wallah, aincher? In for a pip? Well then, how the hell you going to lead men if you don't never have charge of nothing? Now's your chance to learn.'

'Very good, Corporal,' I said.

'Right! Now I got to rustle up the bastard sick.'

Corporal Dexter buckled on his belt and bayonet and left the room. He could be heard downstairs getting the sick together, threatening them with thickuns. I went over to the fire and tried to thaw out my fingers. They were frozen stiff. It was December.

The orderly corporal sat writing, surrounded by stacks of sick reports. There was a big route march on that morning and nearly the whole company had gone sick as a result. The orderly corporal looked up.

'O.C.T.U. candidate, are you?' he asked in a cultured voice.

'Yes,' I said.

'Had your board yet?'

'Which board? I've had two.'

'That's nothing, I've had three. And another fellow I know's had four and he's still waiting.'

'God!'

'It takes some time.'

He borrowed ten bob off me and I went down the stairs into the street where Corporal Dexter had the sick lined up at last.

'Don't forget—0920,' he yelled after me. 'And get a crease in them slacks 'fore you come on parade, see?'

'Very good, Corporal,' I said.

At 0920 hours I reported back to the company office. A squad of men shivered sullenly on the kerb outside. Their denim suits, buttonless, flapped open in the bitter wind. My heart sank when I saw them. Dexter must have got them together on purpose. All the worst janker wallahs were there, mixed with a few well-known malingerers and a man just back from detention barracks who had no top teeth. Behind them was the frozen grass plot facing the office and beyond that again the sea. Against this background they looked terrible. But their faces, covered with pimples and blue with the cold, brightened when they saw me.

'Squad! Squad, 'shun!' shouted out a bloke at the back. They all clicked to attention while the man with no top teeth gave a wavering salute.

'What're you doing?' Corporal Dexter roared out, appearing from nowhere. Grins vanished immediately and all stood at ease. 'Shun!' Dexter shouted. They shunned. Dexter came across to me and shouted: 'That how you keep discipline? Letting 'em salute you? Ain't got your bleeding pip yet, y'know!'

'No, Corporal,' I said.

'Now let's see them slacks.' He inspected the crease in my trousers minutely but couldn't find anything wrong: I'd just pressed the bloody things. 'Right. Got to look after you O.C.T.U. blokes, y'know,' and: 'What you got to laugh about?' he bawled at a recruit in the rear rank, who'd got on gym shoes. 'Where's your boots?'

'Excused boots, Corp.'

'Excused marching?'

'No, boots.'

'Right.' Dexter turned to me. 'Get cracking now. They're all yours.'

'Dressing,' I told them in a weak voice. 'Get your dressing.'

They shuffled about shooting out their arms. They were in two ranks by the time they'd finished, and had to be sorted out in threes again.

'Come on, come on,' Corporal Dexter shouted. 'You're wasting time.'

Meanwhile heads had appeared at the office window, watching us. The company clerk and two of the runners and behind them the C.Q.M.S.. They were all having the time of their lives.

'Good as a play,' the C.Q.M.S. was heard to say. 'Beats cockfighting.'

At last they were properly fallen in and I tried to shout 'Shun.' Nobody moved. 'Louder!' Corporal Dexter shouted. 'Louder! They can't hear you.'

'I can't shout any louder. I've got a cold.'

The Company Commander came on the scene. The heads at the window withdrew. Corporal Dexter shouted 'Shun!'

They heard him all right.

'What're all these men standing about for, Corporal?'

'Fatigue party, sir. That there furniture.'

'Well, for God's sake get them marched off before they bloody well take root. Who's in charge?'

I stepped forward and saluted. 'Short of N.C.O.s, sir,' Corporal Dexter explained.

'Right. Well, get moving, you should've been there by now.'

'Right—turn,' I managed to get out. They all turned left.

'Oh God,' the Company Commander said, and he went in.

'As you were. Right turn. By the left.'

The heads at the window appeared again to watch us march off. The man in gym shoes was limping.

'Pick up the step,' I told him.

'You ain't in step yourself,' called back the man with no top teeth. It was true; I'd slipped on the pavement again. 'Stop talking,' I said.

'Barlocks,' they said.

I gave it up. They were all chatting merrily as we came round the Pavilion and the empty bandstand, enclosed now by Dannert wire. 'Left wheel,' I gave them. They broke into a trot. The P.T. instructor, on the steps of the pavilion, stood astounded.

'Stop!' I shouted. 'Stop!'

No use; they only slowed down when they were all out of breath. 'Nice little run,' remarked a man who'd gone sick with blisters the day before.

Now there was the hill to get up. They embarked on the climb with enthusiasm. One fell down half-way up. 'I've broke me bloody leg,' he said. Everyone halted to examine it.

'Fall in!' I shouted. 'March!'

'*I* can't march. Broke me bleeding leg.'

'Fall in the rear, then.'

I didn't dare take them up the town, so getting them to the house took some time. A small man in civvy clothes, from the Garrison Engineer's office, awaited us outside.

'Thought you was never coming,' he said. He led the way into the house and pointed at various pieces of furniture piled up in the hall. 'Start on this first,' he said.

There was an immediate scramble for the less heavy articles; they staggered about laden with chairs; one had hold of a leather poufé.

'Where we take 'em to?'

'Out back, round the corner. First house on the left.'

They disappeared out with the load, all except the man who'd fallen down on the hill. He'd changed his broken leg to a sprained ankle now, and sat on a wooden chest nursing it.

The blokes came back again and looked about them in despair. All the chairs had been taken and the heavier pieces now confronted them. Three fellows, seeing there was nothing for it, tried to tackle a table. They got it wedged in a doorway.

'Careful,' the man from the Garrison Engineer's shouted, you'll scratch the paint.'

'Sod the paint,' they said.

Eventually the table was manoeuvred out sideways. I lent a hand with it myself, resisting an attempt on their part to drop the table on my foot.

'Now this chest.'

The man with the sprained ankle was dislodged from on top of it after a lot of talk, during which I threatened him with jankers.

'You can't get me jankers. I'm on 'em already.'

'Well, you can have another lot.'

That shook him, and four chaps got hold of the chest. The man from the Garrison Engineer's watched their struggles in disgust.

'Last war we had to handle double that lot, and with full kit on,' he said.

At last the hall was empty.

'That the lot?' the man in gym shoes, asked wiping an icicle of snot from his nose.

'Not by no means. Look in the next room.'

'Ah, sod it,' they said.

More chairs were shifted out by the back door. But this time the men didn't return. After they'd been gone ten minutes, I went to have a look. They weren't in the other house. I couldn't see them anywhere. They'd all vanished.

'Having a tea, likely,' the man with the sprained ankle said.

'Don't blame 'em, poor sods.'

The Y.M. was not far off. I rushed up the steps and looked inside. They weren't there. I turned into the next street. A wireless was blaring in one of the houses. I looked up at the window. There sat a sailor, waving a pack of cards at me and grinning. Two more sailors sat with him, and one of my fatigue party dodged out of sight just as I looked up.

'Come out!' I shouted. 'Come out at once. I'll have you all on a...' I couldn't remember the number of the form you wrote out charges on, so I finished: 'I'll have you all on thickuns.'

That fetched them. One by one they filed out, swearing; the sailors grinned from the window. I thought I saw a woman in a brassière lurking in the background, but I'm not sure it may have been a mirage.

'Come on,' I said. 'Back to work.'

'Ah hell. What about a break first. We're bleeding froze.'

'All right,' I said; it was break-time. But then it turned out they couldn't have a break because none of them had any money and no fags.

'Lend me half a dollar,' the man with no top teeth said coming up with his fist clenched.

'I'll be damned if I do,' I said. Lending the orderly corporal ten bob had left me short myself. So he unclenched his fist and said 'Fuck.'

The man in gym shoes produced twopence and disappeared into the Y.M. 'Bleeding capitalist,' they said.

Finally I got them back to work. Slowly the furniture changed its abode. The men blew on their fingers and swore.

'That the lot?'

'That's the lot.'

'Thank Christ.'

'Fall in on the road,' I said. This time they obeyed promptly: they wanted to get back. 'Wait a minute,' I said. 'What about that man in the Y.M.'

'Oh, *he's* gone. You won't find *him*.'

They were right. I looked all over the Y.M., but he wasn't there. He must have dodged out the back door.

They'd started off already when I got back: I had to run to catch up with them. The man with the sprained ankle ran, too. A small crowd collected in front of the company office to watch us dismiss. Corporal Dexter was there, of course. They broke off before I'd time to finish the word of command. All of them ran straight for their billets, including the man with the sprained ankle. I stood there watching them run.

'Well, me old cocker,' Corporal Dexter said, coming up. 'How d'you like being in charge of a squad?'

'Fuck the squad,' I said.

I thought he'd put me on a charge for insolence, but he didn't. He only burst out laughing. I walked away.

Somehow I don't think I'll ever make an officer.

The Swag, the Spy and the Soldier

Part One

The Story

Then war broke out and the amusement park closed down. The swings and roundabouts were silent, covered in tarpaulin. From dismantled stalls the painted faces of the Aunt Sallies grimaced, gaping in vain for flung coconuts. The bumper cars no longer jolted round the track striking electric sparks; the distorting mirrors reflected nothing. Dead bulbs in daylight still spelt out ZOO over the papier-mâché entrance, but inside the cardboard grottoes echoed with emptiness; the animals—the polar bear, the Algerian rat, the owl, the shrieking savage cockatoo—had been evacuated.

And Sandy O'Connor, like the rest of the staff, was out of work.

When I first met him he was shouting numbers hoarsely from the housey-housey stall, wearing a long white linen coat and a leather pouch containing change slung by a strap from his shoulder. Some of the shillings and coppers occasionally found their way from this pouch into Sandy's pocket: the fairground boys called this fiddling. You couldn't blame him, working fourteen hours a day (fifteen on Saturdays) for a wage of two-ten a week. By fiddling Sandy made this salary up to about six nicker and a few hundred fags. It was a recognized practice: the bosses shut their eyes to it; sometimes, very rarely, someone was made an example of and given his cards.

Sandy at this time was nineteen, rising twenty. He was stockily built and square jawed. His oblong face had a fresh colour and his eyes that lashless look peculiar to people with reddish hair. His thick pink lips, which seemed puffed up, bee-stung, twisted sideways when he spoke, always out of the corner of his mouth and very quickly in a Scotch-Irish accent. He came from Glasgow, where his home life had not been happy. Most of his time there seemed to have been spent knocking out his elder brother, who was a right bastard. He got fed-up finally and cleared out to earn his own living. This he had done in various ways up and down the country. He'd worked on a race-track, in a pin-table saloon, in a glass-blowing factory, where for some reason the faces of the workers eventually turned yellow; in the intervals of these occupations he had lorry-hopped and slept in casual wards all over England. He had been in the army, but not, so far, in prison.

II

I was passing the amusement park the day Sandy got sacked. I saw him come out. He was smoking and he snapped away the butt of his cigarette and spat back over his shoulder at one of the gigantic grinning cardboard dummies that stood on either side of the entrance. He scored a direct hit. Then he muttered: 'Fog 'em.'

'What's wrong, Sandy?' I asked him.

'Got my cards,' he said. He had them in his hand. He spat again, this time into the gutter, and said: 'I'm for a cup o' char.'

We walked in brilliant sunshine down the deserted esplanade. Pillboxes had already been put up and a dannert-wire, apron fence encircled the pier arcade. Sandbags were stacked round the shops and notices announced CLOSED on all sides.

We sat down in a café that wasn't closed. 'What d'you mean to do?' I asked him.

'Oh, I'll make out all right,' he said, stirring his tea. 'Once I get up the Smoke. Plenty graft going up there. Smashing jobs.' He'd two weeks' wages on him, plus a quid he'd fiddled. 'I'll take some time off first,' he said. 'Reckon I've earnt a rest.'

He never had it. He got boozed up instead. I met him next day; he hadn't a bean. 'Dead skint,' he said. 'Somebody rolled me. If I could only get my hands on that bastard!'

'Where'd you sleep?' I asked him.

He jerked a thumb towards the amusement park. 'In the dobbies.' But despite this he still looked natty, his trousers were knife-creased, his sandy hair as usual brilliantined back. The only thing, he wasn't shaved. The blond stubble glittered along his chin where the sun caught it. He said: 'I'm off to sign on the Labour.'

'What'll you do meantime,' I asked, 'without money?'

He shook his head. He slouched along, hands in pockets. He was depressed. I said: 'You anywhere to stay the night?'

'Oh, I'll find some place to kip down, don't worry,' he said.

I'd have lent him a quid but I was hard-up myself. The money I'd earned that summer writing radio plays had nearly run out, and I'd no idea where the next lot was coming from. The Jansens, whom I shared a bungalow with, were hard-up too, but on the other hand we had a spare bedroom.

'You'd better put up with us,' I told him.

He shook his head: 'I wouldn't want to be a trouble.' It took the hell of a time to persuade him, he was stubborn as a mule. But in the end he came. 'I'll pay you back first fifteen bob I draw,' he said.

'That's all right,' I told him. 'Come on.'

'I got one or two things to pick up, first,' he said. 'Be back right away.'

I watched him walk rapidly off towards the amusement park. He disappeared inside and came out a few moments later lugging an enormous valise, which he'd evidently parked there. 'All set now,' he said. We boarded a bus bound for Greenleaves.

The bungalow stood isolated at the end of a long rutted road which in winter, when it rained, became almost impassable: a lake of liquid yellow mud. This condition had its advantages for us. Creditors hesitated to approach. Cars got stuck halfway up, bicycles were no use at all. Now, in September, the road was baked hard with sun and Greenleaves showed no signs of life as we neared it. It was practically in a state of siege. We came in the gate, up the path, Sandy changing hands with his valise. Except for a few bushes in the back garden, there seemed no reason why the bungalow should be called by that name. Sun-dried grass, mowed by Erik Jansen into the semblance of a lawn, surrounded it. The mower itself, rusty and decrepit, stood up abandoned by the porch. The green paint of the front door had broken out in blisters.

I banged on the door. Subdued voices inside the house ceased instantly. There was dead silence. I banged again and shouted through the slit of the letter-box. There was a shuffle of slippers in the hall and the door opened a chink. Jansen peeped round it at us. He wore Russian silk pyjamas with an eagle embroidered on the chest. A curious small smoking-cap was perched on the back of his head. A lock of yellow hair fell forward into his eyes from under the cap. He pulled the door wide and said: 'Thought you were the Macfisheries' man again.'

'This is Sandy O'Connor,' I said. 'He's coming to stay with us.'

'Splendid!' Jansen said, shaking hands. 'Splendid! Welcome to Greenleaves.' He led the way into the living-room, shouting 'Food' and 'Eva'. Eva, Jansen's wife, sat in a chair by the fireplace, with a turban round her head, darning a sock. She sprang up, startled. For a moment she thought the bailiffs were in.

'Food!' Jansen shouted. 'Food for our guest, Sandy O'Connor.'

Eva shook hands with Sandy, who in these surroundings seemed subdued. Books were piled up everywhere, there was an easel in the corner; the remains of a meal and the manuscript of Jansen's novel littered the table. Sandy looked round furtively at the gramophone, the typewriter, the colour-prints on the wall. He swallowed. He muttered something about a wash and shave.

'That can wait,' Jansen said. 'You must be famished. Eva! Food! We must prepare a feast.'

Eva was at a loss. 'There's only bread and cheese,' she said.

'Bread and cheese?' Jansen said in surprise. 'That all?' He looked round at the table as though expecting a colossal spread to materialize before his eyes. Bread and cheese confronted him instead. He coughed.

'There may be some jam,' Eva said. 'If you haven't eaten it all.'

'Jam!' Jansen said, recovering. 'Of course there's jam. Bread and cheese and jam. Which will you have?'

Sandy hesitated. Then he said: 'I'll have bread and cheese and jam.'

'Fine!' Jansen said. 'Fine! Sit you down.' He started to saw at the loaf. 'It's all very informal here,' he explained. 'Bohemian. We lead a Bohemian existence.' He poured out some tea. 'It's a bit stewed,' he said. 'Black as your hat.' Sandy said he liked it black. Jansen said: 'Splendid. Very fortunate, especially as there's no milk.'

Eva said: 'No more milk until we pay up. Man told me this morning.'

'Money-grubbing materialist,' her husband said. 'We'll take our custom elsewhere. We'll go to Sait's.'

'We owe Sait's two pounds ten.'

'Do we? That's a blow. Still, there must be other dairies.' With a sweep of his hand he dismissed the subject as sordid. Little Eva, his daughter, aged two, toddled in from the passage dragging a decapitated rag doll by the neck behind her. She was introduced to Sandy, but did not pay much attention. So many strange people came in and out of the house that the presence of this new additional uncle passed her by almost unnoticed. Sandy ate bread and cheese and jam steadily. Jansen picked up his manuscript and read out a chapter of the novel. Sandy stopped chewing. He said: 'Did you write that?'

'Yes,' Jansen said. 'I'm a writer. So's he,' pointing at me. 'We are both writers.'

'What about your wife?' Sandy asked. 'She a writer, too ?'

'She's a sculptress.' Jansen pointed at a masked harlequin, carved out of wood, which stood gloomily staring down from the top of a bookcase. Sandy looked at the harlequin and nodded. He jerked his head towards Eva, playing on the couch with her doll.

'And her?' he said. 'She a writer?'

'Writing runs in the family,' Jansen said. 'When she gets a little older she'll be a great writer.'

'She may be a sculptress,' Sandy said.

'She'll be a sculptress and a writer,' Jansen said proudly.

So the future of little Eva was settled.

Sandy stood up from the table. He slapped his pockets in search of cigarettes, but found none. He went over and opened his valise. It seemed to be principally full of bright-coloured shirts and bottles of Brylcreem. He dug underneath these and produced a hundred Players. We were overjoyed; there were very few fags in the house.

'All I could get me hands on,' Sandy said. 'I'd rather have Craven A by rights.'

He dug in the valise again; he hadn't finished. A giant panda was fished out and handed to little Eva. I'd seen it before, as one of the principal prizes on the housey-housey stall. There were cries from the Jansens of 'Say thank you.' Little Eva didn't respond. She put a finger in her mouth and stared at the panda with an awed expression. Sandy was still fumbling among the shirts. He started to fling them backwards as a dog, digging, flings earth back from a hole. Two bottles of perfume came to light next. But just as Sandy was offering Eva Jansen one of them a knock came at the door.

Everyone went immediately to ground, Jansen under the table. Further knocks followed, then the sound of footsteps crunching away down the gravel path. From a crouching position Jansen peered out through the window. He stood up. 'All clear!' he said as the gate closed.

'Who was it?'

'The wireless man.'

This was one of our most frequent and importunate visitors. He was always on about the instalments we owed. To celebrate his departure Jansen switched on the wireless itself. The news came through on National. It was nothing much. Sandy asked if he could take off his coat. It was a sign that he was settling in. He sat there in his shirt-sleeves, smoking and nodding his head in time to the dance music which followed the news. Jansen did the honours. He showed Sandy his hunting trophies, the silver riding cup he'd won at the *Concours Hippique*, the hole a rat had gnawed in the living-room door last winter.

In the middle of this my girl friend, Helen Baker, arrived. She was mistaken for a creditor at first, but at length admitted. She'd brought us a chocolate cake. Sandy presented her in return with the second bottle of perfume. She accepted it, but was suspicious. She stared in astonishment at the shirts, the cigarettes and the panda.

'Where's he get all this stuff?' she asked me while Sandy was being shown his room.

'Ask no questions, hear no lies,' I told her.

She shook her head gloomily. 'You'll all end up in jail.'

And as things turned out she was very nearly right.

III

Sandy slept on a camp-bed in the attic, among the mouldering boxes full of false hair, tinsel crowns and sticks of grease-paint, relics of the time when for a short period Eva Jansen had been on the stage. Jansen had formerly used the attic as a refuge, a place to retire to in moments of stress, when creditors made a mass attack or his wife, during a family quarrel, flung the bread-board at him. It was reached by a trapdoor and a ladder which could be drawn up after ascent, like the drawbridge of a castle.

Sandy used the attic for sleeping in only. During the day, between signing on at the Labour and looking for jobs, he used to walk restlessly about the living-room or sit hunched up in a chair smoking Craven A and snapping the cork butts into the fireplace. He became more and more restless as the prospect of getting work receded. He handed all his dole money over to us, only keeping back enough for a packet or two of fags. He often talked of joining up. Only the fact that he'd already deserted from the peace-time army deterred him from this course. He stood for hours staring out of the window and swearing softly under his breath. Often he'd cross over and peer closely at the books on the shelves. These seemed to fascinate him. He'd stand there and gaze, his thick lips moving silently, spelling the titles over to himself.

One day he actually took a book down. It was *Brighton Rock*. He read it through at a sitting. This started him off. He became a tremendous reader. He read book after book, anything that came to hand. The tough books and those dealing with working-class life were the ones he liked best. He used to comment on the authenticity of the slang used in the dialogue. Expressions he used—'Charva', and 'Scarper' and 'Palone'— became part of the lingua-franca of Greenleaves. There was also rhyming slang: a thief became a tea-leaf, tea itself was Rosy Lee. Sandy climbed the apples and pears to bed; we ate at the Cain and Abel.

Meanwhile the late summer broke up; rain poured down in a solid sheet outside; there was a flood; when this subsided, the road leading to Greenleaves had resumed its winter condition and the hire-purchase touts employed by typewriter, gramophone and radio companies could no longer get at us. Visits from the local tradespeople also ceased; on the other hand, our letter-box became choked with bills, solicitors' letters, demands and threats which we did not bother to open.

The financial position had not improved. Jansen's novel wasn't finished; my short stories returned regularly; the job I'd been promised at the BBC did not materialize owing to war-time curtailment of staff; moreover, I was expecting my call-up papers any moment. But even these didn't materialize.

The Great Bore War went on. We heard Haw-Haw on the radio; 'We'll Hang Out Our Washing on the Siegfried Line; gallant little Finland; *on les aura*. We took it in turns to go out in my mackintosh and Jansen's rubber boots; I used to wade downtown in these to see Helen, as it was now almost impossible for her to visit us. I'd come back to find Sandy crouched over the fire reading and the others gone to bed depressed.

Then one evening when we were all together Sandy suddenly announced that he'd like to try his hand at a short story himself. He licked the stub of pencil and bent determinedly over one of my abandoned notebooks, which had a few blank pages in it. He wrote steadily for about an hour. When he read us the result we were astounded. It was a story called *The Spike*, about life in a casual ward, and told entirely in dialogue. We thought it very good indeed.

Sandy was encouraged. He set to and wrote several more stories. He used to write three or four short stories in an evening. He filled notebooks with his pencilled script, printed always in block letters and abounding in spelling idiosyncrasies and contractions that none but I could decipher. I typed some of the best stories and sent them round to editors. They came back, but then so did mine. Undeterred, Sandy started on his autobiography. It was called *Dog-End*. It seemed to us to have the makings of a best-seller, or at any rate a banned book.

Then as a sideline Sandy took up surrealism. A book he got out of the public library began it. He sketched out some extraordinary designs of his own and Eva painted two of them for him. One was called *Birth of a Nation*, the other *The Parson Preached a Sermon on Palm Sunday*. The *Parson* had to be painted on plywood, as Eva had only one canvas left, and the *Birth of a Nation* occupied that. I planned to take these down to the owner of the local art shop, who was keen on modern painting.

Then everything fell through. We struck a particularly bad patch. The tradesmen with one accord cut off our credit. We were behind-hand with the rent. There were no fags and very little food in the house. Outside it was freezing hard. We'd plenty of coal, but you can't eat coal. Sandy got restless again and began to walk up and down, muttering 'Fog it' through clenched teeth. He gave up reading and writing; he didn't even sketch.

'Art don't seem to be much cop,' he said.

One night he put on my mackintosh and went out. He didn't say where he was going. By midnight he had not returned; I began to fear he'd done himself in. Then I heard him crunching ice underfoot on the path. He tapped on the window for me to open the door.

'Where in hell have you been?' I asked him.

He held a finger on his lips for silence. His face was flushed, and at first I thought he'd been on the beer. He closed the living-room door and leaned against it, breathing hard. Then, speaking even more rapidly than usual in his thick, slurred voice, he said: 'I done a job.'

He began without further ado to empty his pockets. In a trice the table became completely covered with a miscellaneous collection of bracelets, wrist-watches, alarm clocks, shaving sets, cosmetics, scent sprays, jars of sweets, slabs of chocolate and boxes of cigarettes. I gaped down at these in a daze.

'Where'd all this come from?'

'Ssh!' Sandy said. 'Don't make a loud mouth about it.'

Then out came the whole story. He'd done a bust, burgled the amusement park. Apparently they had the whole stock stored up there. Sandy had eluded the nightwatchman; he knew a way in via the Zoo. He'd cased the gaff; he wasn't no amacher tea-leaf; no one'd be the wiser. It might be days before they found anything out. Meantime we were all sitting pretty.

He offered me a fag from one of the stolen boxes. Tomorrow he'd think up ways and means of selling the stuff. There was the barracks, for instance. One or two of those watches'd go over big, tosheroon apiece. He wanted to wake Jansen and cut him in a three-way split then and there. I said no, Eva'd be furious. Sandy said maybe you're right. He snapped away his cigarette butt and shovelled the loot back into his pockets, leaving a hundred Players for me on the table.

He said: 'See you in morning,' and climbed to his attic. He pulled up the ladder and closed the trapdoor behind him.

IV

Next morning an uproar in the passage outside awoke me. It was Jansen locking his wife and child in the kitchen. Eva shouted and hammered on the door. Little Eva shouted too, but joyfully. I could hear her dancing up and down. She thought it great fun.

I got out of bed and put my dressing-gown on. The living-room door was also locked. 'What the hell's going on?' I shouted.

Jansen opened the door. 'Come in quick, I don't want Eva to know.' He locked the door again behind me. 'What you think of this lot?' he said. 'Look, watches!'

'I've seen them,' I said. I was feeling a bit sour. The stolen goods were spread out on the table and Sandy sat there arranging them in separate heaps. 'These ought to fetch a tidy packet,' he said.

'What's my cut?' Jansen said. His eyes shone. He evidently fancied himself in the role of a fence: Fagin or Jonathan Wild.

'Ten per cent,' Sandy said.

'Not enough,' Jansen said. 'After all if the swag's found here, I take the rap.' He lit a stolen cigarette and started to wind up the alarm clocks in a row. He wound up a watch and held it close to his ear, listening to the tick. He buckled it on to his wrist, broke off a bar of chocolate and sprayed scent on himself. He and Sandy began to argue about his cut. Jansen waved his hands and stroked an imaginary beard. All the alarm clocks went off at once. I said: 'For Christ's sake!'

We could hear both Evas shouting and hammering in the kitchen.

'I'd better let her out now,' Jansen said. 'Hide the loot quick.'

'I'm away,' Sandy said. He gathered the stuff up and disappeared aloft.

'What's the idea?' Eva asked indignantly as the door was unlocked. 'Why'd you shut us in? What were all those clocks going off?'

'None of your business,' her husband told her. 'Here, take this lipstick and shut up.'

'Where'd it come from?' Eva said suspiciously. 'Not another of your schemes?'

'You want to know too much,' Jansen told her.

That afternoon Sandy borrowed a bike and rode over to the barracks. He sold seventeen watches at half-a-crown each, an alarm clock, three bracelets and a scent spray. Out of all this I got seventeen and eightpence cash.

'A pretty good day,' Jansen said, pocketing his share. 'Now we'll have tea.' He went to let Eva out.

'What is this?' she said. Nobody answered her.

V

Next day was Helen Baker's birthday. I'd been saving a very elaborate embroidery case, which had belonged to my mother, as a present for her. Helen herself met me at the door of her house. At sight of the embroidery case she started back in horror.

'No, no! Don't bring that here! The police have only just left.'

'Police?' I said. 'What police? What're you talking about?'

'The burglary!' Helen hissed. 'For God's sake hide that thing and go quick.'

'I don't get it,' I said. 'What's happened?'

What had happened was this. The police had found a jemmy left behind by Sandy at the amusement park. This tool had the name of Helen's brother engraved on it. Detectives had been round asking questions. Since Helen's brother was now in the navy, he'd a perfect alibi; nobody could account for the presence of this clue on the scene of the crime. Only Helen knew that Jansen had borrowed the engraved jemmy that summer to do some carpentering. She immediately assumed that Jansen was the burglar and that my embroidery case was part of the swag. She hadn't thought of Sandy. When I told her she was even more horrified.

'You've got to get rid of the stuff at once.'

'Telling me,' I said. I got on a bus back to the bungalow. I burst in on Sandy, who sat by the fire, head in hands.

'I know, don't tell me,' he said. 'The fogging jemmy. Couldn't think where I'd left the fogger at first. I went back last night when you was in kip, but they'd a copper on the door. I scarpered quick.'

'Well,' I said, 'we've got to get busy. They'll be along here any minute.'

We carried the swag out into the back garden. Jansen and Sandy started feverishly to dig a hole. I kept an eye on the gate. Little Eva, locked with her mother in the kitchen, left off playing with the panda, to which she'd by now become accustomed, and watched with interest from her high chair overlooking the window.

'Mummy, mummy,' she said. 'Look, Daddy dig.'

'Yes, darling,' her mother said bitterly. 'Buried treasure.'

The ground was hard as hell and digging a hole deep enough took ages. I felt it was good practice for the hard labour to which we might all soon be sentenced. At last the loot was buried; by that time it was dark. We kept only the cigarettes.

Afterwards we sprawled exhausted by the fire. Eva could be heard singing her daughter to sleep next door. Once Sandy said: 'I never been in the nick.'

'Now you'll have the opportunity,' I told him.

'Ah, for fog's sake,' he said.

After this nobody spoke. It was a night of terror. We started at every sound, listening for the clump of official boots. But no one came.

No one came next day either. We gathered glumly round the local rag. 'An arrest may be expected at any moment.' Nobody expected it more than we did. But after two days it began to look as though we weren't going to be arrested at all. After a week we deemed the danger past. We started to make a joke of it. Only Helen didn't seem to find it funny.

Sandy was never quite the same either. He felt he had brought disgrace on the house. He did no more writing or sketching; he just sat about. One day he came in with a letter in his hand. The letter was from a mate of his, geezer called Cohen, who'd been a ponce and was just out of jug. He offered Sandy a smashing job in some gaff up the Smoke.

Two days later this man drove up to Greenleaves in an enormous scarlet racing car. Sandy climbed in with his valise; we assembled at the door to wave goodbye. The car splashed and jolted off through the puddles with Sandy waving from the back seat. It turned the corner and we heard the whine of its powerful engine receding in the distance out of sight. It was the last we expected to see of Sandy.

He said he'd write, but he didn't. *The Parson* and the *Birth of a Nation* remained propped up on the easel in the living-room for a time, until Eva got fed up dusting them. There was also the danger that little Eva would scrape off some of the paint and eat it. So the paintings vanished upstairs to the attic and were soon followed by his notebooks and the manuscript of his autobiography. The swag mouldered in the earth outside.

Weeks passed and we often wondered what had become of him. But it was not for another month, when Jansen looked round for his hunting trophies and silver riding cup in order to pawn them, that he discovered the disappearance of these.

Part Two

The Sequel

I

Looking out from the window of our hut, you could see, over to the left, craters in the chalk where the bombs had dropped. Jerry used to come over and drop them on the camp every night.

I'd been in the army about two months. During the day, when we were not being bombed, I worked as a clerk in the company office.

One morning the Orderly Corporal came in with the mail. Only one letter for me, forwarded on from Greenleaves, a long official envelope with OHMS stamped on top. It looked like income tax. I thought: some hopes. I tore the envelope open. Inside was a sheet of notepaper in unfamiliar handwriting, starting off 'Dear Sir'. At the top it said: 'Ref. Pte. O'Connor, F.' I didn't at once connect this with Sandy. I'd forgotten about him. I had other things to think about.

The letter went:

'You are doubtless aware that the above-named man is to be tried by District Court-Martial on Friday next, 23rd inst., on a charge against the Defence Regulations. I have been detailed as Defending Officer, and in order to assist me, O'Connor has informed me that you hold certain manuscripts of short stories he claims to have written.

It you are able to produce these, will you forward them to me at above address at the earliest possible moment, please.'

The letter was signed 'G. Cook (Major), CC 'D' Coy, Blankshire Regt.' At first I couldn't understand what it was all about. I thought it was one of Jansen's jokes.

The Quarter Bloke sat at another table reading the paper. 'What d'you make of this, sir?' I asked him. He took the letter and ran his eye down it. Then he said: 'O'Connor? Here you are. In the paper and everything.'

He passed over the paper he'd been reading. It was there right enough. PRIVATE SOLDIER ON SECRETS CHARGE. A section underneath was headed: 'DIRECT USE TO ENEMY' ALLEGATION. I read with amazement: 'Details of factories and bombing objectives; two sketches of an RAF station; extracts from notebook read in camera; the court adjourned.'

My name was there, too, misspelt but perfectly recognizable. I didn't care much for the description of myself as 'an amateur novelist'; I had by now certainly published stories, but I'd never written a novel. Still, perhaps that was what they meant.

'This O'Connor,' the Quarter Bloke said. 'Is he a Fifth Columnist?'

'Not so far as I know.'

The paper said Sandy stated he was collecting material for a book about the war when it was over. This seemed awfully likely. That his notebook contained information 'of direct use to the enemy' I didn't for a moment believe. Even in the army, nobody would be silly enough to entrust Sandy with information of this nature. A German dictionary and a driving licence, found during a search of his kit, appeared also to constitute evidence against him: God knows why.

'You'll have to testify,' the Quarter Bloke said.

'Can I use the typewriter, sir?' I asked him.

'Sure. Go right ahead.'

I sat down and slammed out two letters: one to Jansen asking him to unearth the manuscripts and forward them to the defending officer; the other to Major Cook himself. I said I thought things were coming to a pretty pass if writers could have their notebooks confiscated and be put on trial for collating the material necessary to their craft. Suppose my own kit was searched? They might even court-martial me as a Fifth Columnist. I took a very poor view of the whole affair.

While I was typing, the CSM looked in. 'Busy?' he asked.

The Quarter Bloke explained: 'One of his mates is in a jam. On court-martial for a secrets charge.'

'Go on?' the CSM said. 'Not that O'Connor? I bin reading about it. Reckon 'e's guilty?'

'No, sir,' I said. The CSM came behind me and read the letter as the typewriter keys tapped it out. 'Who's that to?' he asked.

'Defending officer, sir.'

The CSM chuckled. He said: 'You want to watch out that you ain't clapped in clink yourself, m'lad,' and to the Quarter Bloke: ' 'Ow about a game o' darts?'

They started to play. I stuck the two letters in their respective envelopes. The Quarter Bloke got double-top. He told me: 'You can fall out now.'

It was 12.30. Cookhouse blew as I came out on the veranda.

II

Next day, Sunday, the news was all over the camp. I was pointed out in the canteen; crossing the barrack-square; in the cookhouse.

'See that bloke? 'E's a Fifth Columnist!'

'Aye, name in the paper an' all.'

'Sunday Pictorial.'

'News of the World.'

'It don't say nothing in mine.'

'Fifth Columnist? Rotten bastard.'

'Nah, mate, you got it wrong. His mate's the Fifth Columnist, not 'im.'

'Private bleeding O'Connor. 'Ere it is: page seven.'

Copies of the Sunday paper were passed from hand to hand. This said that as my presence was essential to Sandy's defence, the hearing had been again adjourned until next Saturday.

On Monday morning I was sent for by the Company Commander.

'You are detailed to attend as a witness at a Court-Martial to be held at Chelsea Barracks on Saturday. You will be ready to proceed tomorrow to D Company, Blankshire ITC, and there report to the Officer Commanding. Here are your train-timings, rail-warrant, and other documents. Sergeant-Major, see this man has a haircut immediately.'

'Yessir. About turn! Quick march!'

Out on the veranda the CSM said: 'Now you nip over to the barber's and have all that 'air off. All of it, mind, else you'll be on a bleeding court-martial yourself soon's they see you.'

I went over to the barber. 'Cut it short,' I told him, 'I'm on a court-martial Saturday.'

'Fucking hell. What you bin up to, chum?'

'Nothing. I'm only a witness.'

I reported back to the CSM.

'Now go and draw equipment from the stores. Get it scrubbed and brasses shining like buggery by tomorrow. Parade here, full pack, the whole works.'

Inwardly I cursed. The thought of lugging that load across London in this hot weather was intolerable. Besides, I hardly knew how to connect it up. One of the blokes in our hut, who'd been a batman, came to my rescue. He polished the brasses, packed my kit, and got everything ready.

Next morning, after a heavy raid and a night in the trenches, I dragged myself across the square to Company Office. It was drizzling damply. The pack on my back bowed me double beneath its weight. The straps cut into my shoulders. I'd been issued with fifty rounds of ammo by the CSM: an injudicious action on his part, considering my present mood. I felt quite capable of shooting up the camp with it.

At last I embarked in a truck with a corporal bound for the same destination as myself. He'd been detailed to bring back an absentee apprehended in that area. We drove through the drizzle and got on a train which was a long time starting.

Later the drizzle ceased and sunlit fields flowed backwards past the windows of our compartment. The corporal, taciturn at first, suddenly became communicative and showed me a snap of his wife and kids. 'What're you on, chum?' he asked me.

'Witness at a court-martial.' The story was too long to tell, so I took out a press-cutting and passed it on to him. The corporal read it carefully.

'But this don't say nothing about you. This says a novelist. You ain't no novelist.'

'No.'

The corporal gave it up. He sat back in his corner looking a little offended. He thought I was taking the piss.

Presently we reached a station where we had to change. The platform was crowded with soldiers who'd just been released from detention. These assumed at first that I was a prisoner travelling under escort. One of them shared a compartment with us on the London train.

'Got a fag, mate?' he asked me. I gave him one. 'Ta,' he said. 'First smoke I've had in twenty-eight days. I'm shit out, see? Ain't got bugger all. Give me a bob they did, the bastards; a bleeding bob, that's all. I bin to Dunkirk and that's what I get: twenty-eight days' glasshouse and a bleeding bob.' He pulled up his trouser-leg and showed me a scar on his calf. 'Shrapnel, see? I bin out with the BEF and that's what they give me. Bleeding glasshouse and a bob.'

'But surely they didn't give you the glasshouse for going to Dunkirk?'

'Nah, course not. I mucked off home for a month, see?'

The compartment was terrifically hot. The corporal went to sleep with his mouth open and the glasshouse man continued to recount his experiences in detention.

'Do everything at the double there. Full bleeding pack an' all. Ain't no ruddy picnic, I assure you.'

We got to Waterloo and into another train. Then we walked about in narrow streets and broiling heat, looking for a bus. Our equipment and ammunition boots weighed us down; the blinding sun got into our bones, melting them to water. At last a bus was sighted. It deposited us some distance from the barracks and again we had to walk. Sweat streamed stickily down our faces. My throat felt as though an iron bar had been fixed across it: I'd a sharp burning pain in my back. We passed a high wall with spikes running along the top. This evidently enclosed the ITC. Summoning up a spurt of energy, the corporal shot ahead, presented his pass to the guard, and disappeared through the gates.

I followed through a doorway stacked with sandbags into the guardroom. Inside it was dark and cool after the sun and the RPs were playing darts. The corporal vanished immediately in the wake of another corporal carrying a bunch of keys. No one took any notice of me. I began to wonder if they would not imprison me as an accessory. I recalled gloomily what the jankers-man had said about the glasshouse.

After a time the provost-corporal returned. I came to attention. 'Reporting as witness in the O'Connor case, corporal.'

'Oh, so you're that bloke. Come this way.'

I followed him down a cold stone passage between cells. I wondered if he intended to lock me up straight away. The corporal stopped in front of a cell halfway down and stooped his head to the square aperture in the door. He called out O'Connor. There was a scuffle of feet inside and

Sandy's oblong face, with the long square chin and thick bee-stung lips, appeared squinting sideways up in the opening.

'Hullo, Sandy,' I said.

Sandy's mouth dropped open. His lashless eyes were fixed in an unbelieving stare. Then his face became animated, the eyes lit up, the teeth flashed in a tremendous grin.

'Be Christ it's good to see you,' he said.

'You look very well, Sandy,' I said. And so he did. Nor was he stark naked and wearing chains, as in my imagination I had pictured him. His reddish hair was Brylcreemed and his face fresh-coloured as before.

'You look well too,' he said.

'My looks belie me,' I told him.

Then we talked about his Defending Officer. 'Smashing geezer. Gives me all I want. Books, everything.'

'Splendid. We'll soon have you out of here now.'

''E won't want to leave,' the provost-corporal grinned. 'They live on the fat o' the land here. Eh, Sandy? Ain't that so?'

'That's so, Corp,' Sandy grinned back at him. 'Fat o' the land.'

He seemed in high spirits. The corporal conducted me back down the passage. 'Satisfied? Everything okay?'

'Fine,' I said. 'What d'you make of this case, corporal?'

'Bleeding balls-up, between you and me.'

He took me over to D Company Headquarters. It was in another part of the ITC and in process of construction. A smell of damp plaster and camouflage paint pervaded it. Pails and ladders stood about everywhere; the stone huts had no doors or glass in the windows and they were not yet wired with electric light.

I'd been detailed to sleep in the Orderly Sergeant's bunk.

The Orderly Sergeant was a corporal. He said: 'I dunno where the hell you're going to kip. We only got three beds in here, and one of 'em's broke.'

Then I was taken before the acting CSM. He viewed me with disfavour. 'So you're here at last,' he said. 'Well, Major's orders are: don't do no talking to no one. 'Bout O'Connor, I mean. Keep your trap shut, see? Get it? Right. Report back here 0800 hours tomorrow morning for interview with the major. Meantime: trap shut. All right. Fall out.'

Well, it was evident I wasn't to be locked up, anyway. I had a wash and went back to make up my bed. It had a large rent in the canvas and one of the legs was splintered, but I felt I'd rather anything than sleep on the floor.

'Am I allowed out?' I asked the Orderly Sergeant.

'Sure. Till 2359. Sign in the gate coming back.'

I went to a cinema and when I came out there was an alert on. The searchlight beams swung and pointed and planes throbbed overhead. I checked in at the gate and crossed the barrack-square, which seemed enormous in the searchlight rays. A dull panting of asthmatic engines indicated the presence of Jerry somewhere in the sky. Ack-ack rumbled over to the west.

I found the Orderly Sergeant's bunk with difficulty. The blackouts were up and it was pitch-dark inside. I struck a match; the hut was empty. Nobody had come in yet. The camp-bed creaked and sagged ominously as I climbed into it. I could feel the canvas splitting. Jerry chugged almost immediately above. It was a sound I'd become used to in the other camp. I'd have felt lonely without it. I fell asleep and was awakened by a man falling over me. This happened at intervals until the hut was filled with a sound of steady stentorous breathing and I went to sleep again.

The hell of a crash woke me. I was certain a bomb had been dropped on the barracks. I sat up and my bed collapsed under me with a splintering sound. A voice said out of the breathing dark: 'Ain't nothing, mate. You get used to that. Nowhere near. Miles away.'

I lay down again but it was some time before I went off to sleep. My bed was now flat on the ground, but I was too tired to do much about it. I woke next morning at eight. Luckily, no one rose early in the Orderly Sergeant's bunk. Breakfast was brought up from the cookhouse by a man called Paddy. After eating I had to brass myself up to meet the major. I started on this task while Paddy, seizing a broom, set himself to sweep the floor, shouting in an unintelligible accent for assistance. No one paid the slightest attention; the Company Runner, seated bolt upright on his roll of bedding, polished and polished a pair of boots, crooning all the time an unending obscene parody of a nursery rhyme, something about Miss Muffit and a spider, a rock and Robinson Crusoe. The Orderly Sergeant sat down at a table and began to write furiously. Paddy continued to sweep up; the air was full of flying particles of dust and horse dung. The Company Runner crooned:

Then up came a spider,
Sat down beside her...

From the other huts issued a stream of men carrying rifles and scrambling in a mad rush to get on parade. The voices of sergeants, shouting 'Outside!' could be heard. It was 0900 hours. I dropped my button stick and made a dash for Company Office. But first came Company Evidence; it took ages. Nearly the whole Company seemed to be on a charge. Then the acting CSM called my name; he shouted 'Shun!' I marched in, right-wheeled, stood to attention in front of a desk.

I liked the major on sight. He looked like Charlie Chan. He had horn-rimmed spectacles and a thick drooping dark moustache. He ignored my salute and stood up to shake hands. He said to sit down. 'All right, Sergeant Major, wait outside.'

'I was so glad to hear from you.' He pushed over a box of cigarettes.

'It'll be an awful blow to the prosecution. They don't really believe you exist. They think O'Connor invented you, to lend colour to his story. By the way, have you brought the MSS?'

'They're on the way, sir.'

'Good. He really does write? The prosecution doesn't believe that either.'

'The prosecution seems awfully unbelieving.'

'Well, it does seem incredible.'

Then he told me the story. It was long and not easy to follow. Sandy had not been a model soldier. He had already absented himself at least twice. Before one of these flights he'd dropped his notebook in a Naffy. Some woman had picked it up and, bewildered by the contents, which she imagined to be in code, had taken it along to the civil police. Meanwhile, Sandy had been picked up by the red-caps, and the notebook, forwarded on by the police, had led to a search of his kit and the discovery of further notebooks, sketches, maps, and a German dictionary.

'Of course it's all rot,' the major said. 'There's no reason why he shouldn't have a German dictionary. Why, I've got one myself.'

'What about the RAF sketches, sir?'

'I'll show them to you.' The major took a few sheets of paper from a tray on his desk. Groups of buildings, pylons and hangars, rather out of the drawing, were sketched on them. There was also an unfinished sketch of a plane, evidently made by Sandy when, with another unit, he had been stationed near a drome.

'These couldn't be of any value to the enemy.'

'No. Does he sketch, normally?'

'Yes. I've two of his pictures at home. Paintings.'

At this the major became tremendously excited. Jansen must be sent for, with the paintings. I suggested that Helen Baker might also be a useful witness. I saw no reason why she should not spend a few days in London at the army's expense. The major said he'd send her a wire.

Then he showed me Sandy's notebooks. I turned the pages. There was no connected narrative, but merely page after page of notes, which Sandy's habit of making contractions rendered almost indecipherable. I could not make head or tail of them. Isolated phrases of stilted German dialogue, plainly copied from the back pages of his dictionary, appeared here and there enigmatically. Columns of figures were scrawled in the margins: a habit of Sandy's when he was thinking something out. There were certain dates and items of information relating to bombed British factories written underneath them in a journalistic style. I was completely baffled.

At this point a lance-corporal, who'd been a barrister in civilian life and was helping to prepare Sandy's defence, entered with some pages of typescript in his hand. These were copies of statements used as evidence against Sandy. One from an adjutant; one from the military policeman who at some time or another had arrested Sandy and who suspected him of having (sic) communistic or fascist tendencies. A lot more statements from people obscurely connected with the case. A letter from a woman whose son had lately been buried. The exact date of the burial was important, I forget why. I think Sandy had absented himself without leave to attend the funeral, but I don't really remember now.

Then Sandy was brought in. He was in splendid form. It was evident he got on smashing with the major. He sat down. He smoked a fag and, like old times, flicked the ash in the fireplace. He said not having smokes was the one thing that got him down in detention. I said: 'Now look here, Sandy, what the hell have you been up to? Are these really notes for a novel?'

'Sure. I was going to write it when the war's over, see? I took notes on everything I seen. Realism; atmosphere; same's you always told me. Bits in the paper too I copied out. All this stuff about factories they're kicking up a caper about, it's all bin printed; they're the dates written down, proof plain. But would they believe that? Not a word. No, they was dead set on me being a spy. Put handcuffs on an' all. I bin waiting on this court-martial a couple o' months now.'

'What about all this German?'

'Oh aye. I got a character, a Jerry, don't speak nothing but his own language. So I got me a dictionary to work out the di-log. I told 'em all that but they wouldn't listen, the ignorant so-and-sos. Would have it I was a Fifth Column. Now is it likely, if they'd the brains of a louse?'

'Well,' the major said, 'I think it's in the bag now. Soon as the MSS arrive I shall want to take down a statement from you both. Meantime,' he said, coming with me to the door, 'make yourself at home. I'll give you a permanent pass so you can go out any time of day. Anything you want, just ask.'

'Thank you, sir,' I said. Out of the corner of my eye I saw Sandy scoop up a handful of fags from the open box and stuff them down the front of his shirt. He winked at me as the door closed.

III

The intervening days passed quietly except for incessant sirens; mornings with the major looking over the MSS and making sure the statements tallied; afternoons having tea with Helen, who'd arrived in answer to the major's wire; evenings at the cinema; altogether a pleasant rest from the usual routine of army life. The major had even provided me with a new camp bed to sleep on.

Then came Saturday; I buckled on my belt and bayonet; we drove to the court in a camouflaged civilian car; a sympathetic RP sitting next to the driver; Sandy and I at the back. A great deal of sun flashed back off glass in this suburb we were passing through; it seemed to be full of gigantic garages; Sandy, with a fag on, talked happily out of the corner of his mouth about his future; he seemed quite confident he would get off. What he wanted to do was go abroad, see some action; parades and bullshit got on his wick; why couldn't they put him on fogging draft.

Only the idea of seeing Jansen again appeared to worry him, as we drove past the furniture shops in the King's Road; I could understand that, remembering the disappearance of the hunting trophies and the riding cup. But Jansen, waiting for us at the barracks with the paintings wrapped up under his arm, wasn't one to bear malice; all he had for Sandy was a hearty handshake. There was just time for this before Sandy was led away through a door with a sign on it: COURT-MARTIAL IN PROGRESS. KEEP SILENCE.

I was the first witness called for the defence. I marched in uneasily, afraid that my belt and bayonet would fall off me. I stood before a table with a crimson blanket covering it. I saluted the President, who wore a crimson sash. He had white hair and smiled at me benevolently. I took the oath and sat down on a form facing the court. Major Cook stood up and said did I see Sandy O'Connor among those present. He nodded towards Sandy sitting between two RPs. I said I recognized him perfectly. I gave my evidence. A snuffy little man, who turned out to be a journalist, scribbled assiduously in shorthand at my elbow. The siren went as I was speaking; the President smiled. I stopped. The MSS were handed up by Major Cook and passed around. The President read a chapter of *Dog-End* with great attention.

Then the Prosecuting Officer stood up to cross-examine me. He coughed and stroked a short fair moustache. Did I really consider it possible that a boy like O'Connor, without—ahem—the advantages of education, could ever become an author? Surely it was necessary to have some—ahem—knowledge of grammatical rules before authorship could be embarked upon? I asked him sternly whether he had ever heard of the proletarian school of literature. He had not. He said was it a correspondence school? I put him right on this point. The journalist asked me if I would mind repeating the name of the school, he hadn't quite caught it. The President chipped in. Was it true, he asked the Prosecuting Officer, that the notes on bombed British factories made by the accused had previously been printed as common knowledge in the daily press? The Prosecuting Officer coughed and said he now understood that to be the case. He sat down deflated. The President smiled at me and said: 'Well, I don't think we need trouble this gentleman—I mean this Private,' he smiled again, 'any longer.'

So I saluted and marched out, and Jansen was called. He turned out to be the star turn. The paintings caused a sensation. 'What did you say this was called?'

'*The Birth of a Nation.*'

They nodded gravely. 'And this?'

'*The Parson Preached a Sermon on Palm Sunday.*'

'I beg your pardon?'

'*The Parson Preached a Sermon on Palm Sunday.* Excuse me, sir, you've got it the wrong way up.'

Then Helen Baker's statement was read out; she didn't appear in court herself. After this it was all over bar shouting. An acquittal on the secrets charge was certain. There were still two charges of absence, but the major hoped to get these squashed as Sandy had already spent two months in close arrest awaiting court-martial. He also promised to send Sandy abroad on the very next draft. This cheered Sandy up no end; we all shook hands and wished him the best of luck and came out into the bright glare of noon where Helen awaited us, wearing sunglasses and twirling a parasol. The All Clear blew as we came out.

Later, we all got drunk at the Café Royal. Jansen paid; he had a publisher's contract in his pocket; besides, he'd put it down as expenses when he sent Major Cook his bill. 'The Army pays,' he said, emptying his glass and ordering another. 'Drink up, it's on the Army.'

'D'you remember the swag?' he said. 'My God, those were the days. Good old Sandy. Remember those watches? And when he pinched my cups, too. My God, he was some lad.'

We all drank a toast to Sandy, solemnly standing to attention: 'To the great Tea Leaf!'

Everyone in the café stared disapprovingly.

IV

Two years later I received a letter from Sandy. It had stamped on it PASSED BY CENSOR and bore an address in the Middle East Forces.

'DEAR OLD PAL,' the letter said,

'I have made many attempt to write you though I have never quite got down to it. The reel reason was to say I have not forgot the great help you give me on my Caurt-Martial. I only hope some day I get the chance of repaying that debt. You must wonder even now how I got myself mixed up in that espial. I only hope we meet again so I can tell you. I expect by this time you will be wearing a pip or two. If not, why not. Have you any news of Jansen, I am always looking for his book out here, but it doesn't seem to have got this far yet.

'How is your own writing coming along, it is hard writing in the army, I know as I have tryed it myself. I have met a great many geezers who do a bit of writing as a hobby, they are all of the opinion you can't write and be a soldier same time. Myself I think that's all balls, though I am sometimes wondering if it is worth carrying on. Well, Pal, cherro and good luck. I will be hoping to hear from you.

S. O'CONNOR,
One of the Tea Leaves
from Green Leaves.'

They Can Have It

There's ways and means of getting on in our mob. Either you go in for football or cricket or you play in the Unit Dance Band. Then there's boxing of course, that's very popular. One of our blokes went in for boxing and got his nose busted, and they gave him a stripe straightaway, so's he wouldn't get downhearted. But getting my nose busted's not much in my line, so it's either crickct now the summer's on or else the dance band. It's a toss-up between 'em. Well I used to play the old piano a good bit in civvy-street, whereas I don't rightly know which way up you hold a cricket bat, so I plumped for the band and now I play the piano in it.

Well that's got its advantages of course. 'Specially when it comes to tarts. You can get to know most any nice bit of stuff when you're in the band and once you know 'em the rest's up to you. But don't think it's all beer and bleeding skittles. There's staying in nights for rehearsals and having a weekend stopped just coz the bandmaster's fixed up a date you've got to play at suddenly and putting off your seven days so the band can all of them be away at the same time. Course you make an extra bit of cash at it now, and again, but what's that amount to? Sweet Fanny Adams when all's said and done.

Take what happened to me the other night.

We were down to play at the jocks' Saturday evening Hop. Well that in itself's no cop, coz these jocks are tough and there's always trouble. Didn't they sling old Smudger Smith through the big drum one night just coz he couldn't play the signature-tune of some clan one of 'em belonged to. And another time they bust in both the double doors down the Pavilion and one of the plateglass windows, they did the window by bunging a bloke through it, though luckily a bomb dropped down by the Pier that night and they stuck the damage down as Enemy Action.

The drum couldn't go down as Enemy Action though, and they had to fork out for a new one. Then they had a weed on us coz they'd all had pay stopped, so they grabbed old Smudger on his way back from the Naffy one night and slung him in the swimming-pool this time. They reckoned slinging him in that wouldn't break it, and they were right, only

Smudger got pneumonia it being Xmas time and lost his stripe through going in hospital and getting Y Listed. Anyhow.

There we were at the jocks' and the dance was in full swing, they had on kilts. No bagpipes though, and nobody'd tried to do the highland fling so far. Nothing'd got busted except a few bottles and glasses, and we hoped we were in for a quiet time. We gave 'em a swing version of *Loch Lomond* to put 'em in a good mood, and that went down a treat. Course when we played for the Irish it was a sight easier, we'd just give 'em old *Mother Macree* and the whole mob'd burst out crying.

Well we were up on the stand, Wells and Geordie squeezing away at their accordions and old Smudger giving the drums all he'd got and me at the old piano. We give 'em two more numbers and comes the interval I says to old Smudger, 'Save some beer for me. I'll be back in two shakes.'

But I when I got outside I couldn't find the place. There wasn't any sign up as I could see. No GENTS, nothing. I wandered out there banging up against things in the black-out, then I come to a door and there's a couple of tarts in there, one of 'em taking her stockings off, and they lets out a yell. I got out at the double and ran slap-bang into one of the jocks at the door.

'It's back yonder,' he tells me, pointing.

'Whyn't they stick a sign up?' I asked him.

Turned out they had, only somebody'd pinched it. In the army they'll pinch anything. Anyhow I came out of there and made for the hall. They'd already begun dancing inside, I must have been out there hours. I went to go in and a couple of blokes on the door gets in my way.

'What's up with you?' I ask 'em.

'Ye canna come in, mon,' one of 'em says.

'Who can't?' I says.

'Where's ye ticket?' he says.

'What ticket?' I says. 'I'm in the band. 'I don't need a ticket.'

'Ye canna come in without a ticket,' this bloke says.

I started to argue the toss pretty strong, I was getting browned-off with all this. They said Buy a ticket. I was blowed if I would. 'Sides, I was broke. I'd only got tuppence.

Then along comes this tart, the one that'd been taking her stockings off, and she lets out another yell soon's she sees me.

'That's him!' she says. 'Come walking into the Ladies bold as bold.'

'*Ladies*' I says. She was a pretty rough-looking bit and I was browned-off, as I say. Anyhow she gets hold of me by the hair. One of the jocks gets hold of her and she lets him have it. Pretty soon we were all at it when out comes the Bandmaster hisself. He's got up posh, with brown shoes and a stick, and you have to call him Mister. Even the officers do.'

'Where the hell have you been?' he says to me. 'I've a good mind to shove you on report. Deserting your post.'

Then everyone chips in, the two jocks and this tart, and here's me with my best battledress blouse with all the buttons torn off it.

'I'll listen to all this later,' the Bandmaster says, and he gives me a pretty dirty look. 'Meantime you get back on that piano,' he says.

So I did and they all say You lousy so-and-so where've you been. And who've they got on the piano but Burrows, who can't play but with one finger?

'We had to get someone,' they said. 'Thought you'd gone absent. And what've you been doing to your tunic.'

See? That's all you get. And it wasn't the finish, by a long way. I gets back on the piano and after they've sung *Auld Lang Syne* and the jocks have started busting everything in sight, I'm coming out carrying the drumsticks when up comes another jock with this tart again, seems she was his missus.

'I'll learn you,' he says, 'Insulting a lady,' and with that he gets up and lands me one. Well I wasn't standing for any more of it. I hits out with the drumsticks and it's in the black-out see, well anyhow old Smudger cops it instead of this jock. And was he wild.

Next day I come up in front of the Major.

'What's this I hear?' he says. 'Fighting. Striking a comrade. Insulting a lady. Disgraceful conduct. And I've a very bad report on you from the Bandmaster.'

So then he fines me a dollar out of my share of the band money for being absent and to pay Burrows for taking my place. Well is it fair? They can stick their ruddy band in future. It'll be winter soon, I think I'll take up hockey.

The High Priest of Buddha

You'd never believe I'd been a Buddhist, would you? It's true, though. I became a Buddhist for the whole of one summer, when I was about twelve years old and lived in the South of France. All the boys I used to play with at that time became Buddhists. To be a Buddhist became the fashion. Later it became the fashion for all of us to wear monocles, but before that came Buddhism; it was Rossignol who really began it.

One day we were all standing round the captured German cannons in the Jardin Albert Premier. We'd just finished playing marbles. The game had ended abruptly because Rossignol had as usual won all the marbles and no one had any left to play with. The pockets of Rossignol's flannel shorts bulged with the marbles he'd won. They clinked and rattled when he moved.

He was a fat boy, not enormously fat but fat enough, and a lot of his prestige among us depended on his weight and the unscrupulous use which he made of this when confronted with any opposition to his will. He would suddenly lower his head and butt whoever opposed him in the belly, at the same time encircling the offender with his arms and bearing him to the ground by the sheer force of his fat. After that he would if necessary sit on his opponent until all resistance was literally squashed out of him.

His face was fat too, but in the centre of it was embedded, surprisingly, a small delicate hooked nose, like a parrot's beak. His hair was thin and fair, it stuck up in a crest at the back of his head. He always wore apricot silk shirts stretched tight across the upper part of his body, which wobbled as he moved.

Now he sat astride the snout of one of the cannons looking down at us impatiently and with contempt.

'Come on,' he shouted suddenly in his thick hoarse voice, 'Let's do something. Don't just stand about like that. Think of something to do.'

Someone, I think Charpentier, suggested a relay race. Someone else a game of Gendarmes and Voleurs. Rossignol shouted these suggestions down at once.

'And your sister,' he said.

He didn't like running about. He always came in last. So any game with running in it was automatically washed out.

'You,' Rossignol shouted at me, 'l'Anglische! You're a foreigner, full of bright ideas. Think up something new. Something we've not done before.'

Something new. It was a facer. I couldn't think of anything at all.

'Come on,' Rossignol shouted, 'quick about it. Else you're in for a razzing.'

My heart sank at this. I knew only too well what a razzing meant. I'd had two shirts torn off my back already, and once Rossignol had wrenched off the brim of my brand-new straw hat. For all these things I'd got into hot water at home.

'Give you till I count ten,' Rossignol said. 'One, two, three..'

I tried desperately to think, but my brain was a blank. Rossignol had got up to seven, the others had closed in and were preparing to pinion me. A razzing appeared unavoidable.

Then suddenly Rossignol stopped counting. I looked round and who should be there but old Hippolyte, as usual with his nose deep in a book. Rossignol started to grin in anticipation, he made us a sign to shut up.

Shortsighted and stooping, absorbed in his book, Hippolyte advanced, unaware of what he was in for. When he was too near to make a dash for it without being caught, Rossignol shouted out, 'Hullo Hippolyte! How's it going?'

Hippolyte started, shot up his head. He saw Rossignol and his face went pale beneath its pimples. He looked round but he was already encircled, his retreat cut off. He blinked up at Rossignol through his big glasses.

'Just the type I've been wanting to see,' Rossignol bellowed. 'The boy with brains. You'll be able to help us.'

Hippolyte breathed again. He wasn't taken in by all this bonhomie but he thought it entailed nothing more than buying ice-cream for the lot of us. He'd often got out of a razzing in this way. His parents were rich, he'd plenty of pocket-money, and he knew that Rossignol himself had a prodigious appetite for ice-cream. He'd been known to consume sixteen ice-cream cornets in a couple of hours. All paid for by Hippolyte, of course.

But this time Hippolyte was soon made to realize he'd have to produce something more than ice-cream.

'Something to do!' Rossignol shouted at him suddenly, with a change of tone that caused Hippolyte to jump. 'Come on! You got brains, always reading books. Think up a new game. We're sick of hanging about here.'

Hippolyte began blinking and shaking his head from side to side. He didn't know any games, never played them, never took part in anything: he just read books. All sorts of queer books, not like those the rest of us read. Books you'd expect the professors in college to read.

'Five minutes by my watch,' Rossignol told him. 'After that you're for it.'

Hippolyte by now was almost in tears. He remembered past razzings; Rossignol had three times fractured his spectacles, on one occasion stamping a pair of them underfoot.

'Five minutes, that's all. Better start thinking. I'll read your book till time's up. What's it about?'

Rossignol reached down his hand for the book. 'Come on, what's it about?' he shouted.

'Buddha,' Hippolyte stammered, 'it's about Buddha.'

'Buddha? What's that?'

'It's a god. A god they have out in India.'

'Yes, I know,' Rossignol roared. 'But what's it do? Can it strike anybody dead?'

'They sacrifice people to it,' Hippolyte said.

'All right,' Rossignol said, 'we'll play that, we'll play Buddha.'

'Play Buddha?' Hippolyte was astounded.

'Why not?' Rossignol roared, 'it's a new game, isn't it? Well, then. What do we have to do?'

'You have to get someone to represent Buddha,' Hippolyte said. He spoke with more assurance as the prospect of a razzing receded.

'All right, I'll be Buddha,' Rossignol said. 'And then what?'

'People bow down and worship you.'

Rossignol nodded, he thought this only natural.

'What about this sacrificing though?' he said. 'When do I start doing that?'

'You don't do it,' Hippolyte told him. 'Not if you're Buddha. The High Priest of Buddha does all that for you.'

'What do I do, then?'

'Nothing. You just sit there.'

'Too slow,' Rossignol said. He started to clamber down off the cannon.

'Come on,' he told Hippolyte, 'get up there. You're Buddha, I'll be the High Priest. Allons, dépêche-toi!'

Hippolyte scrambled up on the snout of the cannon, barking his knees and nearly falling off in his relief at the turn things had taken.

'Get set!' Rossignol shouted. 'Like the picture in this book!'

Hippolyte hastily arranged himself in the traditional attitude of a Buddha. Rossignol peered at the picture closely to make sure everything was correct. Then he flung the book in the dust in front of the cannon and shouted at us, 'Come on! Can't you see it's Buddha! Down on your knees, the lot of you. Bow down and worship Buddha!'

We all got quickly down in the dust.

'On your faces! Noses to the ground! Grovel!' Rossignol roared. He came behind and kicked a few of us who weren't grovelling enough. 'Pray to Buddha!' he shouted.

Hippolyte sat rigid on the cannon.

Rossignol, who had not himself got down in the dust, made a salaam and said, 'What are your wishes, O Buddha? Anyone you want sacrificed?'

Hippolyte didn't answer. He was feeling a bit dazed. He'd never expected to see us all grovelling on the ground in front of him.

'Victims!' Rossignol prompted in a menacing whisper.

'Victims,' Hippolyte mumbled obediently. 'Victims for Buddha.'

'Right! Victims!' Rossignol roared, turning on us. 'You hear that? Buddha wants victims. Stop rolling about in the dirt, you swabs. Get on your feet and find victims for the All-Highest!'

We all got up quickly, Rossignol helping us with kicks here and there.

'Where are we to find these victims?' I asked him.

'Anywhere! All around!' Rossignol roared, waving his arms.

'Out you go and look for 'em, all of you. Get cracking! I'll stay here and meditate in the temple.'

So off we all went to look for victims. I paired off with Cassin, he was my pal at the time.

'You go to the right, I'll go the left,' I told him. 'We'll meet back at the cannon with our victims.'

'Righto,' Cassin said, and he set off.

I went along by the lake and pretty soon I saw a kid going by on a scooter. He was about eight years old and looked a likely victim, so I gave him a hail.

'Here kiddo,' I said, 'how'd you like to play Buddha?'

'What's that?' he asked.

'New game. Come on.'

'Sure,' he said and started riding along by the side of me on his scooter.

But before we'd got very far I heard Cassin hollering out in the distance.

'Here,' I said to this kid, 'give me that scooter. Quick!'

I shoved him off it and paddled along full speed in the direction of the shouts. The kid ran along behind protesting.

Round the corner I came upon Cassin struggling with a group of kids. He had one by the hair and another by the seat of the pants. Two more were hacking at his shins and one was hitting him over the head with a cricket bat. All of them were yelling blue murder. I threw down the scooter and rushed to the assistance of Cassin. Charpentier appeared from out of the blue and threw himself into the scrum. It didn't take us long to subdue the kids and haul them along with us. Cassin followed giving them cuts with the cricket bat or whatever it was.

It was a satisfactory haul: the only snag was that when I looked round for the kid I'd originally got hold of, he'd vanished. His scooter had vanished too. He'd done a bunk when he saw what playing Buddha meant.

'Never mind,' I thought, 'plenty more where he came from.'

We got back to the cannon with our victims and the others were there too, each of them holding a kid they'd caught somehow.

'Good, good!' Rossignol said, rubbing his hands when he saw us. 'Plenty of victims. Now we'll start to put 'em through it.'

One of the kids began to whimper when he heard this.

'Ta gueule!' Rossignol roared at him. 'Shut your trap!' and called up to Hippolyte on the cannon, 'How d'you want 'em sacrificed, O Buddha?'

Buddha mumbled something about burning.

'Burning?' Rossignol said. 'How, burning?'

'Roasted alive,' I told him. 'On a pyre. That's how they sacrifice them out in India. Burnt offerings, see?'

'Like the golden calf,' Cassin said. He was a Protestant and had read the Old Testament.

'How d'you know they roast 'em?' Rossignol asked me. 'How can you know what they do out in India?'

'My grandfather was out there,' I told him. 'As an officer. He's often seen people being roasted in the Temple of Buddha.'

'All right then,' Rossignol said, 'we'll roast 'em. Got any matches?'

'No,' I said.

Cassin shook, his head. Charpentier hadn't any matches either. We none of us had matches.

'Roasting's off,' Rossignol said with regret. 'No matches. We'll have to just torture them. Torture do all right?' he bawled up to Buddha.

Buddha nodded. But at the word 'torture' the kid who had whimpered before now began to bawl at the top of his lungs. Others followed suit.

'Shut them up!' Rossignol shouted. 'Shut them up. Else their bloody mothers'll hear and there'll be hell to pay.'

We grabbed hold of the kids, but at that moment the band began to play, so there was no need. The music crashing out drowned the screaming of the kids. The mothers sat round the bandstand knitting peaceably, oblivious of what their offspring were going through.

Meanwhile the kids were being well and truly tortured. Hippolyte's eyes gleamed behind his glasses as their arms were twisted and they were forced to kneel in front of him.

'Bow to Buddha, you little bastards,' Rossignol roared. 'Lick the dust in front of the All Highest!'

They licked obediently. Rossignol poured some of the dust on their heads for good measure. He turned to Hippolyte and made his salaam.

'How's that, O Buddha? Anything else you want done to 'em?'

Buddha, instead of replying, shifted uneasily on the cannon as though he were getting restive.

'See that?' Rossignol shouted. 'Buddha's not satisfied, he's moving about. Carry on with the torture lest his wrath descend upon us.'

'It's not wrath,' Hippolyte explained, 'It's cramp, I've got cramp. This cannon's uncomfortable.'

'Uncomfortable?' Rossignol roared. 'Cramp? Rot! How can a god get cramp? Keep still or you'll have me up there after you.'

Thus rebuked by his High Priest, Buddha returned to his traditional impassivity.

'Right!' Rossignol roared, turning round. 'Now listen, you kids. From now on you're baptised into the Buddhist faith. You'll worship in the temple, that's this cannon, every day. Worship starts at 2.30. Mind you're on time tomorrow, otherwise you're for it! Got that?'

The kids, covered with dust and streaming with tears, nodded dumbly.

'Okay! Off you go now. Scram!'

The kids scampered off gladly. But one of them in his haste tripped over the book on Buddha which was still lying on the ground, and was hauled back to be given a real raclée by Rossignol himself.

'Kick the Sacred Book, would you, you little scut! I'll learn you!'

With a kick in the pants he dismissed the kid and turned round grinning.

'Not a bad day's work. We made a few converts there. More tomorrow. Meanwhile, the All Highest can buy us all ice-cream.'

He grabbed Hippolyte by the ankle and hauled him down off the cannon. Hippolyte landed thump on his back in the dust.

'Banquisettes!' Rossignol bellowed. 'Get up and buy us some Banquisettes!'

A man was passing with a tray, hollering 'Banquisettes! Chocolat glacé!' Hippolyte got up and ran after him. We all crowded round, he bought us one apiece. They cost a franc each, but Hippolyte didn't mind: it was worth that to be worshipped.

Next day it was raining, so the grotto became the Temple of Buddha instead of the cannon. Rossignol decided to have it there permanently in future. It was more secluded, and the kids couldn't be heard yelling. All of them rolled up in force and periodically we'd sally forth in search of new converts: they were no longer called victims.

The cult of Buddha spread like fascism. Buddhism became the official religion of the public gardens. Pretty soon nearly everyone was a convert. We no longer confined ourselves to kids: André Sorel and his crowd were roped in, although it took three of us and Rossignol himself to sit on Sorel while he was being converted.

Soon only Bertolon's crowd were unconverted. They were tough. They came from the old town and didn't play with us at all. Rossignol often talked about converting them, but even he thought twice before trying it on.

I'd been made Grand Inquisitor, on account of knowing the customs of India. I spent all my time thinking up new tortures: tourists being conducted through the grotto were sometimes surprised to find someone being sacrificed among the stalactites. Still, they never interfered. They probably thought it was one of the quaint local customs.

The most curious thing about all this, though, was the effect on Hippolyte himself. He became quite different. He was no longer shy, didn't stammer, he constantly called for more sacrifices and newer tortures: anyone who crossed him was ruthlessly excommunicated—which meant being driven out of the gardens altogether, after a duck in the lake.

'Buddha's riding for a fall,' I said to Cassin one day. 'He's got swelled-head. He'll get deposed if he doesn't watch out.'

'Who's going to depose him?' Cassin asked. 'Charpentier tried it, didn't he? And what happened?'

'Charpentier got excommunicated.'

'We'd get excommunicated too,' Cassan said.

'How about Bertolon?' I said.

'Bertolon? You mean...'

'Why not?' I said.

'It's an idea,' Cassin said.

But before we could contact Bertolon, he paid us a visit. In the middle of worship, too. One of our sentries preceded him, rolling down the steps of the grotto and landing on his back in front of Rossignol, who was half-way through a sacrifice.

Bertolon followed grinning, with one hand in his pocket scratching his crutch. He wore only a singlet on the upper part of his body, which was muscular and burnt almost black. He had a flat nose and thick lips. His face was almost black too. He came from Martinique and his mother was absolutely black.

Rossignol jumped up and went towards him menacingly.

'Who dares to desecrate the Temple of Buddha?' he roared.

Bertolon grinned and went on scratching. At last he said, 'I represent Brahma.'

'What?' Rossignol roared. 'What's that?'

'Brahma,' Bertolon said. 'I represent Brahma.'

'What's Brahma?'

'A rival god,' Bertolon told him.

Rossignol spat on the ground. 'And your sister,' he said.

'And yours,' Bertolon said. He spat too.

'See that?' Hippolyte howled from the rock where he was sitting with crossed legs. 'He spat! He spat in the Temple of Buddha! Sacrilege! Sacrifice him! Sacrifice him at once, for sacrilege!'

'You hear?' Rossignol shouted to us. 'Hearken to the voice of Buddha!'

He turned and butted Bertolon in the belly. Sorel rushed up behind and pulled Bertolon's head back by the hair. Rossignol threw his weight forward at the same time; Bertolon went down but as he hit the ground with Rossignol on top of him he let out a wild yell.

'Brahma! Brahmins to the rescue!'

Instantly Bertolon's gang, wearing turbans made out of newspaper, came plunging down the steps of the grotto.

A proper free-for-all started up. Hippolyte uncrossed his legs and danced about on top of his rock shouting, 'Fight for the faith! Fight for Buddha! Down with the Brahmins! Beat 'em up, boys!'

And of course the Brahmins were yelling, 'Down with Buddha,' and so on: the din was deafening.

Rossignol got up off Bertolon and dived at the Brahmins with his head down. His weight turned the scale in the end—that and the kids. The kids came in surprisingly useful. They were so small you couldn't get a decent smack at them. Clusters of kid clung to the legs of the Brahmins and brought them down.

Finally all the Brahmins were driven out of the grotto up the steps, except two we'd taken prisoner. These were promptly baptised in the lake and became Buddhists.

The remainder of the Brahmins besieged us for a time, flinging lumps of earth, one of which burst all over Buddha himself. I was rather pleased about that personally, but Hippolyte screamed for vengeance. Rivers of blood, he wanted.

Rossignol told him to shut his trap. 'Wait till tomorrow,' he said. 'You'll get all the vengeance you want then.'

Next day instead of worship he took us all to a bazaar in the old town. This place sold a special kind of pistol that fired small packets of gunpowder instead of bullets.

'There you are,' Rossignol told Hippolyte, 'Buy us one of these guns each. Then we'll avenge you.'

Hippolyte started to count out his money on the counter. It took him a whole week's pocket-money to buy us the pistols, with enough ammunition to go round.

When we got back to the grotto the Brahmins were in there smashing up the altar. We rushed down the steps firing off our packets of cordite; the explosions echoed thunderously in the cave; the Brahmins were put to flight.

But Hippolyte was angry because no prisoners had been taken. He didn't think he'd been adequately avenged. For some reason he put the blame on me. I got angry too. I got so angry my pistol went off. The shot hit a rock by his head and the explosion knocked his glasses off.

At once I was seized and sacrificed. They couldn't duck me in the lake because the guard was watching, but I got kicked out of the grotto for good.

'All right,' I thought. 'That settles it.'

I went straight to the temple of Brahma, a place called Les Sables, on the other side of the gardens, and shouted for Bertolon. I was seized by two Brahmins and brought before him.

'I'm no longer a Buddhist,' I told him, 'I've quit. I've come over to the Brahmin faith.'

'How do we know you're not a spy?' Bertolon said.

'Wait till you hear my plan,' I told him.

'Spill it,' he said.

I did. My plan was simply this: to kidnap Buddha himself. I knew where he lived, it'd be easy. All we had to do was lie in wait for him on his way home.

'Sounds all right,' Bertolon said, 'we'll see how things go. But first you've got to go through the conversion.'

'I'm already converted,' I said. 'I believe in Brahma and in Bertolon his prophet.'

'You've not been baptised though,' Bertolon said. 'Baptise him, boys!'

So I was baptised a Brahmin. It was painful but not more so than some of the tortures I'd invented myself.

No sooner had I been baptised than Cassin came limping in. He'd been excommunicated too.

'I want to become a Brahmin,' he told Bertolon.

'You'll have to be baptised first.'

'Have a heart,' Cassin told him. 'I've only just been sacrificed. Give me time to get over it.'

Bertolon hadn't a heart. 'Baptise him, boys,' he said.

They baptised him.

Then we all went off to ambush Buddha. We waited half an hour and Bertolon began saying if I'd brought them along there for nothing I'd catch it hot.

'Ssh!' I said. 'Here he comes.'

Hippolyte groped his way towards us. His glasses had cracked when they fell off and he couldn't see properly. Suddenly we surrounded him.

Bertolon said, 'The All-Highest himself,' and with a sweep of his hand knocked Hippolyte's straw hat flying. I stamped promptly on the crown of it. Someone else shot between his legs and tripped him up. Buddha went over backwards, screaming for help.

'I'll help you!' Bertolon told him and stuffed a lump of dirty rag in his open mouth. We were having a high old time with him when all of a sudden an upstairs window opened.

'Vagabonds! Camels! What are you doing to my son?' a woman's voice shrilled down at us.

'Watch out!' I said. 'His mother!'

We all decamped just as the concièrge came dashing out of Hippolyte's house with a cudgel in his hand. Bertolon and another Brahmin tried dragging Hippolyte along the ground with them, but the concièrge was hot on their heels so they had to abandon him, Bertolon snatching his glasses and shoving them in his pocket before making off.

When we were safe again, several streets away, he dropped the glasses down a drain and clapped me on the back.

'Good work,' he said. 'You're a true Brahmin. We'll meet at the temple tomorrow and think up some more plans.'

'Have you got any money?' I asked him.

'Why?' Bertolon said. 'You're English, you ought to have plenty. What about all your dollars?'

'I've got a little,' I said, 'but not enough.'

'Daresay I can scrounge some,' he said. 'What's it for?'

'Tell you tomorrow,' I said.

Next day I led them to this bazaar in the old town.

'No good,' Bertolon said. 'We haven't enough to buy these pistols.'

'But we can buy the ammunition,' I said. 'Fire it out of catapults. Better than pistols. Longer range. Like bombs, see?'

Bertolon was impressed. 'You got good brains for an English,' he said. 'I'll make you High Priest for this.'

So I became the High Priest of Brahma and when the Buddhists tried to raid our temple to avenge the attack on Hippolyte, we drove them off easily with our bombs.

Then the Buddhists came back with bombs and catapults too. It was a large-scale attack. A regular religious war raged for days on end after that. All over the gardens. At last the public began to object. They got sick of bombs whizzing about and bursting over their heads. So they complained to the Guard.

But the Guard, a superannuated soldier with only one leg couldn't catch up with us. We'd just dodge out of his way and sometimes fire a few bombs at him, while he hopped about on his wooden leg and cursed.

The municipal authorities got to hear of it in the finish. They had the wooden-legged Guard shifted and stuck in a younger one who could run like hell. He chased us all over the show, caught some of us too. Sorel got hauled off to the police-station, I believe.

The war was driven out into the streets round the public gardens. There it raged furiously for a time and then stopped. It had to stop because the summer holidays were over and we all went back to school again.

It was over a year before I saw Rossignol again. And when I saw him I didn't recognise him at first. We none of us did. I was talking to Cassin over by the cannon one day when this fellow came up to us. He had a check cap on and white flannel trousers: they were long trousers. Like his tennis shoes they were dazzlingly white. And he wore an eyeglass. A horm-rimmed monocle screwed into his eye.

'Don't you remember me?' he said. 'Surely you haven't forgotten? Rossignol.'

'Rossignol?' we echoed.

We stared at him. Could it be? It was. But he was thin. In height he hadn't grown, but all his fat had melted completely away. I don't suppose he could have weighed more than seven stone. His face was thin as well. Under the rakish check cap his delicate beaked nose now seemed quite appropriate. Of course looking back, it must have been glands. But we didn't know about that then. To us it seemed hardly possible.

Rossignol screwed his monocle more firmly into his eye and said: 'Remember Buddha? Those were the days. Nothing like that doing now. None of you blokes got enough go to organise anything. You need me to organise you.'

But his voice hadn't the old assurance. It had lost its thickness too. It was no longer hoarse: a thin voice, quite light and high, like a girl's.

'Remember the tortures?' Rossignol said. 'In the temple?'

Cassin and I nodded. We remembered the tortures only too well.

'All the sacrifices?' Rossignol went on. 'We ought to revive them. Old Hippolyte's not here, gone into a seminary so they tell me. Don't matter, we'll get another Buddha. How about it, eh? How about reviving the tortures?'

'We'll revive them,' I told him. 'Remember the time I got excommunicated?'

'Sure,' Rossignol said, 'I remember.'

'So do I,' I said. 'You remember, Cassin?'

'Sure,' Cassin said, 'I remember.'

We'd edged gradually closer to Rossignol by this time. I shot out my hand and caught hold of his wrist.

'Hey!' Rossignol shouted, trying to pull free, 'What's the game? What the hell you doing?'

'Just reviving some of the tortures,' I told him. I twisted his wrist up behind his back and forced him down on his knees. Cassin hauled him up and slapped him a good one across the face. Rossignol gave a yelp and his monocle fell out. I picked it up and put it in my pocket. Then I caught one of Rossignol's legs by the ankle. Cassin caught hold of the other. We started to bump him on the ground. He tried butting us with his head but there was no weight behind it. Soon he was too exhausted to yell, he could only sob. We dragged his flannel trousers in the dirt and played football with his check cap. Cassin finally scored a goal, kicking it right over the railings on to the war memorial.

Rossignol, who'd been lying face down in the dust, suddenly scrambled up and started to run. His silk shirt was torn and the tail of it hung out of his trousers. He ran and ran. We chased him for a bit but we were laughing so hard we couldn't go far. Rossignol disappeared into the distance, holding his sides and sobbing.

I took his monocle out and stuck it in my eye.

'By gosh that looks good,' Cassin said. 'Suits you. I'd carry on wearing that if I were you. Think I'll get one myself.'

So that's how we all came to wear monocles. Only Rossignol was not allowed to wear one. Whenever he bought a monocle we smashed it for him at once. We stopped razzing him after while, but now that he was no longer fat he became a complete nonentity. In the end he gave up coming to the gardens altogether.

As for Buddhism it was never revived. It just died a natural death. But you see, it's true: I really have been a Buddhist. Brahmin, too.

And now I don't belong to any religion at all.

We travelled down first-class. It cost two quid but I thought we might as well be comfortable.

We were not comfortable. All the first-class carriages were full and we stood in the corridor with people falling over our suitcases and swearing at us.

'Never mind,' Sally kept saying, 'it'll be all right once we get there.'

This trip to Oxford had been her suggestion. Both of us were determined to get away from London for a bit, but at first we could not decide where to go. Brighton was a banned area, Sally's parents lived at Windsor. Wales was too far for a weekend.

So Oxford it was. The idea appealed to me. Oxford was associated in my mind with grey stones and sported oaks and cloistral calm occasionally shattered by undergraduates debagging one another and being sick after bump suppers. I'd never been there, but Sally had. She had in fact been educated there.

She'd come a certain distance since then, via Bloomsbury and Soho and the back bar of the Café Royal where the script-writers sat on high stools drinking Scotch, but no stage of this journey showed in her face. She had her hair done behind her ears and looked about ten years old. I began to fear that no hotel would let us in when they saw her.

'My godfathers, I could use a drink,' she said.

I said: 'Same here.'

Neither of us had had one since the pubs closed at three. It was now nearly half-past six. The train was drawing at last into Oxford.

My mental picture of the place may have been muddled, but I did expect to see from the window a perspective of dreaming spires. I saw instead a gasworks. This was immediately blotted out by an advertisement for timber and a line of trucks filled with coal.

A surge of people down the corridor tore me away from the window before I could see more. A man jolted my ribs with his elbow; I was hit in the face by someone's respirator. The owner of this said 'Thank you' as he pushed past: I could not see what I had done to earn his gratitude.

Hefting the suitcases, one of which was unbelievably heavy, I forced a way down the platform full of uniforms. Trolleys piled high with luggage impeded our passage. People were standing on some of these trolleys signalling frantically to their friends. Getting through the barrier we were almost crushed to death, it was like bank holiday week.

I hadn't expected anything of this sort; I began to wonder whether we'd find anywhere to sleep. But Sally had evolved a plan of campaign. 'Get hold of a taxi, tip the driver ten bob, and tell him to find us somewhere. That always works.'

But in this instance it didn't, because there was only one taxi outside the station and this was already besieged by at least eight American soldiers offering the driver heavy bribes.

Sally remembered a friend of hers who had a bungalow nearby and who might be willing to put us up. 'I'll give her a ring while you park the luggage.'

I re-entered the station and stood in a queue behind several, R.A.F. sergeants checking-in kitbags. When it came to my turn the woman at the left-luggage counter stared in astonishment at my cigarette-holder. It took some time before I could get her to understand what I was saying.

Sally reappeared at my side. 'The station phone doesn't work.'

'Why not?'

'It's out of order.'

'Let's have a drink and then ring.'

'I'm gasping for one,' Sally said.

We walked hand-in-hand down a hill. At the foot of this a hotel loomed up, soot-grey and with its name painted in yellow. I approached it but on the door a notice said simply: FULL UP. We turned away and walked through a short tunnel across a bridge over a canal full of stagnant water. Soldiers clumped through the streets in ammunition boots and people were queuing for a bus. There were no undergraduates visible.

We walked what seemed to me some distance. Sally pointed out Parker's Bookshop. It was shut. The window displayed books by a man with whom I'd got drunk the night before. I felt that one did not come all this way in order to look at his books. Another shop window had trusses in it and a tray of glass eyes. Sally pointed to a building with ivy growing on the walls. 'Balliol,' she said.

'Is that it?' I was impressed. 'Did you ever see Benjamin Jowett going in there?' I asked her.

'Never,' she said.

We went up some steps to a hotel. On the reception desk was a card saying NO ACCOMMODATION. Beyond this was the bar. Staff-officers slapping each other on the back and women with false eye-lashes. One might as well have been in Shepherd's. I got eventually to the counter. A woman was drawing beer at one end of this; another was languidly collecting glasses brought to her by a page-boy.

'Two Scotch,' I said to the languid one.

'No Scotch,' she said quickly, as though calling check.

'Gin then. Gin and orange.'

'No gin. No spirits at all. Only beer.' She smiled and stood back in triumph: it was checkmate.

I reported back to Sally. 'No spirits only beer.'

'Let's get out of here,' she said.

We turned into a square where there were two telephone boxes painted a peculiar yellow. I thought at first on seeing these that I had suddenly become bilious. 'We'll go to the Mitre,' Sally said.

'Will they have Scotch?'

'It's possible.'

We were now in a fairly narrow street lined with shops and packed out with people of all kinds. I wondered if this was the High. I was about to ask Sally when an American negro pushed me off the pavement and almost under a bus. I did not see much difference between this and Dean Street, Soho. I was beginning to dislike the place.

But at the Mitre there were two chairs vacant near the window and they had Scotch. The waiter looked askance at Sally: for a moment I feared a repetition of the time when in a London pub the proprietor had asked us to leave because he said the young lady was under age and he had to protect the other customers. However this time nothing happened.

Sally, reviving under the Scotch, said: 'You know, time's getting on. We'd better look round for somewhere to stay.'

I agreed. Frankly, I was beginning to get cold feet. I foresaw us spending the night under a haystack. Only there didn't seem to be any haystacks around. I parked Sally in a pub up an alleyway and walked down a street which she had told me was full of boarding houses.

There was no indication on the outside of these to show that this was so. They certainly had geraniums in pots and cards in the windows, but the cards said 'STIRRUP PUMP HERE,' 'SAND HERE,' 'WATER HERE': a sort of civil-defence serial which continued ad nauseam down the street.

I screwed up courage at last to knock on the doors. It reminded me unpleasantly of canvassing in peacetime for a vacuum-cleaner firm: there was the same sinking feeling, the same grim faces confronted one.

'Oh, no.' 'Booked right up.' 'Nothing till October.'

Only one woman was helpful: she sent me miles in another direction to a Mrs. Jackson who might possibly have a room. But Mrs. Jackson hadn't: 'Doubt whether you'll find anything in Oxford, not over the week-end. If I was you I'd catch the last train back.'

It took me a considerable time to find the alleyway where Sally's pub was. It was jammed to the door with Waafs and flight sergeants. I came into the saloon bar just in time to see a drunk lieutenant cannon into Sally and knock a glass of Scotch clean out of her hand. He seemed annoyed because the Scotch spilled on to his uniform.

'What the hell's going on here?' I said.

'Let's get out,' Sally said.

The barman picked up the glass. 'It isn't broken, that's one good thing.'

'Pity,' I said. I was in a bad temper.

'No luck?' Sally asked when we got outside.

'None. We'd better try the station and your taxi idea again.'

But we arrived at the station at an inopportune moment: another train had just come in and we were met by a fresh horde of visitors coming down the hill carrying suitcases. There were no taxis. It was gradually getting dark.

I said: 'I'm hungry. What about something to eat?'

'Yes, and I can ring up my friend from the restaurant.'

The restaurant she took me to was the upstairs of a pub. On the menu it said Roast Duck but in the end this turned out to be baked beans on toast. Sally went to look for the phone: it was on a stairway by the saloon bar and unapproachable because of American soldiery in a solid mass making love to girls all the way up the stairs.

'Never mind,' I said to Sally, 'we can phone outside when we've eaten.'

We ate the baked beans and ordered coffee.

'No coffee,' the waitress said. 'We don't serve coffee, not up here. You might get it downstairs, I couldn't say I'm sure.'

'The bill then,' I said.

Getting the bill was another problem. The waitress added it up several times before it came out right. 'I'm not used to this kind of work as you can see,' she said, giggling.

Outside it was by now pitch-black.

Sally led me to the hotel where we had tried unsuccesfully to obtain Scotch. A revolving door, going round at a terrific rate, threw us into the lounge. The one phone box was occupied by a sailor. I thought we might have a beer while waiting for him to vacate it, but everyone in the bar was sitting gloomily over empty glasses and the woman behind the counter now leaned back with her hands behind her head and a beatific smile on her face.

'No whisky. No gin. No rum. No beer. No nothing. All sold out.'

The sailor was still in possession of the phone as we came back into the lounge. From his attitude it was evident that he intended to make it an all-night session.

'We'll try the ones in the square,' Sally said.

The revolving door spun us into the black-out. I missed my footing and only saved myself from falling down the steps by clutching on to Sally's hair. Sally screamed. A voice said disgustedly out of the darkness: '*Drunks*. Can't even stand up.'

Searchlights swinging over the sky showed us that the yellow-painted phone-boxes in the square were also occupied. In one of them were three people: two men and a girl. We walked on underneath trees. We passed a parking-place for bicycles. Hundreds of them ranked in rows, shining nickel under the searchlight's beam. This sight depressed me. I hate bicycles.

We came to a corner where there were two more call-boxes. These two were full up, and a short queue stood outside them waiting. A much longer queue waited for a bus. People overflowed from the pubs on to the pavement. Inside, stern voices could be heard saying 'Time, ladies and gentlemen, please.'

I was shocked. 'Impossible,' I said. 'It's only just after nine.'

'Nothing's impossible in this place,' Sally said.

We'd completely given up the idea of phoning. Our steps were now headed inexorably towards the station. We looked guiltily away from each other and did not speak. A drunk man played a ukulele in the gutter and a quartet of soldiers sang *Bless 'Em All* with their arms about each other's shoulders. 'Time, gentlemen, please,' resounded on all sides from the closing pubs.

The last train for London left at 9.30. We were just in time to catch it.

I was twelve at the time: immeasurably older than Mimile, who was only eight. But after twenty years I can still see in mind that small stocky figure topped with an enormous blunt bullet-head, the weight of which, when he ran, caused him frequently to overbalance and fall down, barking once again his bare knees already covered with scars and the golden-brown crusts of half-healed cuts.

Then he would climb slowly to his feet, his face would crumple and become crimson and a mournful bellow of pain would burst from him while he stood, grubby fists clenched, tears making channels in the dust of his cheeks, blown out to the size of balloons as he bawled, his eyes swollen to slits.

He had a powerful voice, and his bellowing whenever he fell and hurt himself disturbed the concentration of older boys playing marbles after school on the public *Place*, myself among them.

'*Ta gueule!*' one of these would shout, scrambling up furious, having missed a difficult shot through an unexpected explosion of Mimile's misery too close to his ear, 'shut your trap, you twirp! I'll give you something to bawl about seriously if you don't shut down double-quick!'

These threats were often accompanied by a clout that, owing to the hardness of Mimile's skull, caused the hand of the donor to tingle. But a slap of this sort seldom had the desired effect of making Mimile shut up. On the contrary, his bawling became redoubled in volume, with an added note of utter despair that made all the players rise in a body and drive him (unless he fell again) to a distance from which his voice was audible only as a wail.

Mimile's parents, now retired, had once owned a café and had made money. Mimile was their only child, born late in life to a thin bitter woman with social ambitions and a jovial blustering fellow in black alpaca and a straw hat, who wore a watch-chain across his belly. They bought their small son expensive toys which the other boys smashed up and clothes of good material which soon got ragged and torn.

His mother was against him being allowed to play on the *Place* at all, where he might pick up with boys from the communal school, but the father, who was less of a snob, saw no harm in it. He remembered being eight himself, although this was some time ago.

The couple could be seen on Sunday mornings leading Mimile home from a service in the chapel. They were Protestants from Lille originally; and this, in a Catholic community, was one more point against Mimile. Religion was rarely mentioned but all the same it made him different. Why even I, the English, was a Catholic like all the rest!

I sometimes had a feeling of sympathy for Mimile. My foreign birth might so easily have made me an outcast also. As it was I was not allowed to forget it for long. Then, too, undue precocity at school had caused me to be placed in a form with boys two years older than myself. I was sometimes held up by the professors as an example to shame the other pupils with. That a foreigner, younger than yourselves, should write your own language with fewer faults than you, and so on and so forth. This did not at first make for popularity, though I managed to live a good deal of it down. At the same time I had come in for a fair share of bullying and therefore rarely joined the others in clouting Mimile or in giving him a *savon* (the victim's head held between one boy's knees while another rubs his knuckles across the skull in a fierce dry shampoo). Most times I merely stood and watched. I didn't intervene on his behalf. Not I. I didn't want to get my face bashed in. I was waiting till I grew bigger in order to beat other boys up myself.

It was Gaston Lagardere, whose father owned the antique shop on the corner, who first gave Mimile the nickname by which he soon became known to everyone. Mimile's head was initially responsible.

His head, as I've already mentioned, was enormous, thick and heavy: you could have battered down a door with it. It was also shaved all over, like a Prussian general's: the hair never allowed to grow longer than a blond stubble. The rough furry feel of this stubble under the knuckling hand was what made giving him a *savon* such a peculiar delight.

One day, when they'd nothing better to do, the fellows formed a ring round Mimile and started asking him why his head was shaved in this way. Mimile didn't know. He thought he could see a *savon* impending again and his mouth opened to bawl in anticipation.

'Shut up!' Gaston Lagardere shouted. 'Don't you begin that row.

Answer at once and nothing'll happen to you. If not...'

Mimile couldn't answer. He just mumbled that his *maman* made him have it done.

I said: 'At the priest's school I used to go to they made us have our heads shaved, too. It was in case of bugs.'

'Bugs!' Gaston took me up, delighted. 'Bugs! That's it, that's why! Mimile's mamma shaves his head every week, otherwise he'd have bugs for sure. Crawling with 'em!'

'*Les morpions!*' roared another, who didn't know what these were and imagined them to be head-lice.

Mimile began to cry. He tearfully denied the existence of bugs in his home. Some of the fellows started to go through his head to make sure he told the truth. They said he lied. They made out his head was like a jungle.

'Like the prairies!' Marcel Sansault screamed, digging his fingers into Mimile's stubbly scalp.

'Like the Far West!' Gaston shouted, pronouncing it Vest, and capping all. He brought the house down. The boys were doubled-up laughing, slapping their bare thick thighs. They made a ring round the weeping Mimile and danced about delightedly.

'The Far Vest!' they shouted. 'Mimile's the Far Vest!'

They even made a song out of it, to the tune of *Je cherche après Titine*. Mimile didn't know what the Far West was, but he imagined it to be an insult and connected with bugs. He began to bawl at the top of his voice. The boys were in such good humour they didn't mind.

From that moment onwards Mimile was referred to exclusively as the Far West. Cowboy whoops were made whenever he appeared. The boys pranced around on the backs of invisible bronchos, scratching their heads significantly the while. Snatches of the Far West Song pursued him during his Sunday transit with his parents across the *Place*.

On Sunday all the boys wore cloth check caps. I'd pleaded with my father to let me wear a cap too, but he refused. He said he wouldn't have his son going about looking like a cad.

Mimile was more successful. One Sunday a cap appeared pulled down on his huge cropped head. The older boys were outraged by this presumption. First they pulled the cap over his eyes so that he staggered about blinded and bawling, then they played football with it and tore out the lining. His mother appeared while this was going on, and everyone fled.

To comfort him for the destruction of the cap, Mimile was bought a big rubber ball, painted crimson, yellow and blue, with a terrific bounce to it. It bounced a bit too close to Marcel Sansault, who got his hands on it, followed by a wailing Mimile. Marcel with a drop-kick sent it soaring over the railings into the road. It was run over by a car, one of its painted sides irreparably deflated. Mimile's howls of grief were louder than we'd ever heard before. They were so loud we were afraid they might bring his mamma on the scene again. We all disappeared off the *Place* at the double.

Things like this were always happening to him. No need to speak of the steam-engine that wound up with a key or the model motor car with a hood you could raise or lower. After these had been disposed of, he became interested in our game of marbles. He was not allowed to take part in it, of course, but he stood about and looked on. His round eyes followed, absorbed, the flight of the marbles: the alleys made of blown glass and agate; those in the ring, of plaster: while the boys waiting their turn watched with the shrewd judicial expression with which they would watch, in years to come, the billiard balls roll down the green baize table, leaning on their cues in the corner café.

Mimile was fascinated. Off he went to Maman and persuaded her to buy him marbles. Of course she got the wrong sort. Huge great things like cannon balls, made of stone. Mimile could hardly get his small hands round them. He didn't have to for long. Gaston got rid of them for him, down a grating in the gutter. He still came to watch us play, though. We tried to drive him off, but it was no use. He always came back.

Then one day we looked up and there was another watcher beside Mimile. It was Luc, a big boy from the communal school, not the one we all went to. He was very tough. Not even Gaston cared to fight him.

For a time he stood there with his hands in the pockets of his shorts, chewing Spearmint gum steadily: a habit picked up from watching American films at the local cinema.

'Want to join in?' we asked him, uneasy under his contemptuous glance.

'Nah,' he said, shifting the gum from cheek to cheek. 'That's a kid's game that is. What you want's this.'

He took one hand from his pocket. He held in it something wrapped round with cord. He flung it through the air. A wooden top fell on the earth and started to spin, released from the end of the cord. We all scrambled up to watch: it was like magic.

'I got another one here,' Luc said without expression, chewing his gum. He produced an even bigger top and threw it negligently to spin beside the other. We were enthralled.

'How d'you do it?' we asked him.

'Simple.' He showed us how to wind the cord, how to hold the top between finger and thumb, how to throw it down through the air. He let us have a go for ourselves; we made a muck of it.

'Nah, not like that, like this.'

Mimile, the Far West, was enthralled too. He squatted on his hams watching the whirling tops with his eyes bulging out. He followed us later to the Bazaar where we all bought tops. We let him trail along, we were far too excited to bother about him. When he'd watched us buy the tops, he trotted off quite happily home to his Maman with his huge head wagging from side to side. He did not even fall down.

Next day we were all on the *Place* hurling our tops through space, we'd already become quite expert at it. Then Sansault came rushing up.

'Seen what the Far West's got? Ruddy great top. Not like ours. Wait till you see it!'

Mimile at this moment came trotting into sight. He carried in both hands a parcel wrapped in tissue paper. He was breathless with excitement. He came right up to us.

'What've you got there?' Gaston asked him sternly. 'Show us quick, Far West!'

Mimile was only too eager to do so. He tore the tissue wrapping off and disclosed a simply gigantic top made of tin and painted luridly, like the rubber ball he'd had before. It must have set Maman back quite a bit. We stared thunderstruck as Mimile stroked its tin surface tenderly with his fingers.

'But how's it work?' Gaston said at last. 'Where's the string?'

Mimile placed the huge painted top down on the ground. His eyes shone with pride. Then he brought out one word:

'Mechanical!'

'Look,' he said, 'I'll show you.'

First he wound the top with a tin key, then he pressed a brass button in it. The top shot from his hand with a loud humming noise and started to spin steadily right in front of our feet. It spun about twice as long as even Luc's largest wooden top, string and all. It seemed as though it might go on humming and spinning for ever. But Marcel Sansault stopped that. He stepped forward and gave it a thundering kick, which lifted it clean off the ground and flung it half across the *Place*. When it came down it wasn't spinning any more. It lay still: again like the rubber ball, one of its sides was dented in.

Mimile's face crumpled immediately. Then it swelled up crimson. His mouth opened wet on an absolute roar. His eyes closed completely, his small fingers curled into ineffectual fists. He bawled as though his lungs were about to burst.

All of us watched expressionless—except Luc. Luc suddenly came striding forward.

'What're you doing to the poor kid?' he shouted.

'Let him alone!' rounding on Sansault: 'You! What'd you have to kick his top for, you little squirt! Eh?'

He grabbed Sansault by the collar of his jersey and slapped him hard across the face, knocking him back against the railings.

'That'll learn you! Let the kid alone!'

The rest of us were too staggered to move. Even Mimile stopped bawling he was so surprised.

'Here, kiddo,' Luc said, turning to him, 'don't you take on so. Maybe it's not broken. Maybe it'll work. Come and have a look.'

Mimile was still sniffing, but the tears had dried quickly on his hot cheeks. He stumbled over and bent down with Luc beside his precious top. Alas, it wouldn't work. We watched in silence while they tried vainly to resurrect it. No use. Mimile's fists clenched. He looked as though about to bawl again. But Luc hastily thrust a hand in his pocket and produced from it his biggest wooden top.

'Look-here, have this one instead. See, it'll go as good as the other, no kidding. Just you see.'

Mimile didn't wait to see. He didn't even say thank you. He clutched blindly at the top and, with it in his hand, set off at a stumbling trot across the *Place*, heading for home. He fell down once, but he didn't cry.

He just picked himself up in silence and went stumbling on.

Luc said to us: 'Now don't let me catch you making that kid cry again, or it'll be the worse for you, see!' and he swaggered off. Not even Gaston said anything to stop him.

But Mimile's misadventures for the day were by no means over: We heard about it later on. Maman caught him coming in, and first she took the wooden top and threw it away, and then she beat him soundly, for exchanging his brand-new expensive top for a filthy dirty object such as boys from the communal school played with.

Mimile wasn't allowed to play on the *Place* for some time after that.

A good thing for him, perhaps. Soon after the incident of the top I started to grow very rapidly. I grew enormous, and seized power immediately. The fellow-feeling that I had for Mimile vanished overnight. I might even have made a victim out of him, but by that time he was no longer about: his parents had sent him to school in another town.

I don't know what became of him. Perhaps—who knows—he grew very big and was able to bully smaller boys in his turn. Let's hope so, anyway.

Happy As The Day Is Long

Directly I came into the shop I saw the Baron was pretty tight. The Baron had been trepanned and had a silver plate in his skull. When this plate pressed on his head and hurt him, he used to drink whisky to dull the pain. At these times he always got tight.

He was a little man with a wrinkled yellow face and supposed to be French, though he spoke English with an Italian accent. He was a dealer in antiques and the shop belonged to him.

When he saw me come in, he staggered forward a few paces, almost overturning the oil stove that stood in the middle of the floor, and shouted: 'Hey, you rascal! Why you not been to see me, hey?'

He swayed to-and-fro, keeping his balance by clutching hold of an antique table. He was wearing a long blue overcoat with a velvet collar. He slammed me hard on the back with his hand and shouted again: 'Why you not been to see me? Where you been hiding, hey?'

'I've been ill,' I told him.

'Hey? Ill? Oh, I am sorry.' The Baron's manner changed. He lowered his voice and putting his hand on my shoulder, said: 'I am so very sorry. But you are better now, yes?'

'Yes,' I said, 'I'm better now.'

The Baron's eyes filled with tears: 'I am so glad,' he said. 'I am so very glad.'

There were other people in the shop besides the Baron. These included Mrs Neville-Stanforth and the Baron's secretary, a small woman who wore a green hat. A middle-aged man whom I didn't know was sitting quietly on a chair in the corner, smiling to himself.

Mrs Neville-Stanforth said: 'Hullo, Sylvester! All right again now?'

'Yes, thanks,' I said, 'going strong.'

I shook hands with the Baron's secretary. She stood behind a table with cakes and cups on it. There was also a bottle of Scotch, half empty, and some glasses. The Baron came forward unsteadily and said: 'I am so glad to see you, my dear friend.' He flung out his hand towards the table and shouted at his secretary: 'Give the boy a drink, no?'

'I was just going to, monsieur.'

The Baron glared at her fiercely. Mrs Neville-Stanforth said: 'Hadn't you better sit down my dear?'

'Sit down?' The Baron stared at her. 'What for I sit down? You sink I cannot stand? You sink I am trunk?'

'No, no, of course I don't think you're drunk.'

'I am not trunk,' the Baron said with dignity. He pointed suddenly at the man in the corner and shouted: 'Why for you grin? You sink I am funny, yes?'

'I think you're very funny,' the man in the corner said with a chuckle. His voice was low and rather husky.

'He sinks I am funny!' The Baron turned indignantly to me. 'You do not sink I am funny, no?'

'That's all right, old chap,' the other man said. 'just you sit down and don't worry your head.'

'Sit down! Sit down! Why for I cannot stand, hey?'

'Don't ask me, old chap,' the other man said, 'ask yourself.'

I took the drink the secretary held out to me and sat down by the stove.

'Would you like some cake?' the secretary said.

'Thanks,' I said, 'just a slice.'

I hadn't had anything much to eat all day, and the cake tasted good. I was glad I'd called on the Baron: when you're down to your last ten bob, a free meal and drink isn't to be sneezed at. It was difficult, though, having to eat the cake as if I wasn't really hungry.

Outside, in the King's Road, Chelsea, it was raw and cold and the cold came in through the half-open door from the street outside. The oil stove didn't do much about heating unless you actually sat on it.

'Will you have another slice of cake?' the secretary said.

'Yes, I think I will, thanks.'

Mrs Neville-Stanforth had at last persuaded the Baron to sit down. He sat astride a hard chair with his arms leaning on the back of it, as though he were riding a horse.

'What about that job you were after?' Mrs Neville-Stanforth said. 'The one with Hatrick I mean. Did you manage to get it?'

'No,' I said.

'D'you know Hatrick then?' the man in the corner asked me.

'I've met him once or twice.'

'I know Hatrick,' the Baron said. 'He is a rascal, that one.'

'I'm sorry you didn't get the job,' Mrs Neville-Stanforth said.

'So am I,' I said. 'Damn sorry.' I finished off the glass of whisky.

'I understood it was all settled,' Mrs Neville-Stanforth said. 'I thought he'd practically given you the job.'

'So he had,' I told her. 'But I got ill, you see. I was in bed three weeks, and when I got up I found he'd given it to someone else.'

'He is a rascal, that Hatrick,' the Baron said.

'Of course I couldn't expect him to wait for ever,' I said.

'What was the job?' the man in the corner asked.

'Painting decorative panels for one of his houses.'

The door came open and two ladies walked into the shop. A blast of cold air came in with them and the flame of the oil stove shot up with a humming sound. The Baron sprang to his feet. He became entangled in the legs of the chair and finally it fell over and he kicked it out of his way. He staggered over to the ladies, who were looking rather surprised.

'Yes?' he said in a menacing manner, 'Yes?'

One of the ladies looked wildly around and picked up a vase at random. 'How much is this, please?' she asked.

'That?' The Baron took the vase from her and looked at it, holding it at arms length away from him. 'That is tree guineas! Tree!' He shook the vase at her and glared menacingly. 'Tree!' he shouted again.

For a moment it seemed as if the lady would he stampeded into buying the vase, but her companion showed more presence of mind. 'No,' she said firmly. 'That is too expensive. Thank you very much.'

'Tree guineas!' the Baron shouted, waving the vase after them as they hurried out.

The Baron's secretary bent forward and picked up the overturned chair. 'Oh, dear, oh dear,' she said. She looked very distressed.

Mrs Neville-Stanforth said in an undertone to the man in the corner: 'Can't you get him out of here? He'll drive everyone away in his present state.'

'Leave it to me,' the man said.

The Baron closed the shop door with a great deal of noise and replaced the vase on the table where it stood. He said: 'All day they come in, they look round, they buy nossing. I am sick of such peoples. They are no good. I tell to them "Get out" if they will not buy. So!'

He came back to the table and stood swaying to-and-fro. I reached out and took the last piece of cake from the plate. I was still damned hungry.

The Baron's secretary said: 'Oh, I'm so sorry. I didn't offer you… will you have another drink?'

'Thank you, I will.'

'That is right,' the Baron said. 'I am pleased you have come, my friend.' He patted me on the shoulder and grinned. 'I too will have another drink, hey?'

'Come and have one in the pub,' the man in the corner said. 'That bottle's nearly empty.'

'Alas,' the Baron said, 'I cannot leave the shop.'

'I'll look after the shop if you like, monsieur,' the secretary said, trying not to sound too eager.

'No,' the Baron said, 'I must be here myself in person.'

'Come on old chap,' the other man said, 'we'll only be gone a few minutes.'

I finished the cake and my second drink and held out my hands to the stove. It wasn't so cold with the door shut, but the stove didn't give out much heat.

'I consent on one condition,' the Baron said. 'That my dear friend here,' he patted my shoulder, 'come also with us. Yes?'

'Will you come along?' the man in the corner asked me.

'Sure,' I said, 'I'll come.'

'There you are,' the man in the corner said.

'Wait just one moment,' the Baron said. He tipped the last of the bottle into his glass and drank it off neat. Then he said: 'So!'

'All set?' the other man said. He rose to his feet.

The Baron looked at his secretary. 'You will see after the shop?'

'Yes, monsieur.'

The Baron started to give her minute instructions regarding the price of certain valuable antiques on sale in the shop.

'Come on,' the other man said, 'don't be all night about it.'

'Yes, yes, I come,' the Baron said.

'Goodbye, my dear,' Mrs Neville-Stanforth said to me.

'Goodbye,' I said.

'I come back soon,' the Baron said to his secretary, turning at the door. The other man seized his arm and hustled him out. It was bitter cold in the street and the sky was smoky and reddish from the reflected glare of neon-signs. The Baron linked his other arm in mine and we crossed the road. The pub was on the other side, almost opposite the shop.

The landlord was just opening the side door into the saloon bar when we got there.

'Well, well,' the landlord said, 'you're on time you are. And no mistake.'

Evidently the Baron and the other man were well-known to him.

'It's gone five, Joe,' the other man said looking at his watch.

'Only just,' Joe said.

We followed him into the saloon; it was warm and cosy inside. The landlord switched on the lights and went behind the bar. The Baron rapped on the counter with a coin.

'What you drink, hey?' he asked us.

'Whisky,' we both said.

'And me also,' the Baron said.

'White Horse, Haig, Johnny Walker, Black and White,' Joe said. 'Which would you like?'

'It's no matter,' the Baron said. 'They are all whisky, yes?'

'I'll have White Horse,' the other man said. 'Because you can tell it blindfold.'

'And you, sir?' Joe said.

'I'll have Irish,' I said.

'Are you an Irishman?' the other man asked me.

'No,' I said, 'not particularly. Why?'

'I thought I'd discovered a fellow countryman,' the other said. 'Are you Irish then?'

'Sure I am,' the other said. 'I come from Dublin. My name is Casey.'

'Not so!' the Baron said banging on the counter. 'You not Irish. You are a Jew!' He said to me: 'Do not believe this man. Always he tell he is Irish but it is not so. He is an old Jew!'

'That's right,' the other said good-humouredly. 'I am a Polish Jew. I come from Warsaw.'

'Why for you tell you Irish then?' the Baron asked him belligerently.

Joe put the drinks on the counter and watched us with a grin.

'This man is a Jew!' the Baron told him. 'A Polish Jew!'

'That's right,' the other said, winking at Joe.

'Do not believe when he tell he is Irish,' the Baron said. 'It is a lie!'

'Well, cheerio,' the other said, picking up his glass.

'A la vôtre,' I said to the Baron.

'Cherry-o,' the Baron said with dignity.

I had never been able to persuade him to talk French with me. He sat there in his velvet collared coat, his wrinkled yellow face looking almost Asiatic. It was impossible to guess at his true nationality. He was a very small man and his legs dangled short of the ground as he sat up on the high stool at the counter, lifting his glass solemnly to each of us in turn.

'You know,' the other man said to me in his husky confidential voice, 'I'm not really a Jew. That's just his joke. I'm an Irishman from Dublin. My name is Casey.' He put a hand in his pocket and produced a card with 'Tim Casey' engraved on it in big letters. 'You see?' he said.

I took the card and looked at it. Underneath the name 'Tim Casey' was inscribed the address of a firm of interior decorators.

'So you're in the same line as Hatrick,' I said.

'That's right,' Tim Casey said, leaning back against the bar. He said: 'I'm pretty well-known in the trade. Ask anyone you meet if they've heard of Tim Casey. They'll tell you. By God, I've lost a fortune over Art, I have.'

'Is that so?'

'It's been my ruin,' Casey said. 'Are you an artist?'

'Yes.'

'There's no money in Art,' Casey said.

'Don't I know it.'

'I'll bet you do,' Casey said, chuckling. 'Hatrick now, he makes it pay. He's a businessman. I'm not. I haven't the head for it. We Irish rarely make good business men. We're too simple. Too free and easy.'

I finished my whisky, wondering how I could pay for the drinks when it came to my round. I'd only got a ten bob note and that had to last me till the end of the month. There was a calendar up behind the bar, advertising a brand of cider. The date was 15th February.

'Same again?' Casey said, looking at my empty glass.

'Thank you,' I said.

'I'm hungry,' Casey said. 'I want something to eat. Will you have something too?'

'All right.'

Casey turned to the Baron, who hadn't spoken for some time. He sat huddled on his stool, holding his head in his hands.

Casey said: 'Same again, old chap?'

The Baron just nodded, dully.

'What's the matter?' Casey asked him. 'Feeling blue?'

'I have pains,' the Baron said. 'Pains in my head.'

'A spot of whisky'll soon put them right,' Casey said. He gave the order to Joe. 'Let's have some sandwiches too,' he added.

'Cheese, ham, or tongue?' Joe said taking a plate from out of a glass case.

'Ham, I think,' Casey said. 'What about you?'

'Yes, I'll have ham,' he said.

'Have a ham sandwich,' Casey said to the Baron, who shook his head. 'Come on. It'll do your pains good.'

'You sink so?' the Baron said, looking up.

'I'm sure of it.'

'Ver'well. I will have a ham.'

'Three ham sandwiches,' Casey said to Joe. 'Here you are,' he said to the Baron. 'Get outside that. You'll soon feel good again.'

'Sank you,' the Baron said gravely. He took a bite of the sandwich and a gulp of whisky. He said: 'You are a Jew but you are generous. You have pay for my drink. So!'

'That's right,' Casey said. 'We Polish Jews are always generous.' He winked at me as he said it.

'You are a generous few,' the Baron said.

'You bet I am.' Casey winked again. 'That's just his joke,' he explained to me huskily.

I nodded, eating my sandwich. I was wondering if I could perhaps touch Casey for a quid. Of course if the worst came to the worst there was always Fleurette, but I didn't want to go to her. We'd had the hell of a bust-up just before I got ill and it would take a bit of getting over. Besides, I hate borrowing money from women, because they never let you forget it. Especially Fleurette.

So I considered Casey. He might have been a Jew or again he might not. You couldn't tell from his face; there are plenty of Irishman with thick noses.

'Have another sandwich,' Casey said, pushing the plate over towards me.

'Thanks, I will.'

'Do,' Casey said, 'it's on me.'

Joe went along behind the bar and switched on the radio; it played a syncopated tune.

'Are you fond of music?' Casey said.

'Do you mean dance music?' I said.

'No, real music.'

'Yes,' I said, 'are you?'

'And then some,' Casey said. 'You mightn't believe it, but I had a great career ahead of me once, as a singer.'

'Really?'

'Yes,' Casey said. 'I had a beautiful voice. Really beautiful.'

'What happened?'

'The war,' Casey said. 'I was gassed. Now I can't sing a note. Not a bloody note.'

'I say, what rotten luck.'

'It was,' Casey said. 'I'd have been a great singer if it hadn't been for that war.'

'What was your register?'

'Tenor,' Casey said. 'I'd have been a great Irish tenor. Like Count McCormack.'

'Or Jack Doyle.'

'That's right,' Casey said.

'Did you ever meet James Joyce in Dublin?'

'No. Who's he?'

'Another Irish tenor.'

'I never met him,' Casey said. He shook his head. 'Ah, if I could only be young again. I'd give all the money I've got in the world if I could be your age, with your opportunities. I'd be happy as the day is long.'

'Would you?'

'By God I would,' Casey said. 'You don't know how lucky you are.'

'No,' I said, 'you're right about that.'

'How old are you, if you'll pardon me asking a personal question?'

'Twenty-six.'

'Twenty-six!' Casey said. 'Twenty-six! I'd give every penny I possess to change places with you. To be young and carefree and happy again.'

'How d'you know I'm carefree and happy?'

'If you're not you ought to be,' Casey said. 'You've got all the world before you. What more do you want?'

'Lots of things.'

'Such as?'

'Well, money, for one.'

'Ah, that's a thing we all want,' Casey said. 'But remember, money can't buy happiness.'

'It could for me at the moment.'

'You can make money,' Casey said.

'How? You say yourself that there isn't any in Art.'

'No, that's true,' Casey said. 'But there are other ways of making money. If I were you, if I had my life to live over again, I should chuck Art. Believe me, it doesn't pay, and I'm one who knows.'

'So am I.'

'There you are then. Why not give it up? Become a bank manager or something.'

'That's not so easy, either.'

'Everything's easy when one's got youth,' Casey said. 'Look at me. I'm over fifty. The best part of my life's behind me. But what couldn't I do if I were twenty-six again? Eh? I ask you that.'

I couldn't think of an answer offhand and Casey continued: 'When I was twenty-six I had everything—youth, health, strength, the promise of a great future. I was handsome, too. Look at me now and you can imagine what I was like then. Eh?'

I looked at him. There was nothing about his appearance to indicate that he had ever been good looking, but I nodded, for politeness' sake.

'I had everything, I tell you,' Casey said. 'Now I have nothing. All gone. Youth's a stuff will not endure.' He removed his hat sadly and I saw then that he was completely bald. Bald as a coot. He passed a hand over his head and said: 'I had thick curly hair once, as thick as yours. Now even that's gone and I have only memories to look back upon.'

He shook his head again; he looked more like a Jew with his hat off. He said: 'In Dublin they used to call me the Tiger.'

'Why?'

'It was a tribute,' Casey said. 'A tribute to my youth and strength.'

'I see.'

The radio behind the bar continued to play dance music. The Baron sat huddled on his stool, staring vacantly into space. Joe was leaning on the counter, reading the sporting page of an evening paper.

Casey said: 'I'm telling you this so that you'll realize what it means to waste one's opportunities. I've sacrificed myself in the service of Art. See that you don't make the same mistake. You're young and healthy: take time by the forelock. Go in and win.'

'Meantime,' I said, 'I've only ten bob in my pocket.'

'Ten bob?'

'That's all.'

A subtle change came over Casey's expression. He suddenly looked very shrewd. He said: 'Ten bob isn't much certainly.'

'It's got to last till the end of the month.'

'What's the date today?'

'The fifteenth.'

'Oh, that's not so bad,' Casey said.

'It's pretty bad. Thirteen days.'

'Time passes quickly when one's young. The end of the month'll be here before you know it.'

'So will the end of the money.'

'It'll last you,' Casey said with conviction.

'How d'you know it will?'

'I'm certain,' Casey said. 'I've got a feeling it will. We Irish get these feelings you know, and we're usually right.'

'Are you?'

'Nearly always.'

'That's a comfort, anyway.'

'It'll last if you're careful,' Casey said. 'If you don't go throwing it away. That's always been my trouble—generosity. Chucking money about like water.' He turned to the Baron. 'How are you feeling now?'

The Baron shook his head dully.

'Pain's bad?' Casey said.

The Baron nodded.

'Never mind. Have another drink. You'll feel better then.' Casey turned to me. 'Like another?'

'Thanks.'

'Same again all round,' Casey told Joe.

I said: 'I suppose you don't happen to have any jobs going?' Casey looked at me very shrewdly, rubbing a hand over his head. 'No, I'm afraid not, old chap,' he said. 'Of course if I hear of anything...'

'Of course,' I said.

'Well, cheerio,' Casey said.

'Cheerio,' I said.

The Baron lifted his glass and gulped the whisky down.

'Better?' Casey asked him.

'No,' the Baron said.

'Cheer up,' Casey said, 'you'll be all right again tomorrow.'

'You sink so?'

'I'm sure,' Casey said.

'Have you got a feeling about it?' I asked Casey.

'Yes,' Casey said.

'That's all right then,' I told the Baron. 'The Irish are always right about these things.'

'I'll say we are,' Casey said.

The Baron looked at the clock above the counter; it marked a quarter to six.

'I must return to the shop,' the Baron said. He got down off the high stool. His movements were still unsteady, but he was much more subdued; his pains seemed to have sobered him a lot.

'Right-ho,' Casey said, putting on his hat.

'Good night gentlemen,' Joe said.

'I'll be seeing you, Joe,' Casey said.

'I bet you will,' Joe said.

We all went towards the door.

'Wait a sec,' Casey said. He stopped in front of a fruit machine that stood near the door. He said: 'I must try my luck with this. We Irish are like that, you know; we can't resist a gamble.'

He put a sixpence in the slot and pulled the lever; the machine whirred and the numbers clicked into place, 1-7-0.

'Damn the thing,' Casey said. He put in another sixpence without success. He put in four sixpences altogether, without winning anything at all. Then he turned to me. 'Now you put one in.'

'I can't afford to.'

Casey took a sixpence from his pocket and handed it to me. 'Here you are,' he said. 'Go on. You can pay it back at the end of the month.' He chuckled.

I put the sixpence in and pulled the lever. 0-0-7 turned up.

'No luck,' Casey said. 'Never mind.'

He opened the door and we went out into the street where it was still bitterly cold. The Baron turned to me and held out his hand. 'I'm glad you come to see me, my friend. You come again, hey?'

'Certainly.'

'Soon?'

'Soon,' I said.

'You not forget?'

'No, I won't forget. And I hope your head gets better quickly.'

'Sank you,' the Baron said, 'You are kind.'

In the dim smoky light of the street his face looked yellow and strained, but he seemed much soberer now.

'So long, old chap,' Casey said to me. 'Look in sometime, you've got my card. If there's any jobs going...'

'Yes,' I said, 'and I can pay back the sixpence.'

'Don't worry about that,' Casey said with a wave of his hand. 'And remember,' he tapped my chest lightly with his finger, 'you've got youth, and that's everything. Money doesn't matter when you've got that. Take it from me. I'm one who knows.'

'So long,' I said.

Casey took the Baron's arm and they crossed the road. I turned up my coat collar and started to walk away down the King's Road, past the cinemas, the tobacconists, and the cheap confectioners, wondering what I should do next. It was damned cold; I could feel it right through my gloves and overcoat.

There was only one thing to do: ring up Fleurette. She'd come across all right, once we'd patched up that row. Walking along, feeling the cold, I cursed Casey for a stingy swine. Still, I'd had two sandwiches and three drinks out of him, even if I had had to listen to his bloody nonsense about youth and health and money not mattering.

It was all very fine for him to talk, but money can buy happiness when you haven't got any. It could buy happiness for me right now, at this very moment.

I turned into the square where the telephone-boxes stood. I went into one of the boxes and the glass door shut the cold out behind me. I hesitated, looking at the telephone, thinking curse him, curse him for a mean goddamned swine.

Then I picked up the phone and dialled Gerrard one-six-double-O.

And did I swear. I'd already typed out the orders three times. It was this big invasion scheme, very secret; everybody in the battalion had been talking about it for weeks. It was due to come off any moment, but when? Not Thursday, because that was the Sergeants' Mess Social; but there was Monday, Tuesday, Wednesday, or would it be Friday? And I typed and re-typed the orders, and we slept for four nights fully dressed, with steel helmets, respirators, and equipment connected up by the bedside, and it didn't come off.

Then a despatch rider fell off his bike in front of BHQ and staggered in with a sealed package from the Scotch. They were the enemy and supposed to invade us. The major tore open the package; inside it said they were sorry, for some reason they couldn't invade us, not just yet. So we disconnected our equipment and took off our trousers before kipping down; everyone said, 'What a muck-up.'

But next morning the major rang for me in his office and there were new orders to be typed. I was working till midnight. At last it was done. I was beginning to run short of paper, my typewriter ribbon was nearly worn out.

That bloody scheme's on again, everyone said. And did they swear.

All leave was stopped, there was an argument about where the bayonet should be worn. And then the bugle. There was a bugle, but only one man who knew how to blow the alarm on it, and he was in clink.

'We can't let him out for that,' the major said. 'You'll just have to shout.'

I was given a nominal roll to type out showing where everyone had to go when the invasion started. Thank God I was on staff, so I didn't have to turn out. All the rest were to go to the golf-links. And what's more march. It was miles.

I didn't mind. I already had my orders. I was to take over the phone; the RSM himself told me. 'You're a key man,' he said. 'Communications, see? Very important.'

'Yes indeed, sir.'

Everyone said: 'That bloody scheme's on tonight.'

It was, or rather next morning.

At 0200 hours in came the orderly sergeant and pulled all the blankets off me.

'Invasion up,' he said. 'Rise and shine. Get your gear on.'

I pulled on my boots. The laces broke; I swore. Everyone swore. Somebody shouted up the stairs: 'INVASION! Chrissake get cracking.'

There was a rush of feet along the landing and roars of 'Stop the bleeder.' One of the prisoners in the guardroom, who'd been let out to go to the lavatory, was now attempting to escape.

The 'phone room was completely empty; the fire had been let out; it was winter and bitterly cold. I sat down by the switchboard with my overcoat on. Outside, I could hear them falling in, the door opened and there was Corporal Stimson with his tin hat on the wrong way round.

'What the hell's going on?' he said. 'Someone says invasion.'

'It's a scheme,' I told him. 'The jocks are invading us.'

'Well I don't know nothing about it. I just come back off leave. Nobody told me nothing.'

The RSM came in. 'Corporal Stimson, you're in charge of the anti-tank gun. Where's your section?'

'I'll go and see, sir.'

'You should be all ready to march off by now.'

Out he went, banging the door. Stimson said: 'What a game. Who's in my section: d'you know?'

'Not offhand.'

'What a game.'

He went off to find his section. I lit a fag and sat on by the phone. Marching feet went by outside the building. The provost sergeant poked his head round the door.

'All on your lonesome?'

'I'm in charge of the 'phone. A key-man. Very important.'

'Bleeding Bellairs tried to make a break for it.'

'How'd he get on?'

'O'Sullivan's sitting on his head.'

'What are you doing in the scheme, sergeant?'

'I'm in charge of summat or other. Blamed if I know what. Give us a fag.'

Back came the RSM unexpectedly. 'Put them cigarettes out. No smoking on duty. Sergeant Malone, you're supposed to be guarding the door.'

'Very good sir.'

'Any message come through yet?' the RSM asked me.

'No sir.'

'Something wrong somewhere,' the RSM said, and stamped out into the hall. I heard the sliding door slam and then his voice in the street asking where in hell were all the men.

I sat and shivered by the 'phone. Corporal Stimson came back rubbing his hands and stamping his feet. 'I'm off the anti-tank,' he said. 'I'm on fire-point now.'

'What's going on?'

'Half the blighters ain't woke up yet. They won't half cop it in the morning.'

'It's morning now.'

'What a game!'

Then he told me about his leave. The missus. The nippers. He showed me snapshots. More men went marching by; it seemed as though things had got moving at last.

The provost sergeant looked in again. 'Everything according to plan?'

The street outside was now completely silent. So was the 'phone. I sat by it for two hours, being a key-man, and nothing came through. My feet were frozen. Stimson had gone to sleep in a chair. The provost-sergeant cursed quietly to himself in the corridor.

Then suddenly the buzzer went. Stimson woke up in the middle of a snore. I picked up the 'phone. 'BHQ.'

A voice said: 'All clear. Invasion over. All informed.'

'How'd it go off?'

'They took us all prisoner.'

I put down the 'phone.

'Is it over?' Stimson asked.

'Yes. Our mob are all in clink.'

'Thank Gawd. Now I can go back to kip.'

'Don't you believe it. We've got to wait till they get back.'

'Stone a crow!'

Well, as I say, the golf links was miles. It was another half hour before they came straggling back. Then suddenly the hall was full of tramping feet; the RSM appeared in front of me.

'All right. You can stand down now.'

'Very good sir.' I stood up. I was stiff with cold.

'What's happened to your boot-laces?' the RSM said.

'They broke, sir.'

'Well, see you get a new pair in the morning.'

'Yes sir.'

I trailed out into the corridor with my laces tripping me up. The major was there; he was plainly put out. Before him five platoon sergeants stood to attention.

'Bad show!' the major was saying. 'A *very* bad show. Frankly I take a very poor view of the whole affair.'

I went upstairs. Everyone was taking off equipment and cursing. I sat down on my bed and pulled off my boots again. I lay down and pulled the blankets up over my head. Two hours left before reveille. A tin hat fell down in the next room. Somebody dropped his boots. Then gradually the noise died down; they crawled into kip. The invasion was over for another week. Lights out. Talk out. Everything under control.

Mandrake

When I was a boy of fourteen, living in the South of France, I became obsessed with the idea of finding a mandrake-root. I was determined to get hold of mandrake, only I didn't quite know how to go about it. Then I thought: Gene Flood. He'll know. Gene Flood used to live next door to me at that time. He was fourteen, too, and when he grew up he was going to be an explorer. That was quite definite.

'But why a mandrake?' Gene said.

I said: 'It's a good thing to have about the place.'

'Why?' Gene asked.

'You can do all sorts of things with it. Magic. I think you can raise the dead with it, but I'm not sure.'

'H'm,' Gene said. He stroked his chin sceptically. He was a materialist. Didn't believe in magic.

I said: 'In a film I saw, a man made a woman out of it. I tell you it's a good thing to have.'

'How'd he make the woman? It show you?'

'No. He was a scientist.'

'Well, we're not scientists,' Gene said. 'We'd never be able to do that. Besides, who wants to make a woman, anyway?'

'What about raising the dead then?'

Gene shook his head. He was still sceptical.

'When you pull it up it screams like a man,' I said.

Gene said: 'Men don't scream. Shouldn't anyhow, less they're cowards.' But the idea of it screaming had interested him and he asked: 'Where's it grow?'

'At the foot of the gallows,' I said.

'There aren't any gallows round here,' Gene said. 'It grow anywhere else?'

'Forests,' I said. 'Swamps.'

'All right,' Gene said. He stood up. He was a man of action. He squared his jaw and started to stuff his most powerful catapult into the already bulging pocket of his flannel coat.

'We taking Phil?' I said.

Gene turned and shouted 'Phil' towards the closed shutters of the villa.
'What about Darkie?' I said.

At the sound of his name, Darkie, the alsatian, who'd been knocked
out by the sun and lay stretched on the ground as though dead, revived
miraculously and beat his tail on the ground.

'Yes, better take him,' Gene said. 'Useful for tracking.'

Phil came running down the steps of the villa with a Wild West
magazine in his hand. On the cover it showed a cowboy shooting up a
saloon. Phil came towards us, shaking his rather shaggy head. There was
a family resemblance, but Phil hadn't Gene's square jaw or steely eyes. He
had brown eyes and was inclined to blush. It was obvious he'd never make
an explorer. Besides, he was scared of snakes.

'Come on,' Gene said to him. 'We're going a walk.'

Darkie sat up and cocked his ears at the word 'walk.' He was
interested.

'Where to?' Phil said.

'Find a mandrake.'

'What's that?'

'Kind of plant. Screams when you pull it up. Grows on the gallows.'

'What we want it for, Gene?'

'Don't ask fool questions,' Gene said. 'Raise the dead, if you want to
know.'

'Ghosts?' Phil said. He'd gone white.

Gene said: 'You needn't come if you're scared.'

'Who's scared?' Phil said, bridling.

'Shut up and come on then,' Gene told him.

Darkie, seeing that something was afoot at last, rushed barking ahead
of us to the gate. Beyond this the road led uphill, deep in white dust.

'Better try the forest first,' Gene said.

The forest was some distance away. It was a real forest. Parts of it were
like a jungle. In these parts it was quite gloomy once you got inside them.
The tree-tops shut the sun out. There were supposed to be orchids
growing, but we'd never come across any.

Gene led us to a clearing full of rotting tree trunks with toad-stools
growing out of them.

'How about this?' he said.

'Not bad,' I said.

'Know what it looks like?'

'Like a man's hand.'

'H'm,' Gene said. He stroked his chin and looked around. 'Nothing like that here.'

'No,' I said.

'We better start searching,' Gene said.

He bent down and laid hold of a nearby root. He pulled and pulled. His face turned crimson and his veins swelled up. I bent down and helped him to pull. We both pulled. The root came up, so suddenly that we were flung backwards and nearly fell.

Gene threw it on the ground in disgust. 'No good,' he said. 'Not a mandrake. Didn't scream.'

Darkie, who'd been absent for some time, now reappeared, crashing through the undergrowth. He stood looking at us and panting. His ears were cocked and his long pink tongue lolled out sideways. He began to whine and look back into the undergrowth.

'He's scented something,' Gene said. 'Maybe it's the mandrake.'

'Maybe,' I said.

'Find the mandrake, Darkie,' Gene said. 'Go on. Good Darkie. Find the mandrake.'

Darkie turned obediently and disappeared into a thicket. We followed him on all fours. We came out at last to a clearing. It was completely silent in this clearing. Not even any birds in the trees.

Darkie dug his claws into the ground and started to dig. Gene danced about, spurring him on with shouts. 'He's found it!' he kept on saying. 'He's found the mandrake.' He was terrifically pleased. Darkie was living up to his reputation at last.

'Must be buried pretty deep down,' Gene said.

'If you dig far enough you come out in Australia,' I said.

'Maybe that's where the mandrake grows,' Gene said.

'Maybe it is,' I said.

Phil didn't say anything. He was getting a bit bored. He'd started to shuffle his feet about and feel his behind where a thorn had torn the seat of his pants.

At last Darkie stopped digging and flung himself down flat beside the hole. He was exhausted. We had to roll him away by force to get at the hole. Gene put his arm down. It went in to the elbow. He withdrew it covered in earth.

'Can't feel any roots,' he said.

I tried also, without success. We started to enlarge the hole with our hands. It contained nothing except soft, fine earth.

'Darkie's let us down,' I said, panting.

'Darkie's a washout,' Gene said.

'Better try the swamp now.'

'Where's the swamp?'

'Nearest one's some way.'

'All right,' I said. 'Let's go.'

'Come on, Darkie,' Gene said. He spoke sternly. Darkie got up guiltily and shook himself. He followed us out through the thicket with his tail between his legs.

The swamp itself was in the centre of a grove of bamboos growing quite thickly together and not far from the seashore. In amongst the bamboos there were a few trees growing, but only a few with leaves on them; mostly they had withered and stuck up out of the swamp, gnarled and dead. The ground became more marshy as we went on, pushing through the bamboos, and water squelched up between our shoes, which sank a little at each step.

Phil kept moaning: 'I've got my feet wet. I'll catch a cold. I'll get *new-monia.*'

'Shut up,' Gene told him. He was looking round for roots. Suddenly he said: 'What about that?'

We were now in the centre of the swamp and there were banks of mud along its sides and in the middle a smooth expanse of mud, almost like sand and solid-looking. On the further side there was a gnarled root growing. It had sort of fingers and was certainly a bit like a man's hand.

'That's it, I think,' I said.

Gene braced himself. His jaw was squared. He took a short run back and then charged forward. He leaped the mud in the middle and landed with both feet just clear of it. The root was a little too far for him to reach and he started to pull himself up the bank until he got his fingers round it. He started to pull, digging his other hand into the mud to get a hold.

I jumped and landed beside him. I got a hand on the root, too, and we pulled. The root came clear of the mud. It didn't scream, but there was a sucking sound and then a yell from Gene. His braces had given way. He slipped and went sliding down the bank to the bottom. His feet were at once stuck in the sand-like mud that we had thought solid. It wasn't solid. It wobbled and one of his feet slipped down into it. He tried to pull it clear and the other one went in. The mud closed round it immediately.

Phil began to dance about on the other bank. 'Quicksand!' he shouted. 'It's quicksand!'

I dropped the root I was still holding in my hand. It didn't matter. It wasn't a mandrake, anyway.

I slid down the bank and grabbed Gene by the collar and the arm.

The sleeve of Gene's jacket tore under the armpit. I got the jacket bunched up in my hand and by levering on his collar pulled him backwards out of the mud. Gene was half choked, but both his feet were out, the mud clogging his shoes up to the ankles, and he could get hold of me from behind.

The mud released my foot reluctantly. It sucked and sucked and I could smell it stinking. My heel came up and then my toe, and the mud wobbled into place over the hole my foot had made in it. We started to scramble up the bank as fast as we could. Once we nearly slipped down again, but at last we were at the top, Phil giving a wild yell of triumph from the other side.

We turned to look down at the mud. It was perfectly smooth and solid-seeming, not even a bubble on its surface. Gene stooped and picked up a stone. He flung it down. The stone sank out of sight. I threw one. Same result. Phil scooped up a handful of stones and threw them. Then we all went completely mad. We pelted the mud until our arms got tired. Gene threw a rock in. The mud received it gratefully.

After about five minutes we felt better. But somehow we didn't feel like looking for the mandrake any more that day. There weren't any more roots about, anyhow.

Gene said: 'We'll have another look tomorrow. I know a place where there's bound to be plenty of mandrakes.'

But next day we didn't go hunting for the mandrake after all. Gene had looked it up in the dictionary or something and there it said the mandrake was mythical. Didn't exist.

So we never looked for the mandrake again.

And yet I don't know. Sometimes I wonder whether I haven't still been looking for it all my life. One way and another.

That was her name. It took old Dinty Moore, the phone orderly, three days to find it out for me.

At that time I was still in the army, a lance jack working in the orderly room of our Depot Headquarters. One afternoon about 1.30 I was on my way back from the Naffy when I noticed this girl walking ahead of me down the passage with posts across it that served as a short cut. It was summer and she had on a short flowered frock without sleeves. Back-view, because of her smallness and slight build, her thin bare legs and fluffy fair hair, I took at her first for a child of about fourteen.

I watched her circumnavigate the posts and pick her way delicately past the twisted rusting heaps of scrap metal that were piled up further down. With my longer stride I quickly caught her up, but as I was about to draw level she stopped. The backs of shops abutted on either side of this passage and she'd halted opposite one of these. She shook the door-handle but the door was locked. She was half turned towards me and I saw her face. It wasn't a child's face, nor was the shape of her bare arm a child's. Astonished, I almost stopped, but my impetus carried me on. At the end of the passage I glanced back. The girl had disappeared.

Upstairs in the orderly room a row with the ORQMS drove all thoughts of her out of my head. There'd been a typing error in one of the reports; the C.O. had been enraged at the sight of a book on my desk. I was unpopular all afternoon and on duty clerk in the evening.

It was then that I remembered the girl in the passageway. I saw in mind quite vividly the bangle on her bare arm that was not shaped like a child's. I could not recall her face at first, except that it was pale and that she had blue eyes. Then later I remembered more about it: the pointed chin, a large mouth. I thought all these things over and decided, if possible, to date her up. But first she had to be found, so next day I set old Dinty Moore on her track. He undertook to find her for a packet of fags.

Old Dinty was not really old at all, he was still in his thirties. But he'd plenty of service in. He'd once been a sergeant, but then he led a mutiny in India and got busted. Now a private again, he worked the switchboard in the 'phone room and also acted as runner on occasion. We got on well but he was a tough customer. His face was deeply scarred and pitted with pockmarks, as though someone had used it for a dartboard. The structure of his skull showed through the parched skin. He had very fair hair, cropped into a sort of fringe, and a short scrubby fair moustache that grew unevenly. Even in winter he walked about in his shirt, with the sleeves rolled up. His arms were tattooed with pythons and mermaids picked out in faded blue, and on his chest was a heart enclosing the name of a girl not his missus.

I knew that if anyone could find the girl for me, old Dinty could. But she was elusive, and even for him it proved difficult. For three days he trotted round the shops whose backs abutted on the passageway asking for a girl who looked about fourteen and wore a bangle on her arm. Several such girls were produced for his inspection but none really fitted the bill, and he began to get browned-off with the game.

Then, on the fourth day, he came into the orderly room and sat down on the edge of my desk. 'Her name's Lulu,' he told me.

'Sure it's the right one?' I said.

'Dead sure. I chatted her ten minutes. Works at that electric shop, in the cash desk. She's twenty-four. Never think it from her looks, though. Nice kid. Ain't never had a boyfriend, one of the other girls told me. Doesn't walk out as a rule, keeps herself to herself. Reckon you can date her up if you try. I told her a bit about you.'

'What'd she say?'

'Got a bit scared when she heard you was a writer. Too classy she reckoned. I told her not to talk cock. Said you was a bloody good bloke. Tell you what to do, write her a note. I'll slip it her teatime.'

I've a rooted objection to writing girls notes, as a rule. I believe in the sound old saying, 'Fear God and do right, fear women and *don't* write.' This time I compromised by typing the note and sticking an indecipherable signature at the foot of it. The note said that I admired her greatly and would she make a date with me. Just before I knocked off for the evening old Dinty brought back the reply. It was verbal and she'd meet me by the pillar-box at the Naffy about seven o'clock. I was so pleased with this that I gave Dinty twenty Players instead of ten Woodbines as I'd planned.

He banged me on the back and winked. 'Good luck, Rossy. Anything else I can do just let me know.'

Lulu was standing by the pillar-box as appointed at seven. She had a push-bike immobilized in the gutter. She'd not heard me approach and started when I appeared suddenly beside her. She wore a light coat over her summer frock and I could not see the bangle on her arm. I was astonished again at the contrast between her slightness and smallness and the maturity of her face. Her face looked fully twenty-four. It was pale and pointed and she had large pale blue eyes. She wasn't made up except for her mouth. This was painted scarlet, the lips were full and drooped wistfully down at the corners. Her voice when she spoke was flat and slightly metallic.

We talked of this and that for a few moments; she was embarrassed and looked at the pavement while we were speaking. Then I came to the point.

'Are you coming out with me tonight?'

'I can't tonight. I promised to go home. My sister's not well.'

'Tomorrow then?'

'Yes, all right.'

'You don't sound enthusiastic.'

'I want to come. But it's not easy. I hardly know you.'

'You'll get to know me better.'

'I don't mind.' She flushed and glanced quickly up at me out of her large pale eyes. I noticed the thin blue veins at her temples and in her hands. She had very fine bones and her whole appearance was refined almost to the degree of decadence. It contrasted queerly with the flatness of her voice and the way she pronounced her words, correctly but with the air of reciting a lesson.

'I'd like to paint you,' I said.

'Are you a painter? I thought you wrote stories.'

'I do. But I tried to be a painter once.'

'I do drawing,' she said. 'What's your name? I couldn't read it on the note.'

'Julian,' I told her.

'It's a nice name.'

'I like yours, too,' I said.

'Lulu,' she said. 'Funny, isn't it? I've got to be going.'

'So soon? Where shall we meet tomorrow?'

'Down by the big clock. Same time.'

She shook my hand quickly, without looking up, and swung on to her bicycle. I watched her ride away down the street; her legs were just long enough to reach the pedals. She disappeared round the corner bent over the handlebars. I turned into the Naffy and played the piano for two hours. I was very elated with the way things were going.

Next day I was still elated and arrived at the meeting place ten minutes too early. Evening sun flashed off the face of the big clock, which was enclosed in a pink tower and belonged to the catering firm which owned half the town. I walked impatiently up and down underneath a striped awning. Dead on time Lulu rolled up. She was wearing her light coat again and I saw with pleasure that she'd made herself up for the occasion.

'You're very punctual,' I said.

'I don't like to keep people waiting.'

'Well, where would you like to go?'

'Anywhere, I don't mind.'

'What about a meal?'

'I've had one at home. I got off early today.'

'Have a coffee, then?'

She agreed to that, so we went to the Odeon café. Upstairs there was a balcony where you could sit on chromium chairs at glass-topped tables in a dark green décor, with a rubber floor underfoot. We did this and I ordered scrambled eggs and coffee. The scrambled eggs were for me. Lulu refused to eat anything. I offered her a cigarette.

'I don't smoke,' she said. Now that we were facing each other across a table, she was much more embarrassed than she'd ever been before. Her face assumed an almost sullen look. I began to despair of ever establishing contact with her. Snatches of dialogue from the talkie now showing were wafted up to us every time the doors into the cinema downstairs were opened.

'Do you want to see the film?' I asked her.

She shook her head. 'I don't want you to spend money taking me out.'

'How silly. If it gives me pleasure.'

'We can just talk. Or I expect you'd get bored just talking to me.'

'I'd like nothing better. How can we get to know each other if we don't talk?'

She shrugged her shoulders. Sitting there with her hands folded in her lap she looked remote and strangely inbred: again one had the illusion of a decadent aristocracy which might have produced her.

'You look like a Russian princess,' I told her.

She flushed. 'Is that a compliment? I don't know. I've never seen a Russian princess.'

'Some of them are very beautiful.'

'I'm not beautiful,' she said. She wasn't fishing she was stating a fact.

'You're very unusual-looking.'

'I am unusual.' Again she was stating a fact. The flatness of her voice made the statement sound final and without vanity.

I said: 'When I first saw you I thought you were a child.'

'People often take me for younger. I'm twenty-four.' Then she said: 'I've never walked out with a boy before.'

'And now you will?'

'I expect so. But I don't know anything about you.'

'I'm thirty. I'm a lance corporal in the army. I write short stories. I was brought up abroad in the South of France. That's where I saw all the Russian princesses. Later I sold vacuum-cleaners and I've been on the dole. I was on the dole for six months in 1938.'

'How did that happen?'

'I lost all my money.'

'I never had any money to lose,' Lulu said, and laughed shortly.

Later on, as we walked together in the public gardens overlooking the sea, she told me more about herself. She'd been working with this firm of electricians ever since she was fourteen. She had now worked her way to a job in the cash desk and she lived with a married sister just outside the town. Her parents were dead. She usually spent her evenings at night school and at drawing-classes. There'd recently been a move to call her up, but Lulu refused to register on religious grounds. She was a girl of spirit and she'd given the National Service people a piece of her mind. True, the firm that employed her was doing war-work; but it was constructive, not destructive, so she was willing to compromise that far. Any move to shift her into one of the services, however, she resisted tooth and nail.

I was impressed by all this; I saw there was more to Lulu than just a little girl one might come to make love to. 'You're certainly unusual,' I said to her. 'You've got plenty of character.'

She smiled without saying anything. She was much less shy now and I felt that everything was progressing satisfactorily. 'Let's sit down,' I said. We sat on a bench in the gardens and below us stretched the mud-flats with the tide way out and ships that seemed stuck, abandoned, in the mud.

'Take off your coat,' I said to her.

'Why d'you want me to?'

'I want to see you in that frock, the way I saw you first.'

'I'll be cold,' she said. But she slipped off her coat and I looked at her bare arms, round and well shaped and not a child's, with the bangle on one of them and the skin of her shoulders smooth and cream coloured with faint blue veins. 'You've got pretty arms,' I said.

'Like the princesses?' She laughed but her face had gone pink. She stood up suddenly from the bench and put her coat on again. 'I'll have to be going. I said I'd be in at eleven.'

'I'll take you back.'

'It's a long way,' she warned me. It was. We walked through street after street of drab semi-detached houses on the outskirts of the town; I began to wonder if I'd ever find my way back to H.Q. Lulu pointed out landmarks. The soap factory; the baptist chapel. 'I'm a baptist officially,' she said. 'I used to go there once. Do you know the Minister?'

'The one who comes round with the mobile canteen?'

'That's it. I used to fill the tea-urn for him.'

'And don't you now?'

'No. We disagreed on matters of dogma.' And then for some time as we walked along Lulu gave me her views on religion. She felt very strongly about this, but I was unable to discover what conclusion she had come to or to what persuasion she belonged now that she'd renounced the baptist chapel and given up filling the tea-urn. During the religious discussion it had got dark and we were approaching a gasometer. I felt that the subject should be changed, as beyond the gasometer were fields and only a few houses, one of which, she'd told me, was where she lived.

'When shall I see you again?' I asked her.

'I don't know.'

'I thought you were going to walk out with me.'

'I don't know if it's wise. You see, we're not the same class.'

'What nonsense!'

'It isn't nonsense. You're educated. You've lived abroad. All the princesses and everything. I've never been out of this town.'

'All that doesn't matter. If you like me.'

'Yes, I like you.'

'Well, then.' I took her arm; I could feel the bangle under my hand. Her head did not even reach to my shoulder. I let go her arm and slipped mine round her waist. She did not draw away. 'Now we're walking out properly,' I said.

'Yes.' We walked along like that until we came to her gate. 'I can meet you on Thursday,' she said. 'Same time, same place.'

'Splendid.'

She held out her hand. 'Goodnight, then,' she said.

'Aren't you going to kiss me?'

'I'd rather not.' I was taken aback at this, but she added: ' Not tonight, anyway.'

'But you will?'

'I daresay.' She pressed my hand quickly and was inside with the gate between us before I could argue the point further. She ran towards the house, turning to wave back once before the dark swallowed her up. I was inclined to curse, but then I decided to be philosophical. After all, there was loads of time. I determined to press for a decision on Thursday.

But on Thursday no further progress was made. We went to the Odeon café and she showed me some drawings of hers. They were interesting but confused in technique. 'I'm just groping about,' she said. 'I don't really know anything about it.'

Afterwards we walked in the gardens above the sea; we sat on a bench and I put my arm round her, but more than this she would not let me do. Nor would she let me kiss her on the way home. 'I'm not ready for that yet,' she said.

'I've never let a man kiss me.'

'Don't you think it's time you started?'

'Not yet. You'll have to have patience.'

Naturally, my desire to make love to her increased in the face of these refusals. Visions of her bare arms and her large, drooping wistful mouth came between me and my orderly room work; typing errors became more frequent and rows with the O.R.Q. an almost daily event. I used to send her round sweets obtained from the Naffy by Dinty Moore. Dinty himself, kept *au courant* of the affair's progress, was in favour of a big push. So was I, but the opportunities for this never seemed to arise.

Then they put the black-out back and it got dark earlier. This favoured a frontal attack and I had high hopes of success. I took Lulu to the part of the public gardens where there were pine trees and fewer people about. Searchlights swivelled over the sea and the sirens went. It was a lone raider over the coast that kept going round in circles with the ack-ack trying for him. We watched the crimson sparks of tracer drop like falling stars down the sky. Lulu shivered and I drew her against me on the bench where we were sitting.

'Are you scared?' I asked her. 'Would you like to move? '

'No,' she said, 'I'm not scared. It's only that I hate war.'

'Don't think about it,' I said.

'I have to think about it. I hate it. I hate it.'

We sat in silence for a bit and the guns stopped firing. I could no longer hear Jerry either. Lulu's body was light against my encircling arm.

'Lean back,' I said, trying to draw her closer. She resisted this attempt; I could feel all her muscles tense.

'I'm not going to loll,' she said. 'I can't stand girls who loll about.'

'I'm not asking you to loll about,' I said, releasing her.

She put her hand in mine: her thin fingers were cold.

'Don't be cross with me,' she said. The searchlight beam swung across the sky and lit up her face turned towards me, making her eyes seem bigger and her mouth seem fuller than in actuality they were: for a fugitive instant, before it was suddenly switched-off, heightening her sensuous appeal.

'I'm not cross with you,' I said, 'but I think you're being silly.'

'I can't help it,' she said. 'You'll have to give me time.'

Then she said: 'My sister was on about you today. She saw us the other night from the house. She didn't like the idea of it much. She didn't see how it could lead to anything.'

'Oh?'

'She said, "He may be married for all you know. How d'you know he hasn't a wife tucked away somewhere?" I said, "Mind your own business. Of course he isn't married."'

She was watching me while she repeated this conversation, but the searchlights were no longer up and my face was in shadow. I didn't say anything. Two people came up the path between the trees towards us. It was a soldier with a girl and they were linked tightly together. When they had passed our bench, Lulu said again: 'You're not cross?' Her voice sounded a little anxious now. 'My sister didn't mean any harm. She'd only my interests at heart.'

'Of course,' I said. I had my arm back round her and I could feel her hair tickling my cheek and smell the scent she used. But when I leant towards her mouth she turned her face away from me. I stood up suddenly. 'Let's be going.'

'I'm sorry,' she said. 'I am, honest.'

'It's just not any use,' I told her.

'It could be some use. If you'd give it a little while.'

I remained silent. As we walked up the path leading to the promenade Lulu stumbled over a root in the ground and took my arm. The All Clear went shrieking up as we came out among the tank traps that gleamed like white monuments in the dark.

Lulu said: 'Don't you want to see me any more?'

'I don't think we'd better.'

'But I want to go on seeing you.' She still had hold of my arm and now she slid her hand down into mine and held it tightly.

I said: 'It wouldn't work out.'

'But why not?' Her voice sounded miserable.

'Lots of reasons. One is that I want to make love to you and you don't want me to. And then there are other things.'

'Such as?'

'Never mind.'

We walked along in silence past the soap factory, the baptist chapel, the gasometer. As this loomed up I could hear Lulu sniffling to herself and she was still clutching my hand.

'Here we are,' I said. She didn't speak for a moment. Then she said in a stifled voice, 'You're sure you don't want to see me again?'

'It wouldn't make sense.' We'd stopped by the fence that ran along by the fields and it was too dark to see the expression on her face. 'Goodbye, my dear,' I said. 'Kiss me goodbye?'

She leaned forward, and then as our mouths were nearly touching, she stiffened again and drew back. 'I'd rather not,' she said.

I turned and walked away. She was still standing by the fence when I left her.

Old Dinty greeted me from the 'phone room as I got in to H.Q. 'Good time, Rossy?'

'It's all washed up,' I told him. 'Finished.'

'Just as well,' old Dinty said. 'I got a message for you here. Your missus coming down. Tomorrow afternoon, two-thirty.'

I saw Lulu only once again after the visit from my wife. She was standing in the passage that ran along behind her shop talking to two boys on push-bikes, and did not look at me at all as I passed.

A few days later I was transferred to a Depot in another part of England.

It started with a pain in my side. I didn't know I had pneumonia; nobody told me. We were out on the square, first period, 06.55 hours. Arms drill. The C.S.M. himself was taking us. He looked browned off: I don't believe he liked it any more than we did. Drilling before breakfast's a bugger, believe me.

That morning I just couldn't do anything right. I felt sick and also I had this pain. It caught me every time I breathed; you know, like when you've been running and you get a stitch. Only worse than that, of course. At last I couldn't stand it any longer. I thought I was going to be sick over the man in front of me, so I committed a terrible crime: I broke the ranks.

The C.S.M. was outraged. At first he couldn't speak at all when he saw me walking across the square towards him. He went scarlet and his face swelled up. Then he found his voice and shouted: 'Go back! Fall in! What the hell you think you're doing?'

'I'm sick, sir,' I said. 'I feel sick.'

'I'll have you in the guard-room,' the C.S.M. shouted. 'Sergeant Smithson, get hold of that man. Take him to hell out of here!'

'To the guard-room, sir?'

'No, back to his hut. Anywhere. But get him off the bloody square. Out of my sight.'

'Very good, sir. Come on, you! Quick march!'

But once off the square Sergeant Smithson said: 'You don't need to look so scared, lad. He won't stick you in the guard-room. He don't mean nothing, not really.'

'I'm not scared, Sergeant,' I said. 'I'm sick. I've got a pain.' I could hardly stand up.

'Where's it get you? In the guts?'

'No, not in the guts. In the side.'

'Take off your belt, and lie down, then. If you don't feel no better after breakfast you better go sick.'

I lay down on the bed, and lying down the pain didn't seem so bad. In fact I thought it'd gone, till I tried to sit up. Then I found out my mistake. So I lay down again.

The other blokes came tumbling in; they'd been dismissed. The corporal said: 'Dodging the column again, eh? You ought to be under arrest by rights, you ought, breaking the ranks like that. I reckon you got off bleeding lucky myself.'

Then they all went off to breakfast, rattling their mess-tins. I didn't feel like eating anything, so I didn't go. I just lay there until they came back again.

'Ain't you eaten nothing?' the corporal said. 'Cor, you *must* be sick.'

'He *looks* sick,' the other blokes said, examining me. 'He don't arf look yellow.'

I didn't care if I looked green, I only wanted to be left alone. The corporal got concerned and put his hand on my forehead. 'You got a temperacher all right. You better go sick.'

'Oh, fuck off.'

'For Christ's sake. Who're you talking to?'

'You,' I said. 'Anyone. Fuck off and leave me in peace.'

'He's sick all right,' the corporal said, 'Better ring up the Reception Station.'

'Get an ambulance.'

'Get the M.O.'

I didn't mind who they got, it was all one to me. A runner went off to the Reception Station and the others all stood round the bed talking in hushed voices, as though I were already dead.

Presently an ambulance arrived. Two orderlies came in; one shoved a thermometer in my mouth. Then he took it out and looked at the result. The other orderly looked at it and said, 'Cor.' He was impressed. They both shook their heads.

'You in any pain, mate?' the first orderly asked.

'Yes,' I said.

The orderly nodded; he'd expected that. 'Appendix,' he muttered to himself. 'Obvious case.'

The other orderly thought not. He favoured ptomaine poisoning. 'We'd fish for tea last night, remember,' he said. An argument ensued. I could have stopped it by telling them that I'd had my appendix out long ago and that I hadn't eaten any fish the night before, but I didn't feel like a lot of talk.

The corporal said: 'Well, what I want to know is he for the sick bay or not?'

'Yes, he's for the sick bay all right,' they said.

'Right. Get his small kit together, someone.'

The orderlies lifted me on to a stretcher. The sky tilted round as they carried me down the steps of the hut. Someone threw a hastily-packed haversack into the ambulance after me. Then there was the road running backwards behind us and the sky tilted again as they lifted me out at the Reception Station.

The medical officer looked down at me. 'Hullo, you again?' he said.

This medical officer didn't like me. I didn't like him either, come to that. It was a reciprocal dislike. He said: 'A pain in your side? Which side? H'm. We'd better keep you in. I'll examine you later. Can you walk upstairs, d'you think?'

'I can try, sir,' I said. I started to struggle up off the stretcher, but the pain caught me again and I fell back.

'Carry him up to the sick bay,' the medical officer told them.

Upstairs in the sick bay the wireless was on and the patients were sitting up in bed. Other patients, wearing hospital blues, were sitting in arm-chairs round the stove. All looked round as I was carried in.

A nurse came up with some pyjamas. Screens were erected round a bed and behind these I managed to get undressed, holding myself upright by hanging on to the bedrail. It took me some time, but I managed to do it in the end. I was damned if I'd let anyone else undress me. Then I got into bed. I could hardly breathe at all by this time. When the sister brought me a glass of something to drink and I tried to say thank you, only a whisper came out. I thought I was dying for sure, and I should have been frightened, but I wasn't. I felt too weak and too tired to be frightened. I lay back in the cool sheets and went off to sleep almost at once.

I woke up to find the M.O. standing by my bed. I opened my mouth to speak and the sister thrust a thermometer into it. The thermometer was withdrawn just at the moment when I felt I must spit it out or choke and the M.O. said: 'Off with your jacket. Let's have a look at you.'

He put on his stethoscope and listened through it to my chest. 'Say ninety-nine.'

'Ninety-nine.' My voice sounded a little louder since I'd had a sleep. The M.O. said: 'H'm.'

He applied the stethoscope to my back next. 'Take a deep breath.' I did. It hurt and made me cough, and coughing tore something inside me. I tried to cough as gently as possible, but still it hurt. The M.O. said 'H'm' and again commenced to tap my chest with his two fingers. I'll say this for him, I didn't like him, but he could get more sound out of my chest with his two fingers than any M.O. who's examined me before or since. He got a terrific sound out of it. Through the stethoscope it must have sounded deafening. He took the stethoscope off again and said 'All right.' Then he walked away out of earshot with the Sister and started to give her some instructions. I hoped he wasn't telling her to have me chucked out. I didn't feel able to move.

I watched him walk out and then two nurses came up and started to raise me from the pillows. I thought I was going to be forcibly ejected, but I was wrong. A third nurse came and banked up a lot more pillows behind me. Between them they strapped me bolt upright to a wooden rest and put a bolster between my legs, like the Dutch wife you read about in books about the east.

'Is that comfortable?' they asked. I nodded. It wasn't comfortable, but I felt too weak to argue. I went to sleep again straightway. Later I woke up in a sweat and the wireless was on. I'd been hearing it in my sleep; it was playing full blast. The patients were having tea, digging marmalade out of a tin. I didn't want any tea. I'd acquired a distaste for the thought of food and in particular for the thought of chocolate and Horlick's: formerly my staple diet at break-times. But they didn't seem to expect me to eat, so that was all right. I didn't feel like smoking either, which was a minor miracle, because ordinarily not a day passes but I smoke at least thirty cigarettes, excluding a few occasions when for some reason or other I've not had any cigarettes to smoke.

The man in the next bed to me was smoking, and the smoke from his cigarette, blowing across at me, smelt like cabbage soup, and I knew that if I lit one it'd taste like that, too, and I didn't mean to try it. I had a drink of barley water that the Sister brought me, and then they fixed a hot poultice on my chest, that smelt strongly of aniseed.

I went back to sleep, or rather I dozed and once I woke or dreamt that

I woke, I don't know which. My eyes were open, I'm certain of that. I could see the patients in blue walking up and down, but they didn't seem to make any sound; it was as though I were not really there, but looking at a silent film of them or seeing them through glass. I wondered if perhaps I'd died without knowing it. I once read a book where a man died in a hospital ward and afterwards he could see the whole of the ward and the people moving about and bending over his own dead body. I wondered dimly if this had happened to me, but on the other hand the man who wrote the book had never died himself, so he couldn't really know how you felt afterwards. Anyhow, it was like that at first; I could see them in front of me, but they seemed simultaneously at a distance, and then bit by bit I could hear the wireless. It kept fading in and out as though someone was fooling with the set, but I could see it and nobody was anywhere near. It faded on and off, IN and OUT, IN and OUT, OUT and IN, and the people I was seeing began also to fade in and out with the sound, like watching a series of lap-dissolves, and then there was a final fade-out and I woke next in the middle of the night, everyone in the ward asleep and the lights turned low, and I couldn't remember where I was at first. I felt terrible.

I looked round and saw something sitting by my bed watching me, a shape with some kind of head-dress on, and I knew at once that this was Death waiting patiently his chance. Or her chance: it seemed to be a woman. Well, why not? Somerset Maugham portrayed Death as a woman, and I couldn't see anything against it. I began to feel a bit frightened then, but I thought perhaps it didn't really matter because if I died then I shouldn't presumably feel so terrible.

By the time I thought that, my eyes had got accustomed to the dark and I saw it wasn't in fact Death watching me, but the night Sister.

'Can't you sleep?' she whispered to me.

'No,' I said. 'I feel awful.'

'Sick?'

'Yes.' I didn't have to keep my voice down as she was doing; it was a natural whisper.

'I've got some tablets for you to take,' she said. With her arm around me I managed to sit up and take the tablets; they were washed down with barley water. She turned the pillows and bunched them up again behind me, but I still couldn't sleep. It was a terrible feeling of nausea that I had, but it wasn't really like wanting to vomit; I can't describe what it was like. Later I began to shiver, although I wasn't cold. I just shivered and I had a cold sweat on me. The night Sister kept smoothing the hair from my forehead, which she couldn't have liked doing because it was damp and clammy and horrible.

'You're awfully good to me,' I whispered when finally I'd stopped shivering.

She said, 'It's nothing.' She smiled and I could see her teeth gleam white against her face in the dark. I still couldn't sleep, and then I could, and when I woke the eight o'clock news was on and they were all having breakfast.

The feeling of nausea had subsided and also the pain, but later when I sat up they were there again and I started to retch. I tried to hold it back because it hurt, but I couldn't and the nurse fetched me a bowl. What I brought up felt like blood and I looked in the bowl and it was. It was mostly dark, almost black, but there were some bright scarlet threads mixed with it as well, and it was blood all right.

When I saw the blood I got a little scared, but the nurse said there was no need. 'It's quite usual in cases like yours,' she said. I was relieved by that; I'd have hated to do anything irregular. I was so relieved I coughed up quite a blob more blood without minding at all.

The coughing hurt and exhausted me, but I felt much better afterwards. Then the two nurses sponged my face and hands. They wouldn't let me do a thing myself. They even combed my hair for me. 'You mustn't exert yourself,' they said.

'What about shaving?' I said.

They said: 'You'll have to grow a beard.'

Then the M.O. came round. He looked at the blood in my sputum bowl without much interest and asked me a string of questions. Had I ever had chest trouble before? Was there any chest trouble in my family? Did I feel any better today? The answer to all these questions was No. I felt too exhausted to add Sir, but the M.O. didn't seem to mind. Perhaps he wasn't really so bad after all.

When he'd gone they put another poultice on me; it was very hot and seemed to bring the pain out through my back. They gave me two more tablets; I went to sleep. I woke and felt sick again. It was like that all day.

During the afternoon Brailowsky came round. He was a Russian boy, naturalised British, but not related, so far as I know, to the pianist called that. I liked him, and we used to argue about the way Russian slang should be translated into English and also, because he was Russian, about the soul. But that afternoon when he came I didn't feel like arguing about the soul. I had one of my lap-dissolve periods on and the face of Brailowsky, seen as if through glass, seemed to recede and advance, dissolving and re-forming, in and out, in and out, out and in. I couldn't talk; he sat by the bed awhile and then tiptoed away. I slept.

Next morning I felt better. The news was all about Hess and how he'd landed by parachute and all the patients were talking about Hess and how the bust-up in Germany was coming for sure and the war'd be over by Christmas, you mark my words.

There were too many patients for me to sort them all out, but I noticed that one of them had his face painted a bright orange. I'd noticed this before, but thought it was part of my delirium. Now I saw it was real; he had some spots on his face and the stuff they put on turned him this peculiar colour. He looked extraordinary; he was a New Zealander, someone told me.

Well, there they were, talking about Hess, and after this the wireless continued to be Hess, and it was also a little Roosevelt and dance tunes, *Falling Leaves* and *There I Go* and *Yes, My Darling Daughter*, and when I hear these tunes again I shall remember the Reception Station and the poultice drawing out the pain gradually, the orange-faced New Zealander and the tablets that were known as M. and B..

They always made me feel sick and the days were divided up by the times I took them and there were also poultice-changing, temperature-taking, barley water and broth. Then there was sweating and sleeping and coughing, less and less blood by degrees, and the tablets made me feel less sick as time went on.

The nights, when I began sleeping better, were my best time because then the night Sister was on duty. I knew all the sisters by now; the fair, wispy one who was engaged to a subaltern in the eighth, the spectacled, talkative one, the tall, thin, dark one, and the two nurses: the short, dour Scotch one and the grey, elderly, tired one. They were all very sweet and kind to me, but best of all I liked the night Sister.

She was not beautiful; there's a temptation to think of her as beautiful because I was sick and she nursed me, but I like to remain a realist, and she was not beautiful, no. She was a big dark girl with a cloud of dark hair under her coif and she had very white teeth. In the night I sometimes woke and I was frightened. I'd not been frightened at first because I was too weak, but later I was, and seeing her sitting by the bed used to stop me being frightened at once. She had also to wake me during the night to give me two of the tablets and she always did this by stroking my forehead.

'Why do you stroke my forehead to wake me?' I asked her once.

'I want you to think you're at home and wake up happy,' she said.

'No one wakes me like that at home,' I told her.

'Not your girl?'

'No. I haven't a girl.'

'Surely you must have a girl.'

'No, I haven't.'

'You're a poor lonely boy,' she said.

'No,' I said. 'I'm poor, but I'm not lonely. I'm hardly ever lonely.'

'Ssh,' she said. 'We're talking too loud. We'll wake the others.'

Then I'd take the tablets and go off to sleep quite happily. The nights were like that, and in the morning she was gone and there was Bing Crosby and the *Morning Star* on the radio and afterwards Hess.

Now I was better; I no longer coughed up blood, and one day the Sister showed me the thermometer and it was down to normal. I used to lie there and sometimes read, and I used to think of all the sick leave I'd get when I got out of hospital.

I knew now I'd got pneumonia; at first I didn't care what I'd got, but later I became curious and got the orange-faced man to turn round the chart that hung on the end of my bed and this said PLEURISY AND PNEUMONIA. I remembered the company clerk who'd gone down with German measles and how they gave him seven days, and if you got given seven days for measles what'd you get for pneumonia? My mind soared to dizzy heights of sick leave. Twenty-eight days? Two months? The camp with its dust and heat and the C.S.M. shouting seemed agreeably remote —almost a thing of the past. A month anyway, I thought. They can't give me less than a month. I felt so bucked at the thought of a month that I even felt hungry for the first time and ate a piece of chicken cut up into tiny little squares. Hess was having chicken, too, we heard.

Then one morning I'd been asleep and I woke and there was the colour-sergeant rattling a bag of coins and grinning at me; the company commander was with him. It was Friday; I'd been ill for almost a week.

'Here's a quid for you,' the colour-sergeant said. 'Better take it while you can. They'll only pay you eight and six when you shift to the hospital proper.'

So I took the quid and they went round the ward rattling the bag of money. Everyone woke up when they heard it, even the man who'd been carried in nearly dying of something the day before woke up, and all got paid out.

That afternoon Brailowsky came again. He had some news for me.

'D'you remember Collins? In No. 7 Platoon?'

'The one with glasses?' I remembered Collins; he was a country lad and not too good on drill—he just couldn't seem to grasp it somehow.

'A terrible thing happened this morning,' Brailowsky said. 'He had his eye put out; he was blinded. We were on bayonets and a scabbard slipped. It was the corporal's actually, Corporal Evans. It struck Collins and broke his glasses into his eye. It was awful.'

'I should think it was,' I said. 'Poor devil.'

'If only he hadn't worn glasses he'd have been all right. It was the glass breaking that did it really.'

'How awful,' I said. 'Did he faint?'

'No, he was conscious all the time. The corporal's awfully cut up about it.'

'Where is Collins now?'

'At the town hospital. He's to have an operation.'

'Well, there's one thing,' I said, 'he'll get his ticket.'

'Oh, yes, they'll give him that, I should think. And you, d'you think you'll get yours?'

'No such luck.'

Then we talked about the soul. Tolstoy was mentioned, and Dostoevsky. We both got a little exalted and in the end Brailowsky was asked to leave by the sister in charge. He said he'd be back. I felt a little less exalted when he'd gone and I thought a bit about Collins; I thought principally poor bastard. Anyway, he'd be out of the army, that was one good thing, but was it worth losing an eye for? I decided not.

On the Sunday after that I was moved. There was no warning; the M.O. suddenly came round about midday and said I was to go to the town hospital that morning. Immediately I was carried out to the ambulance on a stretcher. It was lovely weather and the sun felt good on my face, but I was worried because I hadn't said goodbye to the night Sister. Later, though, she came round to the town hospital, and I saw her there, and when I came out finally I went to look her up, but she'd been transferred and I never saw her again.

At the town hospital they had huts adjoining it for the military, and I was in one of these. When they carried me in there was lunch going on, and I was hungry. I asked for something to eat.

'Bread and milk,' the nurse told me. 'You can have some bread and milk if you like.'

'They're eating stew. Why can't I have some of that?'

'Not until the doctor's seen you.'

'But I'm eating normally now, nurse. I've had no lunch. I'm hungry.'

'Well, you can't have anything till the doctor comes.'

'When will that be?'

'About three o'clock.'

'Oh Christ.'

The nurse was a little shocked. She went away and I watched them eat the stew. Later the nurse returned with some junket. I didn't like junket; I told her so. She said I ought to be glad of anything I could get these days.

Then there was an altercation when she took down my particulars. She wanted my mother sent for. I said I didn't want her worried and it all ended in this nurse not liking me. I was surprised at the difference in atmosphere. Of course, these were not V.A.D.s; they were trained nurses, and there's the difference between amateur and professional; it's something like that, and there were also more regulations and less food, as I found out later.

The doctor came round about half-past three, and it was a woman doctor. The first thing she did was to knock off the tablets. She said I was progressing satisfactorily. I said could I have something to eat; she said of course. So I ate bread and jam for tea and later stew.

The hut was a long one and stretched down a perspective of beds to long french windows leading on to a lawn. The end beds by the french windows were not filled except one that had a man who had fits in it. We were always waiting for him to have one, but he didn't; we thought he was a washout. Most of the patients were up and about; they used to get free passes to go to the cinema in the afternoons, but at mealtimes they always reappeared and there was a scramble to sit down at the long table that ran down the middle of the room, and the bed patients sat agitatedly up and made desperate signals to the nurses to make sure they didn't get overlooked.

Everyone was always hungry because, although the hospital took military patients, they still had civilian rations and food was scarce. One day we had a major who shouted at us that we were under military discipline and any man misbehaving himself'd damn soon find it out. But we were not interested in discipline; we were interested in food. The food remained unmilitary and we were hungry all the time.

The food we got was mainly vegetable stew with a few shreds of meat in it and beans abounding. The beans had an effect on us that was embarrassing when the matron came round at night; it was like crackers going off all the way down the ward. At each explosion the matron would give a little start as if stung. From the beds behind would come giggles smothered by blankets and a fresh salvo burst out in front, so the matron was caught between two fires, so to speak; it was amusing but embarrassing for everybody.

That was in the evenings; in the mornings there was the wireless, which was now altogether Roosevelt and sometimes Bing Crosby; Hess had fizzled out. Roosevelt made a rousing speech; it was terrific, and the patients all said the war'd be over by October, but some still stuck to Christmas; they were pessimists. With the wireless came washing, and now that I was stronger, shaving, and there was also Yes or No.

At the Reception Station Yes or No had been considered a rhetorical question, but here the nurses began to ask it with increasing urgency, and one came round with potions and pills and various kinds of purges on a trolley. I took a yellow-coloured medicine and several pills without result and they began talking about dynamite.

When I did at last get going it was quite an adventure. The lavatory was just outside the ward, and to get to it you had to pass eight beds. This took me fully five minutes; it was the first time I'd been up. My body felt as light as a blown feather and my legs as though the laws of gravity had altered. I had to look down to make sure that my feet were in fact touching terra-firma. I refused the offer of a stick and a nurse's arm. I set off to float down the ward on my own, the other patients cheering me on. As my head seemed also independent and a separate entity, it was an exhausting experience and tired me out for the rest of the day.

The afternoon was merely an interlude between dinner and tea, and during it there was a blanket bath, which I did myself, and rubbing methylated spirit on my body, which was done by a nurse. I was always embarrassed by this, especially since the nurse who did it was a good-looking one. She was a well-set-up girl, and I used to watch her walking down the ward with detachment, and then one day it was no longer with detachment, and I knew then that I was getting definitely better.

Every day after that I got steadily better, and now that the pain had entirely gone and the doctor said the lung was almost healed, I had great pleasure in breathing; every time I breathed my whole body seemed to expand, and it was very pleasant. I could feel my blood circulating freely and I felt very strong; it was always astonishing that when my feet touched the floor I felt dizzy and so weak I could hardly stand.

Sometimes I was allowed to get up and sit in a chair by the stove, which was not lit now as it was the middle of May and warm weather. I used to send out all the time for food; one of the up-patients got it for me. The colour-sergeant's quid soon went, and I ate always with tremendous appetite.

The orange-faced man turned up, but now you couldn't see his face because the new treatment he had caused it to be swathed in bandages, and he looked like the Invisible Man in the film before he actually became invisible.

And then Collins turned up. He didn't see me at first, but I saw him; he had a black patch over his eye and looked really none the worse. I heard what was said when his doctor came round. We each had separate doctors, and his was a doctor who considered it his duty to demobilise the army, or at any rate such part of it as came under his care. I heard him tell Collins that he'd been recommended for discharge and Collins mutter something in his slow country voice, but he didn't seem pleased about it;

he seemed just indifferent. Later he saw me and we had a talk.

'How'll you like getting your ticket?' I asked him.

'Oh, I dunno. I ain't so keen. I dunno as I want it really.'

'You don't want it!'

'I ain't all that keen. Course I wouldn't mind getting home for the harvest, but still.'

I was astounded. I knew that if I'd been blinded in the army I'd expect my ticket and probably a pension as well. I looked at him and thought he took it so calmly he must have more guts than I had. But then I knew it wasn't guts; it was just that he hadn't the imagination—if something happened to you and you didn't imagine, it had not really happened and even the tangible loss of an eye did not entirely happen until it'd been fully imagined. Well, in his case he was better off like that—and who wants imagination, anyway.

I looked at Collins standing there with his black patch and in his hospital blues that were rather too big for him; the sleeves hung down over his hands.

'Well,' I said, 'it looks as though you'll get your ticket whether you want it or not.'

'Ar,' he said. 'Well, I don't mind much either way.'

I watched him walk back to his bed, and later Corporal Evans came, the one who'd done it to him by accident, and I watched the corporal come walking down the ward with a look on his face as though he were going into action; he was Welsh and emotional, and you could see he was all worked up about it.

Collins was sitting on his bed and he stood up and slowly grinned.

'Hullo, Corp,' he said.

I couldn't hear what Corporal Evans said, but I could see Collins wince at the grip his hand got; it must have nearly cracked the bones. Then they sat down and talked. Corporal Evans gesticulated a lot, and I could see Collins shaking his head slowly from time to time. They talked for quite a while, and when Corporal Evans got up to go he seemed tremendously relieved. He left the ward with a shout of laughter and at the door he turned back to wave a hand at Collins. 'So long, lad!'

'So long, Corp,' Collins said, and he sat there on the edge of his bed for some time afterwards smiling to himself, and I couldn't tell what he was thinking about; perhaps he wasn't really thinking at all.

That afternoon, too, Brailowsky came, but Collins was out by that time; he'd gone to the cinema; it was *All This and Heaven, Too.* Brailowsky said I'd been Y listed; it was on orders, twenty-one days in hospital; but as I wasn't an N.C.O. it made no difference to me, I had no stripes for them to strip.

Brailowsky had brought a book by Turgenev, and he'd brought with him also the same book in Russian. He was showing me how the translation differed from the original Russian when a sudden blood-curdling yell from the end of the ward made us both start round.

The yell proceeded from a bed occupied by an Irishman, who had some kind of stomach trouble. I'd never spoken to him, but I'd never thought that he was really very ill. We looked round and he was sitting up in bed, gaunt and unshaven, with a wild look on his face.

'I want my wife!' he yelled out.

Two of the nurses came running in and immediately went to his bedside, but he waved them away.

'I don't want you; I want my wife. I'm a dying man. I want my wife.'

The nurses said something; he wouldn't listen. He started to beat on the bedrail with his hand and to shout over and over again, 'I want my wife, I want my wife, I want my wife.'

Brailowsky had turned pale. 'What's wrong with him?' he whispered. I said I didn't know. I was watching the Irishman. Everyone in the ward was watching him; the patients from their beds and some of the patients who'd got back from the cinema stood watching him and the nurses. The Irishman glared back at them with his eyes starting out of his head.

'I'm dying, I tell ye!' he howled. 'I'm dying, and ye can't tell me no different, I know it! I want my wife!'

Suddenly there was a commotion at the other end of the ward. It was the man who had fits; he was having one. The Irishman had evidently upset him. Now attention was divided; our heads kept turning from side to side, and all the nurses made in a body for the man with fits. Screens went up round his bed in no time, but the Irishman, on the other hand, feeling himself abandoned, began to shriek at the top of his voice; it wasn't pleasant.

'I'm dying, I tell ye, I'm dying! I want my wife! I'm dying, I'm dying!

I want my wife, I tell ye! I'm dying! I want my wife! I'm dying, I'm dying! The Mother of God have mercy! I'm dying!'

Brailowsky stood up; he'd gone green in the face. You'd have thought that being Russian he'd have been used to this kind of thing, but evidently the naturalised part of his nature asserted itself suddenly and he couldn't take it. He muttered 'So long,' and left the ward promptly and with expedition.

The Irishman was on to a new tack now. He pointed a furious finger at the patients who stood gaping round his bedside.

'Aye, ye can stare, all of ye, ye can stare. Take a good look; I ain't afraid to die. The Lord God strike ye where ye stand. May he strike all of ye dead!' He added: 'And may a dying man's curse be on ye all!'

More patients came in, attracted by the noise from another ward, and two more nurses; they all stood staring. The Irishman included all these newcomers in his malediction.

'Die, all of ye, die!' he shrieked. 'Ye're dead! Why don't ye die?'

He leant forward and waited for them to die. They didn't; they just stood there. The Irishman cast his eyes to heaven and again called on God to strike them dead.

The bed patients further up now began to call angrily down the ward.

'He's loopy! Lock him up!'

'Fetch a straight jacket!'

'Fetch the doctor!'

'Fetch a priest!' this evidently from a fellow Catholic, but delivered in a Scots accent.

The Irishman paid no attention to these exhortations. He was watching the group round his bedside, waiting for them to fall.

'Nothing happens,' he muttered after a moment. 'Nothing happens.' He said this hopelessly, his faith was shattered. He dropped his head in his hands and began to sob.

A doctor now rushed in with a stethoscope dangling round his neck and took instant command of the situation. Up went the screens, and from behind them we could hear the Irishman sobbing brokenly.

'Is he really dying?' I asked one of the nurses, who'd halted by my bed on her way down from the man with fits.

'No,' she said, 'of course not. He won't die.'

'What about his wife?'

'She's in Ireland. Besides, he's separated from her.'

The Irishman quietened down after a while, and later he apologised to all of us. It'd been a mistake, he said, the devil had entered into him. We accepted the apology and also the theory of demoniacal possession, but that night the Irishman had a relapse, and this time he kicked over the screens and hit someone, a sergeant, I think. In the morning when we woke he'd been removed, and I don't know what happened to him because shortly afterwards I was moved myself.

I went to a convalescent home, where I remained for three weeks. And I never got any sick leave after all. An A.C.1 had just come out saying that if you went to a convalescent home you couldn't have sick leave; the M.O. at the camp took great pleasure in explaining it to me.

I did get my seven days' privilege leave, which was, anyway six weeks overdue, and they said I was lucky to get even that, because being on light duties I wasn't entitled to any kind of leave without the M.O.'s okay.

When I came back to the camp I saw Collins. He hadn't got his ticket; they'd graded him B.2 and given him a job in the company stores. They gave him also a brand-new glass eye, which he's very proud of; he can even move it about in its socket. The boys all call him Nelson, but he doesn't mind that; he doesn't seem to mind anything at all.

'Been in prison before?' the Reception Officer asked Hooper.

'Not,' he said, 'unless you count a night in the cells at Savile Row.'

'D and D?'

'I beg your pardon?'

'Drunk and disorderly.'

Hooper nodded. 'Not a man until you've had a bash of that,' the Reception Officer said cheerfully. 'Any artificial teeth, truss, or other surgical appliances? Right! Cooper, isn't it?' He opened a big ledger, apparently similar in purpose to the Black Book kept by Jonathan Wild at the Debtors' Prison, and started to inscribe the name therein.

'Hooper—but I'm only here on remand. My bail's likely to be through any moment.'

The officer glanced from the buff form in front of him to a calendar on his desk and a clock on the wall. 'Looks like you'll be staying the week-end,' he said. It was 6 pm on a Friday evening. 'Empty all your pockets down that passage there, take off shoes and necktie. The hangman awaits.'

Not the hangman, but another officer awaited, writing at a high Dickensian dais. 'Take all your clothes off,' he said. 'Have you been in prison before?'

Presently, measured, weighed, bathed and fully dressed again—having elected not to wear prison clothing—Hooper was issued with kit stuffed in a pillow-case and locked by a warder into a small cubicle already containing a West Indian. On all sides voices shouted and cell doors clanged-to on their occupants. The West Indian rolled red eyes at Hooper: 'Got smoke?' he asked. 'Ah got match.'

It was a fair exchange: Hooper had been allowed to keep his few remaining cigarettes but not his lighter. 'What are you in for?' Hooper asked as he lit up. Already he felt like an old lag.

'Violence,' said the West Indian. 'Was mah landlord. Bad man, he took way mah lectric bulb. Too strong, he say, waste lectricity. Ah tell um "Where mah bulb? Man you gimme back mah bulb, you thief." Landlord doan like ah call um thief. Say "Ah doan give you no bulb you dirty black man." Ah tell um "You blacker man, Nigerian burgher, bad thief sonabitch." Den we fight, he fall down, much blood, police come, say his neck cut, bring me here.'

'What did you hit him with?'

'Side of mah hand. Very hard. Here, you feel.'

'But you couldn't cut his neck that way.'

'Very hard hand. Coppers say done wid chopper, Ah tell um doan have no chopper.'

'Then you should have been in the clear.'

'Yah, but they find chopper wid blood, wrapped in shirt, up mah room in chimney dere. Say him mine, malicious wound. Ah tell um no guilty, dey doan believe.'

'And was the chopper yours?'

'Man, dere's mah story, Ah stick right dere wid dis.'

There was the shuffle of a queue lining up outside, the door was flung open and a warder shouted 'Get ready for your medicals.'

'What's the time?' Hooper asked. The warder pointed to a clock: 'Why worry? In here, time's a thing you got plenty of.'

It was past seven, the last hope of bail that weekend had gone. Hooper said, 'Is the landlord dead?' to the West Indian.

'Him alive. Big pity.'

Prison proved eventually to be a dim-lit high hollow structure, where officers rattled bunches of keys and echoing steel flights twisted up towards tiered galleries with wire netting stretched below. NO SMOKING EXCEPT IN CELLS, a notice announced, and the officer in charge of Landing Three gave Hooper a light before he was faced by a locked door painted yellow, a judas window, and an enigmatic pencilled scrawl: ITALIAN FRED IS A LOUSY GRASS. A BLOKE'S BEST FRIEND IS HIS MOTHER. This was signed 'PADDY': presumably a previous inmate informed upon by Italian Fred.

It was not long after, as he was making his bed down, that Hooper first became aware of Gaffney. He couldn't see him but he heard his voice. Like a voice from the Beyond it was heralded by the sound of tapping, and said quite plainly: 'First time Inside?'

'Who the hell?' Hooper said, startled.

'Gaffney. Next door,' the voice replied. 'Speak close to the pipe.'

Hooper lay down on the bed near the steam-heating pipe underneath the window, which evidently acted as a sound conductor. 'Can you hear me better now?'

'A treat. How d'you find your new digs?'

'I was in the Army for three years.'

Gaffney gave the ghost of a laugh.

'What did they nick you for?'

'Debt. I didn't pay some bills.'

'Section 13. Debtors Act 1869?'

'Wouldn't surprise me. And you?'

'Thereby hangs a tale. Alas too long to tell.' Then he said, 'Light's due out any second. I've been here six weeks. You get to know.

He was right. Almost as he spoke, the bulb above the scrubbed deal table, not at all the high-voltage sort basically responsible for the West Indian's arrest, was extinguished and the moon came on instead, projecting the shadow of the window-frame across the opposite wall.

'May flights of angels sing thee to thy rest,' Gaffney said via the pipe.

They met next morning on the narrow, railed board-walk, between the smell of slops being emptied and that of breakfast being dished up in the hall below, when Gaffney hurriedly thrust at Hooper an armful of Prison Library books including *Point Counter Point*. But the story didn't come out until later, as they trudged round and round on exercise, the circular path worn slippery as a skating-rink and bordered by beds of budding tulips beneath high walls of dun-coloured brick.

'I,' Gaffney said, 'am the bloke responsible for the fact that you can no longer get change for a two-bob piece on slot-machines in the Tube.' A lick of blond hair flopped over his forehead into his eyes. 'Before that I used to write songs. Tin Pan Alley stuff. But by dint of trial and error I managed to produce a coin of the correct size and weight to operate the machines. The milled edge was the main problem but in the end overcome. Result: one and a tanner a time, clear profit.'

Young and pale and serious, he wore prison clothing, grey trousers and a brown sack-like jacket too big for him, so that he clutched his sleeves in his hands while walking and tripped every now and then over trailing turn-ups. 'Needed organization, mind. D'you know how many Underground Stations there are from Acton Town to Woodside Park?

Two hundred and seventy-three—but not all equipped with two-bob machines. We'd to make a planned survey and then my team had only covered a quarter of the territory before I myself was lumbered. A coin got stuck, an officious Tube official, and the whole sweet racket went up the spout. Now they've blocked up the slots.'

'What did you get?'

'Acquitted,' Caffney said. 'Lack of proof. We'd the plant well tucked away and all dismantled before they got to it.'

'Then why are you in here now?'

'The spirit of adventure,' Gaffney said. 'Otherwise called not knowing when to leave well alone. I ought to get three years this time.'

'Inside, one and all!' roared the officer in charge, and soon they were back on the boardwalk where a brisk traffic in paper-bound books went on (one Irish boy even leaping down on to the netting and climbing back again in order to secure a science-fiction mag which had fallen short when flung from the opposite gallery) before they were locked in again until dinner-time.

That afternoon, in the exercise yard, Gaffney continued his story. 'You've heard the Postmaster's radio appeal asking people to cross postal orders more thoroughly? Well that's on account of me again. We made a big haul from a bookie's down the City, no breaking and entering, just me and my girlfriend got up as staff, stopped the postman in the hall, said we'd take the mail up, huge great bag, van waiting, rushed it out the back way before the real clerks arrived. Then special ink remover, my invention. We mucked up two hundred quid's worth of P.O.s before getting it right, had to burn the lot, nearly broke my heart. All cheques sent back, anonymously of course, don't believe in any truck with banks... too risky and there's no point in causing needless trouble to others. Everything going like a dream when I get pinched again. Squad car stopped alongside me one night, two coppers coming the other way; after someone else as it turned out, but like a fool I bolted. Guilty conscience, see where it get you?' And the answer seemed to be this asphalt path, the West Indian walking splay-footed ahead, and the Assizes Gaffney was to come up before the following week.

On Monday afternoon Hooper's bail came through, while Gaffney was downstairs seeing his lawyer, so they didn't say good-bye; but Hooper bequeathed him some cigarettes he'd been allowed to buy, and often wondered how he was getting on when, having paid a large sum into court, he was a free man again. And then one day, in a pub off Charing Cross Road, there he was: green velvet coat, silk shirt, twill trousers and a Havana cigar, ordering Scotch.

'Don't mean to say you got off?'

'Complete acquittal,' Gaffney said.

'I made a full confession, talked for damn near an hour about the spirit of adventure and the raw deal my generation has had, angry young man stuff, you know, and I believe they were glad to see the back of me in the finish. I had to promise to give up being on the bend though, and I'm a bloke that keeps his word.'

'Then how'll you make a living?'

'I've written what the boys up yonder reckon'll be a Top Twenty Tune—and all due to the good old nick *The Exercise Yard Song.*' He hummed a few bars of something resembling *The Banana Boat Song.* 'That West Indian fellow gave me the idea—he got five years by the way. Pity that, rough luck. Meantime, my number ought to start paying off soon.'

Hooper was already late for an urgent business appointment. Wishing Gaffney luck, he plunged down the Tube where a long unmoving queue stretched half across the booking-hall. He crossed to the ticket-machines, but the only change he had was a two-shilling piece and the slots were all blocked up.

Books by Julian Maclaren-Ross

The Stuff to Give the Troops, Jonathan Cape, London, 1944.
Better than a Kick in the Pants, Lawson & Dunn, jointly with the Hyperion Press, London, 1945.
Bitten By The Tarantula, Allan Wingate, London, 1946.
The Nine Men of Soho, Allan Wingate, London, 1946.
Of Love and Hunger, Allan Wingate, London, 1947.
The Weeping and the Laughter, Rupert Hart-Davis, London,1953.
The Funny Bone, Elek Books, London, 1956.
Until the Day She Dies, Hamish Hamilton, London, 1960.
The Doomsday Book, Hamish Hamilton, London, 1961.
My Name Is Love, The Times Press, London, 1964.
Memoirs of the Forties, Alan Ross, London, 1965,1994.

Fear & Loathing in Fitzrovia
The bizarre life of Julian Maclaren-Ross

by Paul Willetts

£14.99 softback
416 pages
152mm x 232mm
ISBN: 1-899235-69-8

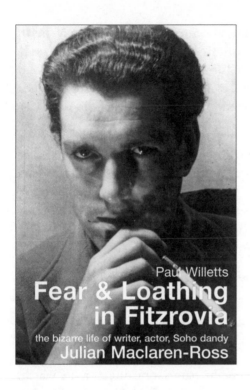

What the critics said:

"Very striking, very strange and altogether fascinating." — Richard Holmes, author of *Dr Johnson and Mr Savage*

"I especially admired [*Fear and Loathing in Fitzrovia* which] breaks new ground and revives [a] remarkable writer in the context of [his] times... Paul Willetts provides a vivid portrait of Julian Maclaren-Ross, the brilliant novelist, short story writer, memoirist, critic, parodist, sponger, dandy and bohemian." — Philip French, *The Observer*, Books of the Year

"An inspiring read." — John King (author of *The Football Factory*), *The New Statesman*, Books of the Year

"Most of the books I enjoyed [this year] were works of non-fiction. They included... Paul Willetts's entertaining chronicle of the Forties literary legend J. Maclaren-Ross." — D.J. Taylor, *The Spectator*, Books of the Year

"Willetts's subtitle 'The bizarre life of writer, actor, Soho dandy Julian Maclaren-Ross' is the perfect precis. His book evokes not just the seedy flamboyance of a man who slept in Turkish baths and railway stations and was immortalised by Anthony Powell as X. Trapnel, but also a long-vanished bohemian world." — Michael Arditti, *The Times*, Books of the Year

"*Fear and Loathing In Fitzrovia* is the proper stuff. Paul Willetts knows how to depress a depressive. It makes me wish I was an accountant, or anything other than a writer. Once, in the early hours, after a too long dinner I asked the poet, autobiographer and *London Magazine* editor, Alan Ross, the entirely dumb question 'What was Julian Maclaren-Ross really like?' Alan didn't demur: 'Better not to have met him.'
I do feel I've met him now." — Jonathan Meades

"Diligent, painstaking and bleakly hilarious." — *The Guardian*, Book of the Week

"Historical profiling of a high order, richly and racily done."
— Philip Oakes, *The Literary Review*

"Willetts's gloriously readable biography paints a picture of a life which, for all its disappointments, was richly lived. I finished the book rather regretting never having had the opportunity to have stood Maclaren-Ross a drink." — *The Mail on Sunday*

"The legendarily catastrophic life of Julian Maclaren-Ross has tempted biographers before. But the task of pursuing him, like the Hound of Heaven, through the sordid backstreets, rented basements and sodden saloon bars of his progress has always proved too much of a challenge. It is an extraordinary story of profligacy and waste which has been told, up until now, only in a million awed anecdotes… I have to take my hat off to Paul Willetts for his sheer industry in following his subject to places where few literary biographers need to tread." — Philip Hensher, *The Spectator*

"[A] lively biography of an archetypal Soho flâneur… Willetts has made a spirited attempt to get under the skin of someone who might have been Jeffrey Bernard's less pleasant brother." — Andrew Lycett, *The Sunday Times*

"Assiduously researched and enthusiastic... a fascinating trawl through Soho's bohemia." — *The Independent on Sunday*

"*Fear and Loathing in Fitzrovia* is an amusing and ultimately tragic account of the post-war bohemian Julian Maclaren-Ross whose self-destruction was emblematic of an age of fire." — Anthony Daniels, *The Sunday Telegraph*, Summer Books Recommendations

"This book is more than just an attempt to rescue and resuscitate a lost reputation. It is also an evocation of a world that most of us never knew and which has, in any case, all but disappeared. Willetts conjures up the 1940s and 1950s, from the frenetic, tense, energetic world of Soho in wartime to the end of an era as the 1960s dawned." — *The Birmingham Sunday Mercury*

"Exhilaratingly depressing." — *The Times*

"Recounting a life made up of lost afternoons, unfulfilled projects and midnight flits is no easy task. Willetts doggedly follows Maclaren-Ross to the bitter end, providing a biography that maintains a careful balance between the broadly sympathetic and the properly sceptical." — Peter Parker, *The Daily Telegraph*

"Later this month Paul Willetts, another fan like myself, publishes Julian Maclaren-Ross's fascinating biography... Debt-ridden, homeless and self-destructive, Maclaren-Ross, 'one of the ruined men of Soho', was a figure of sexual charisma, unspecified corruption and unshockable cynicism. How much more glamorous could a writer be?" — Virginia Ironside, *The Independent on Sunday*'s 'Talk of the Town' magazine

"Very few writers manage to inspire an affection and an intimacy that makes criticism seem like a graceless intrusion. Julian Maclaren-Ross, known chiefly for his short stories, radio plays and literary journalism, was one such. As a short story writer he could make you laugh out loud, particularly in his army stories which drew widespread admiration in the war and after in the heyday of little magazines. Indeed, they could still be read today as a handbook to barrack-room life. As a journalist, he anticipated the likes of Tom Wolfe and Hunter S. Thompson who applied fictional techniques to reportage. As a man he was like no other, as Paul Willetts's new biography, *Fear and Loathing in Fitzrovia* testifies with forensic skill that gets under the skin of the private man... It does not miss a significant detail and is a fitting account of a rare romantic who pursued his literary dreams with courageous insouciance to the very end." — Alun Richards, *Planet*

"Short-story writer, novelist, radio playwright, film scriptwriter and one of the most magnetic bohemians of the 1940s and 50s London, Maclaren-Ross cloaked his talents in dandyism and well-timed prose. This vacuum cleaner door-to-door salesman has finally been awarded a long overdue afterlife: Paul Willetts's scrupulous and moving biography, *Fear & Loathing in Fitzrovia*. Maclaren-Ross's style was on a level with the myth and *Fear & Loathing* matches both. Willetts washes away the stale perfumes of apathy and posterity and Maclaren-Ross's haunted journey stands today as a good corrective to the bland careerists of our time." — *The Buenos Aires Herald*

"Paul Willetts' book will prove an essential tool for researchers of the period... He has so well pieced together the day-to-day life of the wayward Maclaren-Ross that you sense that the author has a greater grip on his subject's life than Julian ever had himself... Willetts has provided us with a finely paced account of a flawed and very human bohemian — and a fiercely dedicated writer." — *The Tablet*

Julian Maclaren-Ross
Collected Memoirs

with an Introduction by
Paul Willetts

Black Spring Press
£8.95, Paperback, 464pp
ISBN 0-948238-30-5

"Only beware of Fitzrovia. It's a dangerous place, you must be careful."
"Fights with knives?"
"No, a worse danger. You might get Sohoitis you know."
"No I don't. What is it?"
"If you get Sohoitis, you will stay there always day and night and get
no work done ever. You have been warned."

(Maclaren-Ross plays ingenue to the wordly J. Meary Tambimuttu,
editor of *Poetry London*, in an account typical of these memoirs.)

Julian Maclaren Ross was one of the most colourful inhabitants of the
Soho and Fitzrovia of the forties, fifties and sixties. He knew and wrote
about its most memorable characters, among them Dylan Thomas,
Graham Greene, Cyril Connolly, Tambimuttu, Nina Hamnett and
Woodrow Wyatt. He was a gifted raconteur, and his life, often chaotic —
and related unsentimentally by him in these memoirs — veered between
the fringes of the literary establishment and homelessness. His
atmospheric stories are a rare insight into a world now gone. His best-
known work of non-fiction, *Memoirs of the Forties*, is included here in full,
along with many less known but no less interesting works, some
published here for the first time in book form. Also included in full is
Maclaren-Ross's collection of childhood memoirs, *The Weeping and the
Laughter*: these are markedly different in tone from his writing about his
adult life, and cast a very different light on him. The *Collected Memoirs* is
a fascinating and rounded portrait of Julian Maclaren-Ross and his world.

For a full list of our publications please write to

Dewi Lewis Publishing
8 Broomfield Road
Heaton Moor
Stockport SK4 4ND

You can also visit our web site at
www.dewilewispublishing.com